MICHAEL MCDOWELL was born in 1950 in Enterprise, Alabama and attended public schools in southern Alabama until 1968. He graduated with a bachelor's degree and a master's degree in English from Harvard, and in 1978 he was awarded his Ph.D. in English and American Literature from Brandeis.

His seventh novel written and first to be sold, *The Amulet*, was published in 1979 and would be followed by over thirty additional volumes of fiction written under his own name or the pseudonyms Nathan Aldyne, Axel Young, Mike McCray, and Preston MacAdam. His notable works include the Southern Gothic horror novel *The Elementals* (1981), the serial novel *Blackwater* (1983), which was first published in a series of six paperback volumes, and the trilogy of "Jack & Susan" books.

By 1985 McDowell was writing screenplays for television, including episodes for a number of anthology series such as *Tales from the Darkside*, *Amazing Stories*, *Tales from the Crypt*, and *Alfred Hitchcock Presents*. He went on to write the screenplays for Tim Burton's *Beetlejuice* (1988) and *The Nightmare Before Christmas* (1993), as well as the script for *Thinner* (1996). McDowell died in 1999 from AIDS-related illness. Tabitha King, wife of author Stephen King, completed an unfinished McDowell novel, *Candles Burning*, which was published in 2006.

By Michael McDowell

NOVELS

The Amulet (1979)*

Cold Moon Over Babylon (1980)*

Gilded Needles (1980)*

The Elementals (1981)*

Katie (1982)*

Blackwater (1983; 6 vols.)

Jack & Susan in 1953 (1985)

Toplin (1985)

Jack & Susan in 1913 (1986)

Clue (1986)

Jack & Susan in 1933 (1987)

Candles Burning (2006) (completed by Tabitha King)

PSEUDONYMOUS NOVELS

Vermilion (1980) (as Nathan Aldyne)

Blood Rubies (1982) (as Axel Young)

Cobalt (1982) (as Nathan Aldyne)

Wicked Stepmother (1983) (as Axel Young)

Slate (1984) (as Nathan Aldyne)

Canary (1986) (as Nathan Aldyne)

SCREENPLAYS

Beetlejuice (1988)

Tales from the Darkside: The Movie (1990)

The Nightmare Before Christmas (1993)

Thinner (1996)

* Available from Valancourt Books

KATIE

MICHAEL McDOWELL

VALANCOURT BOOKS

Dedication: For the Friskes: Roberta and Dave, Mary, Millie, and John

Katie by Michael McDowell
First published as a paperback original by Avon Books in 1982
First Valancourt Books edition 2015

Published by Valancourt Books, Richmond, Virginia
http://www.valancourtbooks.com

All Valancourt Books publications are printed on acid free paper that meets all ANSI standards for archival quality paper.

ISBN 978-1-941147-68-9
Also available as an electronic book.

Cover by M. S. Corley / mscorley.com
Set in Dante MT

Money, you think, is the sole motive to deception and devilry in this world. How much money did the devil make by gulling Eve?

Melville, *The Confidence Man*

PROLOGUE

On Christmas Eve of 1863, at the height of the conflict between the Northern states and the Southern, a nine-year-old girl called Katie Slape sat before the hearth in a set of poor tenement rooms in Philadelphia. She was dressing her doll with scraps of gauze, lace, and silvered cloth – incongruously rich materials in that shabby, dim interior.

The cold December wind blew down the chimney and now and then scattered soot over Katie and her doll. Katie would smile, hold the doll up, and shake the ashes off.

Sitting at the table in the poor room was a woman of about thirty, with harsh lines in her face and no kindness in her eyes. Hannah Jepson was taking care of Katie Slape while Katie's mother, known professionally as Mlle. Desire, appeared on the stage of the Olympic Theater. Katie's father was employed as a railroad savage, either building up the Grand Army's lines in Pennsylvania and Maryland or destroying Rebel lines in Virginia and Tennessee. Katie had not seen him for more than a year.

On the floor beside Hannah Jepson was a wooden crate with eight mewling, scrabbling poodle pups inside it. On the table was a large jug of the cheapest sort of saloon liquor. Hannah would fill a syringe with the noxious liquid, then taking a pup into her lap, inject the full contents down its tiny throat. She repeated this process with each pup. The dogs gagged and spat up over Hannah's apron and struggled against her tight hold – but most of the liquor remained in their distended bellies.

"Why do you do that?" asked Katie once.

"Stunts 'em," replied Hannah shortly.

"Why do you want to stunt 'em?" Katie persisted.

"Meant for the fashionable ladies," Hannah explained. "Fashionable lady don't want a dog that's any bigger'n these pups. So I stunt 'em. Feed 'em this gin, and they don't grow no more. If they live at all," she shrugged.

Katie watched the operation with interest. "Have you ever seen Mar dance?"

"No," replied Hannah.

"When Par was here we'd go every evening to see Mar dance." Katie held up her box of scraps. "These are from Mar's costumes. Mar wears lovely clothes," Katie sighed. "See, I made this doll to look just like Mar. I call her Mlle. Desire, just like they call Mar on the bills."

She held up the doll and Hannah nodded. Hannah was not a woman inclined to be fond of children, but Katie Slape displeased her less than most.

"Want to help me?" she asked the child.

Katie rose eagerly. Hannah filled the syringe with gin and gave it to the child. Katie grinned, took up a pup, and jammed the nozzle down the animal's throat. She squeezed the bulb and grinned.

The animal jerked, convulsed so that its four legs splayed with a comic suddenness that made both Katie and Hannah laugh merrily. But then the gin spewed up all over Katie's dress, and the liquor was mixed with blood.

"Pushed too hard," Hannah remarked. "Likely put a hole in his belly."

"My dress!" said Katie excitedly, looking down at her front. "That dog ruint my dress!"

"Won't live," said Hannah, examining the bloated pup.

Katie lifted her fist high above the table and brought it down hard on the animal's exposed belly. There was a kind of pop, and the animal seemed to deflate. Blood and gin flowed weakly from its mouth and a fissure that had opened between its tiny forelegs.

Katie raised the wind-rattled window beside the table and flung the expiring dog out into the yard three floors below.

She turned back to Hannah. "What's Mar going to say about my dress?" she demanded.

The bill that night at the Olympic Theater consisted of the celebrated Ravels in *Magic Pills! or, The Conjurer's Gift*, the French ballet, *La Vivandière*, and a set of classical tableaux entitled *The Three Gladiators*. Mlle. Desire, Katie's mother, appeared in the ballet as the Baroness de Grimberg. She had two solos, and danced a polka with Robintzec the Burgomaster, played by François Ravel.

Mlle. Desire had first gone onto the stage only three years before as an infernal Zouave in *The Seven Daughters of Satan* but, upon the unexpected confinement of one of the principals during the long run of this show, had been promoted to the role of Sulphurine, the devil's fourth daughter. She had youth and beauty and more than her share of vivacity. She was known for a shining liquid eye, a fire in her steps, and an audacity and wildness that made the other dancers on stage seem mere daubed cutouts. What her audiences did not know, however, was that her fire, audacity, and wildness were almost all the result of a pint of champagne imbibed in the course of her toilet before the performance.

Tonight, in the ballet, her performance was even wilder and more audacious than usual. Some ascribed it to the holiday, but it might more fittingly have been linked to the coldness of the night. To warm herself in the unheated room where she dressed with half a dozen other young ladies, she had consumed an entire bottle of champagne, thoughtfully provided by an anonymous admirer smitten the previous evening.

She was drunk this Christmas Eve, and in the wings she staggered and clutched at the side pieces. But Mlle. Desire had been born a dancer, and her step through the first solo and the polka was unerring.

However, during the Pas de l'Inconstance, to which she and M. Brilliant (who played the Baron de Grimberg) were witnesses at the back of the stage, she quite suddenly lost her balance and to regain it caught hold of a pedestal which supported a large lamp. A portion of the wick of the lamp, which had been saturated with spirits of wine to make it burn brighter, fell upon her gauzy dress and ignited it immediately. Within seconds Mlle. Desire was entirely enveloped in flames.

She rushed off the stage, where all the coryphées stood aghast. Mlle. Hennecart, whose dress was just as volatile, pushed Mlle. Desire back onto the stage with the handle of a broom.

The same anonymous admirer who had sent the bottle of

champagne and had secured a seat in the front row for tonight's performance, leapt onto the stage and, taking off his jacket, flung it over Mlle. Desire's burning shoulders. M. Brilliant knocked her to the floor of the stage and rolled her over and over again until all the flames were extinguished.

The curtain was dropped, but already more than half the audience had fled the theater in horror.

When the scorched coat was unrolled, Mlle. Desire spilled out onto the stage at the feet of the trembling coryphées, burnt and dead.

At that same moment, Katie Slape sat weeping before the hearth. Tight in her hands she held the doll dressed in gauze and silver, which she had christened Mlle. Desire.

"Child?" said Hannah, looking up from the table.

Katie flung the doll into the fire.

"Mar's dead!" she cried.

The doll's dress flared suddenly in the coal and was consumed in a moment's time, but the wooden body began slowly to burn and char.

PART I
NEW EGYPT

Chapter 1

PHILO AND JEWEL

Late one afternoon in March of 1871, two young women happened to meet on the principal street of New Egypt, a village in the central portion of New Jersey. The first, whose name was Jewel Varley, was of slender form and sallow complexion. Her features were mean and insignificant, and her demeanor was one of simpering sophistication that ill accorded with the rural air of New Egypt. Jewel was dressed with more pretension than taste, and though she had hurried forward to overtake the second young woman, it was with haughty condescension that she tapped her acquaintance on the shoulder with her frilled parasol.

"Oh, Lord!" gasped Jewel breathlessly. "I believe it is Philo Drax. Philo, is that not you? Why are you hurrying so? Lightning wouldn't have time to strike you!"

"Good evening, Jewel," replied Philo Drax with a polite smile but no evident pleasure at the meeting. "I have been delivering Mother's sewing for her."

"You are a very dutiful child," remarked Jewel, who was seven months younger than Philo. Nothing more was said for a few moments, and Philo was about to hurry on when Jewel detained her by speaking with sudden urgency: "Do you know where I've just been?"

"I've no idea," replied Philo, who had slowed her walk to match Jewel's languorous saunter. She was as plainly dressed as Jewel was ostentatiously, but Philo's skirt and jacket were neat and scrupulously clean – much cleaner than Jewel's overlong dress, which dragged in New Egypt's dust and would have been much more appropriate to the swept walks of Long Branch or Newport.

"I've just been to the dressmaker's," said Jewel with an arch elevation of her ragged brows.

Philo carried a bundle of mended shirts yet to be delivered, and this she shifted uneasily in her arms. "Your dressmaker?" she questioned. "I thought that Mother was in the habit of making your clothing. I know that in the past—"

"Exactly!" cried Jewel. "That was in the past! Have you not heard?" Jewel glanced demurely aside and rattled the tip of her parasol along the picket fence of Doctor Slocum's house, which teased the doctor's hound to furious barking. He hurled himself at the fence, and Jewel poked at him between the pickets.

"Have I not heard what?" asked Philo.

"Oh!" cried Jewel with a smile that Philo thought malicious. "There is a *new* dressmaker in town, just set up, and I have been to see her. She comes from Trenton and knows all the latest patterns. Ma and I are to be her first customers! She works cheap too. She has just showed me a suit – quite scrumptious – in imitation of a Paris dress. It has ever so much trim, and more bows than I could count in a quarter of an hour, and box-plaiting on the sides, and double quilting round the bottom. There was a waist and a double skirt, and it will only cost me twenty dollars to have done, and it's all to be made up on a machine!"

"It sounds a deal too grand for New Egypt," said Philo. Her voice was low and serious, for the arrival of a new seamstress in New Egypt boded ill for her and her mother's already precarious finances.

"I have no intention of stopping in New Egypt all of my life," simpered Jewel. "It is all very well for you to remain here, Philo Drax. You and your mother are poor as poverty – you won't mind my saying so, for you know it's true – and when you're poor as poverty, your life is already set out for you. I suppose you will live with your mother until you marry some young farmer or mechanic. Perhaps if you are very fortunate you will be taken to New York on your honeymoon. I am told that these days even farmers and mechanics take their brides on honeymoons, in imitation of their betters. Perhaps you will one day see New York, Philo. I was there this last Christmas."

"I recall that," said Philo with hard-won impassivity. Jewel's remarks were cruel, but Philo knew them to be analytically only too sound.

"Ma and I will spend the summer at Saratoga. Saratoga," continued Jewel sententiously, "is the most fashionable place in the world. I think it very unlikely that you will ever visit Saratoga."

"I think you are probably correct, Jewel," said Philo with philosophical calmness. In exchanges with Jewel, Philo's only triumph was never to let the other young woman know how her remarks pained; and after a time, Philo had been surprised to discover, they did not. They had come to the Varleys' home, the largest and handsomest in all of New Egypt. Jacob Varley, Jewel's father, had established the graniteware factory at the southern end of town. This factory employed a quarter of the population of New Egypt, and Jacob Varley owned many of the houses occupied by his workers. He had also bought up the mortgage of the cottage in which Philo and her mother lived, and it was to him that Mrs. Drax paid nearly one hundred dollars interest each year. Jewel knew of this debt and because of it felt doubly secure in her high-handed treatment of Philo.

Philo Drax was indeed poor. She had no fine clothes, she had no hope of travelling to fashionable resorts, and she had no prospects for a good marriage. But all the town of New Egypt spoke favorably of Philo, and Jewel had often suffered the mortification of hearing that young woman's praise – accompanied by the unvoiced comparison and dismissal of her own attractions.

"I must go in now," said Jewel, stopping at the gate. "I've dawdled enough with you for one day, I suppose."

"You stopped *me*," corrected Philo.

Jewel sniffed. "I must go in to see if my cousin has arrived."

"Your cousin? I did not know you had a cousin, Jewel."

"He is my Aunt Maitland's son. His name is Henry Maitland. He is excessively fashionable and excessively rich. He went to college at Yale and achieved top honors there. He lives in New York and moves in excessively lofty circles."

"You will be *excessively* glad to see him, I suppose," said Philo, unable to repress a smile.

"Oh, I shall!" Jewel rubbed her parasol lightly against her neck, lifted her chin, and looked carefully at Philo out of eyes that were almost closed. "Shall I tell you a secret, Miss Philo Drax?"

"Please don't tell me any secrets, Jewel!"

"Why not? Are you not close?"

"Oh, yes, but if the secret were to get out, you would think that *I* divulged it!" Philo knew that nothing would prevent Jewel from saying what she intended to say, but she did not want the young woman to have the pleasure of being begged for a confidence.

"I shall tell you anyway," said Jewel with a shrug. She lowered her chin and her voice. "Mother intends that Mr. Maitland and I should be married one day."

"Which?"

"Which what?"

"Which day?" said Philo. "Which day does Mrs. Varley intend for you to marry Mr. Maitland?"

"Oh, Philo, you are too stupid! Mother intends that I should marry Mr. Maitland *some* day. She has heard Mr. Maitland say that he likes slender girls, and she has advised me to eat chalk and slate pencils and drink quantities of vinegar. That will make me slender as a straw."

"Chalk and slate pencils and vinegar is a fashionable diet, I suppose," laughed Philo. "And may be found on the bill of fare at Saratoga and other exclusive watering places."

Jewel frowned. Her frown was more natural and not much less pleasant than her smile. "You vex me, Philo Drax. Next week ma is giving a little party in honor of Cousin Henry's visit. All the best people in the county will be there. If you like, Philo, I will send word to you what night the party is to be given, so that you may walk by the house that evening and see the lights."

"Thank you, Jewel," replied Philo drily. "But shouldn't you dread Mr. Maitland's looking out one of the windows to see the unfashionable daughter of a seamstress peering over the picket fence?"

"It wouldn't matter," replied Jewel. "He would not know who you are."

"Good evening, Jewel," said Philo, moving away. "I have been too long delayed." She delivered the bundle of shirts to the wife of the manager of the graniteware factory, who lived only a few rods away, and when she came out into the twilit street again, she glanced back up toward the Varleys' house. In the handsome front garden she saw Jewel strolling with a tall, bearded man whose features, in the gloaming and at the distance, she could not discern. Probably that is Mr. Maitland, Philo thought. And at least from the grace of his movement, he seemed every bit as fashionable as Jewel had described him.

Philo turned with a sigh. She knew poverty to be no disgrace, but she could not help but feel a pang that she and her mother should suffer such great and constant unease on account of their slender and precarious means. Philo dreamed waking dreams sometimes of possessing even a quarter of the number of dresses she knew to be in Jewel Varley's wardrobe. She dreamed of visiting New York and of seeing the ocean. She dreamed of a life that would not be *all* toil and privation. She dreamed a hundred dreams a day, each pleasanter than the next – but what she did not dream was that the possibility and the means for such a life were so very near at hand.

Chapter 2

MRS. DRAX

All the important buildings of New Egypt were situated along the single main street of the town. These included three churches – the Presbyterian but newly constructed; the livery stable; the two stores which, in sharp competition with one another, sought to sell everything from vegetable seed to dress patterns to sugar cookies at the lowest price possible; the little house which could hardly be distinguished by the name "hotel" but where the few commercial travellers, drummers, and visitors to New Egypt invariably put up; the doctor's house, the blacksmith's house, Mr. Varley's house; and the town graveyard. On a few short streets that were set at right angles to this principal thoroughfare and which terminated at no great distance in fields to the west of the town and a pine forest to the east, were numerous smaller houses of the less prosperous. At New Egypt's southern extremity, along the railway line, was Jacob Varley's graniteware factory, and clustered around this were a fair number of workers' cottages. These workers, with the farmers of the district, served to boost New Egypt's census to nearly a thousand persons, twice the number which the town had claimed in the years before the War. Because of the factory and the proximity of the railroad, New Egypt was a more prosperous village than many, though some residents complained that it had grown too quickly, or that prices were too high, or that wages at the factory were insufficient to support a family. There were others however who looked forward to the time when the principal street would be paved with bricks.

Philo lived with her mother Mary Drax in a small cottage on a quarter-acre of land on the eastern boundary of New Egypt. For their dark little parlor with its tiny windows, Mary Drax could not afford a carpet for the floor nor china ornaments for the mantel. On the other side of an inconveniently narrow corridor was the kitchen, quite as small as the parlor and just as dark. Upstairs was a single chamber directly beneath the sharply pitched roof. The sloping eaves materially lessened its useable space. Here slept Mary Drax and her daughter, their beds separated by a green baize curtain.

Mary Drax was not a strong woman, neither physically nor in her character. She had performed one brave act in her life: marrying against the wishes of her family. Tom Drax, Mary's husband and Philo's father, had been a carefree man, who ought to have taken more care for his family. His only financial talent seemed to be a knack for getting rid of money in a way that proved to be of no benefit to anyone. After his death in the Battle of the Wilderness, Mrs. Drax had been sorely bereaved, but at the same time she found it rather easier to get along.

She sewed for a living. She was expert with a needle, and women vowed they had never known anyone to get a fuller skirt from a skimpier length of cloth. Her melancholy manner attracted women who felt sympathy for her condition and widowhood, and her meekness commended itself to those like the Varleys, who appreciated a due regard of their superior standing. But even with the principal custom of New Egypt securely hers, Mary Drax stitched but a meager livelihood for herself and Philo. A sewing machine would have assisted greatly, but where were Mary Drax and Philo to come by twenty-five dollars when they considered themselves fortunate if twenty-five cents could be found to spare in their frugal household?

Mary Drax had never taught her daughter to sew. In fact, even when Philo had expressed an eagerness to learn, her mother had dissuaded her. "There's not enough work in New Egypt for two seamstresses," Mary Drax said, "and I don't want to compete with you for custom, Philo." But her real reason was this: Mary Drax cherished an entirely groundless hope that one day she and Philo would be lifted out of their poverty. To train her daughter as a seamstress would give the lie to that sustaining hope.

Yet in the meantime, Philo needed to contribute her share. For three years she had assisted Mrs. Mark, the Methodist minister's wife, in teaching the children of the factory workers. Philo was able and patient, and there wasn't a child in that school who didn't prefer her to Mrs. Mark. When the minister's wife was confined with her sixth child, Philo took over the running of the school altogether. And when Mrs. Mark died in childbirth, Philo had reason to hope that Mrs. Mark's place – and Mrs. Mark's salary – would be turned over to her. But there Philo reckoned without the town's Board of Selectmen, which was headed up by Jacob Varley. These men considered Philo too young and too inexperienced, so they hired a thin, mean-spirited graduate of the Bangor Institute not on his qualifications but on his willingness to accept even less pay than Mrs. Mark had demanded. And this bully of a man, sensing at once Philo's superior knowledge and her recalcitrant spirit, had removed her from the school altogether.

Philo had nowhere to turn in New Egypt for work. It was true that the graniteware factory employed girls her age – and considerably younger too – but those places were reserved for daughters of men and women already working there. To assist her mother Philo would even have gone into service, but there was no household in New Egypt which both lacked daughters and possessed sufficient funds for a hired girl. Money itself was a scarce commodity in New Egypt – very little changed hands each day, and quite often bartering on a well-advanced and long-practiced scale took the place of purely monetary transactions.

Philo's only source of income now was the occasional delivery
of letters from the post office to persons who lived at an inconvenient distance. For this service, which generally entailed a walk
of three or four miles, she received one cent, or sometimes one
cent and an armful of vegetables.

The mortgage on the cottage necessitated a quarterly payment of $22.50. This sum constituted the interest, at six percent
yearly, on an original mortgage of $1,500, which had been bor-
rowed thirteen years before by poor Tom Drax. In that time
the Draxes had managed to pay back only fifty dollars of the
principal, so that almost the entire amount was still owed to
Jacob Varley. All Mary Drax's exertions were wanted to make up
that payment each quarter. The seamstress had unfortunately
taken ill in February. Confined to her bed for seventeen days
without strength in her arms to cut cloth or sharpness of vision
to thread a needle, she had further been forced to make expen-
ditures for medicines and the doctor's visits. Her fragile scheme
of employment and saving had been upset, and Mary Drax was
six dollars and fifty cents short.

It was nearly dark when Philo returned home. A single candle
burned in the parlor, and by its meager, guttering light Mary
Drax was straining her eyes to finish off the collar of a boy's
shirt.

"Mother," said Philo, "I have delivered all the bundles. I am
sorry if I am late, but Jewel Varley stopped me in the road and
would talk." Philo seated herself in the little chair across from
her mother's in the western parlor window.

"Always be pleasant to Jewel, dear," said her mother. "Jewel's
father owns this house, and Jewel and Mrs. Varley keep me constantly involved on their wardrobes."

Philo bit her lip and beat a tattoo on the sill of the window.

"Jewel is a disagreeable companion," said Philo. "She taunts
me because I am poor and have no expectations."

"We *are* poor," sighed Mrs. Drax, "and Philo dear, you have
no expectations at all. It is hard, but—"

"I don't mind what Jewel says about me, Mother. I have known
Jewel too long, and her tongue doesn't get sharp on me. But she
told something that does bear upon us, I'm afraid."

Mrs. Drax put down her work and closed her eyes. They were red and watered and pained her. "What did she say?"

"She said that there was a new dressmaker in town, and that she and Mrs. Varley intended to employ her."

The shirt slipped from off Mrs. Drax's lap and onto the floor. "Philo, this is a very great misfortune! Mrs. Varley and Jewel have been my mainstays. I don't know now *what* we shall do, for I haven't even the money to pay Mr. Varley when he comes tomorrow."

This was unexpected and unhappy news for Philo, but she attended to her mother's distress before giving in to her own. "Something will turn up, Mother. We shall get the money somehow. I only wish it were the summer, for then I could pick berries and sell them."

"We shall be turned out!"

"No, Mother! Of course not. Even if we are a little late with the mortgage payment, Mr. Varley is hardly likely to evict us."

"He is very hard with his other tenants, I have heard. The week before Christmas he turned out one of his workers, and that man had five children. It killed his wife. She died in the street of a broken heart. We will be sent to the poorhouse!" Mrs. Drax cried out, the dreadful possibility occurring to her suddenly. "Oh, I know it!" she wailed the next moment in wretched certainty.

Philo looked sternly at Mary Drax. "We will not," she said defiantly. "Mother, take hold of yourself. I'll get the money somehow."

Mrs. Drax shook her head, unconvinced by her daughter's optimism. It was impossible to imagine that Philo, who had never possessed more than fifty cents at any one time in her whole life, could produce that and six dollars besides before the next day was out.

Mrs. Drax's spirits did not improve over the course of their small supper, though Philo, repenting her earlier harshness with her mother, formulated a hundred small schemes for the getting of six dollars and fifty cents, some of them remotely promising, some very unlikely, some humorously preposterous – such as that they should borrow a little press from the stationer in Trenton and simply print out the needed bills (and some few more as well, as long as they were at it); or that they should sell shares in a coal-mining venture in earnest of which Philo was prepared to dig a tunnel from the root cellar all the way over to the Presbyterian Church; or that Philo should paint her face with lampblack, climb into a yellow pinafore, and allow herself to be exhibited as the "Monstrous African Baby – Six Months Old and Weighing One Hundred Eight Pounds Nine Ounces Avoirdupois."

It was when she had finished washing up the dishes that Philo turned to her mother with an expression of surprise. "Oh, Mother, I quite forgot. We have received a letter! I was walking past the post office, and Mr. Clegg ran out waving this—" She dried her hands, and from the pocket of her skirt she drew out a small but thick envelope.

"Who on earth – ?" wondered Mrs. Drax. "Where was it mailed?"

Philo examined the postal mark. "It was mailed at Shiloh on the day before yesterday. Mother, you were born in Shiloh. Perhaps it is an old friend who has written to you."

Mary Drax took the letter and looked at the writing upon the envelope. She trembled. The letter dropped from her grasp to the floor. "Philo," she whispered, "the letter is from my father!"

Chapter 3

THE INTEREST PAYMENT

Philo plucked the letter from the floor, and her mother begged her to open it. "I cannot, Philo, I cannot," she whispered. "I have not heard from your grandfather for twenty-three years – not since the day that I married Poor Tom." Mary Drax never referred to her husband without the deprecatory adjective, and it was very much in this character that she remembered him.

But just as Philo had taken up a knife to open the envelope, the two women were surprised by a knock at the door. Mary Drax laid a startled hand on her heart, in alarm that was more a result of the letter than of the unexpected summons.

Philo slipped the letter back into her pocket, lighted a small candle in a stand, and after seeing her mother seated anxiously in the parlor, opened the door of the house.

"Mr. Varley!" said Philo in surprise.

"Mr. Varley!" echoed her mother in a voice of terror, and rose precipitously.

"Good evening, Philo," said Jewel's father gravely. He was a tall, imposing man of middle age whose every word and gesture seemed calculated to impart a sense of his own consequence. When his eyes moved they appeared to be searching out whether those around him were granting him the respect due his sublime station in New Egypt. He wore four large rings, and a thief of small stature might have been hanged from his watch chain.

"Please step in, Mr. Varley," said Mrs. Drax deferentially, and raised a trembling hand to point out her best chair. He appeared entirely too large for the small chamber, like an owl imprisoned in a cage meant for a canary.

Philo for the first time saw the man who had stood behind – and had in fact been almost hidden by – Mr. Varley. The flame of the candle was reflected in his eyes – and they were eyes that seemed to smile. He was tall and well-proportioned, with rather shorter hair than was worn in the country and a fine brown beard with large moustachios. "Good evening, Miss Philo," he said pleasantly. "I am Henry Maitland."

It is probable that had Mr. Maitland remained silent, Mr. Varley would not have introduced him, thinking the Draxes beneath his important nephew's notice. For despite his ease of manner and unfailing politeness, Henry Maitland had a fortune that was at least ten times that of Mr. Varley, and Mr. Varley, who was by no means a poor man, knew it.

"I am pleased to meet you, sir," said Philo with a smile. But that smile faded when she remembered that a few hours earlier she had seen him walking with Jewel in the Varleys' garden – and that Mrs. Varley intended that Jewel should marry this very man.

"Please sit down, Mr. Maitland," said Mary Drax. "May Philo bring you two gentlemen a glass of water?"

"No, thank you," said Jacob Varley shortly. "We have no intention of remaining so long. Mr. Maitland merely requested an evening's walk after dinner, and as I saw your lighted window, I thought I might as well stop and collect the money that is owed this quarter."

"The payment is not due until tomorrow," said Philo.

Jacob Varley paused a moment before answering, and when he did speak he addressed Philo's mother. "Mrs. Drax, I am a busy man. Do you mean to make me walk over here again tomorrow morning?"

"I don't have all the money tonight," said Mrs. Drax in a small voice.

Philo glanced at Mr. Maitland. He sat a little apart and behind Mr. Varley and, with a movement that was probably habitual for him, ran his fingers along his moustachios, smoothly turning his head as he did so. But his evident study was Mrs. Drax and herself.

In an aggrieved tone, Mr. Varley said to Mrs. Drax as he rose from the chair, "Then I *must* return tomorrow, I suppose. I shall be here at about eleven o'clock, before that—"

"I won't have all the money then either," protested Mrs. Drax. "In February, you'll remember, Mr. Varley, I was quite ill, I—"

"What do you mean, you won't have the money?"

"We have the largest portion of the payment, sir," said Philo. "So we must ask you to allow us another week to make up the remainder. Mother and I—"

"I will do no such thing!" cried Mr. Varley, incensed. "Don't approach me with such a scheme. I want to know nothing about illness and partial payments and the like! If you cannot meet the interest on the loan, then you are welcome to go elsewhere. Only today I had an enquiry regarding the availability of this house from one of my senior employees. I know his wages, and I am certain *he* would not attempt to cheat me of what is rightfully mine!"

"Cheat!" cried Philo incensed.

"Uncle Varley," said Mr. Maitland, speaking for the first time, "I am certain that these two ladies would have no intention of depriving you of your . . ." He paused. ". . . legal deserving."

Mr. Varley grunted, perhaps realizing that he had spoken too harshly in the presence of his nephew. Grandly, he said, "I will return at eleven o'clock tomorrow and will be grateful to receive your quarterly payment then."

"And if not?" asked Philo boldly.

"Philo, do you set up to speak for your mother?"

"My mother is distressed, Mr. Varley."

"She will have my money for me tomorrow, or she shall be more distressed yet."

"You would turn us out?" demanded Philo, forgetful what effect such a question would produce in her mother.

"Come Mr. Maitland, let us continue our stroll," said Jacob Varley, turning to his nephew.

"Uncle Varley," said Mr. Maitland easily – quite as if there were not a destitute widow openly sobbing in the room – "I am thirsty. I will remain a few moments and then meet you again at your house."

"As you desire," replied Jacob Varley, and majestically departed.

Philo looked grimly at Henry Maitland. His insensitivity to their plight seemed extreme. Philo knew only one rich man – the one who had just walked out of the house – and had always nurtured a hope that he was a prejudicial example of the species. Yet here was just such another. Despite their evident distress, there seemed to be a smile on Henry Maitland's lips. "May I get you that glass of water, sir?" said Philo in rather a harsh voice.

Mr. Maitland nodded his head. And there *was* a smile behind his moustachios.

Philo went to the kitchen. Mary Drax, recalling her manners despite all her troubles, asked, "You are Mr. Varley's nephew, I believe?"

"Yes. My mother is Mr. Varley's elder sister. Mother and I live in New York, and besides one another, the Varleys are all we have to denominate family."

"And how do you occupy your time in New York, Mr. Maitland? Are you in commerce?"

Philo brought a glass of water, which the young man accepted with a word of thanks. "I have no business," he said. "I am entirely idle, I fear. My father left my mother and me well provided for – perhaps a little too well provided for, at least so far as the development of my character is concerned."

"Perhaps you could devote yourself to charitable concerns," suggested Mary Drax.

Philo blushed hotly, thinking of their financial plight. It might seem to Mr. Maitland that Mary Drax was surreptitiously asking for help. "Mother," Philo whispered.

Mr. Maitland glanced at Philo, but remained impassive. She suspected he understood her discomfort.

Presently, he said, "I am afraid I am a wholly unregenerate case, Mrs. Drax. I haven't the stamina for any sort of cause or project. I go where the wind blows me. A few weeks ago I realized that I was weary of being alone, and weary of crowds, and weary of the city, and weary of just about anything I heard or saw or did, and so decided to take a little trip into the country. I happened to meet Mr. Varley on the street in New York and he invited me down. And here am I, installed and introduced about as 'nephew.' "

He smiled, and in this speech and in that smile, Philo realized how great a world there was beyond the reaches of New Egypt, that it could hold – without her having ever heard of them at all – rich young men, world-weary young men, lonely young men, men who travelled distances on so small a pretext as a chance meeting on the street and a vague dissatisfaction with the tenor of their lives. New Egypt had been Philo's entire world for eighteen years, but to this handsome, bearded man, it was a spot of ink on a map, distinguished only by its containing his mother's younger brother.

"Mrs. Drax, how much do you owe my uncle?" Henry Maitland asked in a light voice.

"Twenty-two dollars and a half," replied Mary Drax, "but we have only sixteen of that."

"Do you really believe that Mr. Varley would compel you to leave this house on account of six dollars and fifty cents?"

"Yes," said Philo, "I do. I don't care if he is your uncle. I think him a cruel man. Even if he allowed us to remain here, I would have to say that his treatment of Mother was shameful."

Mrs. Drax made a vague movement, which was possibly meant to suppress her daughter's too evident anger. To speak so of Mr. Varley before his own nephew!

"Miss Philo," Henry said, reaching into his pocket, "here are ten dollars. That will make up what is wanted when Uncle Varley comes round tomorrow." He held out a gold coin for her to take.

"Mr. Maitland!" cried Mrs. Drax.

Philo hesitated. Henry Maitland came toward her and placed the coin in the palm of her hand. "Take the money," he said. "Ten dollars mean very little to me. They mean a great deal to you. I *dislike*," he said, and laid an emphasis on the word that implied a kind of disgust, "to see a lady weep." Philo looked quickly to her mother to see if she had understood Mr. Maitland's deprecation of her hysteria. She evidently had not, for now there were but tears of gratitude in her eyes.

Philo wanted to be angry with this man who had come so unexpectedly and all unbidden to their rescue, for she was astute enough to see that though he might have felt compassion for Mary Drax's plight he also felt contempt for her lack of self-control. But instead, Philo only felt ashamed of her mother's want of strength and was hotly embarrassed that Henry Maitland had witnessed it.

He inclined his head slightly, as if in understanding. "Mrs. Drax," he said, bowing politely in response to her confused and voluble thanks, "I was happy to be of service to you and your daughter."

"We *cannot* accept the money," said Philo in a low voice, holding out the coin. "We have never taken charity."

"This is not charity. This is more in the way of amusement. I wish to see my uncle blocked. He behaved badly tonight, and I was ashamed to witness it. On the other hand I was glad that I was by, so that I might counteract his . . ." He searched about the entryway for a word. ". . . *rudeness*," he brought out at last.

"You must allow us to pay you back then," said Philo quickly.

"Very well. I'll come by here tomorrow at ten with a little note of agreement for you to sign. But I warn you, Miss Philo, I shall charge you quite usurious interest."

It was half an hour, after Mr. Maitland's departure before the letter in Philo's pocket was remembered. Mrs. Drax had talked that long of Mr. Varley's threats and Mr. Maitland's timely rescue.

She now had a semblance of calm but this had been an evening of such surprises and reversals that she jumped at every noise. She wondered whether she ought not put off reading the letter until the morning.

"Mother, if Grandfather has not written in twenty-three years, it seems likely that this letter contains some matter of importance. Shall I read it aloud?"

Mrs. Drax nodded, for she was always persuaded by her daughter and had long given over argument as ultimately ineffectual.

Philo brought the candle and the knife while Mrs. Drax arranged herself in the chair for the receiving of momentous and likely very bad news.

But her – and Philo's – first response to the letter was one of astonishment, for when Philo slit open the envelope, two folded ten-dollar notes dropped out and fluttered to the floor.

These Mrs. Drax turned over and over in her hands while Philo read aloud what her grandfather had written.

Chapter 4

THE LETTER

Parrock Farm
Goshen, New Jersey
March 20, 1871

Daughter Mary,

Because I have neither seen you nor answered your letters for twenty-three years, this missive must be opened by you in surprise. I hope that time and my supposed indifference have not withered the filial affection which was so marked an element of your early character and from which, for so many years, you have had such barren return. I have long hesitated to write to you, for I knew that when I did write it would be to beg not only your forgiveness but also your assistance.

I was wrong in abandoning you, but your marriage to improvident Mr. Drax at so tender an age and entirely contrary to my wishes and those of your mother set my heart against you.

I foolishly attributed your mother's wasting away to that wilful connection. Your brother James was my comfort in my bereavement, and I was soon convinced that I had but one dutiful and loving child. I purged you from my heart. This was wrong of me, but daughter Mary, if you knew the sorrow that has fallen upon me, you would forgive me the wrong I have done you. For truly I have been punished.

James and I lived alone and in contentment for fifteen years. Then, some five years ago, when I was on my way to Salem with a load of plums, a young man, driving his phaeton wildly down a too-narrow road, frightened my horse and overturned my wagon into a ditch. I fell beneath it and my legs were crushed. From that day I have been an invalid, and when I budge I am carried.

Shortly thereafter, James was married. He was thirty-seven years of age and not inclined to the conjugal estate. I am convinced that he married more for my sake than for his. His choice was worse than yours. James married a woman from Philadelphia called Hannah Jepson. Her father had been a fisherman and her mother sewed straw for a living. Hannah herself stunted poodles for the fashionable ladies of Philadelphia, which occupation she gave over when she came to live with us here on Parrock Farm.

From the very first I was not pleased with her. Mary, the Parrocks are plain country people – fair and honest and plainspoken, though we had always taken care that our children should be educated. The strength of a nation is founded in the literacy of its populace, and if some of our neighbors felt we were too "high-toned" for our station as mere farmers, I could only point to Mr. Jefferson who also was "a mere farmer." But the Jepsons were another sort of family altogether – low, certainly, and possibly cunning. Hannah's father, I hear, died in a brawl and her mother of drink. Hannah at first was taciturn although apparently complacent, but after the marriage her true character was not slow to reveal itself. She is unmannerly, hypocritical, avaricious, and ignorant – it pains me greatly to speak so of a daughter-in-law. She became imperious and demanding. James once told me he had married Hannah because she was such a strong woman and could help with the work here, but he was mistaken in her.

She refused to leave the house when the sun was up and even required that we hire a girl to assist her in the kitchen. Needless to say, that girl does all the work. Within two years of James's marriage to this woman, her ascendancy over our household was complete. Your poor brother would sit by my bed for hours with his head in his hands and beg my forgiveness for bringing that woman to Parrock Farm.

Nine months ago James died very suddenly. One night after supper he took ill, and the next noon he was dead. I asked Hannah to write to you, but I suspect she did not do so. Hannah said she feared contagion and James was quickly buried. For three months Hannah wore crape streamers on her bonnet whenever she went out, but so far as I could ascertain, those streamers were the length and breadth of her sorrow for James. One morning she went out without them, and when she returned at noon she informed me that she had married again.

John Slape, her new husband, I consider to be in every way Hannah's equal. I do not know what he did for his livelihood before his marriage, but I would not be surprised to learn that he had spent time in prison somewhere. He has that sort of look about him. By his first wife, he has a girl called Katie, a dark-haired beauty some would say, but I think she has the devil in her. Slape and his daughter came to live on Parrock Farm. I would have liked to object to this incursion, but Hannah said that someone was needed to manage the farm and Slape would be better than a paid overseer or set of rascally tenants.

I am served with a kind of grudging courtesy by my daughter-in-law and her husband, for they know I have money. I am prodded once a day to let be known the contents of my will, but this I have refused to do. In a weak moment I was persuaded to sign over the farm to the Slapes, but I was ill and had become convinced that I no longer wanted the trouble of it. From my window I see only the kitchen garden, and that is in such ill repair that I have not the heart to ask after the fields and orchards, which have always been the Parrock pride. Parrock apples were once asked for in Philadelphia and Camden and Trenton. Now the Slapes are trying to persuade me to settle upon them the remainder of my fortune. If I do, they say I need never again worry myself with matters of business and finance. But I know that if they had all my fortune they would not scruple to turn me out of doors, crippled as I am, without property or means.

When I see the hard-visaged Slapes whom I accepted and remember my darling daughter Mary whom I cast out, I am filled with bitterest remorse. I have had John Slape drive me into Goshen today, and I write this letter at my lawyer's. I gave Slape to understand that I would discuss my testament with Mr. Killip, so he contented himself to lift me out of the bed and carry me downstairs and put me into the wagon. I am not the father you remember!

I have been ill now for several weeks with grievous trouble in my bowels. I have suspicions as to the origin of this illness, and someone less trusting than you reading this letter might have an inkling what those suspicions are. I have determined to try to fight these Slapes, and it is for this I ask your assistance. I want the loan of your daughter Philomela. Though I have never seen her, I have heard something of her, from whom I shall not tell you. I have a spy in New Egypt. Philomela, I am told, is of a strong, generous, frank nature. She is independent and resourceful, qualities not often admired in ladies, but qualities which have often distinguished the Parrock women. Philomela is, I am happy to hear, much more a Parrock than a Drax.

Daughter Mary, if you can spare Philomela and if she be willing to come to the aid of a grandfather who has hitherto ignored her existence, send her to me. Let her come to Parrock Farm in the guise of a servant seeking employment. Hannah has lately discharged a girl who was employed in the kitchen here, and her parsimony and short temper are so well known in this neighborhood that the position is in little danger of being shortly filled. I have a plan which, with Philomela's help, might effect the restoration of Parrock Farm to the sad remnant of our family. If the Slapes can be turned out then I would beg you to join Philomela and me here, in the home of your birth and upbringing.

Your father, erring but repentant,
Richard Parrock

P.S. I enclose twenty dollars to defray Philomela's expenses should she choose to come. In any case, please do not think of returning it. R. Parrock.

P.P.S. I have read this letter through twice and only fear that it may be dismissed as the querulous complaining of an old and infirm man whose reason has been unbalanced by his injuries and his grief. I have not misrepresented the infamy of the Slapes – in fact they are worse than I have painted them. And, what I hesitated to write before I will add now – I have begun to fear for my life. R.P.

Chapter 5

PHILO'S RESOLVE

"I will go to him tomorrow," said Philo.

"No!" cried Mrs. Drax. "What could you do against such wicked people as that? Those terrible Slapes. My poor father!"

"Mother, he is in desperate need. His last words were, '*I fear my life is in danger.*' He asks that I come, and how could I refuse?"

"It is dangerous," said her mother. "Such a journey – alone. And such a mission!"

"Goshen is not three hours by the cars, I should think."

"You have never travelled so far, Philo. You have never travelled alone."

Philo paused, then when she spoke to her mother, it was with calmness and deliberation. "Mother, you are trying to put difficulties in my path because you don't want me to go to Goshen. But here is Grandfather's letter and he asks me to come to him. I intend to do just that, and it would not matter to me if he were in California – I would go all the same."

Mrs. Drax shook her head. "It's of no use to talk to you, I suppose."

"No use at all," Philo smiled, and embraced her mother. "Give me your blessing," said Philo quietly, "and some kind message to take to Grandfather from you."

"Tell him – tell him I know not what, Philo. I suppose tell him to leave those terrible Slapes and come to New Egypt. Our home is fearfully small, but he may be assured that he will always be treated with respect and honor and love by his only surviving child. Poor James. I knew he had married, but I had not heard that he was dead. Philo, this letter has been a sad blow to me. I have lost my brother!"

"But you may have regained a father," said Philo comfortingly. "Mother, come upstairs and help me to pack my clothes. I suppose it is a good thing that I have not such a wardrobe as Jewel Varley's after all – for then I should never be able to leave tomorrow. . . ."

"Philo," said Mrs. Drax with some hesitation, "do you think that your grandfather has some deal of money? If the Slapes are resolved to *kill* him for it, I suppose there *must* be a deal of money—"

"Mother! This is not the reason I have chosen to go!"

"Of course not, Philo dear, but wouldn't it be a fine thing if your grandfather came to live with us, or we went to live with him – without the Slapes there of course – and he happened to have some vast quantity of money!"

Philo was silent, and Mrs. Drax said nothing more but was already looking forward to the time when she might slip her needle into a fold of cloth and never pull it out again.

The following morning, Philo went early to the railway station and consulted a table of schedules. She found that she would be able to leave shortly past noon and would arrive in Cape May Court House, the town nearest Goshen on the line, about eight o'clock that evening. Her hope that the journey would require only three hours had been wholly unfounded. On the way back from the station, she was surprised and happy to fall in with Henry Maitland, who had stopped by the post office in hope of finding a recent newspaper or some periodical he had not yet read.

"Mr. Maitland," said Philo, "I am very happy to be able to return your money." She held out the gold coin to him.

He held up his hands and smiled engagingly. "Miss Philo, no!

I had much rather have the pleasure of your I.O.U. Besides, the money is needed."

"No longer," she said. "Mother and I have the money for the payment on the mortgage and more besides. But we will always be grateful to you for your kindness."

"Ah, you have discovered another benefactor then," said Mr. Maitland. "I hardly think that polite, Miss Philo, for surely I presented myself for that position first."

Philo blushed and explained: "My grandfather sent a letter yesterday which contained twenty dollars."

"Ah! I see now. In that case," said Mr. Maitland, "I suppose I must consent to the return of the ten dollars," and he took the coin from Philo. "I must beg you, however, to apply to me in the case that this situation ever arises again. There is no need to wait until the night before a payment is due either. Sometimes the post is not so opportune."

Henry Maitland begged the privilege of escorting Philo home, and she assented. The morning was warm and tasted more of the coming spring than it did of the passing winter. There were clouds in the west, but in the east the sun shone bright and unobscured.

"Will I see you and Mrs. Drax at Jewel's come-out party, Miss Philo?" Henry Maitland asked.

"I think not," smiled Philo. "Jewel's list of guests is *very* exclusive."

"I see," said Henry thoughtfully. "I will speak to Aunt Caroline."

"Pray don't," exclaimed Philo. "It will not make any difference, for I could not go to Jewel's party anyway."

"Why not?"

"I am going away."

Henry looked at her in surprise.

"My grandfather's letter was also an invitation," Philo explained. "I'm going to visit him in Goshen."

"You are leaving soon?"

"In a few hours."

"I am sorry, Miss Philo, I—"

Just then, as they were passing the larger of New Egypt's two stores, Jewel Varley stepped out the door and into the street, nearly colliding with them. "Lord!" she cried. "Watch out, Philo!" Then she saw that Henry Maitland was with her friend, and she was astonished into silence.

"Jewel," said Henry Maitland, with a small, courteous inclination of his head.

Jewel was dressed in the very teeth of fashion, but her outfit might have appeared to better effect on the upper reaches of Fifth Avenue in New York than in the miry lanes of New Egypt. "Cousin Henry," said Jewel, staring hard at Philo all the while, "what on earth are you doing here with Philo Drax?" Her tone of voice was no compliment to the supposed worth of Philo's company.

"Miss Philo is pointing out to me all the sites of historical and social interest in New Egypt," replied Henry, unperturbed by Jewel's rudeness.

"Do you *know* one another?"

"Your father and Mr. Maitland visited our house last evening," said Philo with a polite smile.

"And you went *inside?*" wondered Jewel.

"If you imply that Mother and I would keep Mr. Maitland on the doorstep, Jewel, you are mistaken in your view of our hospitality." Philo was disposed to enjoy Jewel's discomfiture, which was evident.

"I am escorting Miss Philo home now, Jewel."

"This is outrageous," said Jewel angrily, and kicked her little leather boot in the dirt of the street. "Mother will be beside herself. Mother has invited the best people in the town to be introduced to you this forenoon, Cousin Henry, and when she hears that you have gone to the *Draxes'*—"

"Aunt Caroline," interrupted Henry Maitland, drawing himself up and speaking with some coolness, "will, I suppose, grant me the perspicacity and the freedom to make my friends as I choose."

"Of course, Cousin Henry," replied Jewel weakly, "it's only that—"

"Miss Philo and I must be getting on then," he said, "so good morning to you, Jewel. I will see you at luncheon, I presume."

Jewel Varley nodded dumbly, and stood openmouthed in

the street, staring after the man she had come to look on as her
fiancé walking with the daughter of her former dressmaker!
When they turned the corner, Jewel ran off toward home, her
eyes brimming angry tears, and on her way flung a rock at the
doctor's dog.

"This bag," said Mrs. Drax, with a melancholy smile, "I made
from the scraps of the carpet I brought with me from Goshen.
Generations of Parrocks wore that carpet down. Your poor father
trod on it. And now you're going to take it with you back to
Parrock Farm. I wonder if Father will recognize the pattern."

Philo's few articles of clothing were packed away in the
medium-sized carpetbag that had rested beneath Mary Drax's
bed for as long as Philo could remember. But neither she nor her
mother had travelled anywhere, and the satchel had never been
used. The large squares of carpeting that made up the sides were
of a dark floral pattern: bloodred lilies on black stems, with a
dark green background.

Mary Drax's farewell was tearful. Philo insisted that her
mother not accompany her to the station – she wanted as little
notice as possible drawn to her journey, and her parting words to
Mary Drax were "Remember Mother, not a word to anyone. . . ."

Philo climbed aboard the cars with the carpetbag full of her
clothes. Her ticket was tucked beneath the cuff of her sleeve.
The journey required a change of cars at Philadelphia, and Philo,
never having been to the city, was astounded to see so many
persons – and all strangers to her! – gathered in a single place. It
was nightfall before she reached Cape May Court House, which
was the nearest town on the line from Goshen and about four
miles distant. Philo put up for the night in a small hotel, where
for twenty-five cents she obtained a hall room.

It was not possible for Philo to anticipate the future with un-
alloyed hopes – it might very well be that the Slapes would prove
themselves stronger in mischief than she was in defense. And
the notion of being alone and unknown in a strange place – and
under an assumed name – did not allow her to lie comfortably
in her hard and narrow bed. Her principal consolation was the
thought that she had with this doubtful journey discounted

Jewel Varley's tidy dismissal of her life. It was a pang to have left New Egypt just when the presence of Mr. Maitland had made it so pleasant a place for her, but the sense of adventure and discovery that nearly overwhelmed Philo as she lay alone in her room, wakened every few minutes by the tread of unknown feet just outside her door, pretty well made up for it. And though she had thought ill of her mother's concern for the possibility of getting money from Mr. Parrock, Philo could not help but indulge herself a little, and wonder what it would be to stand equal to Jewel Varley, ribbon for ribbon and flounce for flounce. Philo would like to know who would win Mr. Maitland *then!*

PART II

GOSHEN

Chapter 6

PARROCK FARM

Goshen was a town even smaller and less significant than New Egypt. It was situated just a few miles from Delaware Bay in the northwestern part of Cape May, the rectangular peninsula at the southern extremity of New Jersey. In 1871 Cape May was just becoming popular as a resort. The well-to-do of Philadelphia wanted a place not overrun with grasping families from New York, and in quiet Cape May it was found. There was at this time a great deal of building on the Cape, but principally in the tiny towns along the Atlantic Coast: Cape May, Holly Beach, Wildwood and Stoneharbor. Goshen was unaffected, but in watching how prices rose in the towns where the Philadelphians came and noting the increase in noise and carriage accidents, Goshen's inhabitants were glad to be excluded from the general boom.

If Goshen must be said to have a reason for existence, it was probably for the convenience of the farmers who had concentrated in that area. However the town wasn't *much* of a convenience, since it had no bank, telegraph office, hotel, or dining saloon. For those things one had to travel to Cape May Court House, another five miles toward the coast. The land around Goshen was given over to agriculture, clover and other cultivated grasses being the greatest and most lucrative crop, but also grown were rye, Indian corn, and oats. Larger farms grazed milch cows, and smaller farms had poultry.

Parrock Farm lay a couple of miles to the south of Goshen and fronted Delaware Bay. It was a place of about four hundred acres – more than moderate size for this area – and its principal crops were hay and forage. On the ground gradually rising from the Bay shore was a generous farmhouse, just about a hundred years old. It was a fine, sturdy old building, constructed of stone and filled with the furniture made by the generation of Parrocks who had been sixty or seventy years in the graveyard of Goshen.

During the time Parrock Farm had been managed by Richard Parrock and his son James alone, it had prospered, but the old man's wagon mishap brought an end to three decades of good fortune that had been marred only by the death of Parrock's wife, the marriage of his daughter to Poor Tom Drax, and the War Between the States.

The accident that invalided Richard Parrock was cited as the cause of all their sorrow, not because it crippled the man, but because it was the inducement for his son James to marry. Under Hannah Jepson's reign Parrock Farm started its decline, a decline which began quite at once and so unmistakably as to lead the superstitious to believe that she had cast an evil spell upon it. Field hands had accidents with the plows, work animals took on diseases no one could cure or even identify, violent storms came up just when the hay had been cut and stacked in the fields, and the servant girls hired by Hannah to do work that she ought to have done herself stole money or got into trouble with the fieldhands. It was not easy to judge who was unhappier: Richard the father, confined to his bed and hearing one report after another of the deterioration of the farm that was his very life; or James the son, who made these reports and blamed himself for having brought Hannah to Parrock Farm.

But James's sudden death was only the first peal of the bell that tolled the old man's sorrows. Grief over his son, coupled with his physical infirmity, rendered him defenseless before his daughter-in-law. Before he realized what had happened and how, he found himself the cowering prisoner of Hannah, her new husband, and her stepdaughter. He had signed over to them Parrock Farm, though feeling as he did so that he was betraying four generations of Parrock ancestors who had owned this land since before the War of Independence. Now the Slapes wheedled to have him alter his will in their favor. Slowly the conviction had come upon him that if he did consent to strike his daughter Mary from the document – Mary, whom he had abandoned in all but this – he would not live out the succeeding month. Richard Parrock suspected that Hannah had murdered his son, probably at the instigation of this man John Slape.

He rarely left his chamber now. John Slape was required to

lift and carry him about, and John Slape had let it be known how little this operation pleased him. In Richard Parrock's chamber were but his bed, a dresser, two chairs, and his desk. It once had been a comfortably furnished room but Hannah, upon pretense of cleaning or repair, had taken away the carpet, bed curtains, draperies, lounge, and bookcase. The pieces had never returned, and the old man assumed the Slapes had appropriated them to their own use or had taken them away merely for spite. The Slapes, he knew, had no use for literature, and it was with some particular pleasure that Hannah and the girl Katie refused to bring him anything to read. The hours were lonely and long, and he lay most of the day on his side, looking out the windows toward Delaware Bay. The chamber was rarely swept and the linen infrequently changed, but Richard Parrock knew that his requests for more attention would go unheeded.

It was with the last of his courage that he wrote to his daughter Mary and asked her to send Philomela to him. Daniel Killip, his lawyer in Goshen, had made discreet inquiries into the situation of Mary Drax and her daughter Philomela in New Egypt, and his report on Philo was encouraging. Richard Parrock had now one hope in his life, and that was, with the help of Philomela Drax his granddaughter, to escape the Slapes. He had sent his letter on Monday the twentieth of March, and could not help but expect some reply to it almost immediately. Tuesday and Wednesday passed with no news, and Thursday – when some reply *might* be possible – Richard Parrock was on tenterhooks.

So on Thursday afternoon the twenty-third, though he hated like a dog to do it, he took his cane from the hooks on the wall above his bed and rapped sharply three times on the floor. His chamber was just above the kitchen, and this was the signal that he wanted attendance.

After the lapse of some few minutes   a passage of time meant to inform him of how little consequence he was thought in the house – the door of his chamber scraped open, and in it stood Hannah Slape. She was a tall, raw, overgrown sort of woman with red arms and prominent knuckles. Her strength was probably tremendous, although this would never be known from the amount of work she did about the house. She wore a checked gown, frayed around the hems and not overly clean, a dingy apron smeared with grease and dirt, and a calico nightcap over her strawlike hair. She had no smile for her father-in-law.

"What's wanted, Pa?" she said in no happy tone of voice. She insisted on addressing him so, though they were but tenuously related and not by affection.

"I wanted to know if Mr. Killip had called," replied Richard Parrock. He tried to infuse politeness into his voice, for he had no wish to antagonize the Slapes at present or to put them on their guard against him.

"No one's called. What's wanted with Mr. Killip? Change your will at last, and put your family in? Us who've kept you for so long?"

"Perhaps," replied Richard Parrock evasively.

"Well," said Hannah, "Mr. Killip calls, I'll say you want to change your testament. Save a deal of grief, Pa, if you'd just turn everything over to us now. Give John the trouble of your affairs. Have this chamber till you die, have us to keep you."

"I'll think about it," said Richard Parrock uncomfortably. Hannah Slape's solicitude was worse than her anger, for her anger at least was genuine.

A repulsive grin momentarily altered Hannah's features as she wiped her hands on her apron in grimy expectation of the old man's money. She put her hand on the latch and was turning to go when Richard Parrock asked, "Have you found a girl yet to replace the one that went away?"

"Not yet," she shrugged. "Why are you asking?"

"Oh, I know that when there's no one helping in the kitchen, you and Katie have to do all the work."

"Don't like my cooking, Pa?" The thought appeared to amuse her, as did all the other of Richard Parrock's discomforts.

"No, no, Hannah! I just don't like to see you overworked."

She snorted. "Be someone along sometime. John's left word in Goshen that a girl's wanted at Parrock Farm. Last one run off with three spoons; this one I'll watch close. Next girl comes here won't get away with nothing!"

Chapter 7

THE RABBIT

"What did the old man want today?" asked Katie Slape.

Hannah's stepdaughter sat at the table in the kitchen of the Parrock Farm house. She was eighteen years of age, with thick black hair and fine black eyes. But for the expression of her mouth, which was thin-lipped and hard, she might have been thought a lovely young woman. She held a sharp thin-bladed knife in her hand, and with it she was carefully flaying a rabbit, an operation with which she seemed tolerably familiar.

Hannah grinned. "Wanted to know if the lawyer'd come. Decided at last to give us the money."

Katie smiled too, and it wasn't pleasant to see. "I knew he'd do it, Mar; I said to you he'd do it. Said so in the leaves at the bottom of my cup last night. Leaves in the bottom of my cup said he'd do it today!" The skin of the rabbit was detached, and Katie neatly folded it and laid it atop the four severed feet that stood in a neat row on the tabletop.

The kitchen of Parrock House was of the old-fashioned sort: large and square, with a stone floor and stone walls that sweated in damp weather, with shallow wide fireplaces, and with ovens set into the walls. All round were dark cupboards for storage and in one corner a pump and sink and drain. In the center of the room was a vast deal table, so large that only a portion needed to be kept clean at any one time. It had a variety of mismatched chairs set about it, and it was here that the Slapes most often gathered.

Hannah took the skinned rabbit, and with a knife of her own slit open its belly and dug out the entrails. Katie watched her greedily, as if it were a task she coveted.

"Signed nothing yet," warned Hannah as she dumped the entrails into a pan. "Not agreed yet, but he's thought of it."

Katie banged the heels of her boots on the stone floor. "Oh, Mar, I'd like to have him . . . I'd like to have him . . ."

42

"Have him where, Katie?" asked Hannah indulgently.

"Have him where it was just him and me, that's where! Oh that old man don't care one straw for me. That old man called me a crazy head!" She leaned over to one side, and rummaged in a bloody canvas bag on the floor and in a moment brought up another rabbit.

"Because you went up there one day and looked at his palm, and looked at the frost on the pane, and told him he wasn't going to live to see next Christmas."

"He won't!" cried Katie with malicious triumph. "That old man is booked for the grave. Only he's to sign first, ain't he, Mar? He's to sign and then he's to die, ain't it so?"

Hannah only smiled and put her bloodstained finger to her lips. Katie was a wild girl, thought by some to be simpleminded, by others to have the power of looking into the future and knowing things it wasn't for the sober and whole-brained to know. Katie, even more than Hannah, relished tormenting Richard Parrock.

At the signal for lowering her voice, Katie grinned and lopped off the feet of the second rabbit. She spoke in a low energetic whisper to her stepmother: "Oh, Mar, how you think that old man'll die? Won't be easy, no ma'am! That old man's tough as a ten-year-old chicken. I took down his curtains, and I took off his coverlets, and I sneak in when he's sleeping and open the window, and he don't no more take chill than if he was a stone in the riverbed. Anybody else would have yards of sore throat, but not him. I put ashes in his beans but he's fat as butter. I watch that old man like he was the weather, but there's nothing disagrees with him!" she exclaimed in her exasperation.

They were silent for a few moments as Katie turned her attention to the skinning of the second rabbit. When she was finished Hannah took it. "Old man," said Hannah, resuming the conversation. "Lots happens to folks who's old."

"Sometimes," said Katie with a wink, "their bedclothes catches fire." Hannah nodded and split open the rabbit's belly. "Sometimes," said Katie, "they gets their arms chopped off with a axe."

Hannah laid back the skin of the rabbit and uttered an expression of disgust. Just within the belly of the rabbit was an

immense pale tumor overspread with distended veins. It had
crowded the organs of the rabbit aside and rendered them black
with bad blood. Hannah let go quickly and wiped her tainted
fingers on her apron.

"No," cried Katie, "open it again."

Hannah reluctantly pulled apart the flaps of the rabbit's flesh.
Katie reached across the table and experimentally pressed the
cyst with the flat of her knife blade. It bulged and looked about
to burst.

"Oh, lord!" cried Hannah.

Katie turned the blade and pricked the tumor. Noisome bile
sprayed a foot into the air. Worms flooded out and swarmed over
the blade of the knife. Hannah withdrew her hands suddenly
and the flesh closed over it. The worms began to squirm out of
the rent made in the rabbit's flesh.

"And sometimes," Katie said, "old folks get hold of a bad piece
of flesh. . . ."

That day John Slape had been absent on business in Cape May
Court House. His business was an attempt to sell off a hundred
acres of timber that belonged to Parrock Farm, and he had been
successful. Men would come within the week to hew down the
fine cedars that grew on the northern part of the farm. John
Slape had no intention of telling Richard Parrock of this transaction, and as the old man could not see that portion of the farm
from his chamber, he would know nothing of it. The noise could
be attributed to similar work on an adjoining property.

John Slape was city-born and city-bred. He knew nothing of
farming and hadn't the intelligence or inclination to learn anything of it. He could not do a thing himself, and the pay he offered
anyone else for the job was so ridiculously low as to attract only
those who sought to cheat him of that little by doing nothing
to earn it. The returns on the farm decreased every season, and,
unknown to Richard Parrock, already half the land had been sold
off. The fields which the old man had plowed for thirty years were
now in the possession of a neighbor whom he detested.

It had become apparent to John and Hannah Slape that their
fortunes were not to be made in agriculture. They had given

up on Parrock Farm and now looked toward the other assets which the old man still possessed. James Parrock had once told Hannah that his father was worth $25,000, most of which was held in railroad stocks and government bonds. Hannah's careful investigation had informed her that such investments were not negotiable by the mere possessor – they must be endorsed first – so that there was nothing to be gained by robbing the old man of the paper. Hannah had considered forgery, but she was not expert with a pen and mistrusted hiring a third party. Since Richard Parrock was old, the best plan seemed to be the legal one: that of convincing him to alter his will in their favor. Once that was accomplished, who knew but that the old man might die suddenly and soon?

When John Slape returned to Parrock Farm that Thursday evening, his good news of the sale of the timber was over-matched by Hannah's pronouncement that Richard Parrock had determined to sign over to them his property.

"Oh, this is good news!" said John Slape, and sat heavily at the kitchen table. He was a large-framed man, with thick black hair, a black beard, and a black moustache that looked as if it had been gnawed by rats. His principal pleasure in life was attending the theater, a habit he had formed during his first marriage to the unfortunate Mlle. Desire (whose real name had been Mary Tompkins). He looked forward to the death of the old man, not only for the anticipated possession of his money, but for the return to a city where he might indulge his theatrical passion. John Slape wore a large, drab surtout, with loose, drab clothes beneath, and heavy, rough boots that made his presence known from one end of the house to the other. "I'll go up to thank him."

Hannah and Katie laughed, and John Slape grinned at what he thought an excellent witticism at Richard Parrock's expense. So far as they imagined, the old man was entirely fooled by their hypocritical solicitude.

A few minutes later, John Slape pounded up the stone stairs and entered Richard Parrock's room without knocking. "Pa," he said, "Hannah says you're turning it all over."

Richard Parrock sat up slowly in the bed. "I'm thinking of it, John."

"It's good you've decided, Pa, we're—"

"I'm *thinking* of it, John," repeated Richard Parrock. "But first I have to speak to Mr. Killip. I expected him today but he has not come. When I've talked to him, then we shall see what's to be done."

John considered this a few moments. He was not a quick-witted man, and brute strength and cunning must answer for lack of intelligence. "Hannah says—"

Richard Parrock shook his head. "Not yet," he said firmly. "I've made no decisions yet, but I'm thinking of it." Richard Parrock prayed that the Slapes never learned to what extent he feared them. The sight of massive John Slape filling the doorway of his room always made the old man wonder on what day his neck would be broken by those brawny, soiled hands, or he be lifted and hurled through the casement.

John Slape's disappointment was intense. He stamped his feet on the floor, clenched his fists, and whirled about, nearly colliding with Katie, who appeared in the doorway bearing a tray. She deftly stepped out of the way and allowed her father free flight down the stairs, where he called out loudly for Hannah.

Katie came into the room with a smile that made Richard Parrock every bit as uneasy as her father's anger.

Richard Parrock gave her nervous greeting. "Hello, Katie," he said, attempting to ignore John Slape's impassioned yelling below stairs. "Are you not early? Or have I lost track of the time? When do you suppose my clock will be repaired? It's a shame not to have it on the mantel any longer."

"Oh, that!" said Katie. "Tossed it away. In here you've no need of the time, Grandpa."

Richard Parrock shuddered each time this young girl addressed him so.

Katie placed the tray across the old man's lap, and seeing that the spoon was dirty, wiped it off on the scarcely cleaner hem of her skirt.

"What's this today?" he asked, eyeing the deep plate that had been placed on the tray before him.

"Oh, it's delicious," said Katie with a grin, "go ahead. It's rabbit stew."

Chapter 8

A DOLLAR A WEEK

Early the following morning the Slapes were at their usual meager breakfast of coffee and mashed potatoes. The morning was damp and the kitchen smelled of rotting hay. The fire in the hearth was sluggish and smoky. "Which of you took up his food?" demanded John Slape, looking first at his wife, then at his daughter.

"I did," said Hannah. "Old man don't like the girl."

"That don't signify," replied John Slape. "You ask about the money? What'd he say to signing?"

"Said he was waiting for the lawyer," replied Hannah. "Wouldn't say more'n that."

"He's a wicked old man!" exclaimed John Slape. "To keep us waiting the way he has – there's no forgiveness for it."

Lifting her plate closer to her mouth in order to shovel in the last shreds of potato, Katie grinned. That grin promised no happiness for Richard Parrock when at last he did endorse the railway shares and the government bonds.

There was a knock at the kitchen door. From where they sat the Slapes could not see who called. They were in general chary of visitors, fearing that someone should find how closely mewed up they kept Richard Parrock.

"Maybe it's Killip the lawyer," said John Slape, making no move to rise.

"Who's there?" called Hannah loudly. "What's wanted?"

The knock was repeated, and, casting her plate aside, Katie rose precipitously and jerked open the door. Without, and beginning to sink in the mire of the dooryard, stood a young woman of Katie's own age carrying a carpetbag. Whether she was actually prettier than Katie would have been a matter of individual judgment, but there could be no doubt that the physiognomy of the young woman in the doorway was expressive of self-reliance, honesty, and intelligence. Her dress was plain but wholesome, and she peered curiously beyond Katie into the kitchen. Her mouth tightened a little, evidently in disapproval of the uncleanliness she noted there.

"What's wanted, girl?" demanded Hannah. "Never seen you before."

"I was told you had a place open here."

Hannah regarded her closely; the young woman's eye was unflinching and this surprised Hannah, for most were afraid of her.

"Maybe. Willing to work?"

"I am."

"Are you willing to work hard? Are you willing to do what you're told to do?" cackled Katie, who had taken an instant dislike to the young woman seeking employment.

"I am willing to do what's required of me," the girl replied with perfect self-possession. She came boldly into the room and looked about. "It appears that you've not had anyone in some time."

"Hard to get girls that are honest," sneered Hannah. "You honest, girl?"

"I hope so. I have never had complaint on that score."

"Then you have papers? You have letters?"

Philo – to make no mystery of her identity – took two folded letters from the pocket of her skirt and held them out to Hannah. Katie snatched them away and roughly opened them. She stared at them a few moments but in such a way to make Philo think that she did not know how to read, then handed them to her stepmother. Hannah began to look over the letters, but the effort was almost as great for her as it had been for Katie, and she soon gave it over. Philo realized that she need not have been so careful in preparing these false recommendations, the writing of which had caused her some pangs of conscience as being the first deliberate deceptions she had ever perpetrated.

"You'll do, I suppose," said Hannah. "What are you called?"

"My name is Mary Dracut," replied Philo, who thought it imprudent to give her real name, which might not be unknown to the Slapes. Then, to maintain her assumed character as a servant seeking employment, she asked, "What are the wages?"

"Dollar a week," replied Hannah. Here John Slape took up his shotgun, which was propped beside the door, and made his departure without a word or a second glance at Philo. The hiring of servants was woman's domain, and he took no part in it.

"That's very low," said Philo, who would have taken the position if only a quarter of that sum had been offered, so anxious was she to see her grandfather.

"You've nothing to spend it on," laughed Katie. "Not here. We'll keep you busy enough."

"Sweep out chambers," said Hannah. "Have the care of the poultry yard. And cook – you cook?"

"Does someone else live here?" asked Philo.

"What made you think that, girl?" demanded Hannah sharply.

"I was told in Goshen that four persons lived at Parrock House. I've seen only three."

"There's only the old man upstairs," laughed Katie. "But he won't be troubling you long."

A cloud passed over Philo's brow, which did not go unnoticed by Hannah and Katie.

"Is he ill?" asked Philo anxiously.

"Took sick last night," replied Katie with a smile. "Turned out his stomach five times over."

"I'm sorry," said Philo with an effort to appear indifferent. To betray too great an interest in her grandfather might raise suspicions in the minds of the Slapes.

"Oh, it's nothing to us," Katie assured her.

Hannah regarded Philo closely. "Where you from, girl?"

"Woodbine," replied Philo readily, naming a town about fifteen miles distant at which the cars had stopped the previous day.

"Why don't you bide at home then?" demanded Katie rudely.

"My family are poor," replied Philo with dignity. "And out on my own, I am less a burden to them."

Hannah was apparently satisfied with this explanation and opened the door to the tiny room beside the pantry in which Philo was to sleep. "Hearth wall," said Hannah, laying her hand against the stones, "warm enough in here." She left the girl alone.

Philo sat on the edge of the little cot, which with a rickety table was the only furnishing of the room. She was unhappy with the necessity of disguise and prevarication, but reflected that all was done for the sake of her grandfather, who lay ill, crippled, and practically imprisoned in one of the rooms somewhere above. It was sobering to think that if he had not been able to send the letter which had arrived in New Egypt only two days before, Philo and her mother would never have known of his plight. Since Philo had never met her grandfather and knew him only by his name and the fact that he had rejected his daughter twenty-three years before, it was impossible to think of the old man without thinking of his fortune. Implicit in his letter, Philo considered, had been his intention of settling money on the Draxes. This excited Philo, and the prospect of being raised to Jewel Varley's position in the society of New Egypt was a happy thought indeed. As she opened the carpetbag and set out her meager wardrobe on the rickety table, Philo vowed that the Slapes, having already secured the farm, should not have another penny that belonged rightfully to her and her mother. Even upon so slight an acquaintance, they had impressed Philo unfavorably, and she would not be sorry to thwart their plans.

Philo spent all that morning cleaning the kitchen, and even with so much work she only managed to make it presentable. The Slapes disgusted her with their disregard for cleanliness and order. Hannah and Katie took their leisure sitting at the table, cracking nuts left over from the previous winter's harvest and directing Philo sharply about. Philo would happily have foregone their company, but she forced herself to be polite and subservient.

She attended to the conversation of the mother and daughter, which was coarse and vulgar in the extreme. Hannah and Katie spoke without reserve of the money they imagined they would come into soon, and the dark hints that related to the old man's death were not lost on Philo as she scrubbed the hearthstones and lugged out pail after pail of ashes from the fireplace. When she realized the contempt in which the Slapes held her grandfather and the complacency with which they looked forward to his demise, Philo became ever more anxious to see him.

Toward noon Hannah remarked, "Time to take him a little more rabbit stew," and to this perfectly reasonable speech, Katie replied with a gale of laughter that mystified Philo.

"Oh, let me take it up to him," said Philo, unable to disguise her eagerness.

Katie and Hannah did not remark on Philo's plea for more tasks, but merely signified that she should fill a plate with the stew that had simmered all morning in a thick black pot at the back of the hearth.

Philo hastily ladled out a plate of the stew, set it on a tray with a spoon and a napkin – this last a luxury she had no way of knowing her grandfather had been many many months without – and carried it upstairs. She paused a moment before the door of Richard Parrock's chamber, and when she knocked it was with a slight hesitancy born of the reflection that she was about to see her grandfather for the first time in her life.

"Walk in," cried a feeble voice.

Philo lifted the latch and pushed the door open with her foot. She entered into a large, spare chamber with whitewashed walls, dark wainscoting, and simple, old-fashioned furniture. The chamber windows however made up for the deficiency of decoration by presenting a fine vista of Delaware Bay and the edge of the great cedar swamp to the south. The noon sun had burned away the morning's dampness.

In the great four-poster bed against the wall, Philo made out the enfeebled form of an old man. His eyes had been closed, and when he opened them they were filmed. His face was pale and blotched, his white beard discolored with illness. As she neared the bed she was struck with the unpleasant odor of invalidism, so nearly akin to the odor of death.

The man was startled to see her. "Who are you?" he demanded.

"I'm the new girl," Philo replied, and glanced behind her to make certain that she had not been followed up the stairs. She placed the tray on the edge of the bed, put her finger to her lips, and hurried to the door, shutting it softly.

"Are you Philomela?" the old man cried in wonder, and the tears sprang to his rheumy eyes.

"Shhhhh!" cried Philo with a smile, and came to the old man's side. "It is I, Grandfather. But you must call me Mary. I am known to the Slapes as Mary Dracut. I thought it would be easier for you to remember if I assumed Mother's given name." She took Richard Parrock's hand. "I have come to take you away."

"You have seen them downstairs?"

"They have hired me," replied Philo, "for a dollar a week."

"Philomela," said the old man, "I will give you thousands!"

"I am Mary," said Philo sternly. "If the Slapes discover I am your granddaughter—"

Richard Parrock shuddered. "They must not," he said in a whisper.

"We haven't long," said Philo. "They will wonder what keeps me."

"Your mother, how is she?" asked Richard Parrock with some diffidence.

"She sends her love, and urges you to come to New Egypt. We are not wealthy by any means, but we mean to take care of you there."

"Oh . . ." He paused. ". . . *Mary*, you have come in the very nick of time, for they have almost got me to promise that I will turn over to them my property. But now nothing will induce me—"

Philo heard steps upon the stairs without the room. "Hush, grandfather!" she cried in a low voice, then stepped back from the bed. As she heard the door open behind her, she said in a normal voice, "You seem very weak, Mr. Parrock. Please eat the stew; it is sure to make you stronger."

Richard Parrock smiled at Hannah Slape, who stood in the doorway of the room regarding Philo suspiciously. "I have just made the acquaintance of the new girl," he said in a weak voice. "I am certain that she will work out." And with that he took up his spoon and began to eat of Katie's stew.

Chapter 9

PHILO'S FORTUNE

More work awaited Philo downstairs. The Slapes' chambers wanted sweeping out, and after that she was to take the plumpest chicken the poultry yard afforded, wring its neck, pluck it, and fricassee it for the Slapes' dinner. It was fortunate that Philo's poverty had prepared her well for this masquerade as a hired girl. By six o'clock all was done, however, and the chicken was sitting in a pan of cold water to draw out its toughness before it was cut up. Weary and troubled, Philo stood at the casement window of the kitchen, alternately slicing winter beetroot and staring at the sinking sun. Her grandfather was almost directly above her, but she dared not return to him. She felt that, despite her precautions, Hannah Slape suspected that she was more than she seemed. Philo was determined to give the woman no cause to doubt her simple identity as a meek and impoverished servant.

Presently Philo heard steps on the stairs. She paused in her task and nodded briefly to Katie. This was a girl whom Philo in her turn mistrusted; she hadn't intelligence but cunning in abundance. And perhaps there was something the girl possessed which was more than either.

"Hey, girl!" said Katie loudly.

"My name is Mary," replied Philo quietly. "I'd prefer you to address me by my name."

"Well, girl," said Katie with a sneer, "so you've come to Parrock Farm to make your fortune."

The knife in Philo's hand sliced awry. "What do you mean?" she asked evenly, fearful that Katie had guessed her secret.

"I mean that on your wages – a dollar a week – you'll be the Queen of Sweden before you can count to twenty-five."

Philo was relieved. Katie had meant something else altogether. "Wages of a dollar a week are better than no wages at all," remarked Philo philosophically – and she could afford to speak so, with the prospect of Richard Parrock's wealth before her.

"Come sit by me," said Katie, placing herself in her father's chair at the head of the kitchen table.

"Why?" asked Philo. "I've work still to do."

"Sit beside me," said Katie, whose smile – unpleasant and unsettling as it was – seemed never to desert her. "I'll tell your fortune."

Philo turned and looked closely at the young woman, who beckoned her with a wink and a crooked finger. She put down her knife. "I don't believe in such things. I don't believe it's possible to read the future."

"No more do I," replied Katie, unabashed. "I merely tell what I see, what I've already seen – no more'n that."

Philo's brow furrowed. Her mistrust and dislike of Katie grew by the minute, but she was reluctant to offend any of the Slapes.

"Take a cup of coffee," said Katie, pointing to the pot that was keeping warm in the embers of the fire.

The day was dwindling, and the sun at that moment fell behind the dismal line of cedars at the edge of the great swamp. The kitchen became suddenly darker, and as Philo reached down for the pot of coffee, the embers seemed to spring to fire before her – glowing like molten rubies. She filled a cup up to the chip in its rim, and would have brought it to the table, but Katie commanded, "Drink it off!"

Philo swallowed the coffee quickly, the liquid being little more than lukewarm.

Katie reached out and greedily took the cup. She set it on the table and, placing one finger against the handle, turned it gently round and round. She tilted the cup and poured off a few remaining drops of liquid, then turned the cup three times more, muttering beneath her breath words which Philo could not make out.

"This is superstition," said Philo, seating herself in the chair next to Katie's at the side of the table. But fascinated, she peered into the cup and saw that the grounds of coffee had settled themselves into a pattern of spirals. Katie looked at it, looked at Philo, looked back at the cup and smiled.

Then suddenly, she shoved the cup aside. It spun across the table and over the edge. Philo lurched to save it, but the cup smashed on the stone floor.

"I don't need such," said Katie, frowning. She looked hard at Philo. "There was nothing in there I don't see in your face."

Philo made no reply. She really feared the girl, feared the knowledge she saw in Katie Slape's eyes. "What is my fortune then?" Philo asked bravely.

All at once Katie's hard black eyes appeared to glaze. The whites became a milky, striated gray, and Philo drew back in alarm. Katie looked away and then answered in a voice that was soft and hollow and not her own, "I see a mound of gravel and I see a grave."

"What does that signify?" demanded Philo.

"I see that in your cheeks and in your eyes," replied Katie without looking at Philo. "I see a woman holding a bloody needle, and a girl on a staircase slipping in blood, and a woman opening a case that's brimming with blood. I see them all tangled in your hair." Still she did not turn. "You open your mouth and I see—"

"You see what?" cried Philo when she would not finish.

The girl seemed in a trance. She would not respond, she would not turn to look at Philo. Philo took her by the shoulders and shook her. Katie looked round at last, and her face was filled with fear. She drew in her breath sharply, and her head snapped back on her neck. She murmured inarticulately, and Philo demanded again: "What did you see when you looked in my mouth?" She opened it wide in the girl's face.

Katie jerked away her gaze. After a moment she appeared to recover herself. "You'll marry a limping fiddler," she said at last with a malicious smile. "And your first child will be born an idiot."

Philo burned to know what Katie had really seen.

The fricasseed chicken was a celebratory indulgence for the Slapes, and they were lively and merry throughout the meal, making many jesting references to the money they should soon have through the generosity of the old man upstairs. Philo – who was allowed to reserve a wing for her own supper – affected not to understand the obvious references to the fortune that was rightfully hers and her mother's. She was instructed to carry to the old man upstairs another plate of the rabbit stew, but warned at the same time not even to taste it herself. "Specially for him, Mary, hear?" Hannah cautioned. Philo sought permission to take her meal in her grandfather's chamber, saying she had just as soon keep the old man company for half an hour. To this Hannah assented with a nod, but behind Philo's back she exchanged a knowing glance with her stepdaughter.

When Philo brought Richard Parrock his supper he was rather more ill than he had been in the morning, and she assured him that they would leave Parrock House as soon as he was well enough to travel.

"We must not wait, Philo," he advised her. "I will *never* be well again until *I* have left this house – and that family – behind me. We should leave this very night."

"It is true," said Philo seriously, "we cannot be here long. The Slapes do not entirely trust me, I think. Katie told my fortune earlier, and it seemed to anger her. She is very queer."

"Beware that child," said Richard Parrock weakly. "If that child ever prays, it is for my death. Philomela, we *will* leave this house tonight. We will take one of the wagons."

"But," said Philo hesitantly, "does that not belong to the Slapes?"

Richard Parrock managed a small smile for his granddaughter's scruple. "Philomela, they have taken from me the entire farm. Do you think they have the right to object to the lending of a wagon for a few hours? In Goshen we will hire a boy to drive it back."

Philo must be satisfied. "But won't they hear us? And if they hear us, they are hardly likely to let us get away."

"They sleep sound," replied Richard Parrock. "The last girl employed here told me that. The stable is on the other side of the house from their chambers. If we are quiet about our business, they won't know till the morning that we've gone."

"Won't they know our destination?"

"Perhaps," replied the old man. "But once we are on our way, I shall feel safe. It is only in this house, behind their locked doors with John Slape and that terrible gun of his, that I feel myself weak and defenseless. But once outside, I know I shall feel free and protected. Protected, Philomela, because you're with me."

Philo smiled. She wasn't convinced that they would be able to leave the farm without drawing the Slapes' attention, but since she had no alternative to propose, she acquiesced to her grandfather's plan. "The Slapes are certain to be asleep by midnight," said Philo. "I'll return to you then and help you to pack your things."

"No," he replied. "There is no need of that. I leave everything behind. I am ashamed of the clothing in which Hannah Slape has kept me for the past two years. I shall declare myself independent of trunk-makers and carry my clothes upon my back. I'll manage but one burden—"

"What is that?"

The old man, who seemed to be gaining in strength as he talked of his anticipated liberation from the Slapes, put a finger to his lips, drew himself painfully over to the edge of the bed and, pressing his hand under the sheet and between the mattresses, withdrew a thick sheaf of bank notes. Others, dislodged from the much larger cache there, fluttered to the floor. Richard Parrock smiled feebly and shook the money in his fist.

"This is your future, Philo," he said. "This is hard cash. This will get me out of this house, and this will protect you and me for the rest of our lives."

Philo hurried forward and gathered up the notes from the floor. She was fearful that one of the Slapes would enter the chamber and see that her grandfather had such a sum about him.

"Why did you get it in bank notes, Grandfather?" she asked. "Your fortune was in bonds, I was told."

"Don't trust bonds, didn't want to carry bonds about with me. Oh, Philomela, you and I will show up at your mother's door, and I'll put this money in her hands and pray it begins to atone for my neglect of her."

"Mother would be happy to have you, Grandfather, if you came penniless."

"But I don't come penniless. Philomela, how much money do you suppose is here, beneath this mattress?"

"Five thousand dollars," Philo guessed, wondering whether the sum could possibly be so high.

"Twenty-nine thousand eight hundred and forty-five dollars!"

Philo gasped. "Put it away! Hurry, Grandfather, what if one of the Slapes should come up?"

He nodded, handed the notes to Philo, who quickly shoved them back between the feather mattresses.

"How did you get it past them into the house?" Philo asked curiously.

"Daniel Killip drove me to Cape May Court House one day – I let them think I might be going to alter my will in their favor – and I cashed in my bonds. These are bank notes, drawn on the Bank of Cape May Court House, where the Parrocks have done business for fifty years. They are solid as these walls. Philomela, my dear daughter's daughter, this is hard cash. I brought it back hidden in the pockets of my greatcoat. It is yours now – yours and your mother's. You and Mary have had a hard time of it these twenty-three years, have you not, Philomela?"

"We have," said Philo soberly.

"Do you blame me?"

"I blame no one," Philo replied. "I've learnt many hard lessons, Grandfather. And sometimes it seems that the first premise is always: *The Draxes are poor, the Draxes have no money, therefore . . .*"

"You should blame me, Philo. I have always had the money and I've done nothing to help you."

To this Philo had no reply. It was as if she could forgive the man but not the deed.

"Once we are away from this place, Philomela, we will be very happy! I am very eager to see my daughter again!"

Philo thought of the fortune secreted between the mattresses beneath her grandfather's enfeebled form. It seemed impossible that she could see and hold in her hands that which would keep her and her mother free from want and worry for the rest of their lives. Money itself wasn't happiness – of that Philo was certain, even if it was only from the example of the Varleys; but the lack of money was certainly unhappiness – that she knew from her own experience.

"Grandfather," she said at last, "I have been too long here.

The Slapes will wonder what keeps me. Drink your soup quickly – if it is not already too cold – and let me go down to the kitchen again."

"Philomela, no," he replied, "I have no appetite. And we must work quickly. Have you a bag with you, or a case?"

"I have my carpetbag."

"Bring it up here and put the money in it, then take it down-stairs with you and keep it there. If the Slapes become alerted to our flight, they would doubtless attempt to stop us. And though they would certainly find a way of searching through *my* be-longings, if I were to carry any, they would never bother going through those of a hired girl."

"Grandfather, I hope they don't see us!"

"No more do I," sighed Richard Parrock. "But that young woman . . ."

Chapter 10

KATIE AT THE DOOR

The Slapes remained at the table an hour after Philo came downstairs, drinking more beer, talking of money, and offering gratuitous insults to their new servant. Philo cleared the table, washed the dishes, and prepared the kitchen for the morning, though she was confident it would not be *she* who made break-fast for the Slapes. Then, with a little speech expressing the hope that she had proved satisfactory on her first day of employment, Philo retired to her room.

She closed the door of her little chamber, which communi-cated directly with the kitchen, and, kneeling behind it, peered through the keyhole. She soon had the satisfaction of seeing the Slapes yawn and hearing them tell their readiness for bed. At ten o'clock – John Slape reading the time aloud from his pocket watch – they left the kitchen, taking with them the candles. Noiselessly Philo crept up to Richard Parrock's room with her carpetbag. She opened the door, signified for her grandfather to remain silent. He rolled over to the far edge of the bed, and

Philo quickly removed the bank notes from between the mattresses, stuffing them carelessly into the bag. Then, after deciding with him that they should not attempt to leave the house for another few hours, when it was certain that the Slapes would be fast asleep, Philo crept downstairs again. She sat on the edge of her bed and, by the light of the moon through her window, neatly stacked the bank notes and tied them with string so that they would take up the least room in her bag. She was careful but quick in her task, though she trembled every few moments when she counted out, say, thirty fifty-dollar notes – which sum, in her hands, would have paid off the mortgage on her mother's house. When she was done, she packed her clothing atop the cash, then watched for a passage of time that by the rising of the moon she judged to be about two hours.

She knew that the Slapes had chosen their chambers at the greatest distance possible from her grandfather, so as not to be disturbed by him in case he should call in the night. Tonight this cruelty would be made to work against them. They would be much less likely to hear her exertions in getting Richard Parrock downstairs. Though Philo was by no means weak, she could not be certain that she would be able to lift him from his bed, carry him downstairs, and out to the stable. Very probably the best maneuver would be to take him a few rods at a time, perhaps on her back with his arms clasped about her neck – first from the bed to the hallway, where he could rest in a chair for a few moments, then down the stairs (that most difficult of all), then across the kitchen and into the dooryard. From there, she would take him just round the corner of the house and leave him there while she fetched the wagon. This was, indeed, the *only* plan which suggested itself to Philo. So, no longer admitting trepidation and second thoughts, Philo decided to make a few preparations before she went up to her grandfather's room.

She opened the door of her chamber cautiously and stepped out into the kitchen. Despite the chill of the night, she went in her stockinged feet. She carefully closed and bolted the door of the passage leading to the Slapes' wing. Then cautiously opening the outside door, she crept along in the shadows of the house and out to the stable. As quietly as possible, she opened the doors of the stable – which fortuitously faced away from the house – went inside, and harnessed the horse to the wagon. The animal seemed disposed to quietness and docility. Philo took a moment to stroke the horse and whisper words of encouragement and gratitude. She crept back to the house, wishing that the moon were not so near to full or that clouds would blow up to darken the landscape. The carpetbag which contained her grandfather's fortune – her own future – she had placed in the back of the wagon. Now all that remained was to bring her grandfather down.

She wedged open the outside door with a piece of kindling so that they might get out quickly. At the foot of the stairs she placed a chair so that the old man might rest there when they had gotten that far; a second chair she carried to the top of the stairs and placed just outside his door. The stair and hallway were perfectly dark. She had not dared light a candle or a lamp for fear that the Slapes – even if they heard nothing – would yet see the glow from their chambers.

She tapped softly on the door of her grandfather's room. There was no response. Possibly Richard Parrock was asleep, or his hearing was impaired, or he feared to call out. She tapped a little harder and lifted the latch.

A single candle burned in a sconce beside the bed, but accustomed to the dark already, Philo could see Richard Parrock propped against his pillows.

"Grandfather!" she whispered. "I've come now, I've come—"

His face, she saw now, bore an unflinching expression of horror. She came closer but he did not move. "Grandfather!" she said again, this time more loudly. He was gaunt and still, and Philo was afraid.

When she touched his hand that lay atop the soiled sheet that the Slapes had not changed in weeks, she knew that he was dead.

The door of the chamber slammed shut behind her, and she heard the key turned in the lock. There was a loud cackle of laughter in the hallway.

"Who is it?" Philo demanded, rushing to the door and trying the latch.

"It's me, Philomela Drax!" cried out Katie Slape. "You thought you had fooled us; you thought you could fool me!"

Trembling, Philo knelt at the keyhole. A sharp whistle of wind blew suddenly through it and Philo fell back. Katie Slape was directly on the other side. She hissed through the keyhole.

"I hate you!" she cried. "And I hated the old man. The old man is dead, and I wish you were dead too!"

"You killed my grandfather!" cried Philo, glancing back at the bed and half surprised still that Richard Parrock did not speak to her.

"I did kill him!" shrieked Katie, and there was a loud thumping at the bottom of the door as the girl banged the heels of her boots against it in a drum roll of triumph. "Mar let me, and I wanted to do it, and I did it!"

"Open the door," demanded Philo. She stood, beat upon the door herself, and called out loudly, "Mrs. Slape! Mr. Slape!"

"Oh, they can't hear you," said Katie softly through the keyhole. The girl's fingernails lightly scratched the panels of the door.

"Why not?"

"They're outside, bringing round the wagon."

"Why?" cried Philo.

"Oh, for we're going away tonight. Now that we've got the old man's money."

"No!"

"We do. It's in your satchel. I saw you put the money in there."

"You couldn't have!"

"I did," cried Katie. "What don't I see?"

Philo made no reply, but she wondered at Katie's powers.

Down below, John Slape called his daughter.

"You hear me?" hissed Katie through the keyhole.

"I hear," whispered Philo.

"I have to go," remarked Katie to her prisoner. "I wanted to kill you too, but Mar says you're to stay here and be blamed."

"I won't be blamed," said Philo stoutly. "I'll tell everyone that you did it. You did do it."

"No one'll believe you," said Katie. "Who're you?"

"I'm Philomela Drax, and it's my grandfather you've murdered, and it's my fortune you're stealing."

"You and I – we're cousins then," laughed Katie.

"No!"

"You and I – we'll meet again. When you're out of jail. And then I'm going to beat you with a knotted clothesline until you bleed, and then I'm going to cut you in twenty pieces with a hatchet!"

"How did you do it?" cried Philo. "How did you murder my grandfather?"

"I tried with the stew," said Katie in a hurried whisper, for John called her with impatience now. "The meat was bad, but it only made him ill. So I—"

"So you what?"

"Oh," said Katie, with a harsh little laugh, "then I remembered your fortune . . ." And a moment after this, Philo heard Katie clattering down the steps. A door was slammed shut downstairs, and only a few moments afterward Philo listened to the sound of the wagon wheels along the track to the south. In the distance, over the chill night air, she could hear Katie's laugh.

Philo was left alone in unvisited Parrock House, on isolated Parrock Farm, locked in the room with the corpse of her grandfather. The moon shone in through the window, casting its cold pallor into the mirror over the mantel, to be reflected once more in Richard Parrock's glazed eyes. He seemed to stare at his granddaughter.

Philo dried her tears with the hem of her skirt. She rose to go and shut the dead man's eyes. She still did not know how he had died – Katie was so obviously crazy that even her testimony that she had killed him was not to be relied upon. Certainly the girl's statement, "Then I remembered your fortune . . ." made no sense. What had that fortune been? Philo found it difficult to recall, though she and Katie had been together in the kitchen scarcely six hours before. There had been a woman with a bloody needle, and a mound of gravel, and . . .

The moonlight reflected from the mantel mirror lighted the breast of her grandfather's nightshirt. It was stained, not with blood or sickness, but with soil. Philo touched her fingers to Richard Parrock's staring eyes, but just as she did so a small stone fell from between the dead man's lips.

The staring eyes remained open, but the head of the corpse lolled forward. With a soft hiss, pebbles and small stones fell from its mouth and mounded in its lap.

Philo jumped back and, in so doing, overturned a small pail and a small scoop such as are a child's toys. More sand and stones spilled out onto the floor.

Katie Slape had shoveled gravel down the old man's throat until he had strangled on it.

Chapter 11

DESTITUTE

Philo knew that she must not wait until the morning and the arrival of the field hands before she attempted to get out of the room. She could not even know for certain that the workers would appear on a Saturday. But more than this, her poor grandfather deserved that she do all she might toward the apprehension of his murderers. Though she had no doubt that it was Katie alone who had killed the old man, Philo considered that the entire family was guilty of the crime. If Hannah and John Slape had not themselves shoved gravel down Richard Parrock's throat, they had prompted the act, they had condoned it, and in the end they had applauded their child's terrible deed. A second and scarcely less important reason for haste was Philo's scant hope that the Slapes might be apprehended before they had the opportunity to secrete or dispose of the fortune which her grandfather had left her.

Philo went to the casement, raised the sash of the window, and peered out. All was quiet on moonlit Parrock Farm, but there was a quietness still more terrible in the bed behind her. It was impossible for Philo to be oblivious to the fact that she was alone in the room with a corpse, alone in the house, without a living being for perhaps two or three miles – but her position demanded that she not give way to superstitious fear. The ground, hard and stony, was fifteen feet below the window, too great a distance to jump without fear of injury. However, a pipe for drainage had been raised at a corner of the house about three feet from the window, and it might be possible, if she could grab onto it, to let herself down to the ground slowly.

Kneeling on the sill and holding on to the sash for balance, she leaned far out and only just managed to grasp the drainpipe. It was inconveniently large, and pricks of rust bit into her hand. But no other way of escape presented itself, and Philo was determined not to remain in Parrock House while her grandfather's murderers – and the thieves of her fortune – got away. Still with her hand against the drain, she rose and prepared to spring from the sill. Taking one large breath, she leapt, and with both hands grasped the drain. Her legs knocked painfully against the cold stone of the house. Unfortunately, the thrust of her weight detached the rusting pipe from its pins at the roof of the house, and the drain began to pitch out over the ground. Philo, though frightened, had the sense to shift her body so that the drain fell along the line of the stone wall. She was able then, by scraping her poor stockinged feet against the stones, to slow the descent. But in the dark and in her concentration, she could not see and thus avoid the protruding casement of one of the kitchen windows, and she knocked her head against a corner of it.

That night Philo knew no more.

When she was shaken awake, her consciousness at first was only of cold and stiffness. She looked up and around her, bewildered. The sun had risen and she lay on frosty ground. She could not at first remember where she was.

"Who are you, girl?" asked a man of about thirty years who was bending over her. Other men and a young boy were gathered curiously behind him.

For a moment Philo did not reply. She had first to puzzle out her whereabouts and the identities of these men. When she realized that she was on Parrock Farm, she concluded that they were the farmhands – and the memory of the previous night's terrible events returned to her. After a few moments Philo said, "My name is Philo Drax. Richard Parrock is my grandfather. The Slapes have murdered him for his money, gone away, and left me here."

One of the men looked at the fallen drain. "Were you trying to break into the house?" he demanded suspiciously. "I never heard before of a girl thief."

"No!" Philo cried. "I am Richard Parrock's granddaughter, I—"

"Slapes is the only family Richard Parrock's got," somebody said triumphantly, thinking he had caught Philo in a patent lie.

Philo no longer attempted to explain. She pointed at the window through which she had come. "My grandfather lies dead up there," she said. "He was murdered. Is there someone to take me into Goshen to inform the officers of the law?"

The field hands – for these were the men, shiftless and cagey, whom John Slape had hired to work Parrock Farm – looked at one another, hoping perhaps that one of their number would step forward as a leader.

"Let's see him!" cried the boy who was with them. "Let's see the old man dead!"

"Where's Mr. Slape?" demanded a man who had not hitherto spoken. "Where's his wife? Did you kill them too?"

Philo, now that her dizziness was beginning to wear away, was becoming alarmed. These five men and this boy were improbably dense, and if she spoke five declarative sentences, they seemed incapable of taking in more than one of them. And it was as Katie Slape had predicted – though on this point Philo had had no fear the night before – Philo herself was thought to have committed the murder.

Philo repeated her explanations at least thrice more. She led the men into the house, up the stairs, and into her grandfather's bedroom. They crowded round the bed and wondered at the mound of gravel in the dead man's lap. One of their number went into the hallway and called sheepishly for the Slapes. It was only when Philo dragged open the doors of the stable and showed them the wagon gone that the men were persuaded that indeed, Hannah and John and Katie had departed.

While two of the men hitched a little cart to one of the horses, Philo washed herself as best she could and rubbed generous amounts of Pond's Extract onto the cuts and scrapes she had sustained in her fall. Her boots were still in the little room beside the pantry, but the remainder of her clothing had disappeared in the carpetbag that had also taken away her fortune and her future. She had only the dress she wore now.

She was driven into Goshen by the man who had first shaken her into wakefulness. The others loitered about the door of the house, and when the wagon was only a few dozen rods along the road, they hurried inside. Philo was certain that these men and the boy were after plunder, but since it was more important that she get to Goshen with news of the Slapes than protect what little remained of her inheritance, she made no remonstrance to the man who drove the horse.

It was with a sober brain and weary body that Philo Drax entered Goshen that morning. She had arrived at Parrock Farm at just about the same hour the day before, full of ambitious hope and determination to free her grandfather from the terrible family who had wound themselves about him. Now Richard Parrock was dead, she was destitute, and the Slapes were richer by almost thirty thousand dollars.

Chapter 12

MR. KILLIP

Philo's bedraggled condition and her request to be directed to whatever officer of the law was resident in the town excited much comment in Goshen. Of her grandfather's death and the perfidy of the Slapes Philo thought it prudent to say nothing as yet, though her caution was to no avail. The hired man who brought her into town spread the news quite as effectively as if it had been written in the sky. To what Philo might have said, however, he added his opinion that she had killed the old man herself, murdered the Slapes into the bargain, and buried their bodies somewhere about the property. The improbability of this tale did nothing to prevent its being widely accepted.

Goshen was but a scrap of a town, and its ranking officer of the law was a justice of the peace. This gentleman, however, was absent in Philadelphia, so Philo went instead to Mr. Killip, her grandfather's lawyer. She found him at his home, at work in his study.

Mr. Killip was a man about fifty years of age, tall and thin – almost gaunt – with white hair and white brows and skin so pink it looked as if he had been scrubbed all over with a wire brush just before the door to the room was opened. He had a kindly expression, and Philo felt no hesitancy in confiding her story to him.

"I am Philo Drax, sir."

He smiled. "Miss Philo," he said. "I am glad to see you here. But I am sorry to see that you had such a poor journey," he added when he noticed the state of her clothing. "But in any case, I know that your grandfather will be happy to see you. Though I should say it was perhaps a mistake to seek me out. You were to come to Goshen in the character of a girl seeking employment, and the Slapes might be suspicious if they learned that you had visited Mr. Parrock's lawyer." He cocked an eye at her and sighed, as if disappointed not to find her cleverer.

"Sir," replied Philo gravely, "I have already been to Parrock Farm. I was to take Grandfather away last night. But the Slapes murdered him and then locked me in the house. When I tried to escape from a second-story window I suffered a fall and did not regain consciousness until this morning."

This terrible news was a shock to Mr. Killip, who had respected Philo's grandfather greatly and had been friends with him many years. After pacing about the room for several minutes and holding up his hand to enjoin Philo to silence, he seated himself in a chair beside the window and, turning away his face, begged Philo to describe all that had happened since her arrival in Goshen.

Philo provided what she hoped was a straightforward account, though once or twice she halted for excess of emotion. Now that she was out of that room, away from Parrock Farm, and safe in the presence of a man who evidently believed her, the full misery of the events of that terrible day broke in upon her.

When she had finished, Mr. Killip turned and said, "Miss Philo, I must beg your forgiveness."

"For what?"

"For not having taken your grandfather away from those terrible Slapes myself."

"It is not your fault, Mr. Killip."

"It was not until recently that your grandfather confided to me his unhappy situation with his daughter-in-law and her new husband. When he told me, I asked him to come and live with me here, but he would not. It was about that time that he conceived of the idea of writing to Mrs. Drax, whom he considered he had fearfully wronged. I said that I would wait for you to appear, but that if you did not, or if you were not successful in removing him from the house, I should take him out myself. I ought not to have waited, but I did not know that the Slapes were so bad as they were." He shook his head ruefully.

"Mr. Killip, my grandfather thought highly of you. I wish that you would advise me what I should do now."

"It is a bad piece of business, Miss Philo. Richard made a great mistake in cashing those bonds – it was not prudent to have so much hard cash about him."

"No," Philo agreed grimly, "it was not."

"If he had simply taken the bonds from the bank and carried *them* home, your fortune would be safe at this moment. The Slapes could not have cashed them without his endorsement. If only Richard had confided in me."

"I wish that he had," cried Philo, unable not to think a little ill of her grandfather. "But the bonds were not the whole of his property. What about Parrock Farm?"

"Legally, that belongs to the Slapes."

"But they murdered him!"

Mr. Killip shook his head. "That has not been proved, and if the Slapes have gone away beyond our reach – as appears to be the case – it may never be proved. It will be possible to institute proceedings against them *in absentia*, but such a procedure will take considerable time. I will of course undertake it for you, but I would not expect much – and I would certainly not expect it soon, Miss Philo."

"What should I do now?" the young woman asked, almost despairingly.

"I think you should go back to your mother in New Egypt and tell her that her father is dead. I will take care of things at the farm. I owe that to Richard and yourself for my unpardonable laxity in this matter. My poor Richard!" he exclaimed.

That afternoon, Mr. Killip drove Philo to Cape May Court House, where news of the terrible murder of the rich farmer had preceded them. Rumors of the crime having been perpetrated by a servant girl came also, and Philo was pointed at and shunned as she waited beside the lawyer for the cars to arrive at the station. A prim, cold sort of woman murmured, not entirely beneath her breath, "Why is she not arrested?" Mr. Killip paid her fare and gave her five dollars besides, but there had not been time to provide another outfit, and she wore the same torn and mud-stained skirt and jacket she had put on at Parrock Farm. A piece of disturbing news had arrived at Mr. Killip's house while Philo took a quiet dinner with the lawyer: John Slape had over the past six months sold off more than half the best acreage of Parrock Farm, so that the value of the property was substantially decreased. Even if through litigation Philo and her mother regained Parrock Farm, there would be little enough of that left for them.

"Philo," said Mr. Killip, just as the train was pulling in, "a word of advice."

"Yes?"

"Don't come back this way."

Philo looked to the left and to the right. Everyone on the platform appeared to stare at her, and she knew what information was conveyed in their incessant whispering.

"I won't," she said.

"You're suspected of the crime, and *I* may be brought to task for 'harboring' you."

"Mr. Killip, I hope—"

He shook his head reassuringly. "I can take care of myself, but I warn you now – take care with this business. And when you change cars in Philadelphia, try to stay below notice."

She nodded understanding. Not only was she to return to New Egypt with empty hands, she was to return sneaking.

From the cover of some brush on the other side of the tracks, a little boy, emboldened by her dejected aspect, flung a stone at her head. "Murderer!" he hissed, and then scampered off.

Philo spent that Saturday night in the Philadelphia railway station. The evening was chill but all the places near the coal stoves had been taken by loafers whom mere gallantry couldn't induce to give place to a powerless girl. She was stiff from the cold, sore from the fall she had sustained, and desperately uncomfortable because at Mr. Killip's she had had the chance for only a superficial washing. She reflected bitterly that perhaps the only legacy she would receive from her grandfather was the dirt of Parrock Farm which she carried away on her clothes and body.

Once she was roughly shaken awake by a policeman, who, suspicious of her jumbled attire, demanded reason for her presence. She carried no baggage or proof of her innocent identity, and it was only by dint of long persuasion, humiliating to herself and greatly amusing to the loafers at the coal fire, that she convinced the officer that she only waited for a morning train to New Egypt.

After this, she remained awake and huddled in the darkest and coldest corner of the station. Reflecting on Mr. Killip's warning, she had begun to fear that she would be arrested for the murder of her grandfather.

She breakfasted on a biscuit and coffee and boarded the eight o'clock cars that would leave her in New Egypt.

It was a sad journey for Philo. Not only was her grandfather dead – and she reflected bitterly that he might not have been killed by the Slapes but for their fear that she had come to take him away – but the fortune that he had meant for her and her mother was gone. She would slip noiselessly back into New Egypt, and never have hope again of raising her head above brackish poverty. Philo dreaded the years to come with her mother, whose sewing never did and never would support them comfortably. Jewel Varley's prediction for her life was a bitter recollection. But Jewel Varley, who had never known poverty, did not even know the worst of what such a life entailed. Jewel imagined poverty only as a meager wardrobe and prohibitions against fashionable travel. She never thought of scanty meals, and the worried watching of the calendar for the mortgage payments, the pennies carefully hoarded and spread out each night on the counterpane and jealously counted, the terrors of illness, and never the prospect of a tomorrow brighter than yesterday. Poverty bound the Draxes in cords, and as the cars rolled through the black New Jersey countryside toward New Egypt, those cords seemed to tighten until Philo felt she could scarcely breathe.

And all was the doing of the Slapes.

Philo was a young woman of strong if usually mixed and compounded emotions. If she loved her mother she was also frequently contemptuous of Mary Drax's emotional frailty; if she had felt superior to Jewel Varley's meanness, she was also jealous of that young woman's luxuries of opportunity and wardrobe; if she had respected her grandfather, she had also looked to the fortune the old man would have bestowed upon her. But the Slapes were a different case altogether. Philo hated them with a hate that was without alloy, hated them as she had hated nothing in her life before. And if the Slapes – together or singly – should ever present themselves before her again, Philo vowed they would receive no quarter of mercy.

PART III
NEW EGYPT

Chapter 13

PHILO'S HUMILIATION

Philo arrived in New Egypt at the most inconvenient time, lacking a quarter of ten o'clock, when all the respectable population was on its way to morning worship. The way to her home would take her past the doors of each of the town's three churches. She wondered briefly whether she ought not sit at the station until all three congregations should be inside, but then considered that though she might be poor, might be a dupe, might be the unluckiest girl in the world – she was not a coward.

She would walk past the three churches, doubtlessly encountering those known to her, and if they asked how she came to be in such a state on Sunday morning, in ragged, filthy clothing, with her face and arms scratched, and looking for all the world as if she had sat up all night in a railway station, she would reply simply, "I have met with accident."

This plan she formulated while still at the station, and she had not even stepped off the platform before it was rendered useless to her. The stationmaster, whose name was Kilcrease, came out of his little office. He was less a friendly man than a curious one. He had a high, protruding forehead, little red eyes that seemed to seek deep refuge beneath it, and a livid scar that cleft his chin. He beckoned Philo over.

"Hello, Mr. Kilcrease," she replied politely.

He looked at her dress quizzically. "You don't dress much like a girl what's come into money," he remarked.

"I beg your pardon?" she asked with surprise.

"I say," said Mr. Kilcrease, with the air of one pressing his finger to the spring of a mystery, "you don't look much like a girl what's gone off to collect seventeen thousand dollars from her grandfather what's she's never laid eyes on before." He stretched his neck, as if to peer round her. "You got the money sewed in your dress? You got a secret pocket what's got bills in it?"

"Mr. Kilcrease, I don't know what you're talking about." Philo knew, with a sinking certainty, that her mother's tongue had been loose in her absence. Mr. Kilcrease was known to the Draxes only to be spoken to; he was by no means their intimate. If he had heard of the Parrock fortune, then all the rest of the town knew of it too.

"We didn't look to see you back so quick," said Mr. Kilcrease. "Did you bring the old man with you?" He needlessly looked around the empty station platform.

"Mr. Kilcrease," said Philo, trembling. "Please, I don't know what you are talking about."

"Didn't you just visit your grandfather what's living in Goshen? Nobody round here ever heard of Goshen before," he added parenthetically. "Seventeen people come by here yesterday to find it out on the big map inside the station. Wasn't the old man to give you money? Should have give you a change of clothes too. P'rhaps he didn't think of it, what's never been round girls before."

Philo understood that she would gain nothing by answering any more of Mr. Kilcrease's questions. If she answered truthfully, he would extract the entire terrible story, and she would have been as guilty of broadcasting the tale of her misery as her mother had been culpable in prematurely and unadvisedly giving out the promise of their good fortune.

She was hot with embarrassment and alarm. Her one consolation since she left Goshen was that New Egypt would never learn of her misfortune: her grandfather's murder, the loss of their inheritance, the suspicion that had fallen upon herself for the commission of the crime. That meager consolation was now denied her.

"Mr. Kilcrease," she said hurriedly, "I must go. Mother is waiting for me."

Mr. Kilcrease called after her but she did not heed him.

In the street she was much regarded. Though Philo passed on the opposite side of the road and did not look at the Presbyterians standing outside the door of their church, she heard their exclamations of surprise as she went by. Someone called after her, but she did not recognize the voice and refused to turn around.

Farther down the street, the Methodist Church was separated from the Baptist by only the parsonage, and it was the custom in New Egypt for the two congregations to mix in the street before services. Philo nervously skirted the edge of the crowd, peering this way and that, watching for Mary Drax. The double congregation, alerted to Philo's unlooked-for presence, turned and stared at her. She could hear their comments, not at all hushed, which attempted to reconcile her shabby dress and forlorn appearance with the recent acquisition of a great fortune.

Mary Drax stood in the center of the crowd, at the foot of the steps of the Methodist Church, talking with the Varleys. Philo was so surprised by this – the Varleys rarely vouchsafing her and her mother more than a distant nod on Sunday morning – that she stopped and stared. Then she realized the basis for this social revolution: the Varleys had discovered that Mary Drax stood to get some large amount of money from her father. And the weight of that inheritance (or the prospect of it, which in a town as small as New Egypt, did quite as well) set in the scales of social commerce, raised Mary Drax far higher than she had ever been lifted before.

Jacob Varley, his wife Caroline, and Jewel stood in a crescent before Mary Drax and listened to her politely. Philo came close enough to hear what her mother was saying.

". . . sure that Philo will bring him back with her. We would so dislike to leave New Egypt. We've been so happy here."

"You will of course give up sewing," said Caroline Varley, inclining her head in a fashion that was friendly if still a little condescending. She was a short, imposing woman, who showed a great deal of neck to whomever she was speaking and whose taste in dress her daughter Jewel had inherited.

"Oh, I'm sure Father will not want me to continue working," said Mary Drax with a smile.

"Good," said Jewel with a smile that was probably intended to charm, "for you know, Mother and I have already engaged another seamstress."

"Do you know the extent of your father's fortune, Mrs. Drax?

It is spoken of as being considerable," said Jacob Varley in as pleasant a tone as Philo had ever heard him employ. Jewel and Caroline Varley stood by smiling complacently. They would have preferred that someone rich and entirely unknown to them had moved into the neighborhood, but an old impoverished acquaintance who suddenly inherited money would do almost as well.

"Oh, it *is* considerable," said Mary Drax. "Parrock Farm was always the best piece of land in the state south of Trenton. And Father was always a close man. I shouldn't wonder—"

Here Philo thought best to interfere before her mother spoke any more nonsense. She stepped forward, reached between Jacob Varley and Jewel, and laid a hand on her mother's arm. Mary Drax looked up with a smile. She had been much courted in the past two days and evidently expected more congratulations on the turn her fortune had taken.

But it was Philo who stood there, looking as ragged and dirty and forlorn as the most neglected child of any of Jacob Varley's improvident graniteware workers. Mary Drax and the Varleys looked on her with astonishment. For several moments no one said anything.

"Mother," said Philo at last, "please come home with me now."

"Philo!" cried Jewel Varley. "Look at you!"

Philo did not reply, but pulled gently at her mother's arm.

Mary Drax regarded her daughter uncomprehendingly. "Your clothing, Philo," she said at last. "What happened to your clothing? And where's Father? Did you not bring him back with you?" She looked round her. Though the bells of the two churches were ringing for the congregations to enter, both Methodists and Baptists (and even some very curious Presbyterians who had followed Philo down the street) stood in a loose circle around them.

"Mother," said Philo quietly, and with an attempt to catch Mary Drax's eye, "come home now. I'll answer your questions at home."

Mary Drax caught at her daughter's sleeve. The dirt of Parrock Farm came off on the new gloves Mary Drax had purchased only the day before in expectation of her rising fortune. She stared for a moment at the dirt, then quickly brushed it off.

"Philo," she said in a trembling voice, "what's wrong? Something terrible happened in Goshen, didn't it? We're still poor, aren't we? Father turned you away. The letter was a vicious hoax, I knew it, I was sure when we opened it, I knew it when you read it aloud to me, Father sent—"

The Varleys exchanged knowing smiles and glances, and Philo flushed with shame. She pulled her mother away, but in the cruel disappointment of her expectations Mary Drax resisted, and her voice grew louder. "Philo! Tell me now, have you brought anything to me from Father? Has he sent us anything, or has he determined to abandon me for *another* twenty-three years? If poor Tom were alive this moment, we—"

Philo pulled her mother's hand roughly. Mary Drax was caught off-balance, and when she fell forward, Philo caught her and hissed in her ear, "Mother, be quiet!" She pushed Mary Drax upright again, and now made no pretense of her eagerness to be away from the crowd.

Perhaps this was the best and easiest way, Philo considered. Three-quarters of the persons she and her mother knew in New Egypt surrounded them now. Everyone had heard that the Draxes had sudden expectations of money because of a letter received on Wednesday; everyone evidently had learned that Philo had gone away on Thursday; now everyone could see that Philo had returned in rags on Sunday morning. If everyone could not reckon that the promised fortune had not been forthcoming, then he hadn't the sense of a creeping baby.

Philo had nothing left to hide, not even her intense humiliation.

She let go of her mother's arm and turned in a little circle with a grim smile. She backed up onto the steps of the Methodist Church and stood alone. She spoke loudly. "Mother is right. We have no money. But Mother and I have never had any money, and you all know that as well. My grandfather had intended to give us money; he intended to come here to live with us. But my grandfather was murdered—"

Here Mary Drax gasped and grabbed her daughter's hand. Philo jerked away.

"—was murdered," she repeated in a hard voice. "And the

money that he would have left us was stolen by his daughter-in-law and her family."

She took a breath and would have continued, but the voices of those round her rose to so high and breathless a pitch that she could not have been heard. Mary Drax clawed at her arm. Philo looked round and saw that the Varleys had backed away, and only they of all the crowd did not speak. Jewel actually smiled.

Philo came down from the steps and led her mother away, grimly accounting the worst to be over.

It was not: Henry Maitland stood on the edge of the crowd, and as she passed, gazed at her with impassive, curious eyes.

Chapter 14

ANOTHER LETTER

Several days passed during which neither Mary nor Philo Drax was to be seen on the streets of New Egypt. Neighbors sympathetic and neighbors merely curious came to call and were received by an unsmiling Philo at the door, thanked for their solicitude, and told that Mary Drax was unwell.

That was the truth. It was the old story with the mother and daughter: Mary Drax gave in to her emotions to the extent that Philo, who was just as sensitive as her mother, must deny her own feelings. Mary Drax was free to moan in bed all day only if Philo would answer the door and see to their meals. Philo would have liked to give in a little to her own depression of spirits, but her mother's anticipation of that wish carried to an extreme repulsed her, and she gave no sign of how deeply she felt her triple loss of grandfather, fortune, and expectation.

Philo sat in the parlor at the window, wondering that spring could come at a time of such heavy misfortune. The days became longer and warmer, and the calyxes of the daffodils, though still unopened, were the color of egg yolks. The house was surrounded by a green mist of new growth, which irritated rather than soothed Philo's unhappy spirit.

They wouldn't have the house much longer, Philo knew. Before this hope that had proved empty, Mary Drax had been content to work with her needle. But Philo knew her mother too well to expect that she would willingly return to it. Mary Drax's spirit had been broken by this disappointment – she had said as much. Philo knew that her mother would conceive of some illness – some palsy in the hands, some weakness in the eyes – that would prevent her from resuming her livelihood. The financial burden would then rest solely on her, and this was a burden Philo had no way of discharging. She wished that her grandfather had never written, that he had simply handed over to the Slapes the thirty thousand dollars, and that she and her mother had never been set up with expectations of money and comfort. At the worst he would have been murdered by the Slapes after they had taken possession of his fortune – but that is what had happened anyway.

Jewel Varley had talked of travel to Saratoga and New York and said that Philo would never travel. Well, Philo *had* travelled: She had gone to Goshen, New Jersey, been hired as a servant at the princely salary of one dollar a week, locked into a room with the corpse of her murdered grandfather, accused of the crime, and deprived of her rightful inheritance. It was perhaps more colorful than a sojourn in Newport but without doubt less to be desired.

Philo sat at the window, simply waiting for something to happen. At first, she was filled with lassitude and bitterness, but gradually her pride and innate strength reaffirmed themselves. Inaction troubled her more than outright misfortune. She was no nearer a solution to her problems, but at least she had determined that if her situation could be remedied through courage, hard work, and perseverance, she would not shrink from the attempt.

Only a couple of hours after she had made this resolution and conceived endless and improbable schemes for the getting of money or the supporting of herself and her mother on as little money as possible, Mr. Clegg came to the door with a letter, posted Goshen. This made Philo tremble until she realized that it must be from Mr. Killip.

"The Slapes," he wrote,

are not to be found. No one saw them go, no one knows where they went. Hannah (Jepson, that was) is said to have relatives in Ohio and in Indiana, settled along the Wabash. I have sent their descriptions to the capitals of these states. But the West is a wild place, and I should be surprised if we ever heard of them again. On your mother's behalf I have instituted proceedings for the recovery of Parrock Farm. This is a tedious process, but I may hope that something will come of it that will be beneficial to Richard's rightful heirs.

Your grandfather was buried on Monday, here in Goshen. Many of his friends were in attendance and testified to his goodness. I visited Parrock Farm on Tuesday and discovered to my dismay that some pack of vandals had entered the place and taken away most that was of any value. I have arranged that the house be locked and sealed. The animals I have taken the liberty of selling to a neighboring farmer, and I herewith enclose a draught for the amount of $282. Had the horses not been stolen, the sum would have been more. The money by right belongs to the Slapes, I know, and they may come to me for its restoration. I would be very happy to see them. I trust that this money will be of service to you and your mother.

Miss Philo, I must add a word of caution. You would do well not to return to this part of the state. Not all in Goshen and Cape May Court House are of the opinion that the Slapes were the murderers of your grandfather. Some blame the servant girl. There was a suggestion that you be found and arrested, but fortunately your true identity was never publicized. I was approached, for it was known that I drove you to the station, but I said merely that you had come to me for a position which I could not provide, and that you rode with me to Cape May Court House and took the cars for Philadelphia.

Truly this business involves only unhappiness for us all. I would do you a disservice if I led you to hope that the Slapes will ever be brought to justice, or any substantial part of your fortune recovered. If I may be of assistance to

you or your mother in anything, do not hesitate to write
to,

Y'r ob'd't servant,
Daniel Killip

One of Philo's schemes had been to move with her mother
to Goshen to live at Parrock Farm, where at least they might
raise their own food and perhaps, through the cultivation of the
orchards or the livestock, even manage to make a little living.
Philo took a grim satisfaction in Mr. Killip's message. If there
were no new avenues opened to her by it, at least there were a
few definitely closed, so that in the end her choice would be just
that much easier.

This letter Philo did not show to her mother. Mary Drax,
reading it, would seize only upon the slender hope that some of
the money would be recovered by Mr. Killip through the courts,
and that expectation, constantly put off, constantly dwindling,
would kill her as outright disappointment would not.

Likewise she planned to keep from her mother's knowledge
the funds that had been enclosed in the letter. Philo feared that
Mary Drax, with even this little sum as their protection, would
indefinitely put off the time when she must resume her work as a
seamstress. Such a sum, in their straitened condition, was almost
a fortune – though compared to the thirty thousand dollars they
had lost to the Slapes, it was little enough. Two hundred eighty-
two dollars would see them through almost eighteen months if
it were managed properly.

But if she were to keep the money a secret, it would be
necessary for her to exchange the draught for cash in some place
other than New Egypt. There was no bank in the town, and it
was unlikely that any shopkeeper would have such a sum. The
office of the granite ware factory would doubtless have the cash
to cover the amount, but Philo did not want the transaction
known to Jacob Varley. She therefore determined to walk to
Cookstown, four miles distant, and apply at the bank there.

She went upstairs and told her mother that she must be
absent for the afternoon. Philo had prepared the little lie that she
would be delivering mail for Mr. Clegg to outlying farms, but

Mary Drax did not even ask what would keep her away.

Mary Drax lay atop the covers on the bed and raised a weak hand to her daughter, "Kiss me, Philo. And when you return I want you to fashion a wreath for the door." She smiled sadly and tugged at the black streamers on Philo's old bonnet. "We are in mourning for your grandfather, you know."

Chapter 15

THE PICNIC

The train which brought the morning mail to New Egypt from Philadelphia had also deposited two visitors to the town: a young woman with a dark, unpleasantly smiling countenance and an older man who appeared to be her father. Of Mr. Kilcrease they asked directions for a lodging house in town, and at the lodging house they asked directions to the post office, and at the post office they asked the direction of the house inhabited by Philo Drax and her mother. This information was given to them by Mr. Clegg with some astonishment at the coincidence that he had delivered a letter to Philo Drax not ten minutes before.

The man protested that he had no business with the Draxes, that he only inquired their address because he had heard that the young woman was thinking of going into service.

"Oh, yes?" replied Mr. Clegg with wonder. Everything in creation was a matter of surprise to the postmaster of New Egypt, and the sun didn't rise in the morning without turning Mr. Clegg out of bed with astonishment at the repetition of the phenomenon. "Well, I don't wonder at it. What a family for reverses! I was never so surprised in all my life as when poor Tom Drax died in the War. And not fifteen years later, his father-in-law is murdered in his bed. It was a terrible coincidence! And now Philo is to go into service!"

Mr. Clegg watched after his visitors when they left the little corner of his shop which served New Egypt as post office, and noted with vast bewilderment that the girl, who had spoken not a word, led her father in a direction which, in a hundred years, wouldn't take them to Mary Drax's door.

John and Katie Slape walked to the edge of New Egypt, climbed a fence, crossed a pasture, and entered the fir forest to the north of the town. They doubled back and, keeping always within the concealing line of the conifers, approached the Drax house. It was recognizable, Mr. Clegg had assured them, by being the only house in New Egypt painted blue with black shutters.

Once they had come within sight of the house, they sat down beneath a tree, and John Slape spread his kerchief on the bed of conifer needles between them. Out of her pocket Katie took a hunk of cheese and a small loaf of bread. These they cut with John's sharp pocketknife and ate with relish and in silence. Both watched the Drax house across the field and were pleased to see no one enter, leave, pass, or even come near the place. When they were finished John Slape wiped the knife clean on his pants, and as Katie tore apart the rind of the cheese and flung the pieces at squirrels, he sharpened it on a flat stone.

"I'll watch," he said to his daughter, and she nodded, brushing the crumbs from her lap.

She held out her hand, and John Slape placed the knife in her palm. She tested its weight and nodded. John Slape took from his pocket a length of string, pulled at it to test its strength, and then tied the knife to his daughter's hand, so that the blade protruded about two inches beyond her forefinger.

"Try that," he said.

Katie stood and waved her arm all about her head. Even when she did not grasp the handle with her fingers, the knife remained in place. She nodded.

"Good," said John Slape. "Now it won't slip off no matter how much blood there is."

Katie scratched her neck with her unencumbered hand and set off across the empty field that separated the fir forest from the Drax garden.

"Mind your clothes!" he called after her.

Mary Drax's screams were heard first by the five dogs belonging to her nearest neighbor. These animals, setting up a fierce howling, secured the attention of Mrs. Libby, who came out into the yard. When Mrs. Libby had succeeded in quieting the dogs, she heard the last of Mary Drax's cries, which did not dwindle into a whimper but was cut off clean.

She hurried to the Drax house, beat upon the door, and called out to Mary and Philo. No one responded. Mrs. Libby, a stout woman, thought it easier to call for help rather than run for it, so she turned from the door and began to shout for assistance.

Hearing with surprise the door opened behind her, she turned back and saw smiling Katie Slape in the doorway, her entire right arm dripping in blood. In her left she held up a dress belonging to Philo, which she was evidently attempting to keep clear of the gore that liberally splashed her own clothing.

"Philo and I are of a size," she said to Mrs. Libby with a smile. "I waited for her," Katie said. "Tell her she can expect to see me again. We're cousins, you know." Katie waved the bloody knife in the air.

Mrs. Libby, notwithstanding her stoutness, ran away. And as she huffed down the lane toward the center of town, Katie Slape scampered across the field toward the evergreen forest, still with the dress held at arm's length from her.

Dr. Slocum was in his garden, and Mrs. Libby encountered him first. She was winded, and though convinced that no one alive remained in the Drax house, considered she might as well bring him as any other. Dr. Slocum had seen men caught in threshing machines, but it was with some trepidation that he ascended the staircase that bore brightly the prints of Katie Slape's feet in blood so thick it was still undried.

Mary Drax lay on her bed on a coverlet whose pattern was obscured by the blood there. A water pitcher and bowl had been broken against her brow, and there was a halo of fragments about her head on the pillow. Across her throat was a single cut, about seven inches long and very deep, which had severed both carotid arteries. Along the left cheekbone was a wound made by the slashing of a knife, which, however, did not go much beneath the skin. On the right arm just above the wrist was a cut two-and-a-half inches long, from which Mary Drax appeared to have lost what blood had not pulsed out of her slashed neck. There were numerous smaller cuts along both forearms, and one long incision along each thigh, sliced through her dress after she was already dead.

Dr. Slocum, coming to the head of the bed to close the dead woman's eyes, stepped on her severed ear. Neatly detached from her head with a single slice of Katie Slape's knife blade, it had slipped unnoticed to the floor.

Dr. Slocum tried gently to prevent Philo from viewing her mother's corpse and the room in which she had died, but the orphan was not to be deterred. She stood silent upon the threshold. With a single step into the chamber, however, Philo's courage forsook her, and she retreated quickly. Downstairs, she heard from Mrs. Libby the description of the girl who had appeared in the doorway and who had taken away one of Philo's dresses. But she did not need to be told that the Slapes were responsible for the death of her mother.

Philo was not even surprised when Mrs. Libby called her into the kitchen and showed her that the girl – obviously *after* murdering Mary Drax, for her bloody prints were on the shards – had smashed all the cups and saucers against the oven door.

Mrs. Libby pointed at the broken crockery on the floor, put her finger to her lips, and whispered in Philo's ear: "She said you were cousins!"

"No!" Philo protested. "No, it's not true at all!"

PART IV
CHRISTOPHER STREET

Chapter 16

CHRISTOPHER STREET

When they had murdered Richard Parrock and locked Philo in the room with his corpse, the Slapes drove their wagon to South Dennis, not more than six miles distant from the farm. They breakfasted at a farmhouse which advertised room and board for weary travellers, sold the horse and wagon to the owner for a sum small enough to be irresistible but not so small as to excite suspicion, and took the cars to Philadelphia. It was a city they knew and a city in which they felt comfortable. They took up residence in a small hotel conveniently near the theaters.

The hotel room, which was decidedly poor for a family possessing such a fortune, was furnished with a large bed, a dresser with bowl and pitcher, a broken looking glass, a scrap of worn carpet, a chair with its legs wired together, and three chromolithographs pasted directly onto the wall. Within a kind of closet attached to the room was another bed on which Katie was meant to sleep. The chamber's single window looked out on Twelfth Street.

On the second day after they had taken possession of their room and after they had eaten dinner in the hotel's dining room, the Slapes sat at different corners of the big bed and talked of what had been done on Parrock Farm. They were amused by what must be Philo's predicament.

"Old man'll begin to stink soon," said Katie, "warm day like this."

"She'll be taken up for it," said Hannah, nodding with satisfaction.

"She'll tell that we did it," said John, warning them. The thought had first occurred to him only then.

"They won't believe her," said Katie. "She'll be found with the old man. She'll be found with the pail and shovel. They'll say 'The hired girl killed the old man.'"

"He was her grandfather," John Slape pointed out.

"She is your cousin," added Hannah.

"No!" said Katie. "Mar hired her on. She was the hired girl!"

John Slape said nothing else. It often did no good to argue with Katie, who, when she wanted or when the mood was upon her, was quite impenetrably dense.

"What's to be done now?" said Hannah, looking at her husband. "The money's here." She glanced toward Katie's closet; the carpetbag was secreted beneath the cot.

John Slape shrugged. Richard Parrock had possessed a far greater fortune than they had dared hope. Hannah had tried to count the money but became confused at so great a sum. The Slapes could comprehend the value of one hundred dollars, and two hundred dollars by extrapolation from that. But one thousand, ten thousand, twenty-nine thousand dollars held no meaning for them. And having got so much, they had no idea what should be done with it. With a single ten-dollar bill they could live as lavishly as they pleased for a week – and how many hundreds and hundreds of ten-dollar notes there were in the carpetbag!

A few days after their arrival, John spent the afternoon loafing in a barbershop on Tenth Street. There he learned, through an item in the paper which was read aloud by a man whose neck was being shaved, that the body of Richard Parrock had been discovered, and that the servant who was suspected of the murder had escaped.

He hurried back to the hotel in such haste that the inhabitants of the barbershop could only suppose that he felt an apoplectic fit coming on. He informed his wife and daughter of the item in the paper.

"The girl got away then?" said Hannah.

Her husband nodded his head.

"She did it!" cried Katie, who was lying on her bed, in the unlighted closet, with the door closed. Her hearing was acute however, and her voice piercing.

"Hush!" cried Hannah.

John Slape looked at his wife blankly. "The girl will tell that we did it," he said.

Hannah did not answer.

Katie swung the door open. She lay on her side, propping her head on her bent arm.

"Find her out where she lives," Katie said. "Let me stop her tongue."

From having opened Richard Parrock's mail, Hannah already knew Philo's name and that she lived with her mother in New Egypt.

"If we're found out," said Hannah, "then our money'll be taken away. Girl and her mother will get it. Girl's mother was Father Parrock's daughter."

John Slape blinked. "They'll not have it."

Katie Slape echoed her father, but she smiled. "They'll not have it."

So that afternoon Hannah went to the railway station and consulted maps and timetables. Next morning Katie and John took the cars to New Egypt. After Katie killed Mary Drax, she went to the kitchen to wait for Philo's return and there began amusing herself by smashing crockery. She was disturbed almost immediately by the beating at the door, and after fleeing, she and her father walked through the forest to Cookstown. An hour later they boarded the cars that returned them to Philadelphia. Katie wore Philo's dress.

Hannah was disappointed that Philo had escaped.

"She's not much," said Katie contemptuously.

"Ought not to live," Hannah warned. "Girl lives, we may be taken up."

"I'll go back there, Mar," said Katie with a grin. "This time I'll get her."

Hannah shook her head. "You were seen. Your par was seen. But we'll find her, and she won't live to speak our names. We'll find her out."

"Are we to stay here?" John asked apprehensively. Philadelphia theaters were very fine, in his opinion.

"Not so near," replied Hannah. "Not so near Goshen, not so near New Egypt." She pondered for a moment. "Go to New York," she said as if with sudden inspiration. "You've been in New York," she said to her husband.

John Slape nodded slowly. "All right, Hannah," he said. "We'll go to New York."

Two days later the Slapes were installed in a rooming house on Christopher Street. Upon leaving the ferry it was the first house they had seen advertising chambers to let. Their three rooms on the third floor were dingy, inconveniently small, and relatively expensive. The house was located so near the ferry that the traffic of dock workers, Jersey travellers, and heavy carts was constant on the street from dawn till after dark. But the Slapes were as content as if they had lived instead in a mansion on the corner of Fifth Avenue and Thirty-second Street – this latter address the pinnacle of fashion in the spring of 1871. They liked the noise and the strangeness of the city; their hostess's food was no worse than Hannah's own cooking; and in general, their sensibilities were not such as to require much in the way of the amenities of civilization.

The other boarders in the house were two girls who worked in dollar stores on Eighth Avenue, a brokerage house clerk and his recent bride, a seamstress and her crippled daughter, and a distracted Civil War widow who foolishly attempted to subsist solely on her pension. They thought Hannah tolerably pleasant, and her husband, though slightly her social inferior, a fairly civil being. For Katie, however, none of the lodgers had a good word to say. They didn't like the way she looked at them. They didn't like the way that, after passing them on the stairs, she would turn and whisper something at their retreating backs. She somehow found out their secrets, and her smile was devilish.

The family, despite their way of keeping to themselves, excited some comment in the household. The Jepsons, as they were known, had no work or known source of income, yet the rent was paid on time, and often Hannah and John were seen returning from a shopping excursion with an armful of bundles. In the evening after supper all three of them would go out together and later be seen on the Bowery purchasing tickets at the dime museum, listening with stolid attention to a mud-gutter band on the corner, or winning prizes at a shooting gallery.

Within a week of the Slapes' arrival, the distracted Civil War widow found that she could not afford even so low a boarding house as this one, and moved to a place on Mott Street that operated on the European plan. That is, she paid one dollar a week and got her meals where she could. But her Christopher Street lodging was left empty, and everyone was surprised when the Slapes rented it out for themselves, even though it was only a hall room and on the floor below theirs.

Something about the family discouraged gossip, and though all wondered, no one said a word the following week when the crippled daughter of the seamstress passed round a copy of *The New York Clipper* with this notice circled in violet ink:

KATIE JEPSON – Best clairvoyant on love, health, lawsuits, absent friends, marriage, divorce, contested wills, contracts, patent rights, lost property, partnership, journeys and business affairs. Miss Katie challenges the world: gives names; readings from cradle to the grave. Ladies 25¢ and 50¢. Gents 50¢. From hair $1. One flight up, No. 251 Christopher St.

The same day a placard reading similarly went up in the ground-floor window where the Slapes had first seen the notice "Rooms to Let to Respectable Parties."

Chapter 17

ANN AND CHARLES CLAYTON

At first, little trade came to Katie. There were too many fortune-tellers in New York already – two had placards visible from the Slapes' third-floor windows. Katie got a new dress – new to her, that is to say – down on Chatham Street, and in this orange-yellow tarlatan she sat all day in the room which had been vacated by the Civil War widow. From the window she watched those who passed pause at her sign, glance up at her, and pass on with expressions of suppressed alarm. Each morning Hannah frizzed Katie's hair with a hot slate pencil, both women thinking that this would heighten the appearance of mystery in the girl. Still no one came.

The fact was, custom for fortune-tellers and clairvoyants was not to be got through newspaper space and placards – it was to be obtained only through recommendation. Consequently Katie, who had as yet read no one's fortune, had no one to sing her praise.

The room which was supposed to be devoted to the exercise of Katie's clairvoyant powers was turned into a kind of second parlor for the Slapes. Here they sat every day, and Hannah read aloud to her husband and stepdaughter from the *Clipper*, a weekly New York periodical dedicated to sporting and theatrical news. Hannah circled with a pencil the notice of any exhibition or show or performance that looked to be of interest. After supper, the family would consult, and then with the *Clipper* folded beneath John's arm, march out to seek diversion with a curious earnestness that was perhaps the only thing about the family which their fellow boarders found amusing. They saw Jonas Cooper, billed as the strongest man in the world, supported lengthwise on the shoulders of two of his daughters, while a third daughter, seated straddling his legs, lifted a sledgehammer and smashed a large rock that reposed on his chest. They saw Sheridan & Mack's Special Combination Variety Show, featuring Lola LaTosca and her twin pythons; and at the New York Pavilion they saw a troupe of Circassian maidens, dressed in Oriental costume, languorously draped before a backdrop meant to suggest the interior of a harem. They attended a hop of the Gentlemen's Sons of the Sixth Ward, and on Saturday night they took the Third Avenue Railroad up to Harlem village to see a performance by Blind Tom, the most celebrated Negro musician in America.

This was what the Slapes wanted out of life, and this was why they had murdered Richard Parrock. Now that they had his money – and Hannah calculated that so large a sum as they possessed in the carpetbag would keep them for many years to come – they need never trouble themselves again with thoughts of employment or financial prudence. They had all sat back comfortably in life. John spent his days at the barbershop, Hannah walked the streets and looked in shop windows, and Katie waited patiently for customers. In the evening they went to the theater. They weren't wanted by the police for the murder of the old man, they were far removed from Goshen and Philadelphia, they weren't even known by their former names.

Only Philo Drax could interfere with them, for only she knew their faces and their crimes – but no doubt the girl was in hiding herself. And the Slapes had long before determined that if ever she came near enough to recognize them, she wouldn't long survive that recognition.

It happened that one fine spring afternoon, when Hannah and John Slape had gone out with the intention to stroll through City Hall Park and Katie was alone in her room, Ann Clayton knocked hesitantly on Katie's partially open door. Ann was the newlywed wife of Charles Clayton, who was employed in a Wall Street firm. They occupied the room across the hall from Katie's parlor.

"Miss Katie," said Ann, "are you much taken up just now?"

Katie grinned and shook her head. She motioned Ann Clayton inside the room. Ann closed the door carefully behind her. She was a short, handsomish sort of woman, whose dress, if always neat and tasteful, was noted by the other inmates of the house to possess scant variety.

Ann sat down. After a moment of looking about the room with curiosity – her curiosity was soon satisfied, for there was nothing in it but a table, three chairs, a stack of newspapers in the corner, and a greasy pack of cards on the mantel – she asked, "How is your little business going along?"

Katie did not reply. She threw her arm across the table toward Ann Clayton. The cheap rings on her hand rapped loudly against the wood. The fingers opened and closed clawlike.

Ann Clayton, with some little trepidation, placed her hand in Katie's. Katie clutched it so hard that Ann cried out in surprise and pain.

"Twenty-five cents?" said Katie. "Or fifty?"

"Twenty-five!"

Katie let go her hand, rose and fetched the pack of cards from the mantel. She sat again at the table and began to turn the cards over one by one, stacking them neatly again, in an unvarying rhythm.

"Why did you marry Mr. Clayton?" she asked in an insinuating voice.

Ann was too surprised to reply.

"You married him because you thought he had money," said Katie. "You thought he made sixty-two dollars a week. A friend of his with red hair told you that."

She looked up at Ann and smiled.

She looked down again at the cards and went on: "And he thought you had money. That's why he married you. Your friend in the blue hat told him that you had inherited six thousand dollars from your aunt in Vermont."

To these statements, perfectly true, Ann Clayton could say nothing. She was hot and embarrassed. "Who told you this?" she demanded. "They were lying."

"It was your friends that lied. Mr. Clayton makes seventeen dollars a week. He won't be raised until February next. He'll have nineteen dollars then. Your aunt in Vermont is not yet dead. She'll die watching a parade. You'll get two hundred dollars from her."

Ann Clayton hurried out of the room, slamming the door behind her. Katie continued to turn over the cards. She was still doing so when Ann Clayton returned a quarter of an hour later. The woman put two quarter-dollars on the table and sat down again.

"How can Charles and I get more money?" she said in a low voice.

Katie paused in the turning of the cards, clapped her palm over the coins, and drew them toward her.

"Write to the aunt in Vermont. Tell her you're with child. Tell her that if it's a girl, you'll call the child Maria."

Ann Clayton drew in her breath sharply. Maria was the aunt's given name.

"If it's a boy," said Katie, "you'll call him Woodfin."

And that was her aunt's family name.

To her husband Ann Clayton said nothing of her interview

with Katie, but the letter to her aunt Maria Woodfin was duly dispatched, and she awaited eagerly some reply to it. In the meantime the invisible financial resources of the Slapes had begun to arouse more and more curiosity in the mind of Ann's husband. Charles Clayton was a clerk in a brokerage house with three clerks under him; these three young men made only six dollars a week. But they of course hadn't wives to support on their earnings.

There was some strain between Ann and Charles Clayton on account of their lack of money. It was in Battery Park, on the afternoon following their wedding, that they had discovered that neither the one nor the other was possessed of anything approaching ample means. A friend, hoping to expedite Ann's marriage, had misrepresented to her future husband the size of her dowry, and friends of Charles, only as a joke, had given his salary out to Ann as five times its actual figure, unable to conceive that anyone could really credit a clerk with making sixty dollars a week. The first month of the Claytons' marriage had been spent in recriminations, but these failing of themselves to bring in any money, the couple had declared a truce on the matter: both had been cruelly deceived, and that, unfortunately, was all that could be said. They determined to put a brave front on the matter before their acquaintances – Ann and Charles were not the sort of persons to cultivate actual friendships – being of the opinion that only those who have money, or have the appearance of it (which in New York is the same thing), are apt to get more.

It was obvious to Charles Clayton that the Slapes did not depend on Katie's occult powers to keep them beneath the Christopher Street roof, for her income would not even have kept them in theater tickets or carfare. Therefore he assumed that John Jepson had money put away somewhere, and with this thought in mind he set about to cultivate the man. This was a difficulty, for John Jepson seemed inordinately fond of the company of his family. Yet one Saturday afternoon, when he had returned from Wall Street, Clayton found John Jepson sitting on the stoop of the house, cracking walnuts with his teeth and every few seconds glancing up and down the street.

"Waiting for Mrs. Jepson?" Clayton asked.

John Slape nodded.

"Is she late?"

John Slape shook his head.

Though he could see that his company was not particularly desired, Clayton seated himself on the step just above John Slape and leaned forward with his elbows resting on his knees. "May I have a walnut?"

John Slape handed him one over his shoulder and without looking back. Clayton had nothing to crack it with and feared to employ his teeth – which were rotten – to such a purpose, so he contented himself with turning it over and over between his fingers.

"I'm in a brokerage firm, you know."

"That so? What's that?"

Clayton was momentarily shocked by such ignorance in a man who evidently had money, but reflecting that the ignorant were soonest duped, he went on with energy: "Oh, we're an office that transacts business in stocks, and bonds, and at the Market. On 'Change, you know. For rich people, for people who have money and don't want to put it in the savings bank."

John Slape looked up. "Why don't they want to put it in the bank?"

"Four percent interest. That's why. Four percent interest is nothing! They come to us and give us their money, and we buy stocks, and shares, and interests, and then in a few months we give them back twenty or thirty percent, that's why!"

"How do the savings banks stay in business then?" asked John Slape with a canny leer.

Clayton shrugged. "Savings banks are for small investors. Bootblacks and grocers. Small investors will never make anything. A man with money goes to Wall Street. We – I have one investor, he's doubled his money in seven months. Never saw anything like it. We – I have—"

"What's 'a man with money'?" John Slape interrupted.

Clayton thought for a moment. Evidently John Jepson was going to compare any figure he named with the amount of capital he was possessed of; if Clayton named too high a figure, then Jepson would be discouraged. So at the slight risk of underestimating Jepson's holdings, he said, "About a thousand is the least I'll take on. . . ."

John Slape looked thoughtful at this, and Clayton leaned forward to peer into his face.

"Tell me what it means," said Jepson.

Clayton was confused. "What what means?"

"I take a thousand dollars down to Wall Street . . ." John began.

"No," said Clayton quickly. "You give a thousand dollars to me, and I take it to the brokerage office and invest it for you. I decide what stocks and bonds look best right now, that is, which ones are most likely to rise in value, and I purchase those to the amount of one thousand dollars. Then in a few months, when it appears that the investments may decrease in value, I'll sell them, and bring you your thousand dollars and the profit besides."

"Generous," remarked John.

"Oh, of course we take a commission," said Clayton.

"What's that?"

"You have to pay me a certain percentage."

Clayton could see that this meant little to his friend and was glad that he asked no more questions on that point.

"And I make a deal of money?" was all John said.

Clayton shrugged. "Depends on the market. Could make a great deal, could make only a little, but you'll always get better than your four percent that you take at the bank."

This was of course an outright lie, for there was always risk of loss on the Market, but Jepson's ignorance of finance was so profound that Clayton felt safe in speaking it.

John Slape sat very still for a minute or two. When he looked up it was to see Hannah and Katie not fifty feet away on the street. They had paused at a little cart that was selling hard candies. John Slape turned round on the stoop, and said quickly and quietly to Clayton: "What if I had more than a thousand . . . ?"

Chapter 18

INVESTMENTS

Charles Clayton took John Jepson's one thousand dollars to his employers, giving out that the sum had been entrusted to him by his wife's aunt in Vermont. The money was invested in Canadian silver mining stock, which fortuitously paid off in only eleven days, netting a profit of almost thirty-five percent, or $342. Two hundred of this sum Clayton brought back to John Jepson and asked his permission to keep the principal invested. John Slape, who regarded the two hundred dollars with astonishment – at least after he was made to understand that the original one thousand dollars was his as well – hurried to the barbershop at the corner of Charles and Washington streets, where he had taken to spending the greater part of his afternoons.

Here he retired to a corner near the unlighted stove and gave himself over to some deep thinking on the subject of investments and large returns. He came to the conclusion that he had discovered, through the agency of Charles Clayton, something to do with old man Parrock's fortune.

In 1871 a variety of ways existed for women whose husbands worked in other parts of the city to occupy the leisure that sometimes was theirs in the afternoon. Some paid calls, some patrolled the demi-fashionable streets like sentries, some leaned on their elbows across the counters of dry-goods stores until they had memorized the very nails there, some sat on the stoop watching their children and speculating on their neighbors' secrets, some performed charitable work, the most venturesome conducted affairs with various lovers in discreet houses of assignation that abounded on Bleecker and Clarkson streets, and not a few cultivated an interest in spiritualism.

These last, many of whom were known to one another through meetings at the houses of various mediums then in

vogue, gossiped not about their weak sisters, but about elevated
spiritual planes, clairvoyant demonstrations, prophecy, manifes-
tations of the departed, table-tippings, rappings, and a sounding
trumpet, draped in black, that had appeared near the ceiling of
Mme. Kornfeldt's drawing room.

One of these ladies, a Mrs. Benjamin Crowninshield of West
Sixteenth Street, had visited a dollar store on Eighth Avenue in
search of a cheap shawl for a sister-in-law she detested, and had
fallen into conversation with one of the young women who lived
in the same rooming house as the Slapes in Christopher Street.
The girl behind the counter, who had heard from Ann Clayton
of Katie's powers, told the woman in front of the counter of the
extraordinary new tenant, a young woman with black hair and
wild eyes, who "can read your heart just by taking one look at
the nails of your fingers."

Mrs. Crowninshield asked directions to the house and appeared that very afternoon in the threadbare parlor on the second
floor, sitting at the table across from Katie Slape.

What Katie Slape told Mrs. Crowninshield, Mrs. Crowninshield never revealed, but whatever secret was known to Katie
about her customer was sufficient to prove her prowess in the
matter of divination. Mrs. Crowninshield refused to return to
Christopher Street, but she sent all her friends; and within the
week Katie had doubled her prices, receiving not one complaint
for the increase.

Upon first entering the room and seeing Katie, the ladies
would be disappointed. The chamber had none of the amenities
they were used to: thick draperies, plush carpets, heavy dark furniture, panelled walls. And Katie was dressed in bright, vulgar
colors, with too much ornament about her. She wasn't polite,
her grin was almost insulting, and there was no delicious mystery to the process of her clairvoyance.

Katie looked at you, demanded your money, looked at you
again, touched your hand or fingered the material of your sleeve
– and then told the secrets of your heart.

"You have a lover on Morton Street," she told one woman.
"And your husband has found out his name."

"Your sister," she told another, "was killed by an abortionist in

West Houston Street. Her corpse was sold to a medical student."

"If your stair carpet were to become loose," she told a third, "your husband's father would fall and break his back. You thought he had one hundred thousand dollars, but he has double that."

Katie enjoyed her work, and her parents were happy to see her occupied. The money she obtained in silver and small pieces of gold seemed of more value to the Slapes than that which was hidden away, in such large notes, in Philo's carpetbag.

They began to look for a way to squeeze more from Katie's profession.

"Katie," said her stepmother one evening when the three of them were eating in a German restaurant on Second Avenue, "these ladies that come to see you – do they have money?"

Katie nodded. "Some," she said. "Some have a lot."

"I've seen 'em well dressed," said John, nodding.

"Do they bring the money with them?" asked Hannah.

"Some," said Katie. "I saw a woman carried five hundred dollars in her pocket."

"Five hundred dollars!" exclaimed John Slape.

"Oh, Katie!" Hannah laughed. "We'll coin you, turn you into dollars!"

One afternoon, when Katie was downstairs with one lady and three more waited in the ground-floor parlor, and Hannah was absent with the landlady on an expedition to the aquarium at Battery Park, John Slape pried open the locked trunk in which the carpetbag was kept and extracted from it all of Philo's fortune but perhaps a thousand dollars. He placed the bills in a little tin box and that evening handed over the little tin box to Charles Clayton. John Slape did not even know to ask for a receipt.

Chapter 19

THEFT

With John Jepson's twenty-eight thousand dollars in his possession, Charles Clayton hesitated. He ought perhaps to do with that sum what he had done with Jepson's thousand dollars – invest it under his own name and from the profits take a large commission for himself. But how to explain at the brokerage house the abrupt acquisition of so large a sum? If he claimed it as his own, through the death of, say, his wife's uncle, then his employers would justifiably question him: "If you are possessed of such a fortune, why do you remain in menial employment?"

Neither could he say, "This money belongs to a fellow lodger," for with such a sum to be invested, his employers would insist upon meeting John Jepson and making much of him. And if Jepson talked with the head of the brokerage house, he would learn to what extent Clayton had cheated him.

To deal with another brokerage house would necessitate the further deception of using a false name, and what with constant traffic along Wall Street among brokers, their clerks, and messenger boys, he was certain to be found out.

The simplest solution was probably to steal the money.

Accordingly, Charles Clayton turned in his resignation, this to his employers' indignant astonishment, returned to Christopher Street, and began to pack his bags.

Ann Clayton was no less astonished and indignant over her husband's behavior and demanded of him why he pursued such a course of action.

"We are going to live with your aunt in Vermont," he said.

She started to protest, but Charles pulled from his coat an envelope, opened it beneath her nose, and showed her a thick stack of hundred-dollar bills. He extracted five and gave them to her.

She was silent.

Charles said: "I'm leaving today. I'll take the ferry to Brooklyn, and then to Rye. From there I'll go by the cars to Brattleboro. I should be there tomorrow, and I'll search out a house for us near your aunt. Tell no one where I've gone. If anyone asks, I've been sent to Cincinnati on business. Tomorrow, you will pack only what you need for the trip and follow me to Brattleboro. Abandon everything else – we'll not need it. And above all, Ann—"

"What?" she demanded in an excited whisper.

"Do not speak to the Jepsons."

Five minutes later Charles had kissed his wife, taken up his bag, and opened the hallway door. Directly across the way stood Katie Slape in the doorway of her parlor, picking at one of the buttons on her dress.

She looked up at Clayton and grinned.

He smiled nervously back, said "Good day, Miss Katie," and attempted to slip past her and down the stairs.

Katie reached out and grabbed his hand.

"Want to know what's to become of you?" she asked with an insinuating smirk.

He tried to pull away, but she held him fast. Suddenly her expression altered and she dropped his hand with intense surprise.

Charles Clayton ran down the stairs, but even before he could open the front door he could hear Katie's trampling feet on the stairs. "Par, Par!" she shrieked.

Charles Clayton ran down to Hudson Street, jumped in a passing cabriolet, and was driven to the Houston Street ferry on the East River. He leaned far back in the vehicle, pressed his hand over his heart, and cursed Katie Jepson in his very soul.

Ten minutes later there was a knock at Ann Clayton's door. She opened it cautiously and very nearly slammed it shut again when she saw that it was Hannah Slape who stood there.

"Mrs. Clayton," said Hannah, "Katie and me would be very pleased if you would step up for some tea and cookies. The cookies was sent from over on Sixth Avenue, and they're special good."

"No, thank you," replied Ann Clayton. "I've just eaten, and I fear I've no appetite left me."

"Come anyway," said Hannah. "For the tea – the tea'll aid digestion. And for the company – Katie and me's feeling lonesome as lepers."

Ann Clayton had heard Katie's shouts on the stairs, and she suspected that they had something to do with her husband's leaving the house with a very great sum of money in his pocket. Charles's admonition not to speak to the Jepsons suggested that even if the money had not actually been stolen from the Jepsons the family at least had some interest in it. She decided to accept Hannah's invitation, first because she was curious to learn more than she knew now, and second because a refusal of so polite an invitation would seem suspiciously unfriendly.

When she turned to straighten her dress in a cheval glass, Hannah pushed the door of the room wide open. Drawers were opened, and many of her husband's garments were strewn over the bed.

"Mr. Clayton gone somewheres?" Hannah asked.

"No," said Ann quickly, then amended that too-hasty lie to another: "That is, he's going away tomorrow. To Cincinnati, on business, for his Wall Street firm."

Hannah smiled unpleasantly and remarked, "Reckon it will be a long time before you see him again."

To this Ann Clayton knew not what to answer.

Katie had brought up a pot of tea from the kitchen, and on a little mahogany table near the window that looked down three stories to the brick walk of Christopher Street, she had laid out the boxes that bore the name of a well-known Sixth Avenue confectioner.

Ann took the seat that was proffered her, smiled nervously, and asked, "Is Mr. Jepson not here?"

Katie laughed, and winked at her mother. "He's out trying to catch the ferry."

To disguise her nervousness, Ann diligently brushed nonexistent crumbs from the bosom of her dress.

Hannah was seated near the window. She peered out into the

street and said, "Katie, one of your ladies is below."

"Excuse me," said Katie to Mrs. Clayton, "I'll be back as quick as I can."

"Of course," said Ann. She smiled at both Katie and Hannah, wondering what lay beneath the Jepsons' politeness.

Hannah poured her tea, urged the confectionery on her, and described a reading of Shakespeare given the previous evening by a seven-year-old girl, little Ollie Goldsmith, at Chickering Hall.

Ann grew gradually easier in her mind. Katie returned but made no comment on the session with her customer below.

Having remained in the Jepsons' parlor for a polite half hour, Ann was rising to take her leave when she noticed, on Katie's collar, a little brooch of gold and jet set with diamonds. It was exactly like one that had been made up after the death of her mother and contained, on the other side, a tiny braid of her mother's hair, clipped from her corpse.

Ann stared at the brooch and became convinced it was her own.

Katie Slape had not been downstairs with a guest – she had been in Ann's room.

Hannah and Katie smiled at Ann.

Katie reached in her pocket and took out five hundred-dollar notes. She threw them into an opened box of cookies. "Hid behind the mirror," she said.

"You were in my room!" cried Ann.

"*He* must have taken the rest," said Hannah to her step-daughter. "As you said."

Ann Clayton rose in alarm, but Katie was quicker. She placed herself between Ann Clayton and the door.

"John was a fool to give your husband our money," said Hannah quietly.

"I know nothing about it!"

Hannah shrugged, and Katie stepped closer to the frightened woman.

"I know nothing!" Ann cried again. "Charles went to Cincinnati. He has no money. Miss Katie, you know we have no money!"

"Par'll find Mr. Clayton," said Katie. "I told him where he

should look. I said, 'Par, go down to the Houston Street ferry.' So that's where Par's gone."

"You were listening at our door!"

Katie came closer, and Ann was backed against the window. During the day, because of the effluvia of the docks, windows on lower Christopher Street were kept closed. Ann pressed her hands behind her against the glass panes.

Katie came within two feet of Ann Clayton and extended her arms so that they lightly touched the woman's breast.

Ann tried to brush them away, but Katie was strong and not to be moved. She pressed harder. Ann's back was forced against the window, and she found it difficult to draw breath.

Katie suddenly let go and stood back.

"Can't do it, Mar," she said with a shrug. "Not with the window closed."

Ann stood with her hand against her heaving breast.

"Use a chair," suggested Hannah.

Katie picked up the chair in which Ann Clayton had been sitting, lifted it high, and brought it down swiftly on the woman's head. Ann had watched with horror, but caught between the table, the wall, and Katie, she could not escape the blow. Two legs of the chair broke, and Ann toppled against the table. The dishes and confectionery spilled out over the carpet.

Hannah dragged the table out of the way, and Ann slipped unconscious onto the floor.

Hannah and Katie stood over her, silent for a few moments.

"Open the window and look out, Katie. See if anyone's watching."

Katie went to the window, raised the sash, and peered up and down the street. Christopher Street was busy and noisy. Horses and carts, and vendors with their wares paraded and jostled one another down the center of the roadway while pedestrians on the sidewalk hurried toward the docks or away from them – but no one was bothering to look upward. And directly across the way was only the blank wall of a large warehouse.

"No one," said Katie, after a few moments' examination of the street.

Ann Clayton was moaning. She bled from a cut on her head,

and there were splinters of wood embedded in her cheek. The shoulder of her dress was torn. She opened one swollen eye and looked up at Hannah. Her hand slid across the floor in supplication.

Hannah raised her booted foot and brought it down hard on Ann Clayton's frail wrist. The sound of breaking bones was audible.

"Mar," said Katie doubtfully, "it's not very far down . . ."

Ann began to whimper.

"Then we'll do what we can up here," said Hannah. She lifted her foot again and kicked Ann Clayton squarely in the face.

The woman shrieked, but now Katie had raised her foot and brought it down squarely on Ann's mouth with so great a force that her jaw was broken. Her dislodged teeth were scattered down her throat.

She choked, and despite all her pain, jerked up with the panic of the obstruction of the jagged teeth in her windpipe.

Hannah kicked her in the belly.

Katie picked up the broken chair and brought it down three times against Ann's bloody head.

Ann lay still. Blood flowed onto the carpet out of a large wound on her forehead. Her jaw had become entirely dislodged and sagged far away from the remainder of her face. Her mouth had been torn at the corners and she appeared to have a grin as large as the Negro man the Slapes had once seen who could press two whole apples into his mouth.

Katie pointed out this resemblance, and Hannah concurred.

Katie and Hannah righted the mahogany table and moved it to the window. Then they lifted their victim's body onto the table, and each pushing against one of Ann Clayton's feet, they shoved her headlong out of the third-story window.

Her head was smashed on the brick walk to such an extent that the mutilations that had occurred before the fall were never discovered.

Chapter 20

THE SLAPES SETTLE IN

Neighbors came first and surrounded the mangled body of the woman who had fallen from the third-floor window of No. 251 Christopher Street. Workers and loungers on the docks, alerted by the gathering crowd, came after. And then the police appeared, pushing the curious out of the way, covering up Mrs. Clayton with a sheet provided by grinning Katie, and questioning the inhabitants of the house.

Only Mrs. Hannah Jepson was able to explain why the woman had killed herself. "Come up to our parlor – me-and-Katie-here's parlor – looking wild. Said Mr. Clayton had run off with all their money and was intending to leave her. Took away everything they had. Couldn't live without him. Sat down at the table next the window, fanned her face, said could she have some tea and cake. Sent Katie down for tea, myself to get the cake out of the tin. Turned my back. Pulled up the sash and sailed out. Don't know what my John will think – comes home to find that lodgers been jumping out of our windows."

Charles Clayton was never found. His employers' testimony that he had quit his job quite suddenly and without sufficient or apparent motive confirmed Hannah Jepson's story of a man bent on abandoning his spouse.

On the day after Ann Clayton perished on the sidewalk of Christopher Street, a body was discovered in the water beneath the Brooklyn ferry pier. The unidentifiable man had died when a spike, such as might have been easily picked up in the vicinity, about eight inches long, rusting, but filed to a useful sharpness, was pounded through his right eye and deep into his brain.

The Slapes had recovered the money John had so foolishly entrusted to Charles Clayton, but at the dangerous expense of killing both the man and his wife, whom Hannah and Katie had rather liked than not. Hannah did not berate her husband but patiently explained that this was why *she* had kept the money.

John Slape was penitent, and that night the family went out to see Bryant's Minstrels, the Clodoche Can-Can, and Little Mac as Mark Twain's Jumping Frog. Afterward, at a German dance hall in the neighborhood of the theater, they sat out of the way of the dance floor and the orchestra and talked of their plans.

"Thieves and robbers," said John. "We shouldn't keep the money about the house."

"Don't leave it on Wall Street," Hannah warned. "Wall Street takes people like us and swallows us whole."

"Clayton said the savings banks give four percent. I don't rightly understand what that's tokened to mean, but p'haps a bank would be the place."

Hannah looked doubtful.

Katie said with a grin, "I'd like to see thieves and robbers come past me!"

"Well," said Hannah, "can't be on watch all the time. Might be somebody in the house wanted to steal the money – like Mr. Clayton."

"Maybe," said John, "we ought to have a house ourselves."

Hannah and Katie considered this, and Hannah, who was the quickest of the three, agreed after only a moment. "But what house?" she asked.

"I like the one we're in," said Katie. "I like being near the river. I like the noise."

Hannah and John agreed.

"Why don't we just buy it?" asked Katie. "And if she don't want to sell . . ."

They offered the landlady three thousand dollars for the house, which was considerably above its market value, though the Slapes had no idea of this. Having been for some time of the mind to move to Syracuse, where her son was living, and distressed by Mrs. Clayton's ugly death, Mrs. Bracken signed over the deed of the house to the Slapes, packed her belongings, and was gone before the other tenants had time to wonder who was going to cook their meals.

Hannah wasn't.

Even as Mrs. Bracken was still visible on the sidewalk, walking toward the Christopher Street ferry, Hannah was knocking on the doors of the house, giving notice. The two girls who worked in the Eighth Avenue dollar store shrugged and indicated that they knew of a place on West Thirteenth where they might room together as cheaply as here – and where the company, they remarked pointedly, was more congenial. Only the seamstress and her lame daughter expressed distress at being turned out on the street, and at their pleas, Hannah allowed them to stay for two days more, until Monday – though they would have to get their own meals in the interim.

On Monday the seamstress walked the street with a newspaper, looking for rooms, but could find nothing suitable and sufficiently cheap. She returned to Christopher Street, determined again to throw herself on the mercy of the new owners of the house, but found, when she reached Christopher Street, that all her belongings had been tossed onto the sidewalk and that her crippled daughter sat weeping on the stoop.

A pack of dirty little boys was rummaging through the seamstress's trunk and scattering all the piecework which was her livelihood. The seamstress, who was a frail woman, attempted to beat them away, but they only laughed. Finally she slammed the lid down on their hands and went and sat beside her daughter, joining her in tears.

The Slapes had the satisfaction of being rid of the seamstress sometime on Monday night, for they returned from a play to discover her and her daughter gone and nothing but a few scraps of cloth and some empty spools littering the stoop to remind them of her. Where she went and what she did with herself they never learned or cared.

The Slapes did not alter their manner of living. The rooms that had been vacated they simply closed off and were happy in knowing they were not being spied upon. Katie continued to see her clients in the little bare room on the second floor.

Hannah had no intention of cooking for her family, so two servants were hired, one for the kitchen and the other for the chambers. She insisted that these two young women do all their work in the morning and leave as soon as the dinner dishes were done. Most of Katie's business was in the afternoon, and the Slapes had decided that they wanted the house empty then. In addition, to guard the house while they were away, John Slape purchased a large mongrel dog of vicious temperament which they called Little Dick – after the play which followed the fortunes of a New York bootblack. During the day this dog was kept tied to a ring in the cellar wall, but at night he was allowed to roam the house. He barked at nothing and everything and would leave off only when beat over the head with a stick.

By way of experiment, Hannah took five thousand dollars and deposited it in the Seaman's Bank around the corner on Washington Street. Thereafter whenever they left the house or returned to it the Slapes would go out of their way to walk past the Seaman's Bank, as if they suspected that the edifice, once it had swallowed their money, would pick up its foundations and saunter away in search of other gullible victims.

All in all, the Slapes lived agreeably, and they considered that their present comfort was worth all the trouble that they had gone to in Goshen, getting the money out of that old man and preventing him from giving it away to the Draxes. They could not conceive of anything that would interfere with their present, genial enjoyments. But then, they could not know that Philo Drax was then lodging scarcely seven streets away from them and that it was only a matter of time before their paths crossed once again.

PART V

WEST THIRTEENTH STREET

Chapter 21

"WHAT WILL YOU DO?"

Ben Gillow, the principal carpenter in town, had made coffins for New Egypt's dead for twenty-three years; as a matter of course he had taken over other functions for the preparing of bodies for burial. He was summoned to the Drax house, took one look at Mrs. Drax on the bed, and called out the window for Dr. Slocum, who was loitering in the yard and chatting with the curious over the fence, to send for Mrs. Gillow. With her help the carpenter lifted Mrs. Drax's mangled body onto Philo's bed, cut away her clothing, sponged her body clean, sewed up as best they could the wide cuts in her neck and cheek, and then put her in a high-necked dress. The dress had to be slit up the back, for Mary Drax's corpse had quickly stiffened with rigor mortis.

Mr. Gillow's assistant and Mrs. Gillow's hired girl brought over, in a little goat cart, a plain wooden coffin that had "Female" lightly pencilled on the bottom; for Mrs. Drax, a woman of common height and size, no coffin need be specially constructed. Ben Gillow and his assistant placed Mrs. Drax in the coffin and brought it downstairs, no easy operation considering the narrowness of the turn in the staircase. Upstairs, Mrs. Gillow and the hired girl folded the bloody linen, washed down the walls, and took away with them two mantillas that were all that was left of Mrs. Drax's meager wedding trousseau.

The funeral on Sunday was brief, quiet, and well attended. Despite the damage to her face, Mary Drax's coffin was kept open at the front of the church, with a bunch of violets covering the place where her ear had been sliced off. It was Philo herself, during the last hymn, who pried off the coffin plate for a souvenir and pushed down the lid.

Everyone was respectful of Philo's grief, but even at the graveside, she heard a low voice behind her ask, "What will she do . . . ?"

Philo could not remain in the house where Mary Drax died. It was unthinkable that she should attempt to sleep in a room whose walls had been clotted with her mother's gore. It would do no good either to bring her bed below, for she could not pass the narrow stairs or cross the hallway without seeing the prints of Katie Slape's feet, dyed in her mother's blood. These considerations occurring also to Mrs. Libby prompted that good neighbor to offer Philo refuge. Philo accepted gratefully.

Philo knew that Katie Slape had come to murder her, not her mother. To Philo belonged rightly the inheritance that the Slapes had usurped, and Philo was also witness to the murder of Richard Parrock. Philo, not Mary Drax, had been Katie's quarry in New Egypt. She could not even be certain that Katie was not still waiting in the fir forest for another chance.

On the evening after the funeral, Philo sat silent at Mrs. Libby's table, smiling absently when she was addressed by one of the children, but scarcely able to follow their prattle. She retired to the little room two of the Libby girls had vacated for her, threw herself onto the bed, and wept for nearly an hour, remembering her mother.

Eventually, she undressed and got beneath the covers. She began to examine her predicament in detail. Within a week she had lost both grandfather and mother, and they had been all her family. Her only responsibility now was to herself. She had wondered how she might support herself in New Egypt when work was not to be had for a young woman, when she hadn't her mother's expertise with a needle, when the interest payment on the mortgage would roll inexorably around in another few months – and then realized that there was no reason why she should remain in New Egypt at all. No ties of affection kept her here. If she remained, she would be forever no more than Mary Drax's daughter. *Poor Philo, how do you suppose she keeps body and soul together?*

Philo would have liked to remain for some few days with Mrs. Libby in order to recover herself and indulge her grief over Mary Drax's death; but Mrs. Libby's household was as straitened as her own had been, and Philo knew that she was a burden on the widow with her four children. On the following morning at breakfast, Philo said to her, "I'm going to see Mr. Varley."

"Oh!" exclaimed Mrs. Libby doubtfully. "Philo, do you think he'll have work for you?" She was hesitant to discourage the orphan, but had heard only the day before that the graniteware factory was taking on no new hands.

"No," said Philo, "I'm going to sell him the house."

Mrs. Libby threw up her hands but said nothing.

Philo did not further explain her plans. She went to Mr. Varley's office at the factory, found him in, and offered to sell him the house for two thousand dollars. Fourteen hundred fifty of that would be assumed in the mortgage he held, and Philo would receive only five hundred fifty dollars. Jacob Varley, though he knew that Philo was without funds and that her mother could have left her nothing *except* the house, offered only one hundred dollars over the amount of the mortgage.

"Mr. Varley," said Philo placidly, "you know that the house is worth much more than that."

He shook his head. "No, Philo, the house is no longer worth two thousand dollars. Perhaps last week, but this unfortunate . . ."

"I beg your pardon?"

He turned round and spoke plainly. "A house loses value if there's been a murder in it."

Philo considered this a moment. She did not believe Mr. Varley and knew that he, who seemed to her to have all the money in the world, only wanted to cheat her of what little she possessed. On the other hand, she wanted the cash and she wanted broken those ties that bound her to New Egypt. Her pride, however, kept her from giving in to this avaricious man. "I will keep the house," said Philo, and rose.

"Philo," said Jacob Varley quickly, "you should not remain in that house. You should take lodging elsewhere. There's a room to be had, I think, above Mr. Clegg's store. He'll want no more than two dollars a week for it, I should imagine. That house, you should be rid of it. You'll be forever reminded of what happened there. And of course you won't have any way of keeping up the payments on the mortgage."

"I will not sell the house to you for a sum that would leave me only one hundred dollars," said Philo, and coldly thanked Mr. Varley for his time, and left the room.

Jacob Varley was irritated by the girl. She hadn't money, she hadn't the opportunity of getting any money except by the sale of the house – and still she had refused his offer. The house was of course worth the two thousand dollars she had suggested – his own foreman had offered him twenty-five hundred dollars for it, if he could get it from the Draxes. But if he could buy it from Philo for fifteen hundred, he could sell it to his foreman for only two thousand, make five hundred dollars' profit, and gain the undying gratitude of his employee.

Philo was still young. What need had she of five hundred dollars? The difference between fifty and five hundred would probably not even be evident to her, Jacob Varley told himself. And he could also afford to wait when she obviously could not.

On her way back from the graniteware factory to Mrs. Libby's, Philo stopped at Mr. Clegg's store with the intention of purchasing apples and candy for the kind woman's children.

Mr. Clegg was astonished to see her and wondered that she could be out on the street so soon after her mother's death.

Philo thanked him for his condolences and attendance at the funeral.

"What will you do?" he asked, and even in this mild gentleman's mouth, the question did not please her.

"Yes," said a familiar voice behind her, "what will you do, Miss Philo?"

It was Jewel Varley, in a dress of corn-colored barege with matching boots and gloves and a hat that was no bigger than a cockleshell. She might have been on her way to tea with the President's wife, except that it was ten o'clock in the morning and the President's wife was in Washington.

"I don't know," said Philo, unable to hide her gloominess.

"My goodness," Jewel exclaimed, "but your life is just one long railway track of misery, Miss Philo! Ma and I are certain we don't know what's to become of you! P'rhaps if you could sew we would let you mend some of our things – some of our things get so frightfully torn. The countryside is rife with briars, Miss Philo!"

"I don't sew," said Philo glumly.

"I had intended to invite you to my come-out party this evening, Miss Philo. But I don't think I can now. Why, you're in double mourning! You won't be out of mourning, I'll vow, for another two years! I couldn't have you sitting like a statue of grief in the corner. It would drag on everybody's spirits."

"No," said Philo, "I would not be much inclined to attend a party this evening."

"So you can just sit at home and mope, I suppose," said Jewel. "But I will tell you one thing, Miss Philo: I couldn't sit at home in that house and mope, not when my mother had been hacked to pieces at the top of the stairs. No!" She shook her head vehemently. "I for one couldn't do it!"

"I don't intend to do so," said Philo. "I have decided to sell the house."

Jewel considered this a moment. "Then you will have some money," she said. "I know my father will wish to buy it. His foreman offered him ready cash for it."

"Oh, yes?" replied Philo, with interest.

"I heard Pa tell Ma so," said Jewel. She cast her head about, trying to think of a way to denigrate Philo, who had been un-avoidably raised in her estimation by her having become, in however insignificant a way, an heiress to property. "If you do sell the house, Philo, you will be involved in a business transaction."

"I do not think I shall mind that very much," Philo replied.

"Business transactions are not ladylike. Ma says it is common and vulgar for a lady to know anything about money."

Notwithstanding Caroline Varley's dictum regarding women and business, Philo, as soon as she had made her small purchases and taken leave of Jewel, hurried over to the house of Mr. Varley's foreman. Philo had often delivered sewing to Mrs. MacMamus and was known to both her and her husband.

"Mrs. MacMamus," Philo said when the requisite exchanges of grief and consolation had been made, "I am told that Mr.

MacMamus is interested in purchasing the house in which Mother and I lived."

Mrs. MacMamus, a pleasant woman whose principal fault was an unquenchable desire to rise in the world, said, "Why, yes, Mr. MacMamus has interested himself in the matter. We want the house for Mr. MacMamus's sister, who has decided to come to live near us in New Egypt. Dolly – that is her name – is an estimable woman, but . . ." Mrs. MacMamus hesitated, cocked her head, and concluded apologetically, ". . . but she was once married to an Irishman. I thought it best if we found her some place to live other than this house, but as you know, there is not much building in New Egypt, and there are so many workers at the factory! We despaired of finding a place, and at last I had to ask Dolly to come here."

"Mrs. MacMamus," said Philo. "The house is mine now, and I intend to sell it. Would your husband still like to have it?"

"I'm sure of it," said Mrs. MacMamus. Philo smiled. She was certain at least that *Mrs*. MacMamus wanted it very much.

"How much would he be willing to pay for it?"

"He offered Mr. Varley twenty-five hundred dollars, I believe."

"So much as that!"

Mrs. MacMamus nodded.

"Please tell Mr. MacMamus," said Philo after a moment, "that I will sell him the house for two thousand two hundred and fifty dollars."

Mrs. MacMamus looked very pleased indeed, and asked Philo if she would not wait with her until noon, when Mr. MacMamus would come home for his dinner.

She did so. Mr. MacMamus seemed every bit as pleased as his wife at Philo's offer and, drawing up a bill of sale himself, exchanged Philo's signature for two draughts on the Cookstown Bank. One of these was made out to Philo Drax for the sum of $800, and the other, for the amount of the unpaid mortgage, to Jacob Varley.

That afternoon Philo again appeared at the graniteware factory and again was admitted to see Jacob Varley. He was certain that she had come to accept his offer and was struck dumb with astonishment when Philo merely handed him the bank draught across his desk.

"May I have a receipt please?" Philo asked. "And the original note."

"This draught is signed by my foreman!"

"It is to Mr. MacMamus that I have sold the house," said Philo unperturbedly.

Jacob Varley flushed. He suspected that Philo had found him out, but if she had, she did not betray her triumph in either her voice or her countenance.

"How much did you get over and above this amount, Philo?" he asked curiously as he handed over the receipt.

"You must ask Mr. MacMamus that, sir," she replied. "It is not my business to tell."

"What will you do, Philo?" Jacob Varley said. There was in his voice a little note of respect for this young woman who had got the better of him.

"My plans are indefinite," she said.

"Perhaps you would like to invest your money," he suggested.

"With you, sir?"

"I might be willing to hold on to your money for you, Philo."

"I have my pockets," said Philo. "And if they become full, there's always a bank."

Chapter 22

THE HORSEHAIR BLANKET

That afternoon Philo took the cars to Cookstown, where she exchanged Mr. MacMamus's draught for notes and gold. At a millinery store that sold ready-made articles she purchased two neat dresses, and a little farther down the street, a small wicker bag in which to carry them. She caught the late-afternoon train from Philadelphia that would carry her back to New Egypt.

Philo sat looking out the window of the railway car, wondering when she should next see that familiar landscape of careful fields and evergreen forest. The lowering sun glinted on a brook that followed for some distance the path of the tracks, and the water glistened like her own tears.

Yet her tears dried suddenly and she sat very still when she began to catch the conversation of the two gentlemen seated directly behind her in the car. Both men had been in their places when she boarded the train at Cookstown.

"... state marshal ..." was the phrase that first drew her attention.

She turned her head, and listened carefully, holding her hand over her other ear to shut out extraneous noise. "... to New Egypt," the same voice went on.

"Murder there last week, I heard, terrible thing, woman cut up in her bed."

Philo wondered that the tale of her mother's death had travelled so far and so quickly. She began to hope that the state marshal – she assumed that the first voice was his – had discovered Katie Slape, and was on his way to arrest her. Philo very nearly rose in her seat to speak to the marshal, but his next words stopped her movement and froze her heart.

"That woman's daughter I'm coming to arrest."

"No!" replied the other.

"Certain true, black and blue," the marshal assured his companion.

Philo closed her eyes tightly.

"Own daughter?"

"Girl murdered her grandfather," said the marshal. "I just found her out. Ten days ago down in Goshen—"

"Where's Goshen?"

"Down on Cape May."

"Oh yes."

"—down in Goshen, girl came to her grandfather's house, and murdered him in his bed!"

"Now her mother's dead too?"

"Yes," said the marshal. "Bit peculiar, that, too. I'm told it was *another* girl that killed the woman in New Egypt, but maybe it was the woman's daughter, in a disguise."

"Dangerous girl!"

"Oh I got a warrant, and I got a gun, in case she comes at me with her knife," the marshal assured his companion.

The sun dropped down behind the fir forest, for a few moments shining a gold-green light through the topmost boughs. The train was no more than a mile outside of New Egypt.

"What'll come of her?" asked the marshal's companion.

"We'll send out invitations to her hanging," replied the marshal.

"Put me down," said his friend with a laugh. "A girl that kills her own grandfather, she—"

His voice was drowned by the locomotive's shrill whistle.

The train had halted at the New Egypt station. Philo sat hunched down in her seat as the marshal stood in the aisle. She listened to his retreating steps down the length of the car behind her, and only when she could hear them no longer did she rise. She hurried to the opposite end of the car, stood on the platform, and peered out.

The marshal, a tall, smooth-shaven man in a green plaid jacket, was in conversation with the stationmaster. Doubtlessly he was asking Mr. Kilcrease where he might find the Drax house.

The train began to move again, but Philo did not get off. She could not have emerged onto the platform without being seen by Mr. Kilcrease, who would immediately have pointed her out to the marshal as the very person he was seeking.

When the train had passed the station and was on its way out of town past the graniteware factory, Philo leapt from the car platform and, still clutching her new case, landed on a soft clay bank.

Not even stopping to brush herself off, she raced toward the fir forest and in another ten minutes found herself within sight of Mrs. Libby's and her own house. She sneaked across the field at its narrowest point and knocked at the back door of Mrs. Libby's house, but Mrs. Libby had already been apprised of someone's approach by the furious barking of all her dogs.

"Philo!" she exclaimed, looking down at the young woman's dress but more alarmed still by the terror in her eyes.

"Mrs. Libby," said Philo quickly, "a marshal has come to town to arrest me for my grandfather's murder."

Mrs. Libby threw up her hands in horror.

"Please help me get away," Philo said in a low voice.

Mrs. Libby went immediately to put the horse to the wagon.

Philo went upstairs and hurriedly packed her belongings. Mrs. Libby sat on the buckboard of her wagon in the dooryard. Philo went cautiously out of the house and crept onto the back. Crouching between two large bales of hay, she drew a blanket over her.

"I'll take you back to Cookstown, and you can take the cars to Philadelphia," said Mrs. Libby.

Philo whispered her thanks, and sank lower beneath the blanket. The wagon rolled out into the lane. Mrs. Libby's four children hung over the fence in near danger of puncturing their abdomens on the pickets, but they had been forbidden to call out farewells.

Philo, well hidden, lifted a corner of the blanket and peered out from behind the substantial form of Mrs. Libby. She saw the house where she had been born and raised and the window of the room in which her mother had been so cruelly murdered. Farther down the lane, she saw the doctor, rocking on his piazza.

The way to Cookstown took the wagon past the Varleys'. All the windows of the house were lighted for Jewel's come-out party. Lanterns had been strung in the garden. And carriages had begun to arrive, bringing guests from all over the county, from towns as close and small as Cassville and as far away and important as Toms River. Jewel was at the open door, lighted from behind, and greeting her guests with her high and peculiar laugh.

And at the edge of the Varleys' garden, with the low iron fence between them, Philo saw Henry Maitland in conversation with the marshal, who had come to New Egypt to arrest her for two murders.

The wagon rolled on, and Philo Drax, who had always held her head high, left the home of her birth cowering beneath a horsehair blanket.

In another hour Philo had reached Cookstown again. She thanked Mrs. Libby, wept on her breast, and then sent the good woman back to her children. Half an hour later she boarded the cars, then changed at Mount Holly for a train going north. The dawn of the next morning saw her, pale and silent, at the Hoboken docks, waiting for the Christopher Street ferry to take her across the North River to New York.

Chapter 23

ELLA LaFAVOUR

As she sat on the Hoboken dock, waiting for the ferry, Philo had only the wicker case she had purchased the previous afternoon in Cookstown and a small satchel with the very few items she had hastily thrown together at Mrs. Libby's. Of her mother, she had no remembrance but the wedding ring that the undertaker's wife had pried from Mary Drax's finger just before she went into her coffin. In her pocket she carried an envelope with the two hundred fifty dollars she had received from Mr. Killip, and the further eight hundred from the sale of the house to Mr. MacMamus. Such a sum – over a thousand dollars – seemed vast to Philo, and she was very happy to have it. It would doubtless take her time to become established in New York. She was not afraid of work and was convinced that in time she would succeed at *something*. But she had no skills, and this money would get her through her apprenticeship in whatever profession she chose to take up.

Philo was not entirely at her ease, even so far away from New Egypt as she was now. Who knew but that someone had seen her board the train at Cookstown, and the marshal pursuing her had discovered her route, and that some officer of the law was bearing down upon her even now. She would feel much safer when she was actually out of New Jersey.

Philo had seated herself on a piling of the pier on which the ferry would dock. After ten minutes or so of cautious looking around, Philo caught the eye of a young woman – tall and slight and perhaps a few years older than herself – who stood nearby. The young woman approached with a quick gait. Her dress was fine, but to the practiced eye of the daughter of a seamstress, showed unmistakable signs of long usage and careful repair.

"Going to stay?" cried the young woman without any other introduction, adding a shrill laugh and a jerk of her shoulders.

"I beg your pardon?" replied Philo politely.

"Stay in New York, I mean? You're from the country." She jerked her shoulders. "I know it." She jerked her shoulders again.

Philo smiled. "I must show unmistakable signs of verdancy," she said, quoting something she had read somewhere.

"Somebody dead?" shrilled Ella LaFavour, eyeing Philo's black clothing.

Philo nodded. "I'm in mourning for my mother and grandfather."

"Leave you money?"

Philo thought this a rude question, and she replied sharply, "Your manners would lead me to believe that you were from the city."

The young woman took no offense at this remark. "Visiting a friend for two days in Pompton Plains. Place is dead as Sodom. Ever been there?"

"No," replied Philo. "I have never travelled much."

"Visited a friend," the young woman said, leaning over confidingly, "said he was in love with me from his hatband to his boots." She spoke in a whisper, but even her whisper was shrill. "Would you have believed him if you was me?"

Philo didn't know what to say and so said nothing.

"I wouldn't have," the young woman went on. "And turned out he wasn't worth the shoes he wears to the polls. Had a fiancée . . ." She spoke the word with two syllables only, ". . . in Murray Hill. Got a look at her too – ugly enough to frighten a horse. So now I'm going back to New York." She turned and gazed at the city. She leaned on the rope, kicked a scrap of paper into the water, and sighed. "Lord! That place is a sight for men and angels!"

The ferry was drawing close to Hoboken pier. Philo watched its approach with much interest and no little excitement. The young woman who had confided so much to Philo introduced herself as Ella LaFavour, and Philo told her name as well.

Philo said, "I've never been to New York before. But I'm alone in the world now, and I thought I might as well try to live there as anywhere else."

Ella stared across the river at the city and nodded her approval of this plan.

"Know anybody?" she asked.

Philo shook her head. "Only you."

"I'll help you," said Ella. "What you need is a place to live and something to do."

"Yes," agreed Philo.

"How much can you afford a week?" said Ella.

Philo thought a moment. "What do you pay?"

"Four, but I share a room. If I lived on my own, I'd be paying seven."

"I could afford seven, I suppose, but I think I'd rather pay four. Besides, sharing the room, I'd have company." Philo smiled sadly. "I'm not used to living alone."

"There's an empty chamber where I'm staying, on Thirteenth Street. Not much I don't think. A view of a dead tree and an old peeling wall, but the window sash goes up and down, and there's a Morning Glory stove in the corner. You pay for your own coals, though you can store as much as you want in the cellar for free."

"Is it a rooming house – the place where you live?" asked Philo. She had heard of rooming houses.

Ella nodded. "All young ladies, happy to say. Been in places where all the parlor draperies smelt of tobacco. That's what happens when you live with young men," she added as a fillip of instruction for Philo. "Landlady's not much in the cooking line but she's honest as a pulpit. You'd have the room next to hers, and I'd best warn you: Mrs. Classon snores as if all creation had the croup. She can shake down the plaster."

"Do you think she'll allow me to live there?" asked Philo anxiously. It would be providential good fortune if she could find a place to live without going first to the expense of putting up at a hotel.

"Don't see why not!" cried Ella. "You're a respectable-looking thing! Little dull around the edges, but get you out of that mourning . . ."

The ferry lurched against the pier, and in another moment the ropes were unloosed. Philo was nearly knocked into the water by the horde of passengers that stormed off the boat. She drew back in alarm, but ten minutes later, pushed and prodded by her new friend, Philo was the first to board the ferry for the return journey.

The boat was a quarter of an hour in the loading, and no longer in the crossing. Philo stood on the prow with Ella, and both young women – one returning to the city as home, the other visiting it for the first time – grew equally excited as they neared the Christopher Street pier.

"Move along! Move along!" shrieked Ella behind her as the ropes once more were loosened. "Or we'll be trampled!"

All those persons who had seemed unoccupied, indolent, and careless on board the ferry turned into dynamos of movement as soon as their feet touched the boards of Manhattan and their lungs had filled with its soot.

Philo stared about her wide-eyed. So great a concourse of people she had never seen before: not only those who had come over on the ferry with them – businessmen, farmers, ladies and their children, excursioners – but the workers at the docks, loungers, sailors, businessmen whose business was here, policemen, and more ill-kempt, scruffy little boys than she could have imagined existed in the entire world.

One of these last ran up to her immediately and began tugging at the handle of her case. "Smash yer baggage, Miss?" he squealed.

In alarm, fearing that the child meant to steal it, Philo attempted to wrest it away from him again, but Ella interfered.

"He means he wants to carry it for you," she said. "Let him. A dime if you'll take it to West Thirteenth Street. No. 224," she said to the boy. With this directive, he gave a final jerk to the bag, freed it from Philo's grasp, and immediately disappeared into the crowd.

Philo protested.

"There's thieves, all right," said Ella. "But that's not one."

And by the time they had reached the house where Ella lodged, the boy was sitting on the stoop with the case under his feet. In the doorway stood a thin lady of middle years, with a pinched nose, a pale washed-out complexion, and limp corkscrew curls.

"She wants to share!" shrieked Ella when they were half a block away and without any other introduction of Philo to her prospective landlady.

"Take the whole," wheezed Mrs. Classon in a voice so breathy it could scarcely be heard by the little baggage-smasher sitting on the steps five feet below her.

Philo by this time had reached the stoop. She took a dime from her porte-monnaie and handed it to the baggage-smasher. He took off running as if Philo had raised an axe over his head rather than paid him for a service contracted for and rendered.

"Seven," wheezed Mrs. Classon, and held up one hand spread wide and two fingers of her other hand. "Now."

"See the chamber first!" shrieked Ella behind her, and poked Philo in the ribs.

Mrs. Classon reluctantly moved aside, and Philo entered a corridor hardly wider than the front door. She ascended a rickety staircase, so narrow she had to hold her bag in front of her. On the second floor, as on the first, she saw only a succession of closed doors, and the paper on the walls was even more dismal up here than below. Ella prodded Philo up to the third floor, where she pushed open a little narrow door into a chamber that was about twelve feet by ten. It had, as Ella had promised, a window looking out onto a peeling wall. Below was a dismal spot of ground that only in the distorted imagination of a New Yorker might be termed a garden. The Morning Glory stove in the room's corner looked as if it had been for some years kept on a very strict rationing of coals. A hole had been roughly knocked through the paper, plaster and brick chimney, and the pipe crudely inserted, so that that entire portion of the room was black with escaped soot.

There was a bed with a rent mattress atop it and a little pile of feathers beneath it; a chair with the legs wired together; a table so lopsided that a pencil placed on it would immediately roll onto the floor; a flawed mirror; and a pine dresser that had been painted black and then decorated with advertising cards.

The walls were covered with a lozenged paper of blue roses, faded more in some places than in others.

It was not a room to delight Philo, but she turned with a smile to Ella, who stood with her arms crossed in the doorway, now and then jerking her shoulders, as if creating periods to her silent thoughts.

"I'll stay," said Philo.

Chapter 24

"EVER HAD A BEAU?"

Nine other young women were resident at Mrs. Classon's boarding house, and at table that evening, Philo was introduced to them. She despaired of learning all their names. What seemed most significant about New York to her was not its size – she had seen but a few streets – but the multiplicity of all that it contained. Not two boys to "smash your baggage" when you got off the pier but fifty; not three rooming houses to choose from but hundreds; not one new friend the first day but a dozen.

The young women all seemed tall and angular to Philo, but then she realized that what she was accounting height and angularity was merely an alertness and a sharpness of demeanor. They laughed and joked in what Philo had always imagined to be quite a masculine fashion. She blushed when they chafed her for her greenness, but Ella LaFavour cried out in her defense, "Hush, you all! When I first come to the city I was grass-green, fast color, and warranted to wash! Thought I was going to live on wedding cake and strawberries to the end of the chapter!"

Her shrill voice had quieted them, and after that all the women promised they would assist Philo in getting a foothold in the city. Philo hoped that this promise was not lightly given.

After supper she and Mrs. Classon and Ella sat in the front parlor, and Philo heard the rules of the house: rent paid on time or your baggage is set on the steps, no begging for the larder key after supper, no late breakfasts, no gentleman beyond the front parlor, no sitting in the windows on hot nights. Only this last precaution Philo did not understand the necessity of, since it did not interfere either with Mrs. Classon's ease or the economy of the house, but the landlady only replied mysteriously, "Gives the place a bad air," and nodded sagaciously. She was given a latchkey. "Street door locked at ten, but girls, I know, is sometimes out later than that. . . ."

At this, Ella laughed convulsively. Mrs. Classon laughed herself, as if suddenly seeing the humor of her own remark. Philo was bewildered.

Two other young women were in the parlor, both of them waiting for gentlemen who had promised to call; this was the situation as well with Ella.

To pass the time Philo was asked to tell of herself. However, when Philo began to speak of her mother and New Egypt, Ella cried out, "Oh, that's old stuff! Tell us, Philo: ever had a beau?"

Philo blushed, then smiled. "No," she replied, "I never have."

The other two young women, Laura and Ida, expressed their disbelief.

Philo blushed again. "Just once," she admitted.

"Was he fair?" asked Laura.

"Was he rich?" demanded Ida.

"He had dark hair and dark eyes," replied Philo, "and a dark moustache, but he had no money. It's been a long while since I thought of him."

"What was his name?" said Ella.

"Wesley," Philo replied.

"And he married your best chum, I'll wager!" cried Laura.

"He went off to war," said Philo.

The three young women were silent a moment.

"He fought at Savage Station, Glendale, Malvern Hills, Charles City Crossroads, Bristow Station, Second Bull Run, Chancellorsville, Kelley's Ford, and Wapping Heights. He was taken prisoner at Locust Grove, and he died in Andersonville."

There was silence for a few moments as Philo completed her melancholy recitation. The only young woman at Mrs. Classon's who had not lost a brother, father, playmate, or sweetheart to the War was a young woman who had been orphaned since her second year.

"Papa died in Andersonville," said Laura after a moment.

"And not a beau since the War?" asked Ida of Philo. "Do you keep him alive in your heart?"

Philo shook her head with a smile. "Wesley would have married me – he asked me. I was too young to say yes then, but I would have if he had come back from the War. And after the War, after Papa died, Mother and I were very poor. For my dowry I'd have an old sewing basket and a bolt of cloth – and everybody in New Egypt knew it. Who'd come knocking at *my* door?"

There was only a moment of silence, then the door knocker sounded. The four young women shook off their sudden melancholy. Ella ran into the hallway and opened the street door. Two gentlemen were there – Philo could distinguish so many voices – but they did not enter the house. This disappointed her for she was curious to see the suitors. Ella and Laura went away, with hasty farewells.

"Oh, lord," sighed Ida, "I don't think my gentleman is going to come after all. He was to be here half an hour ago."

"Perhaps he was unavoidably detained," said Philo politely.

"I could weep like a weary child," said Ida Yearance, unconsoled. She was a blonde, of slender figure and graceful form, with blue and dreamy eyes. She was dressed in bright green and wore red boots.

Philo was at a loss how to continue. She had, in truth, almost no experience in dealing with strangers. In New Egypt, she had always known everyone. She picked up and began leafing through an occasional book of short prose, poetry, and sentimental engravings called *The Gem for 1868*. "You're not over-occupied neither," said Ida.

"No," replied Philo with a smile.

"Come out with me then. Let's you and me go for a walk."

To this diversion Philo agreed readily, but then she hesitated a moment and asked of her new friend, "Will we be quite safe?"

"Safe?" repeated Ida.

"Are we likely to be set upon? Robbed in the street?"

Ida considered a moment. Then she said, "Philo, if you have money, I'd hide it in my room somewhere, and take out with you only what you think you'll need. Money can slip out of a pocket without you being aware."

"Pickpockets, you mean?"

Ida nodded.

Philo ran upstairs, took the envelope from her pocket, and looked all round the room for the best place to hide it. She didn't fear for the honesty of the other girls in the house, but tales of New York made her look for a place where the envelope couldn't be easily detected. At last she lifted one of the loose tiles on which the cold Morning Glory stove rested and slipped her thick envelope of bills underneath that. She stood on the opposite side of the room and peered into that corner, but could detect no more than a slight unevenness there. Satisfied, she put on her hat and gloves and came down again.

Ida was waiting at the door, talking to Gertrude Major, the young woman of the house who seemed to Philo the quietest, soberest, and most refined. She had a plain but sweet countenance and wavy auburn hair.

Gertrude smiled. "May I accompany you and Ida, Philo? I feel the want of air this evening."

"Of course," said Philo, "please come." Philo reflected with wonder how easy it was to make acquaintance in the city, when she had heard for so many years what a cold, unfriendly place it was.

Philo was pulling on her gloves when she noticed that Ida's mouth was twitching. "I'll give a little slice of advice, Philo," she said. "Keep your mourning in your heart."

"What do you mean?"

"I mean, you won't get nowhere in New York if you go round like a fashion plate of moping. Won't get hired, won't even hardly get looked at. Maybe some folks like a widow or a orphan, but you'll do much better being just regular."

"Ida is right," said Gertrude softly. "Dear Philo."

To Philo this seemed good advice, and it accorded with her own wishes in the matter. She went back upstairs, changed out of her black clothes into a blue dress, and, to assuage her conscience, attached black mourning bands around her arms, but invisibly, beneath the sleeves.

Ida wanted to go to the Bowery, but Gertrude suggested that since Philo had never been in the city before, a better impression would be given her if they went instead up Fifth Avenue to Madison Square and then down Fourth Avenue to Union Square – and arm in arm, this was the route the three young women took. The casual journey was filled with wonder for Philo: so many buildings, persons, carriages, horses, noises, odors, lights, and diversions. Gertrude and Ida talked incessantly, telling Philo of the buildings they passed, commenting on the clothing of other young women they encountered, and recounting romantic tales of other young women, just like themselves, who had married wealthily, happily, and with honor.

"You'll want some kind of work, I suppose," remarked Gertrude when the young women had stopped for rest on one of the benches on Madison Square directly across from the Fifth Avenue Hotel.

"Oh, yes, if I can find it," said Philo quickly. "Have you a job?"

"I work in a dollar store on Eighth Avenue," said Gertrude.

"I hope this is not a rude question," said Philo after a moment's hesitation, "but do you make enough to support yourself at Mrs. Classon's?"

Gertrude hesitated before answering, and on the other side of her Ida snickered.

And it was Ida who answered: "Gertrude does all right for herself."

"I will ask tomorrow," said Gertrude, "and see if there is a place for you."

Philo was joyed at the prospect of finding employment so soon, but Ida warned her: "Oh, Philo, you may not find the place to your liking . . ."

Chapter 25

THE DOLLAR STORE

At breakfast, Philo regretted aloud that her mother had always discouraged her from learning the seamstress's trade, for then, she said, she would have had no trouble in finding employment. At this, all the other young women laughed, and replied that there was no surer road to poverty and degradation than that taken by young women who armed themselves with a needle and bodkin.

"I don't understand," said Philo.

"Do you know how much a girl who sews can make in this city?" asked one young woman whose name Philo had forgot.

"She makes thirty cents a day – if she's fortunate," exclaimed another. "And that's for going at it twelve, thirteen hours. Her fingers go raw, and her eyes go out, and then there's not even thirty cents a day . . ."

"My mother supported us on her sewing," Philo pointed out. "For many years."

"Ah," said Ella, with a jerk of her head, "that's in the country."

"Life is different in the country," said Ida.

"This is the city," said Gertrude.

All the young women of the house were employed, it seemed, in shops, and printing houses, and stands, and in ways Philo didn't at first discover. At any rate, nearly all of them had disappeared by eight o'clock. Philo sat alone in the front parlor and read the advertisements in the morning *Tribune*. She found countless notices for the employment of young women, but none of the offers was either to her taste or her capabilities:

WANTED – A kitchen girl to work in an oyster saloon, one who understands plain cooking. Apply 39 Green St

WANTED – One good machine operator on coats on Wheeler & Wilson machine; one good pocket maker. Apply 255 W 19th St

WANTED – 150 Protestant girls for private families; first-class help furnished for beach, mountains, houses; cooks, table, chamber, store, room, kitchen, laundry girls. Apply Cole Agency, 223 Broadway

WANTED – A lady compositor acquainted with job work,

and who can also feed a steam press. Mercantile Printing
House, 32 Canal St

WANTED – A good dining room waiter and chamber girl;
also a good barber. Phoenix Hotel, close by Union Square

Philo had no desire to go into service. Her one day under the
Slapes was too painful a memory to allow her to do that. However, before she had picked up the *Sun* to go through its advertisements, a little ragged girl came to the door with a note for
Philo. It was from Gertrude and begged that she come immediately to No. 173 Eighth Avenue, that a position was open in her
store, and that if she passed muster with the manager she would
be hired.

Philo hurriedly put on her bonnet, received explicit directions
from Mrs. Classon to find the address, and set out. Philo could
scarcely believe that the streets were more crowded during the
day than they had been the evening before, when she had considered them almost impassable. But now the traffic was in-
estimably greater, dust and dirt filled the air to such an extent
that she could not always see across the street, and the noise
of Eighth Avenue was deafening – the squawling of newsboys,
the hammering on new buildings, the neighing of horses, the
loudness of the passersby in conversation – all was bewildering
to Philo.

The establishment to which she had been directed did not
have a prepossessing exterior: merely two large windows which
displayed a number of handkerchiefs, cravats, and scarves on the
one side and combs, stockings, mantillas, and embroidered slip-
pers on the other. Aachen's Dollar Emporium was a single room
thirty feet wide by seventy deep, lined to a height of almost
twenty feet with shelves stocked with just such goods and many
others as well, and with long tables spaced out over the floor like
pews in a church. Nearly two dozen young women were employed, either presiding over the counters and tables or standing
on ladders that moved laterally down the length of the shelving.
In addition, there were two fourteen-year-old boys who ran constantly back and forth from the young women to the cashier at

the back of the store who gave change and stamped bills *PAID*. The cashier was also the manager, and it was to him that Gertrude brought Philo.

His name was Charles Litchman. He had slick black hair and a slick black suit. He looked at Philo with a cold eye and nodded to Gertrude. "She'll do. Four dollars a week."

Philo was dismayed. Four dollars a week was less than what she paid to stay at Mrs. Classon's. She would lose three dollars a week, plus whatever she must expend on clothing, entertainment, and sundries. She was about to protest that she could not accept a position that paid so little when Gertrude gently pulled her away.

"I know what you think," said Gertrude in a whisper. "Take the job, and I'll speak to you of the business later."

"But—"

"I get along, don't I?" said Gertrude.

"Perhaps you've been here longer," said Philo.

"I'm paid five dollars a week," replied Gertrude. "Now come stand by me here at my counter. I handle gentlemen's gloves. I will show you what's to be done. Hours are eight in the morning until seven, with half an hour to take your dinner."

The work was not difficult. It consisted simply of standing behind the counter, awaiting the approach of a gentleman who wished to purchase a pair of gloves, discovering his size either by questioning him or by experiment, showing him the different styles, and, when he paid, handing the gloves and the money to the cash boy, occupying the waiting gentleman with a little conversation while the cash boy was absent, and handing over the change and the gloves when the cash boy returned.

Despite the great crowds of gentlemen and ladies who thronged the place, Philo had no difficulty in making this much out.

And she made out much more. The gentlemen who came to buy were more numerous than the ladies, and they were much more disposed to linger and try on more than one pair of gloves. Sometimes they tried on as many as seven or eight, talking cleverly and flirtingly with Gertrude all the while they did so. Some of the gentlemen who came in were evidently quite well known to Gertrude, for they called her familiarly by her given name and asked who Philo was and when she had come to town and where she lived; and then they turned directly to Philo and asked how she liked the city and whether she had visited the Bowery Theater yet, and when she replied no, demanded, "But wouldn't you like to?"

"Yes," replied Philo truthfully, "I would."

"Shall I accompany you tonight?" one man asked with shining eyes.

"No," said Philo quickly, "I meant that I should like to go alone."

The man laughed. "Unaccompanied ladies are not allowed in theaters in New York. You must have an escort . . ."

Philo blushed. "I didn't know, I—"

"Philo is *quite* new in town," said Gertrude, and no more was said.

At dinnertime, two o'clock, Philo and Gertrude adjourned to a little eating place on the other side of Eighth Avenue, where for fifteen cents Philo obtained a plate of meat with a potato and a small budget of bread and butter.

As they sat together, Philo had a sudden darkling suspicion. She looked up at Gertrude and said, "Tell me, please, how *do* you manage to live on the five dollars a week you get at the store? Your dress is very fine." She hastened to add, "I don't mean to appear inquisitive – only I'm so ignorant of New York life that I want to be certain I'm going about things in the correct manner."

Gertrude paused before answering. She said at last, "The gentlemen who come in the store?"

"Yes."

"They are – what shall I say? – generous."

"Generous?"

"Generous to young women," Gertrude explained. "Like ourselves."

"I see," said Philo.

"Many of them are young men, unable as yet to support wives, or unable to find a wife who is entirely to their liking. But they desire companionship, just as young women sometimes desire companionship."

Philo said nothing at all.

"One of them may wish," said Gertrude carefully, "sometimes to accompany you to the Bowery Theater and to supper afterward. On Sunday morning he may invite you to an English breakfast on Staten Island. And as you may not possess the wherewithal to purchase clothing which is appropriate for such diversions, appropriate clothing is sometimes purchased for you. Philo," said Gertrude, turning her head a little aside, "do you understand me?"

Philo understood only too well, and blushed for her comprehension.

Chapter 26

ANYTHING YOU WANT FOR A QUARTER

When she returned to the dollar store that afternoon, Philo was set in charge of the "Anything-you-want-for-a-quarter" table. Since it involved goods already slightly damaged, of odd sizes, or soiled, this place required the least experience. It would have been pleasant to spend these hours in the presence of so many bustling strangers – this included her fellow workers and the shoppers alike – if she had not been constantly apprehensive about the possibility that she would be approached with a compromising offer.

And approached she was – by half a dozen men of various description, a parade of fine moustaches and coattails, offering her theater tickets, oyster suppers, and jaunts up the North River on *The Young Widow* steamboat. Philo invariably blushed, stammered, and declined.

A gentleman might pay for a pair of kid gloves with split seams, give her a five-dollar note, and when she gave him his change again, maintain it had been only a one and would she meet him at the corner of Nineteenth Street when she got off work?

By seven o'clock she was exhausted, not only from standing all day but from the strain of so much polite refusing. She realized that the job quickest and most easily got was perhaps not the job most to be desired and determined then to look out for something better. This resolution she did not relate to Gertrude, who had suddenly conceived a desire to see George Fox in *Humpty Dumpty*, and parted from her just outside the door of the shop. Philo wondered if she were headed for the corner of Nineteenth Street.

Philo was glad that the way back to Mrs. Classon's was so simple: down Eighth Avenue and turn left on Thirteenth Street. She hurried along, scrutinizing the street indicators on the corners of buildings and paying little attention to the crowds that passed her by. But she stopped suddenly when a hand was laid on her arm.

"Miss Philo?" a man's voice said in surprise.

Philo looked up into the face of a man she did not immediately recognize. She had seen so many hundreds of strange masculine faces that day that she was now hard put to believe they each maintained an exclusive identity.

"Miss Philo," said Henry Maitland, "why are you in New York?"

As soon as Philo realized the identity of this man who had accosted her, she recalled the humiliating scene before the Presbyterian Church. Then a moment later she remembered seeing Mr. Maitland speaking to the marshal who had come to arrest her in New Egypt. She blushed deeply and looked away.

"Philo," he said, dropping the Miss, "I was very distressed to hear about your mother. She was a good-hearted woman, and I know that you loved her very much."

Philo thanked him for his solicitude. "I'm here in New York because there was no reason for me to remain in New Egypt," she said. "There was no work for me there. There was no one to keep me there. Now that Mother's dead, I'm completely alone." She shrugged and added with a brave smile, "Besides, in New Jersey, I am wanted for murder."

He smiled at this. "I for one am tolerably sure of your innocence."

"I wonder if your cousin Jewel is?"

To this, Henry made no reply.

The pedestrian traffic along Eighth Avenue was still heavy at a quarter past seven, and Henry Maitland had actually to hold onto Philo's arm to keep them from being separated by the hurrying throng. They had to speak very loudly to be heard by one another at all.

"Are you hungry?" he asked.

She nodded automatically and was about to add that she was expected at supper in a quarter of an hour. But before she could do so, Henry had hailed a cab and assisted her inside. He called a destination to the driver, climbed in after her, shut the door, and they were off.

He took her to a restaurant on Twenty-third Street between Fourth and Fifth avenues, not the best he could afford by any means, but one in which her plain attire would not show her off to disadvantage. The food was simple by fashionable New York standards, but Philo was in amazement at the bill of fare, which contained so great a variety of dishes, each priced separately. A simple dinner might cost one as much as a dollar and a half. Henry insisted that she order whatever she wanted.

When the first course was brought – it surprised Philo that not all the dishes were put onto the table at once – Henry Maitland said, "I was in Philadelphia the day your mother died, and did not return to New Egypt before Jewel's come-out party. A marshal from Trenton, I believe, came round that evening looking to arrest you – but fortunately you had already left."

"Mrs. Libby took me away in her wagon. Mr. Maitland, I want to assure you: I did not kill my grandfather."

"Miss Philo, I never believed it – and neither did anyone else in New Egypt."

"No one?"

"A few," Henry Maitland admitted. "The few who prefer interesting gossip to mundane truth."

"What did the Varleys say?" Philo asked curiously.

Henry hesitated, then only asked, "Why did you come to New York?"

"I don't know," she said, tasting her meat and realizing suddenly how very hungry she was. "Everyone comes to New York, I suppose."

"Have you a place to live?"

Philo described Mrs. Classon's.

"Excuse me, Philo, but I am not prying to no purpose. How much do you pay for your room and board?"

"Seven dollars," she answered readily. Already she was becoming used to the fact that in New York, amounts of money, large, small, or middling, seemed the focus of much of casual conversation.

"That is reasonable," said Henry, nodding. "Have you found work?"

Philo described the dollar store.

Henry Maitland beat a tattoo on the table, rattling the silver. "Philo," he said after a moment, "I know that store."

"I was there only today," said Philo, blushing. "I don't intend to go back."

"Good. And you know why, don't you?"

"Yes."

"This can be a dangerous city, Philo. Especially for an unprotected young woman."

Philo made no reply.

"Do you think you will be able to secure other employment?"

"I hope so."

They continued to eat, and nothing more was said for several minutes, Henry Maitland giving the appearance of being in deep thought.

"Philo," he brought out at last, "I would like you to accept something from me."

Philo looked up but said nothing.

"I want you to accept a draught on my banker for a certain sum."

"No, Mr. Maitland!"

"You must, Philo. Listen to me. You have said yourself that you are alone. The city is dangerous, and you must quit your work at that store until you can find something that is totally respectable. I'm sorry to say, however, that total respectability in employment is usually a synonym for poverty. But by perseverance, I am certain you will come across something that is both to your liking and your financial advantage. I have no real fear of your future – but I do have fear for your present. I would like to lend you a sum of money that will keep you until you have found a situation."

Philo held up her hand and smiled. "Mr. Maitland, it really is not necessary. I am quite solvent now, and have—" She started to name the sum, but instead said only, "—an amount of money which seems a fortune to me. I have received a little money from the sale of my grandfather's livestock in Goshen, and I have the proceeds of the sale of Mother's house. I—"

"How much is that, Philo?"

"I have a little more than a thousand dollars altogether."

Henry Maitland laughed. "Well then, Philo," he said, "perhaps you would consider making *me* a little loan."

"Mr. Maitland, I would be pleased to accommodate you." And she nodded over her plate of boiled meat.

"You are more resourceful than I had thought. And I must tell you, Philo, that my opinion of your resourcefulness has never been low. . . ."

Philo was serious a moment. "I wasn't resourceful enough to prevent Mother and Grandfather from being murdered in their beds."

Dessert was brought – two large slices of peach pie – and when Philo and Henry resumed their conversation, it was with more levity.

"I will trust you then to Mrs. Classon for four months, Philo."

"Four months?"

"I go away tomorrow. I am sailing with a college friend to Brazil, in his pleasure boat. I don't expect to return until August or September."

Philo did not feel she had the right to be disappointed, but that disappointment was apparent in her face.

Henry Maitland saw it and was glad to see it.

"I think you should be able to make your thousand dollars last you until August, will you not?"

"I imagine so," said Philo, smiling.

"And if you have not found any employment by then," said Henry, "I will assist you in your search. Where are your lodgings?"

He took tablets from his coat pocket and wrote down the address of Mrs. Classon's boardinghouse.

"If you should happen to leave there, make certain that you leave word where you can be found."

"You are very kind to me," said Philo seriously.

"I am merely grateful," he said, "for your having made my stay in New Egypt as pleasant as it was. I wish—"

"Wish what?" Philo prompted.

He thought a moment, then said, looking out the window at the rain that had begun to fall in earnest a quarter of an hour earlier, "—that George would postpone this voyage for a week or so, till fairer weather."

And after supper, rather than accompanying her straight back to Mrs. Classon's, Henry took Philo to Niblo's Garden, not far from the restaurant, where Philo was enchanted to see *La Belle Sauvage*. Henry tried to point out the splendor of Mrs. John Wood's performance in the title role, but Philo had to admit that she was most delighted by Slocum's Minstrels in the Ethiopian scene.

She had never spent so pleasant an evening, she thought, though at the end of it she was exhausted. Any three years of her life in New Egypt seemed not to have encompassed the variety and excitement she had experienced in the thirty-six hours she had spent in New York.

Henry brought her back to Thirteenth Street in a cab. He politely escorted her to the door, shook her hand, and said that he would come after her again in August. Philo waved farewell and went inside the house.

Three of her fellow lodgers were sitting in the parlor and interrupted their conversation to ask Philo all about the gentleman who had seen her to the door. She said merely that he was someone whose acquaintance she had formed in New Jersey and that she had run into him on the street quite by chance.

"Was Mrs. Classon angry that I did not appear at supper?"

"Ha!" laughed Nellie Stanwood, a blonde girl who was in the chorus at the Union Square Theatre. "She's used to it. And the fewer of us there is at table, the more everybody gets!"

Philo had thrown herself wearily into a chair and listened with only half a mind to the three women's conversation, which wondered at the abrupt departure of one of their number earlier in the evening. No one could determine why Ida Yearance had so suddenly decamped, and they speculated that she had received good news or bad news, or a proposal of marriage, or a summons to appear in court. Not much later Philo went up to her room to bed.

She sat at the little rickety table by the window, stabilized somewhat by a book pushed under the shortest of the four unequal legs, and wrote a note to Gertrude declining to return with her to the store the following morning. Then she took off her dress, shook it, turned it inside out, and hung it up on the back side of the door.

When she turned, however, she looked into the corner where the Morning Glory stove was tilted awry – tilted because several of the tiles beneath it had been pulled out. And crumpled on the floor beside the misplaced tiles was the empty, torn envelope which that morning had contained, in hard cash, the entire of her fortune – the thousand dollars which she had told Henry Maitland would see her through August.

PART VI
CHRISTOPHER STREET

Chapter 27

KATIE'S LITERACY

Maud Merrill was a young woman dependent entirely upon herself in a society that hadn't much use for unattached females. But Maud was luckier than most in her position: she had employment, she had a beau, and she had the prospect of marriage. She worked from eight until six Monday through Saturday at Wagner's Carpet Salesroom on Waverly Place, and on Sunday a clerk in a bookseller's on Eighth Street squired her to City Hall Park and held her hand during the concert.

The bookseller's clerk had even asked Maud's hand in marriage, though his offer was contingent upon their obtaining sufficient funds to set up housekeeping. This money unexpectedly came their way through the clerk's inheriting from an uncle dying in Maine a legacy of fifteen hundred dollars. One thousand of this sum was put immediately into a savings bank, but the young clerk, ravished by his love for Maud Merrill, gave over to her the balance. With it she was to purchase her trousseau, and locate a place for them to live.

Accordingly, every morning before work, Maud would knock at the door of various rooming houses and ask to see chambers that were to let; and after work, she would do the same. Nothing was right: in too many cases the chambers had already been secured, or they were on the hall, or too dark, or too exposed to the street – and Maud felt that, with five hundred dollars' fortune behind her, she could afford to wait for the place that would exactly suit her and her husband to-be.

One evening, following an advertisement in the *Tribune*, she found herself on Christopher Street, near the ferry. The To Let sign in the window of the house she had searched out was removed even as she was mounting the steps – again she had been only just too late. She looked round her and realized that very probably she wouldn't have liked this neighborhood anyway. All of New York was dirty and noisy, but Christopher Street seemed particularly so, even at half past six on a Thursday evening. She shrugged her shoulders and turned toward her own rooming house on East Seventh Street.

She had not gone twenty feet, however, before she was accosted by a man sitting on a stoop. "Miss, Miss!" he cried, and raised a finger to stop her.

She paused but said nothing.

"Miss!" said the man, whose appearance was not prepossessing. "Come inside and have your fortune told." He pointed to a sign in the window of the house before which he sat.

Maud read the sign, which testified to the prophetic powers of Miss Katie, Extraordinary Clairvoyant.

"What's her charge?" said Maud.

"Fifty cents."

Maud might have gone directly in, but she didn't like this man on the stoop. "She's my daughter," he said, but that was no inducement either.

The door of the house opened, and a young woman with black hair appeared on the stoop. She was eating an apple, and the juice spilled out over her bodice.

"Here's Katie," said the man on the stoop.

"Tell your fortune," said Katie with an insinuating grin.

"No," said Maud, who liked the daughter even less than she liked the father.

Katie eyed Maud closely. "Let me touch your hand," she said, and came down the steps.

Maud wanted to run away, but she stood still as before the basilisk. Katie flung the apple into the street, and with her sticky hand she grasped Maud's fingers and twisted them.

"Par," she said, "go inside and light the lamp."

With alacrity, John Slape rose from the stoop and disappeared inside the house.

"I don't want my fortune read," said Maud weakly.

"I won't charge you," said Katie. "Where's your friend this evening?"

"He's—" Maud began mechanically. Then she stopped. "Who is my friend?"

"The man with the black hair and the ears that stick out so far."

Maud drew her breath in quickly; the fortune-teller had described her lover exactly.

Katie pulled her up the steps, but Maud held back.

Katie leaned over and whispered in Maud's ear. "You'd best be married soon," she said. "You'll have a boy on Christmas Day."

Then she laughed loudly, and Maud burned crimson.

"No!" Maud cried.

"Come up! Come up!" cried Katie, and drew Maud toward the door.

Maud trembled as she sat across from Katie Slape. The lamp had been lighted on the mantel, but the principal illumination was the vast spring twilight that burned in the windows behind the clairvoyant, filling the room and Maud's consciousness with its shining opalescence.

"I'm not with child!" Maud whispered.

Katie shrugged.

"He'll be born on Christmas Day, and he'll be called Clifford."

Clifford was the name of the bookseller's clerk. Maud pressed her hand against her belly with the sudden desperate certainty that what this young woman said was true.

"Will he still marry me?" Maud demanded.

Katie shrugged and smiled.

"You know!" cried Maud. "Tell me!"

"Do you have money?"

"Fifty cents. Your pa said give you fifty cents—"

"Pay to be rid of the child," said Katie, waving away with a sneer the coins that Maud held proffered.

"Where . . ." began Maud in a whisper.

"Let me write the direction," said Katie, and rose from the table.

"How much will it cost me?"

"Twenty-five dollars," replied Katie, standing at the mantel and scratching on a scrap of paper with a pencil. She folded it twice, then handed it to Maud.

"This is where I should go? What should I say? Will Clifford ever discover what I've done?"

"Read the direction," said Katie.

Maud stood and went to the mantel. Holding the paper before the light, she unfolded it.

On the paper were only scribbles.

Maud turned, about to speak, but her question was lost forever.

Katie knocked her once over the head with a hammer, and she crumpled to the floor.

Katie leaned down, took off Maud's shawl, and put it under the young woman's inert head, a precaution against blood staining the carpet. In fact, there was no blood at all, and the fatal wound was not even apparent on her scalp. Katie went through Maud's pockets and in the first found a small yellow envelope containing three hundred ninety-three dollars in bank notes and gold.

Katie grinned, then leaned down and whispered in Maud's ear: "I can't read nor write, you see!"

On page three of the *Sun* for Thursday, 8 June 1871, there appeared this article:

A DEAD BODY DISCOVERED NEAR
THE CHRISTOPHER STREET PIER
SUSPICIONS OF FOUL PLAY
A Coroner's Jury Fails to Determine
the Cause of Death

Last Friday afternoon between 1 and 2 o'clock a young man named Earl P. Mason, who resides with his mother on Jane Street, went down to the North River just below Christopher Street pier to look after a boat and discovered there the dead body of a woman caught between the pilings. The police were notified, and Coroner Bule was summoned and took charge of the body. A memorandum book found in the pocket of the dead woman gives her name as Maud Merrill, residing at No. 31 East Seventh Street. Subsequent enquiries have determined that the young woman was recently arrived from the country, it is thought from eastern Pennsylvania. She was employed as a binder in the carpet salesroom belonging to Mr. Wagner on Waverly Place. She was last seen alive on 1 June, leaving Mr. Wagner's establishment at six o'clock with the intention of "seeing about some rooms to be let."

Dr. Oliver Shaw made a postmortem examination of the dead woman. The results were as follows: a slight abrasion was found on the forehead, also a small patch of extravasated blood beneath the scalp at the back part of the head; the brain, kidneys and liver contained an unusually large amount of blood; the lungs were filled with air, and the bronchial tubes contained a frothy fluid. Death must have occurred during the night of Thursday and might have been the result of exposure. The injuries to the scalp were so slight as to render it improbable that they could be regarded as causes for death. From the postmortem examination, there is no evidence that death resulted from drowning.

E. A. Burgoyne, hospital steward at the Tenth Street Arsenal, testified as an expert that in the War he had seen death caused by concussion of the brain produced by a blow which left no more visible outward injury than appeared in this case.

Upon the above evidence the jury was not satisfied as to the cause of death and accordingly adjourned until next Wednesday evening.

Chapter 28

HAMMER VS. SANDBAG

Maud Merrill was not the first young lady of New York to leave Katie Slape's parlor in a canvas bag. Before Maud, three other young women had died, victims of Katie's hammer. All three had been slipped into the North River by John Slape while Hannah kept watch for him. From the murder of these four young women, the Slapes had gained nearly six hundred dollars, which was considerably more than could have been accrued through interest – even on so great an amount as twenty-nine thousand dollars – and a great deal more than could have been accumulated through fifty-cent and one-dollar fees for sessions at Katie's clairvoyant table.

Not all women who came to Katie were in danger of their lives – only the ones with money about their persons, and of this small group, only those with few friends in the city. Of course questions pertaining to these two important points, put to a prospective victim, would have aroused suspicion – but Katie never bothered to ask them. She knew already whether her ladies had money or not. Her ability to decide who was to die and who was to live was as unerring as it was uncanny. When a young woman such as Maud Merrill had dropped dead to the floor beneath Katie's hammer, her pockets were searched with perfect assurance that some substantial amount of money would be discovered there.

Hannah and John never asked their daughter for an explanation of this lucrative efficiency.

However, having come across the notice of the finding of Maud Merrill's body, Hannah wondered aloud to her daughter if the use of the hammer were not an aspect of her ritual that might be improved upon.

"Leaves a mark," said Hannah, and read aloud that part of the article which described the bruises on Maud's head.

Katie shrugged. "What does it matter to them? They're dead."

"No, Katie," said Hannah patiently, "hadn't been for them bruises, police would have thought for sure she just throwed herself in the water. But them bruises – someday," she said darkly, "somebody might be coming after us."

Katie grinned, which grin signified *Let them try*.

Though Hannah alone continued to be uneasy about the hammer, it was John who provided a solution. He had continued his afternoons at the barber's around the corner, and there obtained sundry information. And one piece of information that looked to be valuable to the Slapes was the existence of a weapon of mayhem that didn't leave any mark.

"Sandbags," John said. "Take little canvas bags and fill 'em with sand and pebbles till they weigh five pounds or so. Then hit someone over the head, and it knocks 'em into the middle of next week."

Hannah shook her head in doubt. "Sand!" she exclaimed. "Can't kill a man with sand."

"Katie's dealing with ladies," said John.

"Same thing," said Hannah. "Can't kill a lady with sand in a canvas bag."

"It shakes their brains up," said John. "Maybe it's to be done three or four times in different places, but it don't leave a mark."

"No," said Katie, who had listened with interest to this conversation between her parents. But her *no* did not signify doubt, it only expressed her unwillingness to abandon the hammer. Katie liked the hammer very much.

The experiment at any rate was tried. John prepared several canvas bags with sand and gravel that he got from an empty parcel of land up on Twentieth Street, and Hannah sewed the tops together. Two of them were placed in the drawer with the hammer in Katie's parlor, and when next a young woman appeared on Christopher Street who had a little money and no friends to speak of, Katie first astounded her with her knowledge, and then while the young lady was standing at the window (Katie told her her true love was standing before a shop half a square down), Katie took out one of the bags and hit her over the head with it. The young lady collapsed, but breathed still. For several minutes Katie beat her about the head and shoulders with the canvas bag and desisted only when one of the lady's earrings caught in the canvas and ripped the bag open, spilling sand into the battered cavity of her ear.

Katie stood and called her parents.

"There's bruises on her face," said Katie with satisfaction. She wanted to stick with the hammer.

"You're not to hit her in the face!" cried John. "Just on her skull!"

"Had to hit her eighteen times," said Katie sullenly.

"She was dead before," said Hannah, looking hard at Katie.

Katie made no reply.

"Search her pockets," said Hannah then.

Katie did so, and after a moment brought out thirty-six dollars and some odd silver.

Hannah and John grimaced. "Not much," said John. "Certain there's not more hid?"

"There's no more," said Katie. "I wanted to show the sandbags didn't do the job."

For this Katie was scolded. They weren't so far from the law that they could afford to murder for the pleasure of it. The sandbags and the hammer ought to be carefully reserved for those young women who had substantial amounts of money on them.

"One hundred dollars, Katie," said Hannah. "Make a limit."

"How do I know how much they're carrying? I don't see the money till I've emptied their pockets."

"You know," said John. "Do as Hannah says, Katie."

In order to make their operation less liable to discovery, John Slape purchased the adjoining house, which had been unoccupied for about eighteen months. Its windows were boarded over.

He knocked a hole in the fourth-floor wall common to the buildings, thereby giving them access to the newly purchased house without the necessity of entering it from without. It had been John's first thought to leave the bodies of the women there until the time for disposing of them in the North River was propitious. But he discovered, in a little ramble through his new property, that the cellar of the house had an earthen floor. Experimentally, he turned that earth with a spade, and found it dense and wet, but workable. Against the next victim he dug out a hole approximately five feet long, a foot-and-a-half wide and four feet deep. It was the most work that he had done since the War.

The next victim was a prostitute, a tall, handsome girl with auburn hair and deep brown eyes, who had received a proposal of marriage from a gentleman and wanted to know if she ought to accept.

"He has a wife in New Haven," Katie replied, and hit the woman over the head with a sandbag.

Katie administered but one blow, with the intention of showing her parents the ultimate inefficiency of that method.

The prostitute slipped out of her chair to the floor, and Katie took from her one hundred and seven dollars.

John and Hannah came into the parlor. Katie handed over the money with a sneer. "She's still alive," she said.

"Out cold," said Hannah, eyeing the woman on the floor.

John shrugged, lifted the woman on his shoulder, and with Katie and Hannah following, carried her up to the fourth floor, ducked her through the hole in the wall, and descended with her to the cellar.

With some difficulty he squeezed her into the grave – Katie's previous victims had never been of so great a stature.

Katie and Hannah stood to the side and watched with interest and admiration.

Hannah had brought the sandbag with her. "I should hit her again," she said to her husband. "She's still breathing."

"Don't bend down," said John to his wife, whose girth would have made such an operation awkward. "You might slip in." He motioned Hannah and Katie to step back, then began to shovel in the damp earth over the living woman.

Chapter 29

COUSIN PRINCE AND HIS GIRL SUE

No one discovered what was happening within No. 251 Christopher Street and its unoccupied neighbor to the west. Many in this neighborhood of transients were of more recent vintage than the Slapes, who had arrived there on the last day of March. It was known, generally, that a single family dwelt in what had previously been a rooming house and that the daughter told fortunes. In this there was no mystery. Certainly there was no neighbor with either sufficient time or interest to compare the number of women who went into the house with the number who came out again.

Katie, through her legal efforts, had made somewhat over five hundred dollars in three months. By murder and robbery she had made a little over two thousand dollars, and eight young women were dead. Of the four who had been slipped into the North River, only Maud Merrill had been found. Three bodies had been washed out into the sea. No one was likely to discover anytime soon the four bodies buried in the cellar of No. 253.

Dozens of young women disappeared each year from the streets, rooming houses, and carpet salesrooms of New York. The cartes de visite of these young ladies – truly a spectrum of beauty – filled three boxes at the Missing Persons Bureau down on Centre Street. Even had all Katie's victims been reported missing – and not all of them were – eight more young women lost in the three months of April, May, and June of 1871 would scarcely have been noticed. It was assumed that any missing young woman was most likely to have run off with a handsome young man; if that were not the case, it was most probable that she had descended to a life of infamy and had voluntarily renounced her former connections; although, it was finally acknowledged, there were a few true victims – of robbery, of rape, of the abortionist's knife.

The papers, finding this so common an item, did not even bother to print three lines announcing "Young Lady Missing in Twenty-first Street." However, should her interesting corpse be washed up onto the shore of Staten Island, to be discovered in horror by a boating-breakfast party, she might rate a full column, which would invariably end with a moralizing paragraph execrating the villain who seduced her, murdered her, and threw her into the water, and drawing our attention once again to that "fair young form lying in the sad-colored robes, which proved its grave-clothes below the gurgling waters, its beautiful ringlets matted with sand and its cheeks empurpled by a death of violence."

All such items Hannah read aloud to her husband and daughter, and John and Katie nodded sagaciously for their length. A number of plays then on the Bowery recounted the plights of young female victims, and over the second-act terrors of these young women, Hannah and Katie and John would weep into their handkerchiefs.

It was characteristic of the Slapes that they never thought of the past. John Slape actually couldn't remember the time when he had been married to Katie's mother, and in truth, nothing remained of that alliance but the girl and John's infatuation with the theater. Hannah might have been able to remember her childhood if she had bothered, but why should she? Katie's memory was purely sensate: of the actions of the previous week she could recall only those moments when she'd taken the hammer and sandbags from the desk drawer in her parlor.

The time, so recently past, when they'd lived in Goshen, when old man Parrock had been alive, when they'd angled for his cash, were scenes vague and confused in their minds – even Hannah's. They were even more than half convinced that it was Philo Drax who had murdered her grandfather. Sometimes Katie would say, "Wonder what's come of her? Wonder if they've strung her up yet?"

And John would say, "Who?"

And Hannah would reply, "Hired girl. Should have done away with her in Goshen."

"I wanted to," Katie would say. "I wanted to hit her over the head with my hammer."

"Didn't have a hammer then," Hannah would point out.

And a week later, the same conversation would be repeated.

In a peculiar way, they were very happy.

A single incident disturbed the equanimity of the Slapes, and that occurred on the evening that they attended Tony Pastor's Theater on the Bowery to see Fanny Herring in *The Female Detective* – they had much enjoyed, earlier that week, her performance as *The Dumb Girl of Genoa*. The Slapes generally took box seats, though these were the most expensive in the house. Their dress and their manners would have made anyone think that they would get no higher than the pit – or no lower than the gallery – so in the boxes they appeared a distinct anomaly. Though they did not realize it, they had come to be known by managers, actors, and other regular patrons.

But Hannah and Katie and John liked the privacy of the boxes, they liked the superb view of the stage, and during the intermissions and before the play began – no fashionable lateness for the Slapes – they liked to look over the crowds.

On this particular evening early in June, Hannah grew suddenly agitated and pulled at her husband's sleeve, at the same time drawing back into the shadows that the box afforded.

"What is it?" said John.

"Down there," said Hannah. "It's Cousin Prince and his girl Sue."

John and Katie peered over the edge.

"No!" hissed Hannah. "Don't want to be seen!" And she drew Katie quickly back.

Prince Jepson was from Camden. His father and Hannah's father had been brothers, and he had known Hannah from childhood. His daughter Sue was perhaps fourteen years of age.

"He don't know Katie and me," John pointed out.

"No," said Hannah, "guess he don't." However, she stayed hidden at the back of the box.

The Slapes remained for the play and the afterpieces, but Hannah didn't enjoy herself as usual. Afterwards she hurried John and Katie outside the theater, and they went directly home.

"He was visiting," said John, "I don't doubt. He didn't come looking for us."

"Suppose not," said Hannah. "But, John, tell you the white truth, did scare me to see him there."

At that very moment there was a knocking at the street door, and Little Dick set up a ferocious howling. John and Hannah retreated quickly into the darkened parlor.

The knocking grew louder.

Katie crept up the stairs.

Hannah whispered to her husband, "Sure to be Cousin Prince. Saw me, followed me here. Saw us come in the house. Knows we're inside."

"He can't break in," said John consolingly. "There's the law."

The knocking suddenly left off, and Hannah heard her name called loudly several times: "Hannah! Hannah Slape!"

Hannah did not answer, and presently the knocking and the calling left off.

Hannah and John remained as they were.

Katie came down and said, "It was your cousin, Mar, and his girl. They went off down the street."

"Angry?"

"No," said Katie. "Like they wasn't sure of something. Went away just talking."

That night the Slapes did not light any lamps or candles in the house. They hoped that Hannah's Cousin Prince had become convinced he had mistaken either Hannah or the house. But if he had taken up a post of observation in the neighborhood, they wanted to make certain that he did not see that the house where he had knocked so persistently was inhabited.

They were not visited again that night, nor the next night either. Hannah refused to leave the house for three days altogether. Katie wanted to know if she should ready the hammer and the sandbags for Cousin Prince and his girl Sue, but to this Hannah would give no answer.

After a week, even Hannah allowed herself to become convinced that Cousin Prince and his girl Sue had returned to Camden and given over their sighting of Cousin Hannah Slape as a mystery of mistaken identity.

Ten days later, however, a letter arrived at No. 251 Christopher Street addressed to Hannah Slape and bearing the mark of the postmaster of Camden, New Jersey. This letter Hannah refused to accept of the postman, and it was returned marked "Recipient Unknown."

There was no way for the Slapes to know how very serious an error this was to prove.

PART VII

WEST THIRTEENTH STREET

Chapter 30

THE FASHION IN HOOPS

Philo felt a fool to have left so great a sum of money in her room, which did not have a lock on the door, in a house of whose inhabitants she now realized she knew nothing. She had instinctively trusted Ida Yearance because she had never been taught to distrust. And Ida Yearance had taken advantage of Philo's gullibility by instructing her to leave her scanty fortune somewhere in the room, where at the first opportunity Ida had searched it out and carried it off.

Philo did not know what to do. Her first thought was to go to Henry Maitland and explain that she had suddenly lost all her money – all, except for the fifteen dollars that she had carried about with her that day – and was nearly destitute. But then she reflected that although Henry Maitland knew where she lived, she had no idea where to find him. And if she did not see him this evening there would be no point in trying, for tomorrow morning he would sail for Brazil, there to remain for several months.

She did not even suspect that Mrs. Classon kept a City Directory in the parlor which contained the address of Henry Maitland's lodgings less than two miles distant.

Philo sat despondently in the single chair of the room, which she had drawn up close to the door. She peered out into the dim hallway and waited for her friend Ella to return.

In the main, Philo was a sturdy girl, not prone to self-pity. She could spend hours turning a thing this way and that until she had found its brightest side, and thereafter it was this aspect that she kept always before her. But this night, while she waited for Ella LaFavour, Philo was at a loss to discover any bright side at all to her predicament. She was without family, she was without money, her only employment – of itself insufficient to keep her in lodging – was in a place of doubtful morality, and the single friend who possessed the wherewithal to aid her was sailing in the morning for South America.

Philo listened to the noises of the house: the young women's muffled laughter in shared rooms, the shutting of doors, the occasional loudness of a cab in the street outside, cats on the roof of the carriage house just outside her own window, and Mrs. Classon's promised snoring in the next room. Every noise seemed alien. These were not the noises she had been accustomed to hear in New Egypt. At night, New Egypt was so still she could hear the cows chewing their cuds in the pasture beyond the kitchen garden.

She would never hear her mother's voice again.

She dropped her face into her hands and wept, and it was thus that Ella LaFavour found her.

Philo told her story.

"Ida Yearance came in last week," said Ella with a knowing nod. "Never told what she did. I'm not a bit surprised. There's a kind of girl goes rooming house to rooming house looking out for what she can find. She finds it, takes it, and goes away, and tomorrow takes up lodging somewhere else."

"But isn't she recognized?" cried Philo, finding a spot of hope that Ida Yearance might be apprehended.

Ella shrugged. "New York, it's so big . . ."

Philo sighed and nodded.

"From now on," said Ella, "I'm going to call you Miss Green." This epithet referred to the ease with which Philo had been taken in. "Miss Green, I'm going to put you up to a wrinkle or two. Have you ever been in a saloon?"

"No!"

"There's a sign over the bar in every one, no matter how high, no matter how low."

"Yes?"

"The sign reads: No Trust."

Philo understood. "Miss Green is the name I deserve," she admitted grimly. "Let me tell you about the dollar store." And to Ella, she told with indignation what she had discovered of the ways and means of young women employed on Eighth Avenue.

Ella didn't appear in the least surprised, but just before Philo finished, she interrupted. "Miss Green, you're on a very high horse."

"I beg your pardon?"

"I mean," said Ella, "that you're looking down on me from a height."

"Looking down on *you?*" cried Philo, realizing suddenly that Ella's income might be got from sources as equivocal as the counter of the dollar store.

Ella was silent a few moments. She looked at Philo earnestly. "I came to the city in 'sixty-six," said Ella, all the jocularity by which Philo knew her suspended. "I've been here six years, and now I'm twenty-two. I got honest employment. I made hoops for ladies' skirts. We worked down in the basement below H. F. Claflin's. There were forty girls who were older than me, and forty girls who were younger. Ten of us worked on hoops. I was never lonesome, that much I'll say. We worked by gaslight, but there wasn't a breath of air, and it was so hot that by nine o'clock my whole head felt as if I'd left it overnight in an oven. We had a slow season – that is, from spring until fall, when all the fashionable ladies are out-of-town – and then we worked seven hours a day. The other six months we worked eleven hours, and at holiday time we worked from seven in the morning until eleven at night. And another good thing – when you've been through a day like that, you sleep like the dead. Oh, Lord, I sat and I bent wire for the hoops, and I dreamed someday I'd be the height of fashion. I wore a tin dog collar around my neck, because on Sixth Avenue they were selling them in gold. My shoe had a French heel even though it made my legs ache. I went without my dinner sometimes so that I could buy a manicure set. Then hoops went out of fashion, and as I didn't know how to do anything else, I was let go."

Philo reflected that her own life in New Egypt had been not nearly so straitened.

"What did you do then?" she asked.

"I had a friend," said Ella, "who advised me to advertise in the paper. I said I did not know anything but hoop-making, and now hoops were out of fashion. She smiled and said it did not matter. I was to advertise all the same, and I did so. I had," said Ella delicately, "many replies."

Philo didn't quite understand and said so.

"I had many offers," said Ella. "But none for employment at hoop-making."

Philo now understood. "And did you—" She paused in consternation.

"Fall?" said Ella grimly. "Give in? Destroy at once my character and my chance at salvation?"

Philo was silent.

"Don't speak to me of morality as if you was a big bug's wife in a mansion on Madison Avenue!" warned Ella. "You'll soon enough find what it is to be a lone girl in New York, without family and without friends, and you'll be glad enough it's summer so's you don't have to pay for coals for your Morning Glory stove!"

"There's no excuse for immorality," said Philo softly.

"Oh, dry up your pious talk!" cried Ella. "How do you think we get along in this house?"

"Do you all work in dollar stores?" asked Philo in wonder.

"Go down to Five Points," said Ella. She sat on the edge of Philo's bed, and scratched the coverlet with her nails. "Go down to the Black Triangle, and the houses round the Battery, and walk in 'em. There you'll find the really honest ones, the seamstresses, and the girls who make umbrella ribs, and the ones who fashion silk flowers for the hats you've seen on the Ladies' Mile, and you'll see 'em working without light, and without enough heat to warm their fingers, and without even enough money to buy drink on. Oh, you'll find enough of 'em, and they all die honest. And they all die soon."

"Is it better to be dishonest?" Philo asked the question as if she truly did not know the answer – and indeed, at that moment she did not.

Ella looked away. "Ask me again in three months," she replied. "But in three months," she went on grimly, "you won't need to be asking."

When Ella saw that Philo, once past her initial shock, was willing to attend to the situation of unmarried young women in New York, she told her new friend a little of the histories, a little of the manners of Mrs. Classon's boarders. Four worked in dollar stores, one in a stationery store, two in a millinery shop on Broadway (not quite in the Ladies' Mile but near enough it to hold themselves annoyingly high in their own estimations), one sold cigars and candy to workers in the printing district out of a "seven-by-nine" store, and the most successful was a victorine- and muff-maker especially in demand because of her skill in sewing furs.

These, to Philo's eye, were all respectable occupations, but Ella gave her to understand that none provided funds sufficient for comfortable living but that each gave opportunity for making the acquaintance of gentlemen. It was difficult to repulse forever men who were handsome, *de bon air*, flattering, and willing to give presents to a girl whose every penny was expended on shelter, food, and clothing.

Philo sighed. "Village life is different," she said.

"Are we all to pack up and descend on New Egypt then?" cried Ella. "Five thousand girls with carpetbags climbing down off the cars, looking about for lodging and employment? Are there enough single farmers in New Egypt to marry us all off to? This city belongs to us," said Ella, "as much as to the bankers on Wall Street and the ladies who buy the clothing we sew."

"What is it *you* do?" asked Philo.

"Through the kind offices of a friend . . ." Here Ella paused significantly. ". . . I got employment as a searcher in the Dead Letter Office of Station D."

"Station D?"

"The sub-post office at the Bible House. It's the largest in the city. I work there now."

"I am glad," said Philo, "that you have honest employment."

"I am paid three dollars a week," replied Ella meaningfully, and by this Philo understood that her friend had some other source of funds. Yet what would have scandalized Philo a week before had little power to shock her now. Whatever wrongs Ella and the other young women of Mrs. Classon's house committed, the extremities to which they had been driven were probably no more desperate than those which Philo would herself feel within the month. If Philo could not entirely countenance Ella's way out of her difficulties, it was not from lack of sympathy with her plight, only from an unfamiliarity with the customs and mores of single ladies in New York.

"I apologize," said Philo quietly, "if I have offended you by my thoughtless observations." She smiled grimly. "I realize this can be a hard life."

"I supposed you knew that," said Ella. "Miss Green, tell me about New Egypt."

Of New Egypt Philo said little, but of her mother and her grandfather she said much. And of Katie Slape, who murdered them both, and of John and Hannah Slape, who stole her fortune.

Chapter 31

ON THE BROADWAY STAGE

As the two young women talked late into the night, the house quietened. Voices left off, doors no longer slammed, Mrs. Classon's snoring was stifled in her pillow. Outside there was no traffic along the street, and they could hear no more than a barking dog closed in a neighboring cellar. The breezes that blew through the window from the river were fragrant of spring.

Despite the lateness of the hour when Ella LaFavour left Philo to seek her own chamber and bed, and despite the unaccustomed weariness of her day, Philo did not sleep. She sat at the single window of her room and stared out over the little plots of rocky soil three floors below, and wondered what on earth she was to do with herself.

Ella had advised her to return to the dollar store with Gertrude. "Some work is better than no work, and some money is a vast deal better than no money at all." An archness of Ella's brows was uncomfortably interpreted by Philo as a reminder that there were ways for a young woman to eke out a too-small wage.

This Philo felt that she was unable to do. She had a repugnance to the bartering of her possibly very meager charms. She had no experience in flirtation and suspected the art was one that came naturally to young women like Gertrude Major or Nellie

Stanwood. Philo was certain it had been in the milk that Jewel suckled at Caroline Varley's ample breast. But for herself, she was convinced she would be a miserable failure if she set about to snare a gentleman who stood on the other side of the counter and examined *her* when he had professed interest only in a pair of eighteen-penny gloves.

And if Philo's surmises were correct, she wouldn't have been able to get by on mere flirtation.

The next morning she told an astonished Gertrude Major that she would not be returning to Aachen's Dollar Emporium. "My money was stolen last night, and I must report it to the police. Later I will seek for work which will support me here at Mrs. Classon's. The dollar store wages would have fallen short of my weekly rent anyway."

Here – for this conversation took place at the breakfast table, where the disappearance of Ida Yearance with Philo's money was all the talk – Ella LaFavour said, "Philo, this morning I've been speaking to Nellie."

Nellie, who was Ella's beautiful blonde roommate, nodded her head vigorously and grinned. She wore cheap pearls around her wrists.

"Nellie wouldn't mind having your room, if you'd move in with me. You would save three dollars a week."

"If you're only to pay four," cried Gertrude, "then you can still work at the dollar store!"

Philo looked round in astonishment. She thought that in all of New Egypt the only person who had been really solicitous of her well-being had been Mary Drax, her own mother. The other inhabitants of the town would have been interested, certainly, if Philo had inherited three millions of dollars or had thrown herself down a well (these the extremities of fate to an inhabitant of New Jersey), but there was not one of them who would have put it in the way of duty to be of material assistance to Philo or her mother. Yet here were half a dozen young women, strangers to Philo three days ago, who appeared genuinely concerned with her welfare, who talked about what was best for her, who seemed willing to walk several squares out of their way for her benefit or amusement.

The sensation of being cared about was almost bewildering.

"I hope," said Mrs. Classon in her wispy voice that Philo could hear only because the landlady sat directly beside her, "that you remain with us. You are a pretty girl." And she laid her hand over Philo's on the cloth.

Philo persisted in her refusal to return to the dollar store that morning. She walked out of the house with Ella LaFavour and with a map of New York on which the Centre Street police headquarters had been marked in violet ink. She marveled anew at the size of the city, which was rather larger than her childhood conception of the entire state of New Jersey. Ella took her directly across town to the Bible House, a building whose immensity startled Philo, and then told her very carefully what cars she ought to take to get to Centre Street.

At police headquarters Philo told how her money had been stolen, gave a description of Ida Yearance, and meekly received a lecture on the evils that invariably befell young women who ought to have stayed in the country. She was questioned not very subtly on the subject of her employment and revenues and blushed when she realized the purport of that interrogation. She hurried away without even the reassurance being given her that "everything would be done . . ."

From a newsboy on the corner she purchased three papers in order to examine the advertisements for employment. She consulted her map, intending to walk back to West Thirteenth Street, but was instead attracted to the vast rectangle, shaded in green, that was labelled The Central Park. Of this expanse she had heard the clerks in the dollar store speak, and one man had asked her if she would like to accompany him there some Sunday afternoon. The morning was bright and warm, and for the first time Philo felt a pang for New Egypt, specifically for her garden and the flowers in it.

She returned to the corner where she had purchased the papers, bought a fourth, and asked the boy how she should get up to the Central Park.

"Got a nickel?" he asked.

Philo hesitated whether the information were worth so much.

She had fifteen dollars in her pocket, which, with her now reduced charges for boarding, ought to be made to last her three weeks at least – but could she afford to trade a newsboy five cents for what could not be *much* of a secret?

"Got a nickel?" the boy repeated with some impatience at Philo's country density. "If you got a nickel then you can take the Broadway stage."

"Oh!" cried Philo. "Thank you!"

New Yorkers were less mercenary than she had supposed. When the boy pointed to the west and told her to walk two squares over to catch the stage, she thanked him and purchased yet another paper.

She went west, waited for the stage at the corner of Franklin Street, and was warned of its approach by the tolling of a shrillish bell. She climbed on, exchanged a nickel for a ticket, slipped the ticket beneath her glove, folded her hands across the papers in her lap, and prepared to enjoy the long ride uptown.

What she had seen of New York before was nothing to what she saw now: square after square of immense buildings, each with five, six, or seven floors, each floor with the name of some business plated in a gilded crescent across the window. More persons than she had imagined existed in all the city together streamed along the walks, and the progress of the stage seemed slower than that of the hurrying throng.

At West Third Street the gentleman who had sat beside her got up, and his place was taken by a sweet-faced woman of middle age. Her tastefully sumptuous dress was worn with considerable grace. Moreover, something in this lady's friendly physiognomy seemed so familiar that Philo could not resist a polite nod, which was politely returned.

The Broadway stage had become crowded and the ticket-taker did not get round quickly. However, at his approach, the lady sitting next to Philo opened her bag, but as she did so uttered an exclamation of dismay.

Philo turned to her and in a low voice questioned whether anything were wrong.

"I have foolishly mislaid my porte-monnaie at the shop I just left," said the lady ruefully.

"Oh!" cried Philo in unfeigned sympathy. She knew what it was to have lost money. "Was there much in it?"

"No," said the lady, "no more than thirty or forty dollars, I think. But I haven't any money to pay my fare."

The ticket-taker was upon them. Philo showed her own and then handed the man five cents for the lady next to her.

"That is very kind of you," said the lady.

"It's nothing," said Philo. "Pray don't—"

"Please come to my house and let me reimburse you."

"It's not necessary," said Philo. "I was very happy to be of service to you."

"If you are not busy, I insist."

"I'm not pressed, I'll admit," replied Philo, smiling.

The lady eyed Philo's papers. "Do you plan to sell them on a street corner?" she asked archly.

Philo sighed. "If I don't find employment in the advertisements, I may finish up so."

"You are looking for work?" asked the lady.

"Yes," Philo replied.

The stage had stopped before an immense hotel. On the other side was a park, filled with large trees, with a fountain in the center, and brightly painted benches all round.

"Is this the Central Park?" Philo asked.

The lady laughed. "No," she said, "this is Madison Square. The Central Park is somewhat larger. You have but recently come to the city, I take it."

"Yes, I have been here only a few days."

The stage started up again. "This is Twenty-fourth Street," said the lady quickly. "I live on Twenty-sixth Street between Broadway and Sixth Avenue. I would deem it a favor if you would stop with me at my home now."

"I will," said Philo, amused that this lady – evidently quite well off if the loss of thirty-five or forty dollars meant so little to her – should go to such trouble to reimburse her for a five-cent fare.

"What is your name?"

"Philomela Drax, ma'am."

The lady smiled. "My name is Mrs. Maitland."

Before Philo could express her astonishment – she was certain, hearing the name and looking closely at the woman's face, that this was Henry Maitland's mother – the stage had stopped again, Mrs. Maitland had stood, and the ticket-taker was ushering them down the steps and into the street.

Chapter 32

ON TWENTY-SIXTH STREET

Philo remained silent in the brief walk from the stage to Mrs. Maitland's house. She tried desperately to recall what she had heard of Henry Maitland's circumstances in New York: whether his parents were living, whether he resided with them, any single fact at all – but she could remember nothing.

On each side of Twenty-sixth Street was an unbroken row of brownstone-front houses, each five stories high, each with a wide, high stoop, each with two windows on each floor. The walks were lined with flowering crab apples, and tiny beds of bright spring flowers had been planted before nearly all the houses. The morning sun was dazzlingly reflected off the windows on the northern side of the street. The very air smelled sweet. Philo for the first time was confronted with New York prosperity, and she was impressed.

A female servant opened the door to Mrs. Maitland and Philo, and Philo entered the house curiously. The hallway was richly papered in blue, the furniture was heavy mahogany, and everywhere were purple and white lilacs in white milk-glass vases.

"Philomela – may I call you so? – you will please stay for luncheon?"

The maid smiled and gently tugged at the papers Philo held clasped tightly in her hands. Philo let go of a sudden, and the papers were set neatly on the white marble table in the hall.

Philo hesitated to accept the offer.

"Is something the matter?" Mrs. Maitland asked.

"No," replied Philo quickly, "I'm only not certain . . ."

"I would be glad of company at luncheon," said Mrs. Maitland. "Only this morning my son went away on a long journey. It is foolish of me, but I miss his presence already."

"I don't think it foolish at all," said Philo. Then this *was* Henry's mother. Philo wondered now that she could have doubted it.

When the maid had opened the double doors into the parlor, Philo suddenly became aware of the shabbiness of her dress. The furniture, the fabrics, the pictures in gilt frames on the walls had all been assembled in the richest manner conceivable to Philo.

She was uncomfortable and felt as if she were somehow deceiving this kind woman. If her money had not been stolen the night before and if she had not thought immediately of turning to Henry Maitland for assistance, this fortuitous meeting with his mother would have seemed only a happy coincidence. She sat upon the sofa at Mrs. Maitland's behest while that lady pulled the pins from her hat.

"Where are you from, Philomela?"

"New Jersey."

"My brother lives in New Jersey," said Mrs. Maitland.

Philo looked away. "Your brother is Jacob Varley of New Egypt, I believe." She spoke guiltily, as if admitting having broken into the man's house and stolen his plate.

Mrs. Maitland turned around astonished and stared at Philo.

"Are you seeking employment as a clairvoyant, Philomela?" she asked at last.

Philo shook her head. "I am from New Egypt," said Philo. "And I have met your son."

"You know Henry?"

Philo blushed. "I was introduced to him in New Egypt. And last evening, quite by chance, he saw me on Eighth Avenue. He took me to dinner."

"Ah," said Mrs. Maitland, thoughtfully. "That is why he was so late in coming to say good-bye."

Philo was convinced that Mrs. Maitland, who was evidently very rich, would entirely disapprove her son's prosecuting an acquaintance with a girl so obviously poor as herself.

Mrs. Maitland was a handsome woman and imposing in the

way that her sister-in-law, Caroline Varley, would have liked to be. She seated herself on the sofa next to Philo.

"Why are you not in New Egypt?" asked Mrs. Maitland.

Philo looked away. "My mother is dead. I have no other family there. I have no other family at all. I came to New York hoping to support myself here."

"It is difficult for a young woman alone," said Mrs. Maitland gently.

"I know," replied Philo, "I—"

"Wait!" cried Mrs. Maitland. "Are you the young woman Henry described to me?"

Philo was confused. She suspected she was but did not want to give the impression that she assumed so much.

"Philomela," said Mrs. Maitland, taking the girl's hand, "was your mother murdered?"

Philo nodded dumbly. She was near to tears and felt that to speak at all would be to release them.

"I see," said Mrs. Maitland. She released Philo's hand, sat back on the sofa with her finger on her chin, and thought for several moments.

Philo knew that Mrs. Maitland now regretted having brought her to this house – the daughter and granddaughter of the victims of murder, a penniless girl who worked in a dollar store that was but two steps higher than a house of assignation, a wanton who had picked up her son on the street and attempted to involve him in her plight, a suspected criminal who couldn't cross the North River for fear she would be arrested once she had stepped onto New Jersey soil. Philo rose from the sofa, intending to leave.

"Philomela!" cried Mrs. Maitland, looking suddenly round with tears in her eyes. "You poor monkey!"

The dining table was white, as were the chairs that surrounded it, the china that was set upon it, the carpet that was beneath it, the frames around the mirrors that reflected it, the ceiling that looked down upon it, the paper on the walls that wrapped it round. Two tall windows at the back looked out over a little shady garden with a cast-iron fountain and statuary.

Mrs. Maitland asked many questions of Philo concerning her

life in New Egypt, the death of Richard Parrock, and the loss of her fortune. She did not speak and even delicately cast away her eyes when Philo told of the murder of her mother by Katie Slape. Philo did not seek to hide the fact that she was suspected of murder; rather, she even emphasized the point, so that she might never have to reproach herself with having attempted to deceive Henry's mother. Of all her story she glossed over only Jacob Varley's attempt to cheat her with the sale of her home and her discovery of the real nature of the dollar store.

But of this last, Mrs. Maitland evidently had some inkling. At any rate she seized upon Philo's current predicament – almost penniless and without certain prospects for betterment – as the cheerfullest portion of a history not distinguished by its cheer.

"Philomela," she said, "we must see something done for you."

"You have returned my five cents," said Philo with a smile.

"I mean to do somewhat more than that," said Mrs. Maitland, and rose from the table.

In the parlor again Mrs. Maitland asked Philo to sit at her desk and copy out two paragraphs in a book.

When Philo had accomplished this apparently meaningless task, Mrs. Maitland took the page, examined it, and nodded.

"This will do very nicely," she said.

"For what?" Philo asked curiously.

"For my secretary's hand," she said, and cocked her head and smiled.

Chapter 33

NEW PROSPERITY

Philo began once more to trust her optimism – and her instincts. When things had seemed blackest to her, Mrs. Maitland had descended like an angel of light onto the Broadway stage. And Philo realized with a shudder that if she had returned to the dollar store on Thursday morning, she would never have taken the Broadway stage, never met Henry's mother, never secured employment in the fine brownstone on West Twenty-sixth Street.

Nedda Maitland's intentions were not entirely charitable in regard to Philo Drax. At the first of course, hearing Philo's story and knowing what an interest her son had taken in her (though he had never told his mother the unfortunate girl's name), Nedda had cast about for a way of helping her. And having felt the need of late for someone to assist her with correspondence and accounts, to run errands, and to put off those whom she did not wish to see, she peered at Philomela Drax in the light of an applicant for that position. Philo was neat, courteous, unafraid, unsimpering, and she wrote a fine hand – so she was hired on the spot.

She was to be paid, Nedda told her, ten dollars a week.

"That is too much!" exclaimed Philo, who knew the wages of the other girls in Mrs. Classon's house.

"It is more than most young women of your age and experience could expect, I admit," said Nedda Maitland. "But I will not give you less. In the first place, it gives me pleasure to be of assistance to you. In the second place, Henry would wish it. In the third place, well – it is simply one of the conditions that I place upon hiring you, Philomela. Now," Nedda went on, "open the top drawer of the desk with this key and give me the wallet that is inside."

Philo did so, and Nedda Maitland opened the wallet, drew out five crisp ten-dollar bank notes, and handed them to Philo.

"I want you to go out this afternoon and purchase the beginnings of a new wardrobe. You—"

Philo handed back the bills with alacrity. "No, Mrs. Maitland, you've already been too kind to—"

Nedda Maitland shook her head in warning. "Please don't interrupt. This is necessary, I think. It will be required of you sometimes to make trips to Wall Street in my interest, and I wish your appearance to reflect credit on me." She scanned Philo's dress. "I think you are neatly done up, dear, but the materials might be richer without any harm. You will give interviews in my stead at times, and as my representative, you will need to appear to best advantage. And recall, Philomela, I am rich, and you are not. This money means very little to me and a great deal to you. I could get no greater pleasure from it than handing it over to you now." And she folded the bills in Philo's hand.

"What are my duties to be, Mrs. Maitland?" asked Philo.

"Many and various. I am a lazy woman, I fear, and I like to do as little as possible."

At this Philo smiled. Nedda Maitland, though stately and calm, did not give any impression of laziness such as was prominent in the character of Caroline Varley, her sister-in-law.

"I subscribe to a number of charities and am frequently called upon to attend meetings. Some meetings take place in this house, and I would ask you in some cases to take minutes of them. Many individual applicants for charity apply directly to me, and I am not always successful in winnowing the deserving from those who seek only to cheat me. I think you have a discerning eye, Philomela, and between us I think we can distinguish the shirkers."

"When shall I begin?"

"Now?"

"Yes!" cried Philo, eager to show Mrs. Maitland her gratitude.

"Then I will write a letter—"

Philo raised her hand in protest.

"I will have *you* write a letter," smiled Nedda, "and I will sign it. It will be directed to the manager of the store where I shopped this morning. You will go back down on the Broadway stage and see if you can recover the porte-monnaie that I so foolishly left behind."

The letter, of Philo's own composition, was written, read over by Nedda, signed, and transported downtown. The porte-monnaie, which had been left on the counter of an honest employee, had been taken to the manager. When he was satisfied that it did indeed belong to Nedda Maitland, a good customer of his, and that Philo was her acknowledged representative, he handed over the purse.

Philo returned to Twenty-sixth Street in triumph. The success of her first mission augured well for her new career.

Mrs. Maitland, who had no other pressing work for her that afternoon, dismissed Philo with the injunction that she ought to spend as much of the fifty dollars as she could. Philo took the kind woman at her word and returned to West Thirteenth Street laden with packages.

Each morning thereafter Philo left the rooming house in the company of the other young women on their way to their places of employment, and walked uptown to Mrs. Maitland's. She opened the early-morning mail, attached notes to the missives – the begging letters sometimes ran to twelve pages or more – which denoted what action was requested or seemed appropriate, Philo's opinion of the writer, and so forth. Mrs. Maitland went over these letters immediately, and Philo began the correspondence. In most cases, Nedda had only to tell Philo in a few words the nature of the reply, and Philo composed the letter herself; it was read over by Nedda and signed. Nedda and Philo took luncheon together, and in the early afternoon Philo went on errands for Mrs. Maitland or accompanied her employer on shopping expeditions. On the latter occasions, Philo's wardrobe never went unaugmented.

Perhaps the most difficult lesson for Philo to learn was to accept graciously Mrs. Maitland's gifts. After a time, Philo came to see that she really was of some considerable use to Mrs. Maitland and that charity had become only a small part of Nedda's motivation.

Philo did not move in with Ella LaFavour. She was pleased to be able to keep the single chamber at seven dollars a week. Though this consumed the greatest part of her wages, she was not at a loss for money. Her meals were normally taken either at Mrs. Classon's or on Twenty-sixth Street, and if Philo were out with Mrs. Maitland, Nedda always paid. Other than rent, Philo's sole expenditure was for entertainment, for sometimes in the evening Philo would go to the theater or one of the variety halls with Ella. Nellie Stanwood played half a dozen roles, each of a minor character, at the Union Square Theatre, and for each of these performances, several of Mrs. Classon's young ladies pooled their quarters and purchased a box for the evening – a giggling extravagance. When Philo had first come to New York, she had been burdened with trepidations of beginning a life whose success or failure was dependent entirely upon her own exertions; will-she nill-she Philo was grown up. But in this, the pleasantest spring she had ever known, Philo felt a young girl again, with few cares and many simple pleasures.

Each morning she walked through Madison Square on her way to Mrs. Maitland's and watched the progress of the flowers and trees. In the tiny, neat garden behind the house on Twenty-sixth Street, Philo and Mrs. Maitland would sit in the early afternoon when the sun had come round, take coffee, and listen to the plash of water in the cast-iron dolphin fountain. Philo had money – far more of her own than she had ever possessed in New Egypt; she had congenial employment; she had friends her own age at Mrs. Classon's and an even finer friend in Mrs. Maitland. It was difficult for Philo to believe that her mother was so recently dead. When she thought of Mary Drax, the image that was brought to Philo's mind was of a statue she had seen at the Academy of Arts with Mrs. Maitland, of Niobe weeping for her slaughtered children. Mary Drax, it seemed to Philo now, had always been weeping.

After a few weeks of being in the employ of Mrs. Maitland, Philo fulfilled a duty she had neglected: she wrote to Mr. Killip in Goshen and apprised him of her whereabouts and newfound situation. Until this new good fortune had come upon her, she had been reluctant to trouble the lawyer at all; but now that she could write hopefully, she was willing enough to tell him of her troubles in New Egypt and New York. She begged him to inform her how things progressed with the case for the recovery of the farm, and whether she were still suspected of her grandfather's murder, and whether anything at all had been heard of the Slapes. Philo wrote in conclusion:

Though I am well and (through the generosity of Mrs. Maitland) provided for, I will not be able to rest easy on my pillow a single night until the murderous Slapes have been apprehended, charged with their crimes, and punished. It is as if they had disappeared from the face of the earth, yet I know they are at this moment *somewhere*, doing *something* – but unassailed, unpunished, and uncaring of the difficulties and sorrow they have caused me. They have murdered my family, and they have stolen my fortune. I believe the family have no conscience, and would feel remorse only if remorse were woven into a gallows rope and tied round their necks. I can never forget or forgive what they have done to me. If I hate anything at all in this fair world, I hate the Slapes.

Chapter 34

JEWEL'S DISCOMFITURE

One week late in June, after Philo had been employed on Twenty-sixth Street for somewhat more than six weeks, she arrived at Mrs. Maitland's door at half past eight o'clock, her usual hour. The servant admitting her bore a troubled expression, but before Philo had the time to wonder if anything were amiss within, she had stepped into the parlor and seen, sitting upon the sofa, none other than Jewel Varley. She wore a forest-green morning dress, embroidered round the skirt and up the front in two wide flounces, one hanging over the other, with sleeves and cuffs fashioned to match.

She sat there stiffly, as if the Queen of England, on a portable throne, were in the next room and Jewel only waited for her name to be called by a herald, to enter and be presented.

Philo smiled, remembering how little communication there was between Nedda Maitland and her brother's family in New Egypt. It was unlikely that the Varleys knew of her appointment as Mrs. Maitland's secretary.

Hearing a step upon the threshold, Jewel looked up and cried, after a moment of amazement: "Lord! It's the murderess!" She shrunk into the corner of the couch and timorously demanded, "Do you intend to kill us all?"

"Jewel Varley," said Philo impatiently, "you know very well that I've never murdered anybody."

"It's said you did!"

"You know very well I didn't."

Jewel, though reassured of her safety, rose charily from the couch. "Then what on earth are you doing *here?*" she demanded.

"I am here to see your aunt," replied Philo. She would have been less than human had she not enjoyed Jewel's evident discomfiture.

Jewel looked over Philo's dress: a Swiss muslin skirt in white with a light blue bodice with white spots. It was of much finer quality than any outfit Jewel had ever seen on Philo.

"Well," said Jewel, attempting still to get over the unpleasant astonishment of seeing Philo there, "you would have done better to wear something less ostentatious."

"Why do you say that?"

"Because," replied Jewel, "my aunt is hardly likely to give charity to anyone so well-dressed as you are this morning. I would have thought that by this time, Miss Philo, you would have been well versed in the tactics of . . ." She paused to find a bitter word. ". . . genteel beggary. But perhaps, if I tell Aunt Nedda how needy your case is, she will overlook the opulence of your dress."

Philo was nearly angry, but she did not allow that anger to show. "Your dress is considerably finer than mine, Jewel."

"Of course it is! But I have a position to maintain in this household. Of course I wear a fine dress!"

"But I have a position to maintain in this household as well," said Philo, and seated herself – to Jewel's even greater astonishment – at the secretary against the wall. Philo unlocked the desk and pulled down the writing board.

"Philo," cried Jewel, "leave my aunt's things alone!"

Philo turned slowly around and said, "Good morning, Mrs. Maitland."

Nedda Maitland stood in the doorway of the parlor.

"Good morning, Philomela," said Nedda. "Jewel, it had completely slipped my mind that you two young women were already acquainted."

"Aunt Nedda," Jewel spluttered, "Philo was going through your desk!"

"Of course she was," replied Nedda imperturbably. "Philomela is very industrious."

Jewel turned back to Philo with an eye of horror.

"I am your aunt's secretary," Philo explained.

"Her secretary!"

"And my companion," said Nedda Maitland. "Philomela has kept me excellent company while Henry has been away. I don't know what I should have done without her."

"She is being hunted down in New Jersey as a murderess!" cried Jewel.

"All the more reason for her to remain with me," replied Nedda calmly.

"You *knew* that she killed her grandfather?"

"Jewel!" said Nedda sternly.

"But Aunt Nedda," Jewel protested, taking another tack. "I would have been happy to come to stay with you. You need only to have asked. I could have written all your letters and done whatever it is that Philo does. And you wouldn't have had to pay me, I would have done it for nothing!"

Nedda smiled and said, "I didn't want to deprive New Egypt of your sunshine, Jewel."

Jewel frowned. "New Egypt is a poky old place. I'd much rather be here in New York."

"I'm a cruel mistress," said Nedda. "I run poor Philomela ragged."

"She doesn't look ragged! How much do you pay her, Aunt Nedda?"

"Not a portion of what she's worth to me," said Nedda, and smiled at Philo, who blushed.

"Well," said Jewel peevishly – she was not getting the best of any of this conversation—"I'm certain Miss Philo will be sorry to see us leave for Saratoga. I wonder what she'll do then."

Philo was indeed alarmed – this was the first that she had heard of Mrs. Maitland's intended journey upstate. She had known of course that the Varleys spent time at the watering place every year but had not known that Mr. Varley's sister accompanied them. She did not look up at Mrs. Maitland, for she did not wish her employer to think that she expected anything more than she had already received at that kind woman's hand.

"She will help me to prepare for the journey," said Nedda Maitland, "and when she goes to the terminal, she will purchase three tickets – one for you, one for me, and one for herself."

"You are taking Philo with you to Saratoga!" cried Jewel, but Philo was just as surprised.

"Of course," replied Nedda, who had seated herself in a velvet fauteuil and inclined her face into the warming rays of the sun through the front window. "Philomela – unfortunately for herself – has become indispensable to me. She will have to submit to being dragged off to Saratoga if she wishes to remain in my employ."

"I think I can bear up," remarked Philo softly.

Jewel protested, "But Philo is your secretary. She helps you with your *work*. At Saratoga she'll just be extra baggage!"

Nedda Maitland replied as if she did not understand Jewel's motive in thus deprecating Philo's usefulness. "There are letters to be written at Saratoga as well as in New York. My broker telegraphs me there as well as here. I'll want someone to buy the morning papers and purchase tickets to the concerts for me. I'll still want conversation at Saratoga, Jewel."

"Philo's paid to do those things," sneered Jewel. "She's in your employ. I'd be doing it for love of you, Aunt Nedda. Besides – and I know Philo won't mind my saying so – she'll be dreadfully out of place among so much of the fashionable world. She *couldn't* be comfortable there. Suppose someone found out about her past!"

Philo blushed hot, but said nothing.

Nedda replied, "She has never disgraced either herself or me. That is more than I could say of some."

Now Jewel blushed hot.

Jewel would have liked to remain in the parlor, for she did not wish to leave Philo and her aunt alone together. She was jealous of the intimacy that Nedda implied was between them. It was vastly annoying that Philo was to go to Saratoga, for Jewel had hoped to be the companion of her aunt – her aunt had a position in society far higher than that of the Varleys, and Jewel would have been introduced to everybody.

Nedda however asked that Jewel leave her and Philo alone for a while so that they might conduct the morning's business in private.

"But I'm your niece!" protested Jewel.

Nedda smiled. "All the more reason for you not to have to listen to Philomela and me go on about letters and accounts and so forth."

Jewel flounced out of the room, unable to conceal her disappointment at the whole business.

When she was gone, Nedda closed the doors and came and sat near Philo at the secretary.

"You and Jewel were not the best of friends in New Egypt, I take it?" she questioned.

"Jewel considered the Draxes to be too far beneath the Varleys to admit of much intimacy between us," Philo replied evenly.

"Jewel would perhaps be happier living in England, where views are not so democratic as they are in this country."

"I don't doubt it."

"I'm afraid," said Nedda, "that the news I had been saving for you was sprung rather too suddenly this morning. I had meant to tell you in a day or so that I wished for you to accompany me to Saratoga this year. Do you much mind going?"

Philo laughed. "I think I can get back the deposit I made on the mansion in Newport. Of course I would be very pleased to go with you – and be of any help that I can. Once, Jewel told me that I should never get to see Saratoga. She cannot be happy that her own aunt is going to prove her a false prophetess."

"Jewel is not often happy," sighed Nedda. "I invited her some time since to come up to stay with me for a few weeks before going off to Saratoga, but I didn't have you with me then. I hope you two will be able to get along."

"When she can't get her way, Jewel settles down into reasonableness," replied Philo. "I'm sure we'll rub along all right."

"We shall be in Saratoga most of July and all of August. I think it would be sensible for you to give up your chamber at Mrs. Classon's for that time."

"Yes," replied Philo. "I only hope that when I return she will have a room available to me. I am used to the place, and the young ladies there have always been very friendly to me."

"I had another suggestion," said Nedda hesitantly.

"Yes?"

"I thought that when we returned, you might move in here with me."

Philo was too startled to reply.

"If you don't mind losing your West Thirteenth Street independence, that is. I hope that you would keep up your acquaintance with your friends – but the fact is, I have grown childishly dependent on you." Nedda Maitland had a way of deprecating her strengths and affections that charmed Philo as much as anything about her. "And I'd like to indulge that weakness by having you about me all the time."

"I don't think," said Philo, with an irrepressible grin, "that Jewel is going to be much pleased with this arrangement."

That evening Philo returned to West Thirteenth Street with the intention of telling Ella of her good fortune. Ella, having heard the story of meeting Mrs. Maitland on the Broadway stage and following Philo's progress into the woman's good graces step by step, had always said, "Lord, Philo, you're the only one I've ever met who lost a fortune, and then bought it back again – with a nickel."

But today it was Ella who had the more important news.

Philo was sitting in the parlor waiting for the dinner bell when Ella came bounding up the steps of the house and flung herself panting into the parlor. She held one arm straight up in the air and was waving an envelope like a flag.

"What was the name of those people that robbed you and killed your grandfather and your mother?" she demanded breathlessly.

"The Slapes," replied Philo automatically, wondering at her friend's behavior.

Ella lowered her arm without bending it at the elbow. The envelope was directly before Philo's eyes.

She read the address:

> mrs. hannah Slape
> no. 251 Christerfer st
> new York

Philo reached for the letter, but Ella snatched it away.

"But there's a stamp: 'Recipient Unknown,'" Philo protested, not wanting to believe the Slapes so close by.

"Don't believe all that you read," warned Ella.

"What do you mean?"

"They're here," hissed Ella, with a leer, "they're five streets away right this minute!"

Chapter 35

THE RETURNED LETTER

"How did you come by that?" cried Philo. "That letter?"

"It was a dead letter – refused at the house," said Ella. "So it came to the office."

Ella was a naturally curious and inquisitive young woman – working in the Dead Letter section of the post office exactly suited her talents and inclinations.

"I remembered the name," she went on, "I *thought* I remembered the name, so I slipped it under the front of my dress and brought it to you."

So excited was Philo that she forgot to chide Ella for this obvious infraction of the rules of her department.

"But if it was refused at the house, then obviously the Slapes don't live there," said Philo, eagerly eyeing the envelope that Ella mischievously swung through the air just out of Philo's reach.

"There's a thousand reasons for refusing a piece of mail," said Ella. "It could be they didn't want to be found out."

"Maybe," said Philo, "maybe it was simply a mistake. You didn't open the letter, did you?"

"Maybe I did," said Ella. "Maybe I know something you don't."

"Maybe you do," said Philo eagerly.

"And maybe on my way home from the Bible House today I went a spike or two out of my way and strolled down Christopher Street, and maybe I hung about in front of No. 251, and maybe I saw a placard in the window advertising a fortune-teller, and maybe the name of that fortune-teller was Miss Katie."

Quite suddenly, with the certainty of the Slapes' presence in

New York put before her, all Philo's excitement spun away, leaving an unpleasant hollowness inside her.

The Slapes were in New York. They lived five streets to the south. Katie was telling fortunes, and with them – unless they had managed to spend it all – the Slapes had Philo's thirty thousand dollars.

But Philo was worried; the Slapes were not to be toyed with, they couldn't be approached directly. She couldn't even put the police onto them, because as far as she knew they hadn't been charged with any crime. Philo knew that Katie had murdered her mother and her grandfather, but the law officials of New Jersey were certainly not convinced of that fact.

Whatever Philo was to do must be done circumspectly. She could not allow the Slapes to get away again.

Ella saw in Philo's face the alteration of her thought and mood. She stood still and quietly handed the letter to Philo.

"And this was refused at the door?" Philo asked.

Ella nodded and seated herself beside her friend.

Philo took a paper cutter from the table, and slit open the envelope. Inside she found this letter:

Camden, June the 12 –71

Cousin Hannah – Prince and Sue was in new York Sunday and monday inquirring into passage to Californ. for Judiths boy Charles they saw you at the playhouse and followed you home but got the house wrong and couldnt find you again thow thay beat uponn the door so iam riteing this to you at that number and hoping a kind nabor who knowse you will give it to you Prince and Sue and idid not know you and John Slape and his girl was in new York and we hope this letter finds you very well at this time threw the Blessinges of god their is nothing like helth in this world of sin and tryals ihad a Blind Boil on mye hand but it has got well now ive got an Irishe girl to do my cooking Prince is shingeling houses for one dollar 25 per day ide rite more icant think of Ennay thing thay all sendes there love to you and youres do not forget to pray Every morning and nite imust End for this time iremanne your Cousin untill Deth

Lillie jepson

From this letter Philo concluded that the Slapes were in New York, and that they did not wish that fact known, not even to their relatives in Camden.

The next morning early, Philo borrowed from Nellie Stanwood a hat with a veil, and in Ella's company walked down Hudson Street from West Thirteenth to Christopher. Philo grew more agitated on the way, and despite her veil and bulky dress, was fearful that if she stood before the house, all three of the Slapes would look out their windows and recognize her at once.

Warning Ella not to appear conspicuous, Philo made her cautious way along the side of the street opposite from No. 251. The traffic from the ferry was heavy along Christopher Street, and many commuters from New Jersey who had disembarked were now heading toward the stage that ran along Seventh Avenue. There was no difficulty, Ella assured Philo, of their remaining unremarked in such a crush. They came to a recessed doorway directly across the street from No. 251 and paused there for a moment. As Ella appeared to rummage through her reticule, Philo observed the house across the way. On the placard in the window, she could make out Katie's claims – and from what she had seen of the girl, she thought her capable of that and much more.

The house had four floors, with two windows in each story. Each window was curtained, but even as Philo watched the house, the draperies across one of the second-floor windows were suddenly pulled aside.

Katie Slape stood there in a green dress. She looked directly across the street to where Philo and Ella stood in the doorway.

Philo stiffened.

"She can't see through the veil," hissed Ella. "And she don't know me!"

Katie, in the window, grinned and beckoned them.

She called to them, but her voice couldn't be heard over the noise of a water cart just then passing on Christopher Street between them.

But Philo knew what she said. Katie's mouth formed the words "Come up, Cousin! Come up!"

PART VIII

CHRISTOPHER STREET

Chapter 36

THE SLAPES CONFER

The two women in the recessed doorway across from No. 251 Christopher Street would not come up, though Katie beckoned to them. They would not be charmed by her smile.

Katie watched them scramble furtively away toward Seventh Avenue, and then she called her stepmother. Hannah was in the kitchen, narrowly watching the servants. She wasn't a hard mistress in that she didn't require much in the way of thorough cleaning or culinary skills, but she was suspicious and inquiring. She had accused the two girls of listening at doors, and was impatiently attending to their defenses.

"What's wanted?" said John Slape, who had heard Katie's call from upstairs.

"Par! That girl's back!"

"What girl?" he asked, not unexpectedly imagining that Katie spoke of one of her customers who had not been murdered and buried in the cellar of the adjoining house.

"The old man's granddaughter, Par!"

John and Hannah came together in the doorway of Katie's parlor. John was perplexed.

"In Goshen?" cried Hannah in astonishment. "The hired girl?"

"I saw her on Christopher Street," said Katie. "She was looking up at our windows."

"When?" demanded Hannah.

"Now – just now."

John was still gathering his memory, but he asked helpfully, "Should I go after her?" He felt in his pockets for a knife.

"Katie's wrong," said Hannah. "Couldn't be here."

"What was her name?" asked John.

"Don't recall," said Katie.

"Drax," replied Hannah. "Someone Drax."

"Katie, you certain you seen her?" asked her father.

Hannah and John protested not because they disbelieved Katie – who in such matters was never wrong – but rather because they wished Philo Drax at the end of the earth: in a jail in Cape May, in a California mining camp, in Cochin. There having been no reason to think of Philomela Drax, they had nearly excised her image from their minds altogether.

"What's she want?" said John.

Katie shrugged, then replied, "She wants the old man's money."

"No!" said John.

"The money's ours," said Hannah.

"That's what she wants," said Katie. "It's a sober fact."

One of the servants appeared on the landing below. Hannah turned toward her with a growl: "If you heard a word, I'll slice off your ears and serve 'em up for supper!"

The servant retreated hastily.

"She can't have it," said John, seating himself at Katie's table and peering out the window into the street. "Is she there still?" he asked his daughter. "I don't rightly recall her form."

"Where does she stay?" asked Hannah.

"Don't know," said Katie. "Had on a dress that was too big for her. Had on a hat with a thick veil. Didn't want me to see her. I saw her. Don't know where she lives though. I wish I'd been on the street. I'd have reached out and touched her arm." Katie pantomimed this action, with Hannah representing Philo. She brushed her fingers over the sleeve of Hannah's dress. "I'd touch her arm, and then she'd never get away from us."

"Have the girl fetch tea," said John to his wife. He sat stuporously at Katie's table. Thinking and planning came hard to his occluded consciousness.

Hannah called up the servant girl, who had been cowering in one of the unoccupied rooms on the floor below. She was sent below for tea, and the kitchen girl was to go out for the particular cookies the Slapes most enjoyed.

Hannah and Katie seated themselves round the table. The morning sun was bright through the window. It wasn't yet eight o'clock.

"When she comes here," said John slowly, "Katie'll hit her and then we'll put her in the cellar."

"She won't come here," snapped Hannah.

"Why not?" asked John. "She was looking in the window, Katie said."

"She knows I killed the old man, and her mother too," said Katie. "She won't come in here. She knows what would happen to her."

"Katie'll find her," said John, amending his plan. "She'll find her, and I'll drive something through her brain."

"What if she sends the police first?" said Hannah.

John looked up in surprise. "Why should she send the police?"

"She wants the money," said Katie. "She'll send the police to get the money."

"The police can't walk in and take our money!"

"What if they go up to the top of the house – find the hole in the wall?" said Hannah. "What if they go downstairs – look in the cellar? See your spade and the turned earth? Take our money and take us too!"

This was a distinctly troublesome thought to John. "When they turn, I'll beat them over the head with the spade," he said slyly.

"No, Par!" cried Katie. "There's so many police!"

"What do we do then?" he asked simply.

The tea was brought, and downstairs they heard the door slam – the kitchen girl was returning with the cookies.

The tea was poured, the cookies brought up, the servant girls banished to the kitchen with strict instructions to close the door and plug their ears, and still the question was unanswered: "What do we do then?"

"What if she went off directly to get the police?" asked Hannah in a flurry of alarm.

John peered out the window. "Don't see none."

"No police," said Katie, craning her neck.

"Could be around the corner, waiting," said Hannah.

"Waiting for what?" said John.

"We have to leave New York," said Katie.

John looked up with severe disappointment. The night before

the Slapes had laughed themselves sick over the crushed baby scene in George Fox's *Humpty Dumpty*.

"There's no theaters in Goshen," he said.

"We couldn't go back to Goshen anyway," said Hannah. "Not with the old man killed like he was."

"*She* did it!" cried John, referring not to his daughter but to Philo. "I'm not going noplace where there's not theaters."

"She brings the police," said Hannah, "you're arrested and put in jail. Won't never see a theater."

"They'll hang you, Par."

"Hang me? Why?"

"Because of the girls in the cellar."

"You killed 'em, Katie!"

Katie shrugged. "They'll hang the three of us."

"Is that right?" asked John of his wife.

Hannah nodded.

John swallowed off the rest of his tea quickly and poured more. He wasn't a drunkard, because Hannah had told him to avoid drink – and John Slape wasn't the man to question his wife's directives.

"Leave town for a while," said Hannah. "Go where we're not known."

"Let's go to Philadelphia," said John. "There's theaters in Philadelphia."

"Too close to Camden," said Hannah. "I'm known in Camden."

"Par and I ain't known in Camden."

"Split up?" said Hannah musingly. "Maybe so. I could go to Boston."

"Does Boston have theaters?" asked John. "Don't want to split up."

"Maybe splitting up would be best," said Hannah. "For a time. Mark you a calendar, John, and meet together on a date."

"I'll go to Philadelphia, you go to Boston."

"Where am I to go?" demanded Katie.

"Who do you want to go with?" asked Hannah.

Katie looked from her father to her stepmother. She touched Hannah's sleeve. "You'll take better care of me."

Hannah nodded. John said, "I don't like to be alone."

"Won't be for long," his wife assured him. "Give you money, John. Go to that hotel where we stayed. Put up there, and there's theater every evening."

"What if I run out of money?"

"Give you five hundred dollars. Ought to keep you."

Hannah went down to the kitchen to dismiss the two servants. John went upstairs to board up the hole in the fourth-story wall. Katie went into the bedroom, took out the carpetbag and stood before a cheval glass. She grinned and swung the bag to and fro and made believe that she was walking to Boston with it.

Chapter 37

ELLA'S FORTUNE

As Philo and Ella retreated hastily along Christopher Street away from the river, Ella attempted to convince her friend that with her disguised dress and heavy veil, there was no way in the world that she could have been recognized by Katie Slape.

"She was looking at you from across the street, wasn't she? And how many times has she even seen you? Do you think your own mother'd know you in that outfit, Philo?"

Philo wasn't to be comforted or convinced. "Katie Slape's eyes tore off my veil," she said wildly.

The two young women took refuge in a bakery at the corner of Hudson and purchased half a dozen sweet cakes.

"You know they're there," said Ella. "You know that family is a universe of putrescence. Now let's go down to Centre Street to police headquarters."

"And tell them what?" demanded Philo. "That a crazy girl who tells fortunes murdered my grandfather? The police will telegraph Cape May Court House and discover what? That *I'm* the one who's suspected of the crime. Tell them what? That the family living at No. 251 Christopher Street stole thirty thousand dollars from me? Do I look as if I had misplaced such a sum recently? Tell them what? That Katie Slape sliced up my mother with a razor, and only waited her chance to show *me* a little bit of her knife? Katie's twenty years old and her dress is vulgar – but who's to believe that she's an assassin?"

Ella looked around uneasily. Philo's whispered vehemence was drawing attention.

"Ask your friend what to do," Ella suggested in a low voice.

"Mrs. Maitland?"

Ella nodded.

Philo walked immediately out of the shop and hailed a cab. Ella was aghast at the extravagance, but Philo only said, "Katie Slape murdered my mother. John and Hannah Slape stole my fortune."

In a quarter of an hour they were on Twenty-sixth Street, but there the servant informed Philo that Mrs. Maitland was somewhere down on the Ladies' Mile, shopping with Miss Jewel for their Saratoga wardrobes.

Philo and Ella found the same cab positioned at the corner of Broadway, and it carried them back downtown.

"I don't know what to do," admitted Philo.

"Wait," said Ella. "Just wait."

"Katie saw me. What if they leave town?"

"She *couldn't* have recognized you."

Philo turned away hotly. "You don't know her, Ella."

Ella sat back in the cab and smiled.

"I think I want *my* fortune told," she said.

"No!"

"Why not? She don't know me from the chief Celestial down on Mott Street."

"She saw you standing with me."

Ella shook her head. "I'll change my dress and my hat. I'll borrow a little paint from Nellie. She'll never know me."

Philo was doubtful. "What good will it do? What will you discover?"

Ella shrugged. "I'll keep my eyes open, that's all."

The driver took them to West Thirteenth Street. Ella altered her appearance to an extent that astounded Philo: with a too-tight dress, false curls, and a complexion of chalk and rouge, she didn't look at all like herself.

"You take up a position in that bakery shop," said Ella as they were on their way to Christopher Street once again. "Sit yourself down with a cup of chocolate and a plate of cookies and watch for me to come out again."

The Slapes' two servants had been dismissed summarily, given five dollars in lieu of a week's wages lost, and warned that if they said a word about anything at all they'd have their tongues sliced out of their throats. They did not question Hannah's threat. Katie had taken the placard from the first-floor window and placed it carefully at the bottom of the case that she was to take to Boston.

Hannah was counting out the money John was to live on in Philadelphia when they were all disturbed by a knock at the street door.

"Is it the police?" cried John.

Hannah went downstairs.

Katie followed her stepmother with a hammer.

John went all the way down to the cellar and unchained Little Dick, who barked furiously and attempted to bite his master's hand.

Hannah opened the street door to a tall, angular young woman, who said, in a shrill voice, "I'm come to have my fortune read!"

"Sign's down," said Hannah shortly, and started to close the door.

The young woman thrust her hand inside. "I've got the blues and dumps something monstrous. I'm desperate to know—"

"Go away!" cried Hannah, but Katie, with a smile, reached round and pushed Hannah's hand from the doorknob.

"Walk in," said Katie. "And I'll show you a picture of your true love."

Little Dick came bounding up the cellar stairs, barking hoarsely.

The three women in the narrow corridor fell back in alarm.

Little Dick stopped before them, growling, but Katie lifted the hammer high and brought it down to a spot expertly calculated to crush his skull. The dog collapsed dead at her feet.

The young woman who had just entered turned and tried the handle of the door, but Hannah slammed it shut.

"Walk up," said Katie, waving toward the stairs with the bloody hammer.

"No," the young woman replied nervously, "I don't think I will . . ."

"What's your name?" Katie demanded.

"Ella."

"What other name?" Katie stood on the bottom stair and grinned. Ella stood between Katie and her stepmother, who guarded the door. John Slape had appeared in the cellar doorway, and stared stupidly at the dead dog.

"Ella LaFavour."

"You were born in Canada," said Katie, "In eighteen fifty, under the sign of Cancer. A young man is greatly in love with you and would give all he is worth to marry you."

She turned and ascended the stairs.

"Walk up," said Hannah grimly to Ella. "Walk up."

"The number six is lucky for you," said Katie, beckoning with her hammer. "The number fifteen very unlucky. Beware of it."

Ella followed Katie up the stairs.

"Today is the fifteenth," Katie remarked, and turned at the landing.

Ella hesitated, but Katie reached over the railing and took hold of Ella's arm, pulling her upward.

"If you had married this young man who is in love with you, your children would have been called Ella, Henry, and Philomela."

Ella stopped suddenly.

"Why won't I marry him?"

Hannah and John Slape stood at the foot of the stairs and looked up. Katie grinned down at Ella around the turn in the stairs and, leaning over, fingered the sleeve of her dress.

The smell of the dog's blood filled Ella's brain.

"You'll die on your birthday," said Katie.

"*Today* is my birthday!"

Katie raised the hammer high.

Chapter 38

NO GOOD

Philo waited in the bakery shop half an hour for her friend before she became convinced that something was dreadfully wrong. She stood up hastily to go, but then she reflected that perhaps Ella had been only one of several young ladies desirous of having their fortunes told and was waiting her turn. She ordered another cup of chocolate, another plate of cookies, and waited another half an hour.

At the end of that time, she nervously paid for what she had consumed and walked out of the shop. She went down Christopher Street toward the river, this time on the same side of the way as the Slapes' house and keeping as close as she might to the house façades.

Katie would see her approach only if she leaned far out her parlor window.

Philo came all the way up to No. 251 and stood several moments before the house, wondering how she ought to proceed. She still wore her veil. She spun her horsehair bracelets round and round her wrist in perplexity.

All the curtains of the house were drawn. Philo mounted the steps and knocked at the door. No one answered her summons. She tried the knob and the door swung open.

The morning was hot, and the dead dog had begun to stink. Its blood stained the runner in the dim hallway.

The door closing of its own accord shut Philo in the house.

She called out Ella's name timidly.

There was no response, no movement in the house, and Philo called Ella's name more loudly.

The dead dog seemed a presage of greater evil.

Philo stepped over the carcass and peered into the first-floor parlor. It looked as if it hadn't been swept in weeks.

She descended the stairs to the kitchen and the dining room, which – common to all boardinghouses – were below the level of the street. The fire had only recently died down in the stove. A table in the kitchen, set for two, bore the remains of a poor meal abandoned before half finished.

Philo took the cloth from the dining table, brought it back up to the entryway and draped it over the dead dog.

Calling Ella's name again she mounted the stairs.

Ella lay on the landing. The false side curls she had worn were drenched in blood and hung down over her face.

Philo brushed them aside and closed her friend's filmed, staring eye.

Neighbors had seen the Jepsons depart with their baggage at about half past ten o'clock that Saturday morning, headed toward the ferry. Philo had discovered the corpses of Ella and the dog at half past eleven.

The barber around the corner knew the Jepsons' servant girls, having recommended their employment. The police questioned the young women. They had been dismissed at half past nine o'clock that morning and knew nothing more at all, but they nervously ventured the opinion that the Jepsons had been up to no good for a long time.

The Jepsons' "no good" was found quickly enough. The boarded-up hole in the fourth-story wall led the police into the adjoining house. Their lanterns in that shuttered building showed them spots of blood all the way down to the cellar. And in the cellar were six heaped mounds of earth and a seventh grave recently dug and waiting for its victim.

Saturday night was expended in the exhumation of Katie's victims: one young woman who had died of a cracked skull, three young women who had died of causes yet to be determined, one young woman who had been buried alive, and a three-year-old boy (inhumed with his mother) who had a mouth full of hard candy and a paring knife embedded in his throat.

Notice of the horrific discoveries appeared in Monday morning's papers. There was straight reportage of the findings, interviews with policemen on the scene, neighbors' opinions, a description of the last victim, speculations of the whereabouts of the villainous family, and the appended rumor that their real name was not Jepson, but Slade or Slate.

Readers of the city's newspapers might have found out much more about the Jepsons if the newspapermen had been able to find the young woman who had discovered the corpse upon the landing. Police headquarters had her statement, her name, and her address; but when the reporters called at Mrs. Classon's rooming house on West Thirteenth Street, it was to find a parlorful of somber young women who could only lament the death of their treasured Ella and give the information that Philomela Drax was packed up and gone – they did not know where and would not have said if they did.

In the next week, drawings of the Slapes (still under the name Jepson) appeared in the newspapers. These were taken from likenesses on file in a photographer's studio on lower Broadway where the Slapes had gone to have cartes de visite made up, singly, and as a family group. A substantial reward was posted for their arrest.

They were variously thought to be in Ohio, in Canada, on the Isthmus of Panama waiting to catch a packet to San Francisco. They were disguised as Hindus and living in Delancey Street.

They had murdered a family in Kentucky, they had robbed a bank in Maryland, they had cheated prisoners at Andersonville.

Hannah had committed suicide with a homemade guillotine, John had been scalped by Indians in western Kansas, Katie had been killed by a stray bullet in a tavern brawl.

In fact, John Slape had shaved off his beard and was living in the hotel on Twelfth Street in Philadelphia. His day was spent at the barbershop, where he was vaguely remembered from having visited there some months before, and in the evening he went to the theater – but Philadelphia entertainments, he maintained, didn't compare to what you could get in New York.

Hannah and Katie had rented rooms on Myrtle Street in Boston. Katie advertised quietly as a card reader, and Hannah, merely to occupy her time, did piecework sewing dolls' bodies for a Tremont Street toy manufacturer.

Philo's carpetbag and Philo's fortune had found one more quiet home, beneath the bed that Katie and Hannah shared.

PART IX

SARATOGA SPRINGS

Chapter 39

JEWEL'S DISAPPOINTMENT

Upon discovering the corpse of Ella LaFavour, Philo had fled the house on Christopher Street. She understood several things. One, that the Slapes were no longer in the house, for if they had been she would not have got out alive. Two, that the Slapes had recognized her on the street, for Katie – Philo was certain Katie was responsible for Ella's death – would have had no other reason to murder her companion from that episode. Three, that it was Philo's responsibility to get to the police as quickly as possible so that the Slapes might be apprehended.

Not allowing herself to remember how short a time before she had sat beside Ella in the cab, or watched her as she applied paint at Nellie Stanwood's mirror, or walked with her from West Thirteenth Street, Philo ran toward the ferry, where she supposed a policeman must be on patrol.

She found one without difficulty, and told him of her friend's corpse on the stairway of No. 251. The policeman rapped his truncheon loudly on the sidewalk, alerting other officers in the neighborhood, and hurried to the place where Philo's best friend lay weltering in gore.

Philo took a cab to Centre Street and there related to three detectives all she knew of the Slapes. She was chided for not having come forward sooner, but Philo was certain that her tale – without the ineluctable evidence of Ella's crushed head – would have carried little weight with the harried New York police, who had a sufficiency of unsuppositious criminals to occupy them.

News of Ella's death had preceded Philo to West Thirteenth Street. Mrs. Classon sat with surprised eyes in the parlor and wondered what on earth could have made Ella want to have her fortune told on a Saturday morning. "Fortune-tellers," she said in her wispy voice, "spiritists and mediums – they can't work but at night . . ."

Philo's involvement in Ella's death was not known in the

rooming house, and Philo did not see fit to acknowledge it. Ella had introduced her into the household, and it was through Ella that Philo had allowed herself to feel a part of that strange community. But now with Ella gone – so suddenly gone – Philo felt alien. She looked around at her chamber and stared at the women who peered in at the door and whispered consolingly with as great wonder as if she had gone to sleep in her same bed the night before and waked this morning in a pasha's harem.

She began to pack her belongings, but found that, because of the number of new acquisitions, she could cram scarcely a third of her clothing into the wicker case in which she had brought all her worldly possessions from New Egypt.

Leaving all there then, she departed Mrs. Classon's and walked up to Twenty-sixth Street. A cab would have seemed too confining. She kept recalling to mind the dim, close atmosphere of the stairway on Christopher Street that stank of old grease and newly spilt blood. Distraught and silent, Philo felt that there wasn't enough open air in all the world for her just then.

Mrs. Maitland was in the guest chamber occupied by her niece. Jewel was examining with satisfaction all that morning's purchases.

"Philomela!" cried Mrs. Maitland in surprise when Philo appeared in the doorway.

"Philo!" Jewel's greeting was an undisguised grimace.

Philo started to speak, but her voice choked off.

Mrs. Maitland rose quickly and went to Philo, crying, "What's the matter, dear?"

Even in her extenuated grief, Philo refused to break down before Jewel Varley and so begged a few minutes' private conversation with her employer. Mrs. Maitland led Philo into her own chamber while Jewel sniffed to the maid who was assisting her, "Did you see that dress she had on? Four rags sewed together with a three-penny flounce . . ."

Jewel pretended that she had no interest in the conversation between distressed Philo and concerned Mrs. Maitland, but once or twice she asked the attendant maid what she thought the purport might be.

The maid didn't know, but twenty minutes later that same maid was summoned and sent out of the house.

Jewel was indignant that *her* assistant had been withdrawn to prosecute some senseless errand of that hired person, Miss Philo Drax.

At tea that afternoon Mrs. Maitland said to an ever more astonished Jewel, "Our plans have changed."

"Which plans, Aunt Nedda?"

"We are all going to Saratoga Springs on Monday."

"On Monday!" cried Jewel. Her aunt had promised to take her to the final rout of the New York season, and that was on Wednesday night. "But what about the Stallworths' ball?"

"I am sorry about that, Jewel, but I've decided to go to Saratoga a few days earlier than I had planned. No doubt," she added with a bland smile, "you will find something at the Springs to console you for the loss of the Stallworths' ball."

"You've decided," said Jewel petulantly, "because of something Philo told you. Why isn't Philo down here helping you?"

"Helping me with what?"

"Oh – things."

"Philo is unwell."

"If Philo is unwell," said Jewel quickly, "she certainly shouldn't make the journey to Saratoga. Aunt Nedda, let Philo remain here – let her remain here in the house if you like," Jewel cried with magnanimous eagerness. "I'll be your companion at Saratoga! Besides, I've been there before; I know my way about. In Saratoga, Aunt, Philo will have got herself into the wrong pew . . ."

"Philo is going with me," said Nedda Maitland, and would allow no more to be said on the subject.

The season at Saratoga Springs did not begin in real earnest until August first. Nedda Maitland had little difficulty in securing her suite a few days earlier than she planned, though the management of Congress Hall, who knew her of old, had to expel an upstart family from Cincinnati into quarters that were decidedly inferior.

Mrs. Maitland had taken accommodations on the fourth floor, overlooking not Broadway (which in season was every bit as congested and noisy as the *real* Broadway in New York), but the quiet garden behind the hotel. She had two parlors, four bedchambers, and a bath. Jewel had begged her aunt to let her remain in that suite rather than go to her parents, who were lodged in the less fashionable Clarendon, down on the other side of Broadway. This Nedda Maitland finally allowed, though it meant that all three maids in attendance must share the fourth and smallest bedchamber.

Saratoga Springs was a peculiar place: a hamlet in the tame landscape of the upper Hudson River valley, to which some fifteen thousands of America's rich, fashionable, handsome, ambitious, flirtatious, and mischievous flocked every summer, ostensibly for the opportunity to guzzle vast quantities of mineral water from the town's numerous springs. It was as if Fifth Avenue had been laid down onto the Central Park. Yet there were differences. To begin with, there were no poor in Saratoga. The very bootblacks and newsboys of the place made more money than clerks of ten years' experience in New York. And, quite unlike New York, the place was clean, with walks swept every morning and every night, where white clothes remained white for more than an hour, where one smelled grass and flowers – not horses and rotting vegetables. Saratoga – it was the common remark – was Eden fenced in.

A morning at Saratoga was spent digesting the vast hotel breakfast, visiting a mineral spring for a beaker of water, walking up and down Broadway, changing clothes, speaking to the same people one was likely to have spoken to on that other Broadway the week before, making discreet bets on the afternoon's race, pointing out the famous and the rich, and the mistresses of the famous and the rich, looking in at Tiffany's, stopping to hear the orchestra in the gazebo on the lake, wondering whether it wouldn't have been cheaper to go to Long Branch, scraping an introduction to those who have never invited you to their homes in New York, playing croquet in the hotel gardens, planning excursions to Lake George and Mount McGregor, having your fortune told at the Indian encampment, visiting the picture gallery, or changing your clothes *again* in order to astonish your acquaintance with the extent of your wardrobe.

The afternoons were quieter. Half the temporary population of the place went to the racetrack, and the other half fell asleep in their rooms or in hammocks that were strung out every day at two o'clock.

There were balls and dancing every evening, concerts on the lake, entertainments professional and amateur, small card parties, amorous walks down the moonlit lanes, more changes of dress, a great deal of gambling in the men's clubs, innocent trysts and less innocent assignations, engagements, demands for "bills" (bills of divorcement), confidence trickery, snares and traps for the innocent, drunken revelry, even a few prayers, parties got up for overdressed children, cigars smoked on the piazzas and diamonds flashed beneath the gaslights in salons, oysters and lobsters late, champagne slings, weary maids looking out of windows at the fashionable world below, gossip about those newly arrived or recently departed, and a final sinking into bed with the reflection that pleasure was an exhausting affair.

Chapter 40

AN OLD ACQUAINTANCE

Nedda Maitland rightly calculated that Saratoga was the very place, the very thing, to take Philo's mind away from the terrible incident on Christopher Street. And Philo was perfectly willing to be comforted. Given the slightest excuse, Philomela Drax was a young woman who tended toward cheer. It was only a pity that so very little in her life had been an encouragement to that propensity. She did not feel guilty for having been the indirect cause of Ella LaFavour's death, any more than she had allowed herself to feel responsible for the deaths of her grandfather and mother. On the narrow shoulders of Katie Slape that burden rested entirely.

Nedda Maitland never mentioned the business, wishing Philo not to be reminded of it. Jewel never learned of it and still supposed it was some affair of the heart which had so agitated Philo on the Saturday before they all left for Saratoga. The case of the Jepsons had been followed in the papers, and a few of these articles Jewel had read, but Philo's name had not entered into them. Nedda Maitland's maids knew of the circumstances of course – maids always do know of such matters – but their loyalty was to Philo rather than to Jewel, and they said nothing either.

Jewel all but abandoned her parents at the Clarendon. She infrequently took meals with them, scarcely nodded her head to them when they passed on Broadway, refused to accompany them to the racetrack, and only now and then, for form's sake, begged money from them for certain purchases. She saw that Jacob and Caroline Varley's stature in the shifting Saratoga community was considerably below that of Nedda Maitland, and even below that of Philomela Drax, Nedda Maitland's acknowledged companion. There were wives of rich men who would talk for a quarter of an hour with Philo of an evening but wouldn't exchange nods with Caroline Varley in the street.

Caroline Varley saw this with anger and wondered at her daughter's consorting with that "female counter-jumper."

"Philomela has never worked behind a counter, Ma," sniffed Jewel.

"She's poor as dirt, that girl," said Jacob Varley.

"She has the money she got from selling her house to Mr. MacMamus," said Jewel pointedly, and her father said nothing more on *that* subject.

"She's not a fit companion for you, Jewel. And besides, you never liked her before in New Egypt."

"It's different now, Ma," said Jewel placidly. "Aunt Nedda has taken her on. I don't like it, I suppose, but there's nothing to be done. I'm pleasant to her for Aunt Nedda's sake."

"I hope Nedda remembers you in her will," said Jacob Varley.

"I hope Nedda remembers you to her son," said Caroline.

"When is he returning?" asked Jacob. "Young men gallivanting . . ." he breathed with disapproval. "He ought to have married somebody before he went off like that. What if something has happened to him?"

"He'll be back in September."

"Very annoying," said Caroline, "that he should not join his mother in Saratoga. Very annoying that we should not see him this season. By the time that he returns from South America, you will be in New Egypt again."

"I hope, Ma, that Aunt Nedda asks me to stay with her in New York for a few months."

"Do you think she might?" Caroline asked eagerly.

"I've dropped a hint with Philomela," said Jewel, who had adopted the true form of Philo's name in imitation of Nedda Maitland.

"Ah!" breathed Jacob Varley with disgust. "She has so much influence with Nedda? This is dangerous. Jewel, I will advise you. Persuade Nedda to rid herself of that girl."

Jewel shrugged. "She won't do it, and if I said anything against her Aunt Nedda'd rid herself of me. Pa, you don't know how Philo's tied her up."

"*I'll* speak to Nedda," he said.

"No, Pa!" cried Jewel. She had but a poor opinion of her father's persuasive power. He much more often offended when he intended only to ingratiate himself. "Let me see what I can do. Lord knows I want her out of that house by the time that Cousin Henry returns."

The remainder of that afternoon – this conversation had taken place over luncheon – Jewel cast about for a way in which to alienate Nedda Maitland from Philo. Philo was absurdly faithful to Nedda, and never spoke but her gratitude and affection for the woman. Philo's conduct in all matters was exemplary, and there was not a hook on which she could be caught. Jewel decided she must wait her opportunity – surely something would present itself before the end of August.

Something presented itself that very evening.

Mrs. Maitland was visiting an old friend at the Grand Hotel, and Philo and Jewel sat together in the grand salon of the Congress Hall, underneath hanging baskets of fragrant jasmine, playing draughts.

Jewel didn't like draughts, and Philo was playing only at her friend's insistence. The game was merely an alternative to sitting with their hands crossed in their laps, waiting to be approached by anyone desirous of speaking to them. Etiquette at Saratoga did not allow young women of their age to thrust their company upon others.

Jewel knew everything there was to know about their fellow guests in the hotel. She would lean over the draughts board, cast her eyes to the left, and say in a low voice, moving her lips scarcely at all, "See that gentleman in the red waistcoat? Fought a duel in Spartanburg, South Carolina, killed a man, and will never be allowed to see his mother again. He told a man at Morrissey's yesterday that when the season was over he was going to put a bullet through his brain."

The gentleman in question was laughing until he was purple in the face at something a rich married woman had whispered to him behind her fan.

"And see that lady over there," said Jewel, flicking her eyes to the right. "She was the *young cousin* of Mr. James Onions, the man who owns one-third of the Lackawanna Railroad outright."

"Young cousin?" Philo repeated, looking out for the young woman of whom Jewel spoke but not being able as yet to see her.

"That is to say, she stayed in his suite, as a young cousin might do – but this morning at ten o'clock, he discovered another *young cousin* who was more to his liking – they were placing bets upon the same horse, called, I believe, Country Matters – and this first *young cousin* has been turned out. She looks desperately desperate, if you ask me."

"I still don't know whom you mean," said Philo.

"*I* wouldn't remain here under those circumstances."

"Jewel, I trust you will never find yourself so inconveniently placed," laughed Philo.

"She's right over there, by the table with the newspapers on it."

Philo saw her now, but the lady in question had her back to the two young women at the draughts table. But when she turned, Philo was shocked to find hers a familiar face.

Philo held up her hand to Jewel to quiet her and temporarily halt their game. She cast about in her memory for the name that corresponded to that slightly remembered visage.

In a moment she had it. To Jewel's intense astonishment Philo walked directly across the room and approached the distraught lady, who was surreptitiously examining a railway schedule of departing trains.

"Ida?" said Philo quietly.

The woman looked up startled. "Who are you?"

"You're Ida Yearance, aren't you?"

"That is not my name in the register. I am the cousin of Mr. Onions. My name is—"

She stopped suddenly and stared at Philo.

"I don't know you," she said sharply, and headed for the doors that opened onto the piazza.

Philo gently caught her arm. Ida tried to pull away but Philo did not let her go.

Ida Yearance looked around her. Everyone in the room appeared to have left off conversation and games, put down newspapers and fancywork to look at them. Under the protection of powerful Mr. Onions, Ida Yearance had been tolerated in the public rooms of the hotel; but now that she had been cast aside, she was universally shunned and abhorred.

"Come with me onto the piazza," said Philo in a low voice.

Ida nodded and the two moved out of the room. Philo glanced back once at Jewel's wide-open mouth.

They did not stop on the piazza, for there were too many persons lingering there in the warm evening, but descended the steps into the hotel garden. Philo pointed to the fountain, and they approached it. The noise of the rushing water would cover their conversation.

"Ida Yearance, you stole a thousand dollars from me," said Philo abruptly.

"No!"

"At Mrs. Classon's on West Thirteenth Street. On the fifth of May. It was all the money I had in the world."

Ida looked steadily at Philo. "I guess it wasn't," she said harshly. "I guess it left you so destitute you had no alternative but to spend a month in the country."

"I was fortunate in finding someone to take care of me. If it had not been for that, I would have been left destitute."

Ida smiled grimly. "Does he beat you? Mr. Onions beat me."

"No! I have honest employment! I am employed as secretary to Mrs. Nedda Maitland."

Ida shrugged. "What do you want from me?"

"You stole my money!"

"You want it back?" Ida laughed. "I haven't three dollars to my name."

"You spent so much in three months?"

"I spent so much in two weeks. I bought new clothes, I rented me rooms up on Thirtieth Street – first floor front, looking out right on the Fifth Avenue mansions. I took out a few advertisements in the papers, and I met a few high-toned gentlemen, who introduced me to other high-toned gentlemen, who took me out for lobster and champagne and drove me through the park in their carriages. And last week I came to Saratoga in a private railway car – and tonight I don't even have the fare back to New York. Would you like your money in gold, notes, or a draught on a private bank?"

Philo was silent.

Ida seated herself on the edge of the fountain. The air was warm and heavy with the spray, the scent of the garden's flowers, and an impending rain.

As Philo looked at her, all the brash effrontery seemed to drain from Ida's face. "What will you do then?"

Ida looked up at Philo with a slow, grim smile. "I'll go back in there and take up a collection for myself, what else? I'm certain you noticed how many kindly looks I received. Or perhaps I can find a position as nurserymaid, if there's a lady who'll allow me to touch her children. Or maybe I'll just go for a little swim at the bottom of a mineral well." She turned to Philo with a smile. "You're the lucky one, you know. Three months ago, I may have taken all your money – there's no reason for me to deny it now – but look at you! Here at Saratoga, dressed all in white, sitting in the salon of the Congress Hall, with your virtue intact. And I'll bet you've got more than three dollars in your porte-monnaie."

"I don't know," said Philo after a few moments. "I'll see."

She drew it out, opened it, and withdrew two ten-dollar bank notes, which she pressed into Ida's hand.

Ida looked at her strangely. Philo thought there was almost rage in her eyes. "Why are you doing this? Do you forgive me?" she demanded sarcastically.

"For stealing all the money I had in the world?" said Philo. "For leaving me destitute in a strange city? No, I don't forgive you for that. You were heartless. I'm giving you those bills for myself."

"What do you mean – 'for yourself'?"

"I realize how easily I could have been put in your position. If it had not been for the kindness of my protector, I don't doubt I would have ended up in some similar straits. Only I doubt my dress would have been so nice."

Ida paused a moment, then she said, "Take care of your good fortune, Philo. Hug it to you." She snapped open her reticule and slipped the bills inside it. "I won't thank you," she said, rising. "I never thank the lucky ones."

She hurried away into the night. Philo never saw her or heard of her again.

Turning to go back into the hotel salon, Philo noticed Jewel on a bench that was wrapped about an ancient elm.

Jewel smiled. "An old acquaintance . . . ?"

Chapter 41

JEWEL'S SCHEME

Jewel couldn't wait to get to Nedda Maitland with the tale of Philo's speaking in close confidence (for thirteen minutes, according to the watch pinned to Jewel's breast) with a woman who was scarcely better than a *nymphe du pavé*. She rose very early the next morning – she had slept scarcely at all the night before thinking how soon she would supplant Philo in her aunt's estimation, affection, and will – and knocked softly at the door of Nedda's chamber.

Nedda was already dressed – though breakfast wouldn't be served for half an hour – and seated at her desk before the window.

"Are you awake already?" asked Nedda in some wonder, for her niece was neither an early nor an uncomplaining riser.

"I am here on a very distressing errand," said Jewel sadly, shaking her head.

"I am sorry to hear it," replied Nedda. "Please sit down, Jewel, and tell me what has upset you."

"I fear that *you* will be the one to be upset. I don't really know but that I should keep it to myself . . ."

"I have borne much . . ." said Nedda drily. Jewel was more easily read than she would have been pleased to know. "Say what you have to say, Jewel."

"Last night, in the salon," Jewel began hurriedly, with no trace of the reticence she had just professed, "I was sitting at draughts with Philomela, when into the center of the room, brazen as brass, walks Mr. Onions's 'young cousin.'" Jewel affected to blush. "You know what I should mean to say, Aunt Nedda. She was thrown off by him at the racetrack yesterday morning and then expected that everything should go along quite the same for her when she was no longer under his protection. I turned my head away and cautioned Philo not to look – such women often attempt to insinuate themselves with respectable persons. But, to my complete astonishment, Philo stands from the table, upsetting *all* the draughts, and walks directly over to her, takes her arm, and strolls with her out onto the terrace. Lord, Aunt Nedda, I was ashamed to witness it! Philo took her arm as if she had been a duchess! I blushed for *you*."

Nedda Maitland made no reply, but indicated that Jewel should continue with her narration.

"Of course when I had recovered my composure, and when I was tolerably certain that *I* wasn't being watched after by the entire salon, I slipped out by another door and strolled onto the piazza. The moon was shining, and I could see them standing by the fountain in the garden, talking, intimate as you please. I wouldn't see that again for a dollar bill! And before I had time to shut my eyes, Philo rummaged in her porte-monnaie and pulled out a stack of notes thick as my thumb and handed 'em to her. Aunt Nedda," said Jewel in a solemn voice, "Philomela Drax gave hard cash to the fallenest woman in the entire hotel."

Nedda Maitland was silent a moment, then asked her niece, "Did you get close enough to hear any of their conversation?"

Jewel shook her head eagerly no. "Though I tried. I snuck round the other side of the fountain, but the water kept me from hearing anything, and if I had got closer, they would have seen me."

"The lady to whom Philomela was speaking—"

"Lady!"

"—is called Ida Yearance," said Nedda blandly. "She was a former acquaintance of Philomela's, temporarily embarrassed for funds. The deficiency was made up by Philomela."

"You already knew of this?"

"Philomela came to me last evening."

"And she admitted that she was acquainted with that woman?"

"Yes," replied Nedda imperturbably. "A laundress once in my employ murdered two of her children – twins, I believe – but that does not make me an accessory to the crime. Philomela was acting entirely out of charity. I was pleased to recompense her for the money that she gave Miss Yearance."

"*Miss . . .*" sneered Jewel.

"It is very early in the morning to be casting such large stones, Jewel. By the end of the day you may find that the favor has been returned, with interest."

"What do you mean, Aunt Nedda?"

"Jewel," said Nedda in a serious tone, "what was your motive in coming to me with this tale?"

"I merely wanted to let you know what sort of young woman you had in your employ."

"Did you imagine that I was not well acquainted with Philomela?"

"Philomela was consorting with a notorious – *courtesan!* And was seen by the entire hotel to have done so! You will not be able to remain here!"

"I think I may all the same," said Nedda. "However, Jewel, since the incident seems so greatly to have affected you, I think you may wish to join your parents at the Clarendon."

Jewel stammered, "No, Aunt Nedda, I—"

"Go now," said Nedda. "You'll probably find Jacob and Caroline at breakfast. I'll have your things packed and sent over. Come now, kiss me good-bye, and I'm very sorry that you feel so strongly about this that you're obliged to leave me."

"No, I—"

"Hush! Not another word, Jewel. I couldn't bear to think that I had persuaded you to compromise your principles in remaining in the same rooms with Philomela. No doubt we'll meet one another on Broadway – though since I'll be in Philomela's company, you may not wish to acknowledge me . . ."

Jewel was mortified that her plan should have come out so contrarily to expectation. At the Clarendon, she suppressed the matter of Ida Yearance and told her parents only that Philo had contrived, through a series of elaborate lies, to remove her from her aunt's good graces and from her suite.

"That girl is a worm!" cried Caroline Varley.

"I'll speak to Nedda," said Jacob pompously.

"No!" cried Jewel anxiously. "Say nothing about it, please. Aunt Nedda will quickly come to see that she's nurturing a viper. Please, I want to leave Saratoga, I want to go back to New Egypt."

"We have these rooms two weeks longer!" cried Jewel's mother.

Jacob Varley, however, on whom the expenses of Saratoga were a drain, eagerly took up his daughter's suggestion.

Father and daughter carried the matter, and that evening the Varleys paid a farewell call to Nedda Maitland. Caroline wanted to be cold, Jewel wanted to be sullen, Jacob would have liked to carry himself with offended dignity – but Nedda Maitland was rich, and the Varleys could not risk cutting themselves off from her.

"Ah, Nedda," said Jacob, "shall Jewel visit you in New York this autumn? I know you once strongly suggested such a plan."

"I don't know when I shall return to the city, Jacob, and when I'm back, I don't know how long I shall remain. I suspect my attention will be taken up with Henry, and I fear I would neglect Jewel."

"Jewel would love to see her Cousin Henry again," said Caroline.

"Yes!" cried Jewel, almost her first word that evening.

"Henry will be very pleased to see all of you, I'm sure," replied Nedda. "But when he returns, I think I will keep him to myself for a little while. I have never been apart from him for so long as this, and I miss his presence terribly."

It was apparent to the Varleys that Nedda wasn't to be pushed in this matter. They took their leave, and at the station Jewel wept with frustration.

All her scheming had had the effect only of leaving Philo Drax alone in the field, to acquire without opposition the affection and preferment of Nedda Maitland, and perhaps even the love of Nedda's son Henry.

Chapter 42

LAST DAYS AT SARATOGA SPRINGS

Neither Nedda nor Philo was sorry to see Jewel leave Saratoga, though the two women were left entirely in one another's company for the remainder of their stay at the Springs. They had planned to remain until the fourth of September, a Monday, when all the rest of the fashionable world would return to New York and repopulate the city's streets.

The final few days of the season were to be riotous with balls, soirées, special races, monster croquet parties, mammoth boating excursions and the like, and Nedda intended that she and Philo should see and be seen, do and have done, as the gayest inhabitants of that place.

Philo and Nedda Maitland had found in one another a perfect daughter and a perfect mother. Nedda was handsome, elegant, rich, and unselfish – everything that Philo would have wished Mary Drax to be, for that unhappy woman's sake as well as for Philo's own. And Philo was what such a mother would want in her daughter: handsome too, poised, self-reliant, trustworthy, a fit companion under all circumstances. Neither intended, if it could be helped, to let the other go.

On Friday afternoon when they had lately returned from watching a croquet match between the inhabitants of the Congress Hall and the lodgers at the Grand Hotel, and Nedda was lying on a lounge that had been pushed up directly beneath the windows, there was a knock at the door of the suite.

Philo being closest went to open it. In the doorway stood a tall man with a vast auburn beard, dressed all in white – the white in great contrast to his sunburnt brow and hands.

"Yes, please – what's wanted?" asked Philo politely.

The man did not answer immediately, but stared at her with furrowed, puzzled brows. She could not make out the expression of his mouth beneath his beard. At last he said, "Why were you not on Thirteenth Street?"

The voice she recognized. "Mr. Maitland!" she cried. "Why are you here?"

"I think *I* deserve an answer to the same question," he laughed. "I am here to visit Mother. But why are *you* here?"

"I am your mother's secretary," said Philo with a becoming blush.

"That was not to be expected," replied Henry with some amusement. "May I walk in, please?"

She had stood blocking his way, but immediately stepped aside, again blushing.

"How did you come to be acquainted with Mother?" he asked.

In a few words Philo told him.

"That was remarkable fortune," he commented. "For you both, I suspect. Where is Mother?"

Philo knocked at Nedda's chamber, and at that lady's summons, opened the door. Henry walked in, and Philo closed the door behind him, not wishing to intrude upon the reunion of the mother and her son.

Yet she was called in almost immediately.

"Mother," Henry was saying, "this was the young lady I told you about just before I went away – the young lady I wanted you to take particular notice of."

"Yes, but you neglected to give me either her name or her street and number."

"You found one another easily enough, it appears."

"Philomela has had many trials since you left, Henry."

Henry's brow clouded.

"Have you not protected her?"

"Notwithstanding . . ." said Nedda.

"What has happened to you, Miss Philo?" asked Henry.

"Please . . ." said Philo with a smile. "Tell us about your voyage. Is Brazil an unending jungle, or is it an unending plain?"

And so the afternoon was consumed. Henry related his voyage and sojourn in South America, and later Philo gave a brief recital of her troubles: the theft of her money, the discovery of the Slapes on Christopher Street, the death of Ella LaFavour, and the disappearance of the murderous family.

"Your recent history is considerably more exotic than mine," said Henry. "I was only in South America." Then he added seriously, "What are the chances that the Slapes will be found and tried?"

"Not very good, I fear," said Philo. "They aren't clever, but they are cunning."

"Please," said Nedda, "we are here together for the first time in five months; let us speak of pleasant things." And she told all over again her chance meeting with Philo on the Broadway stage.

Just when Nedda had decided to dismiss her son to unpack and dress for dinner, he held up his hand. "One more thing," he said. "Do you think I have returned from a four-months' voyage empty-handed, Mother?" He took from the pocket of his coat a wooden box, ornately carved of some rare wood. He handed it to Nedda, who found inside it a diamond necklace which quite outshone anything that was on display in Tiffany's cases there at Saratoga. When Philo had admired it, Henry turned to her and from another pocket withdrew a smaller, plain case. It contained a necklace of coral with matching earrings.

"These are not for me!" she protested.

"I went with these to Thirteenth Street, but you were not there. I confess I was angry with you then—"

"Angry? Why?" Philo asked with some alarm.

"Because you were gone and had left no word where I might find you."

"Ahh," said Philo, "but I was with your mother. . . ."

"I did not know that," Henry reminded her. "At any rate these are for you."

That evening the three went off to a ball at the Columbian Hotel, and Henry danced with Philo and his mother all evening long. He was an object of much comment, for his beard and his sunburnt face forestalled immediate recognition, and he had not been in the Saratoga habit for several years past.

By morning however, it was known all over Saratoga that Henry Maitland – whose eligibility was treasured by Every Mamma from Washington Square to the Reservoir – had come to Saratoga to visit his mother. Every Mamma was enthusiastic, but Every Daughter pointed out that at the ball he hadn't even looked at a girl other than Philomela Drax. Every Daughter didn't even have the comfort of seeing Jewel Varley's discomfort, she who had always boasted the inside track with her cousin.

More than the coral he had brought her from Brazil, Philo treasured the thought that Henry, so soon after his return to New York, had gone searching for her on West Thirteenth Street.

These last three days at Saratoga were a dream and a delight for Philo. All the plans that she and Nedda had made now included Henry, who was as faithful to them as Philo was to Nedda. Philo and Henry's engagement began to be talked about as almost a sure thing. It was fortunate that Philo heard none of this gossip, for she would instantly have withdrawn herself from consideration.

After all, she was poor, and Henry Maitland was very rich. She had a privileged position in the Maitland household as secretary to his mother, and she would never have allowed herself to betray Nedda Maitland by setting herself up as a match for her son. It would be only a reversal of the common tale of the apprentice who married his master's daughter. Philo felt the impropriety almost as strongly as the Varleys would have.

But with the conviction that she would never be to Henry more than his mother's secretary – she felt she knew him well enough to be convinced that he would never betray Nedda Maitland either – Philo allowed herself full enjoyment of Henry's company. She was stirred to be his partner on the floor, felt privileged to walk by his side down Broadway, was more edified by his idle conversation than by the sermons of Henry Ward Beecher.

It was perfectly apparent to every other female in Saratoga –

from the governor's wife to Jim Fiske's mistress to the laundress of the hotel – that Philomela Drax was in love with Henry Maitland.

Chapter 43

PHILO'S VOW

Philo did not regret leaving Saratoga. The sylvan beauty of the place was too much at odds with the studied artificiality of New York fashion. So far as opulence of dress went Jewel Varley herself was scarcely a contender at Saratoga, and such vagaries were more suited to a city, Philo thought, which itself was studied and artificial. And too, at Saratoga she felt useless. All of Nedda's correspondence and all of Nedda's errands never required more than an hour's effort – and Philo had an inkling what a month at Saratoga might cost. She wished to return to New York, where she might do more for Nedda and where her upkeep as an employee would be less.

On the morning of the day they were to leave, while the maids were packing their bags, Philo knocked on the door of Mrs. Maitland's parlor and was admitted. Nedda turned and was about to speak, but stopped when she saw Philo's appearance.

"Dear, you look haggard," she said at last. "Are you so very sorry to leave Saratoga?"

Philo shook her head. "Bad dreams," she replied. "No more than that."

"Well," said Nedda with a smile, "this is morning, and dreams do not pursue us beyond the pillow."

"Mrs. Maitland," said Philo slowly, "last night I dreamt that Katie Slape murdered you. I dreamt that she killed you with a razor that was tied to her hand."

"Of course you dream, Philomela," said Nedda hastily, but the image was discomforting to her, "and we all dream terrible dreams. But you needn't—"

"And I woke up," Philo went on, "and I realized that Katie Slape had murdered the three people in the world who meant anything to me: my grandfather, my mother, and Ella LaFavour. Now I have only you, and I was frightened that Katie would come and . . ."

Nedda shook her head.

". . . and take you away too," finished Philo bravely.

"She won't. She doesn't know I'm alive."

Philo laughed. "You don't know Katie Slape. There's nothing she doesn't know, nothing she can't find out. I think we ought to be on our guard," she concluded soberly.

"They're running from the law," argued Nedda. "They're fugitives. They've stolen your thirty thousand dollars and they've killed at least ten persons. They've not the time to come to Saratoga and find us out. And we'll be just as safe on Twenty-sixth Street. They dare not return to New York. The police know them, know their names, know their appearance. They—"

"They don't think like you or I, Mrs. Maitland. If they were concerned with the punishments of the law, would they have murdered seven women and a child in their own house? Would they have left me behind at Parrock Farm alive? Would Katie have butchered my mother, whom she had never even seen before, when they already possessed the fortune that mother was heir to? What they've done – in Goshen, and New Egypt, and New York – none of it makes any sense. Even supposing you and I were criminals, we would never act in the same manner. They're not rational – and that's what frightens me."

Nedda's brows contracted. "You're still frightened? I didn't know . . ."

"The police will never find them," Philo went on feverishly. She hadn't spoken about these matters since Ella's death, but now her anger and her fear spilled out. "I've been reading the papers every day. There's a report of a girl in Kentucky who does card tricks, and they go after her, ready to collar Katie Slape disguised as a Quaker. Hannah's in Mexico and John's in Canada, trapping. They split up, they stayed together, one of 'em's dead of the fever, one was drowned in a sack like an unwanted kitten. The Slapes won't let themselves be found – but they'll find me! They'll come after me the way they came after my mother."

Nedda drew back stiffly, but Philo laid her perspiring hand on

Nedda's arm. There was a wildness in Philo's eye that Nedda had never seen before.

"They're demons!" whispered Philo. "A family of devils out of a smoky hell come to lay waste to me and mine. My grandfather's face was smeared with the soil that choked him to death. The walls of the room where I slept every night for eighteen years I saw covered in my mother's blood. In all my life I had one friend my own age, and two months ago I saw her brains spilled out on the stair carpet that the Slapes had worn down with their footsteps. I've been poor all my life – I've thought myself rich if I had a nickel in my pocket that didn't have to be set aside to pay the rent – and the Slapes stole from me thirty thousand dollars in hard cash! The law doesn't know all this – all the law knows is a dead girl on the staircase and seven persons dead beneath the cellar floor – but the Slapes know well enough what they've done to me. And the harm they've done already is inducement enough for them to harm me more. I'm here at Saratoga with you and Henry, and every night we dine together, and every night we dance, and I smile and I know I've never been so happy in my life – then I remember the Slapes. And I think: 'Katie Slape may murder me tomorrow.' I've made a vow – and that vow is to see every one of them dead. I'll turn hound, and I'll track 'em to their lairs. I'll see 'em hanged, and that night I'll sleep at the foot of the gallows. Their rotting bodies will smell sweet to me!"

For several moments Philo and Mrs. Maitland stood opposite one another, stock still and staring; then Nedda held out her arms, and Philo fell into them, sobbing.

Chapter 44

THE WEST SHORE LINE

Philo remained sequestered with Nedda Maitland an hour more, by which time she had regained her composure. They breakfasted with Henry, assisted the maids in packing, made one final promenade up and down Broadway, and departed that afternoon on one of seven scheduled trains on the West Shore Line to New

York. Besides three English cars with private compartments, there were four regular passenger cars for the accommodation of those whose drive toward economy, necessitated by a month spent at Saratoga, began immediately upon leaving the place. An extra car for baggage had been added to the train. And despite the fact that the cars were filled with persons acquainted with one another, who had perhaps even been intimate at the Springs, there was little conviviality. It was always a sadness to leave Saratoga and a depression to return to the city. Yet even on this day of departure the custom of the place prevailed, and individuals wore their best – though by the end of the journey dresses were sure to be soiled and creased, suits rumpled and stained, and at the New York station the crowd would appear but a tawdry assemblage.

But if their fellow passengers seemed preoccupied – businessmen thought of their businesses and their wives of servants and provisions, and even children were subdued in remembering how quickly they must return to school – Philo and Henry and Nedda were cheerful enough.

They sat together in a comfortable compartment in the second English coach. Just after the cars had stopped at Albany to let off a band of legislators who had gone up for the last few days of races, Nedda declared her intention of visiting a friend whom she had glimpsed at the other end of the car. After squeezing Philo's hand, she opened the doors of the compartment and made her way down the narrow corridor. Philo was left alone with Henry.

She affected to watch the scenery, but she was very much aware of Henry's proximity. He leaned forward.

"Philo," he said, "I want to thank you for taking such care of Mother."

"There is nothing to thank me for. Mrs. Maitland took me in when I had no other recourse."

"She has no regrets, she tells me."

"I hope not."

"And I hope you will never leave her."

"She will have to chase me away with a broom."

He leaned back and seemed to consider for a moment.

"I have rooms on Stuyvesant Square," he said.

"I have heard so."

"They are dull. The square is noisy. I am thinking of giving them up and returning to Mother's house."

Philo blushed. "She would be very pleased to have you there, I know."

"Cousin Jewel," he said, "would not think it proper for you and me to live beneath the same roof."

Philo blushed deeper, but said nothing.

"Do *you* think it would be inappropriate?"

"I could very easily return to Mrs. Classon's," said Philo hesitantly. "I would not like to offend your family. . . ."

"Ah, but you couldn't return to Mrs. Classon's," said Henry. "I was just there on Friday, and Mrs. Classon told me herself that all her chambers were let. You *must* remain with mother."

Philo looked out the window a few moments.

"I am bound to say," said Henry, "that I also think it might be inappropriate. You are a pretty girl. It might lead to talk in the city."

Philo tried to hide her disappointment in him. Though it was a scruple she no doubt would have felt herself, it was a consideration that seemed mean in him. Certainly it *was* mean for him to speak the matter so boldly to her.

"There is a way around the difficulty, of course," he went on after a moment. She wished his beard weren't so thick, so that sometimes she could see the expression of his mouth behind it; his eyes were too well trained to give him away. "So that you can remain with Mother – I hardly think she can do without you now – and so that I may have a quieter place and better food than may be had on Stuyvesant Square."

"Yes?" asked Philo, watching the gleam of the Hudson River as it appeared now and then through the trees that flew by.

"You will have to marry me."

Philo jerked around.

"You are joking with me, Mr. Maitland," she said hotly.

He shrugged. "It *is* a solution. Even Jewel could hardly object to my remaining under the same roof with my wife. And besides, I'm very much in love with you."

His smile was so broad that even beneath his beard she could see it. And his eyes no longer hid their laughter.

But Philo couldn't laugh at all. "I can't marry you," she said.

"Why not?" Henry asked. "Have you entered upon a previous engagement? Do you object to sunburnt skin?"

"I owe too much to your mother," said Philo.

"Well," said Henry, "here is a way of discharging part of that debt – by taking me off her hands. I must warn you however, she is not likely to give you up – even if you did marry me. You'll end up taking care of both of us."

At this Philo did smile. She could not help but remember how she had always thought of herself as "taking care" of her mother – and of how she had hated the thought. And now she wondered what she wouldn't give to be in just such a place of responsibility toward Henry and Mrs. Maitland, although Henry's plea of helplessness was as spurious as Nedda's.

"I cannot go against your mother's wishes."

"How do you know what my mother's wishes are?"

"She cannot want her son to marry a penniless girl. I have nothing but what Mrs. Maitland has given me."

"You have the coral I brought from Brazil."

"And that would be the extent of my dowry. Mr. Maitland, I am your mother's employee, and I—"

"If you possessed your carpetbagful of bank notes the Slapes stole from you, would you consent to marry me?"

Philo stopped, confused. She couldn't truthfully answer no, and a yes would only get her deeper into this discussion, which was already embarrassing and might become painful.

"I see," said Henry after a moment. "You know, Philo, you are doing my mother a *dis*service."

"How?"

"By not giving her the opportunity to express her opinion."

"Please don't speak of this to her," Philo pleaded.

"My opinion of what?" asked Nedda Maitland, pulling farther apart the doors of the compartment.

"Mother," said Henry, "I've asked Philo to marry me, and she refuses on account of you."

"On account of me!" said Nedda in surprise, sitting down beside Philo. She took Philo's hand. "Is this true?"

"Mrs. Maitland, I—" She had no idea what to say.

"I realize," said Nedda, "that Henry is not good enough for you, but for that you mustn't blame me too much. He *will* go his own way."

Philo looked at Mrs. Maitland in astonishment.

"Mother, Philo took it upon herself to make objections in your name."

"What objections do I have, Philomela, to your marrying my son, pray?"

Philo was too confused to answer.

"Mother, Philo says that you say she is penniless, and you feel that if she married me she would be no better than a female fortune hunter."

Nedda laughed. "Philomela, is this true? Is this your low opinion of me?"

Between mother and son, Philo was lost, and could make no reply at all.

"Philomela, why should it possibly matter that you have no money? Haven't Henry and I between us enough to satisfy you?"

"Yes!" cried Philo. "Oh, but that's not what I meant, I—"

"Now that we have disposed of *my* objection to the match, I suppose we ought to get over your own. I can't suppose that you actually love Henry – I think only a mother could love him – but you might see your way, as a favor to me, or even considering it part of your secretarial duties, to take him off my hands."

"My very words," said Henry.

Defeated, Philo smiled.

"I do love him though," she said softly.

"Good!" cried Henry. "Now how quickly can we be married?"

"Wait, Henry," said Nedda, "there is the marriage settlement still to be agreed upon."

"Settlement?" asked Philo.

"Ah, yes," said Nedda, "as you are an orphan, I suppose I must stand in for your parents. And I must have recompense for giving you up – you *are* a daughter to me, you know. . . ."

"How much do you want, Mother?"

"More than you have, Henry."

"Well, then, I suppose I can't afford her. Can't you be per-suaded simply to give her over to me?"

"No," said Nedda.

"Then," said Henry, "you will have to continue to live with Mother, Philo. I suppose I'll join you, if Mother doesn't charge an exorbitant chamber-rent."

"I'm a reasonable woman," said Nedda.

"Then we're all to be together?" asked Philo incredulously.

"Well," said Henry, "neither Mother nor I will give you up, so it must be that way, I suppose."

"Now for the wedding," said Nedda.

"As quickly as possible," said Henry.

"Perhaps I should ask the conductor if there is a minister aboard the cars." Henry and Philo smiled. "But if you will wait a little longer," Nedda went on, "I will help Philomela to purchase her trousseau and arrange for the wedding."

"Shall we have Cousin Jewel for a bridesmaid?" asked Henry mischievously.

"She might not accept the honor," said Philo, and could not repress a smile at her rival's expense.

Mrs. Maitland had brought a small case with her onto the cars which had been placed beneath Philo's seat. Mrs. Maitland requested her to bring it out now.

As she opened it, Nedda said, "Philomela dear, I don't know yet what your dress will be like, but when you're married, I want you to wear these." She held up the diamonds that Henry had brought from South America. "If Henry doesn't mind my giving them away so quickly, I'd like to make them my wedding gift to you."

"No, they are too valuable, Mrs. Maitland!"

"Philomela, when I die you and Henry will have everything I own. Please let me have the pleasure of giving these to you now."

Philo humbly thanked Mrs. Maitland for her gift. The dia-monds were put back into the case, which contained the rest of Mrs. Maitland's valuable jewelry, and the case replaced beneath the seat.

The next hour was taken up in a continuation of the conversation. Philo discovered that Henry's proposal had come as no surprise at all to his mother, who had quickly found out the secret of his affection, taxed him with it, encouraged him in his decision to marry Philo, and had even left the compartment on purpose to give him the opportunity of speaking to her alone.

The cars had just passed through Highland – after Albany the train had become an express – and they were two-thirds of the way back to New York. It was dark outside, and the lamp inside the compartment had been lighted by an obliging trainboy, who had also left them sandwiches. It seemed to Philo that the greatest part of the happiness she had experienced in the entire of her life had been concentrated into this single railway journey. She wished it never to end.

Then, quite suddenly and without premonition, there was a terrible jolt. Their exclamations of surprise were swallowed by a second, even greater jolt, and then they were thrown from their seats with a terrible crash. The lamp was extinguished, and the car was tilted sideways. Philo fell heavily against Nedda Maitland, whose soft moan she heard beneath her.

In the midst of the appalling darkness, she heard the roar of rushing steam escaping from the boilers of the engines ahead, and an instant afterward, the heat from the furnaces permeated the compartment.

Then she heard Henry's agonized voice, "Mother! Philo! For God's sake, let's get out of here before we burn up!"

Chapter 45

THE OVERTURNED COACH

The engine Bristol lay on its side at the bottom of the deep ditch that ran parallel to the track. Its headlights still flared dreamily into the dark landscape ahead. The burning coal of its boiler had spilled out into the ditch, and all the brush there had caught fire. The steam from the broken pipes hissed toward heaven.

Directly behind the engine, the baggage car was only splinters. Here and there a burst trunk or case spilled Saratoga finery in the mud. The right side of the first English coach had been shirred off in the impact, and within there could be no one left alive. The second and third English coaches had been knocked together at an angle, then overturned into the ditch. One of them had caught fire, and the flames at one end of it were a fitful orange.

Passengers in the latter coaches, shaken and bruised and hysterical, were not otherwise injured.

Beneath the panoply of night, with the black Hudson moving silently and deep on the one side, and the dense Catskill forest on the other, the wrecked train gave more than a suggestion of Pandemonium. The white glare of the locomotive lamp, the fitful orange light of the smouldering fires, the will-o'-the-wispish gleams of the trainmen's lanterns as they searched out the injured and the dead provided a gloomy illumination. To the groaning and shrieking cries of the wounded, the bereaved added their own wailing anguish and convulsive hysteria.

Inside the compartment that had been occupied by Philo, Henry Maitland and his mother, all was dark. The coach leaned precariously to one side. Nedda and Philo, who had sat beside one another, were slid along the cushions and fell against the door of the compartment. The panes of ground glass in this door had shattered in the second jolt.

"Mother, are you all right?" Henry called anxiously. He had kept his place on the opposite side of the compartment.

"I'm here," said Mrs. Maitland, "but I think I've cut myself on some glass."

"Take my hand," said Philo, and reached through the pitchy darkness. "I'm going to pull you away from the door."

Philo felt her hand taken, but Nedda's grasp was weak; and when Philo inched upward on the seat, intending to pull Nedda away from the door, Nedda cried out in terrible sudden pain.

"Mother!"

"I think I've broken a bone in my leg," she said weakly. "Philomela, please don't pull me."

"Mother," said Henry, "we're going to have to get you out of this coach. Do you feel the heat? I'm afraid that the stove at the front of the car may have overturned."

"Henry," said Philo, calling him by that name for the first time, "try to open the doors."

She heard Henry begin to move about, but just as he did so there was another jolt and shaking of the car. It was tilted even farther on its side. Nedda was again precipitated against the door, and she shrieked in agony when her leg was caught beneath the seat.

"Mrs. Maitland!"

Philo reached out and took Nedda's arm.

"The coach is sinking deeper into the ditch," said Henry anxiously. "If the stove overturns completely, the car is certain to catch fire."

"Try the windows," said Philo.

But before Henry could do any more, the coach shifted once again. Now there was a terrible cracking and splintering of wood. Philo felt a great *whooosh* within inches of her head, and she realized that the roof of the car had buckled and broken. One of the timbers had fallen into the interior of their compartment. And with that release, the coach settled entirely on its side. The corridor that ran along the side of the coach had been torn away, and now the door of the compartment lay against the bottom of the ditch. The windows of the car looked directly up into the sky, and the roof was wedged against the muddy embankment.

"Mother!" called Henry, but now Nedda did not answer even with a groan.

By taking hold of the rack on which some of their luggage had been placed and swinging from it as she might have swung from the branch of a tree, Philo succeeded in getting her feet out of the hole that had been opened in the roof. Her feet were pressed into the mud of the embankment, but the aperture, dimly illumined from outside, was not large enough for her to get through.

With her feet still planted through it, and retaining her hold on the rack with one hand, she tore out more boards in the roof, and finally succeeded in squeezing herself out of the coach. She lay for several moments in the wedged space between the muddy embankment and the torn roof of the car. Within she could hear Henry moving about, reassuring an unresponsive Nedda; and about her on all sides, she heard the groans and pleadings of the injured. In that moment of dense confusion, when she wasn't sure where she was and hadn't any idea at all what she should do next, the moon rose over the lip of the embankment and shone down full upon her face.

She roused herself and climbed onto the side of the car, and through the unbroken windows peered down into the shattered interior of the coach.

Henry looked up at her. "Philo!" he called, in a calm sad voice. "Mother is dead."

The moon shone ghastly pale over Philo's shoulder and through the windows of the coach. At the bottom, against the shattered doors, lay Nedda Maitland, white and rigid.

Henry stood over her, his feet braced against the broken doors, leaning against the upended cushions. The timber that had fallen from the ceiling had mashed her head to jelly.

"Henry," Philo cried, beating upon the windows with her fist, "come out! come out!"

Henry turned aside and sought out the hole in the roof of the coach. When he put his arms through, Philo took them and quickly pulled him out.

She scrambled up the embankment before him, lay on its lip, and helped to draw him up to firm ground.

The affianced couple's first embrace was on the edge of that ditch, and the cries of the injured and the wailings of the bereaved all about them, with Nedda Maitland crushed to death ten feet away and the fitful fire of the first English coach lighting their faces.

"My poor Philo," said Henry, with his eyes tight shut, "ours will be a melancholy honeymoon. . . ."

Chapter 46

AFTER THE WRECK

In the first six cars of the train at least twenty-seven persons were dead, twice that many grievously hurt. In the last cars, the injuries were of a minor nature, with the exception of a ten-year-old girl who, standing in the aisle at the time of the crash, had fallen against the stove and suffered severe burns.

The employees of the railroad and the male passengers who were uninjured did what they could to rescue the wounded and extract the dead. The casualties lay moaning on cushions removed from the cars, and many fashionable doctors who had vacationed with their families in Saratoga and hadn't in a long while attended to such unfashionable injuries as these, were busy with improvised anaesthetics and bandages. The dead were placed on planks from the smashed baggage car. Lifted stark and white into the moonlight, they were carried away from the train and laid in rows beneath a vast elm. Their hands had been folded across their bosoms and their serious injuries covered with cloth pulled from broken trunks – but there was no disguising the violence of their deaths. Lanterns were hung from the lower branches, and by that light the survivors made a mournful inspection of their friends and families.

In the latter cars many persons moved about and talked in a dazed manner and seemed unable to comprehend the nature of the accident. They asked continually, "When *will* this train start . . . ?" Others, who thought themselves too shaken to be of material assistance, looked on in terrible fascination, gripping one another's hands and weeping.

Within an hour, carriages and farm vehicles began to arrive from Highland. A farmer living nearby had heard the noise of the accident, hurried to the scene, and immediately sent his eldest boy off on a fast horse to alert the town. The farmer remained, and it was through his efforts that the engineer of the train was dug from beneath the wreck of his machine, both legs shattered and his arms burned with steam but still alive and conscious.

In the second English coach, four men were at work extricating a man buried under the timbers of the wreck. He was in imminent danger of being crushed to death, but his cries – which could be heard from one end of the train to the other – were not from pain, but from his grief to be thus embedded atop the corpse of his wife.

Even on a train populated by the most prosperous families of New York – perhaps *especially* on such a train – there would be sharpers and those who prey upon society, the dangerous element who could dress as well as their neighbors but possessed not a penny that had not been taken from someone else's pocket. These men – and these women too – took advantage of the wreck, the darkness and confusion, to steal what they could from the wounded and the dead under pretense of helping them.

Thieves smiled into the faces of those they robbed, who, conscious but severely injured, could make neither articulate protest nor give resistance. By the morning, not a single object of value would be found on any of the dead.

However, when tolerable order was restored to the scene, this outright theft subsided. The ring of spectators, all eagerly watching, made detection probable, and besides, by that time almost everything of any worth had already been seized.

Two brakemen, when it seemed that the wounded were being sufficiently attended to, went ahead of the train a few feet and, by the light of the lantern still burning on the dying locomotive, examined the track. They discovered that the spikes had been drawn from the ties and the bolts from the fish joints. The train had been wrecked deliberately, and the perpetrator of that crime was responsible for some untold – and probably untellable – quantity of misery. This news quickly circulated among the passengers and added horror to a scene already possessed of a sufficiency of that quality.

Philo and Henry, as soon as they had recovered themselves a little, sought help to remove Nedda Maitland from the wreckage of the car, but no one could be found who would assist. People were distracted, or concerned only with their own families, or protested that the wounded were of greater moment than those who were past help. Philo and Henry removed Nedda themselves.

They found a lantern and reentered the compartment. They were dry-eyed, silent, and efficient. The timber that had crushed Nedda Maitland's head had fallen from the roof in the overturning of the car, but once this had been removed, Nedda's body slipped aside and slumped against the door. Her head was little more than a misshapen lump of bone and bloody flesh. Her limbs were already stiffened, and with her contorted hands she appeared to be supplicating them.

Philo shuddered, and Henry took off his jacket and draped it over his mother's head.

It was difficult to maneuver themselves in the overturned compartment, but Henry managed to lift his mother's body away from the door so that Philo could take her feet. Henry scrambled round behind Nedda's corpse, cutting himself several times on broken glass, and took his dead mother beneath her arms. Philo carefully backed out through the hole in the roof of the compartment.

They laid her out with the rest of the dead, stood before her for a few minutes, grasping one another's hands and weeping. Then they turned themselves to the succor of those who still lived, but the incessant labor of the next hour did nothing to alleviate their grief.

Henry worked with a shovel and his hands to free passengers still trapped in the overturned coaches. Philo went to the rear cars of the train and begged liquor for the relief of the injured, but very few were disposed to give up their flasks and bottles. Philo was shocked and indignant over this display of inhumanity.

Finally, when the carriages and wagons had arrived from Highland and the most seriously wounded had been taken away, Philo and Henry stood aside to rest for a few moments. Out of the way of the majority of the spectators, they stood silent, grim, and exhausted near the embankment where their own car had been wrecked.

They were startled by a noise within the overturned carriage.

"Someone is still inside," cried Henry, and began to slip down the bank.

Philo tried to hold him back. "Henry," she whispered, "that noise was from our compartment."

Just as Henry was sliding down the bank with the lantern in his hand, a black-sleeved arm emerged from the hole in the roof of the car. It carried the white bag in which Nedda Maitland had kept the diamonds that were Philo's wedding gift.

"Henry!" Philo cried in alarm.

Henry looked back, but because he did so he lost his footing and fell painfully against the wreckage of the car.

The man holding Nedda Maitland's bag emerged from the hole in the compartment roof. By the light of Henry's lantern Philo could see his face.

The man was John Slape.

Chapter 47

OLD BEN

"Stop him!" cried Philo, even in her first surprise at John Slape's presence, wondering if Katie and Hannah were nearby.

Henry, still dazed six feet below her, shook his head to clear it, then raised the lantern high. The lamp shone in the angered, frightened face of John Slape.

As he struggled to disengage his foot, which was caught beneath a spar of the roof, Henry said evenly, "Sir, I think you have mistaken a piece of my baggage for your own."

John Slape growled inarticulately and looked quickly around. Seeing no one but a young woman in the darkness at the top of the embankment, he put down the case and from the roof of the car pried up a board full of twisted nails.

Henry saw his intent and worked even more diligently to extricate himself, but John Slape was quicker. The board he held was about a yard in length; he carefully judged which side had more nails, turned that toward Henry, and then swung it with all the force he could muster at the young man's head.

When he was hit, Henry had just managed to free himself from the spar. He was knocked unconscious and slid down into the narrow space between the roof of the car and the embankment. He lay there wedged, unmoving.

John Slape threw the board down on the man he had assailed, picked up the bag, and began to climb the embankment.

Philo searched for a weapon. But at that place no wreckage of the train had been thrown, and the underbrush was not of sufficient size or weight. John Slape's arm appeared over the edge of the embankment. He set down the case and began to pull himself up.

Philo ran forward, and as soon as he had raised himself farther she kicked him, hard as she could, in the side of his head.

Yelling in pain, John Slape tumbled down into the embankment again.

Philo called out "Thief!" and help was not long in coming. The dead were laid out not far away, and the farmer who lived nearby and several of the employees of the train, uninjured, were keeping watch over them.

By the time they got there John Slape had recovered himself and, growling his anticipated revenge, was crawling back up toward Philo.

The farmer and the railroad employees had brought lanterns, and at Philo's direction they held them over the embankment. The light shone on John Slape's upturned face. His ear was bloody and all his hair matted with mud and blood.

"That man," said Philo, "was stealing the baggage from the compartment in which we were riding. This case is very valuable. He attacked my fiancé, who is still unconscious."

Philo had anticipated that she must say no more than this against John Slape. It was best not to confuse the matter by protesting that his evil nature and criminal deeds were already known to her.

John Slape, when he saw that he was to deal not with a single woman but with five or six men, hesitated. He slid down the embankment, landing against the inert form of Henry Maitland.

One of the conductors said, "I seen him hanging about the

dead. I seen him with his hand in their pockets. I chased him off, but lost him in the dark. . . ."

John Slape looked right and left, but the wreck itself blocked his escape. He might as well have been at the bottom of a well.

The ticket-taker of the Saratoga Springs train said, "I don't recall him from the train. I don't recall you, Mister!" he called out to John Slape.

"I do," said the farmer. "This man has been hanging about the neighborhood for two, three days. Asking my boy questions about the cars."

John Slape's eyes grew red in the light of the lantern.

"I was on the train," he said.

"No, you wasn't," the ticket-taker declared again.

One of the conductors concluded, "This is the man who wrecked the track."

"No!" protested John Slape.

"My girl, out to pick berries, seen him down here this very evening," said the farmer. "My girl said he was carrying a hammer and a bar."

"No!" protested John Slape, filled with terror.

"You was the one," said the head conductor grimly.

Philo cried, "Please get Henry up! He's badly hurt."

"We'll get 'em both up," said the farmer. He lay down on the edge of the embankment and reached down a hand. "Take it, Mister, come on up."

John Slape hesitated. The men on the edge of the embankment all smiled at him. Philo was frightened. She looked about her uneasily for Katie or Hannah.

John Slape took the proffered hand and was pulled up.

When at last he stood erect, one of the conductors hit him so hard in the stomach that he doubled over in pain. Jewels fell from the pockets of his coat onto the ground.

A grinning brakeman took a pistol from his pocket and aimed it at John Slape's head. "Move back a little, Mister, we've got an injured man here."

Two men went down into the embankment and lifted Henry from the wreckage. From above two more men grabbed him tenderly and set off immediately toward the place where the wounded were being loaded into wagons and carriages. "Come with us, Miss," said one of the men.

Philo followed immediately.

"Don't forget your case neither," said the other.

Philo ran back for the case of jewels, but she had to step within the circle of light afforded by the trainmen's lanterns to do so. She looked up once more at John Slape.

There was sudden recognition in his eyes.

"You!" he cried.

Philo took the case and ran off after Henry.

The two men carrying Henry called out after a wagon that had just started off toward Highland, crying, "Another one!"

The wagon stopped and, there being sufficient space for Henry, he was handed inside. A surgeon began immediately to examine his wounds.

Philo watched after the wagon as it moved down the moonlit road toward the north. There were only a few wounded remaining, and these were not serious cases. A number of the uninjured had decided to walk to Highland, and others had returned to the coaches. A number of men were beginning to clear the track of wreckage, and news was that another engine was on its way up from Marlboro. Yet the misery was not yet done. The wrecked engine still smouldered, and the dead were still laid out in orderly lines beneath two vast elms. The mourners were on their knees among the dead, sobbing. Around a fire built well to the side, a dozen drunken men were singing songs they remembered from the War.

The two trainmen conferred for a time, and one went off toward the train. The other remained with Philo.

"Are you certain that man was the one who wrecked the train?" Philo asked.

The trainman nodded.

"Wasn't on the train," he said. "Seen by the farmer's children loitering about the tracks, seen with a hammer, found with jewels in his pockets."

Philo shuddered. It appeared that there were degrees of heinousness even when the crime was murder. To conspire to kill an old man when you knew he had thirty thousand dollars hid in his mattress was one thing; to wreck a train filled with strangers and families on holiday in order to loot the wounded and dead was altogether another.

"What will become of him?" she asked. "Will he be taken to New York with us? Or will he go back up to Highland? Or Albany?"

"That's a man," her companion replied with a contraction of his brows, "who don't have much of a future."

At this moment he was rejoined by his companion, who carried in his left hand a long coil of rope. Philo stared at it.

The two men started off again toward the embankment. Philo made to follow, but they signalled her away.

"Sit and rest, Miss. And if you have any dead, weep over 'em."

Philo remained as she was, and the darkness swallowed up the two men.

She looked around her once more and then, taking a round-about way, sneaked up toward the embankment from another direction.

She nearly fell into the party of trainmen again, for they, with the farmer and John Slape, were moving in a group away from the wreck and into the forest. Philo hid behind a tree until they were past, then followed at a discreet distance.

They stopped at a vast oak – in the dark night all that could be seen of it was the massive trunk and the underside of the lowest branches. But these created a black tent that was more than fifty feet wide.

The farmer said, "This is Old Ben. He won't be the first man that's been hanged from Old Ben's branches."

"Hanged!" cried John Slape.

The lanterns were ranged in a circle about twenty feet across beneath one of the greatest and lowest limbs of the tree. John Slape, with his hands tied behind him, was set in the middle of the circle. The trainman who had fetched the rope stood a few feet before him, and John Slape stared in fascination as a noose was fashioned at one end of the rope.

Philo watched from a little distance, and she moved so that she could see John Slape's face full.

She knew that what these trainmen intended to do was wrong, that John Slape ought to be tried in court, that he ought to have benefit of counsel and clergy, that he ought to have opportunity to declare himself penitent. It even crossed her mind that if he were taken before justice, he might even be forced to tell where the money was that he had stolen from her.

Yet Philo did not interfere. And she did not *want* to interfere. John Slape's daughter, under his connivance and abetting, had murdered Philo's grandfather and mother. He himself had been the cause of Nedda Maitland's death, and Philo had watched him attempt to kill Henry.

Now she found herself at the foot of his gallows, and she had no intention of looking away.

John Slape began to plead. He claimed he hadn't wrecked the train, that he had boarded the cars at Saratoga; but the ticket-taker again denied this, and the farmer testified, before God, that he had seen the man near the tracks that very morning.

"And in your pockets," said the ticket-taker, "we found watches and rings, and rolls of bills, all kinds of jewelry, and even stock certificates."

"They was mine!"

The rope was thrown over the limb of the tree, then the free end secured to a stake the second trainman had pounded into a vast root of Old Ben. The noose was placed about Slape's head. The knot of the rope was placed just beneath his left ear.

"Where's Bill?" John Slape cried in terror.

"Who's Bill?" demanded the conductor.

"Bill told me what to do! Bill's the one should be hanged. I—"

"Did Bill tell you to wreck the track?" the conductor demanded.

John Slape nodded vigorously. "Yes, he said we'd—"

"Gentlemen," said the conductor, "you are witness to this man's confession."

"No," cried John Slape. "Get Bill."

"How will we know him?" demanded the farmer.

"Black boots, red shirt. Hang Bill, not me, I—"

"Who marred the tracks?" one of the trainmen shouted. "You or Bill?"

John Slape paused, evidently trying to determine what answer would profit him most.

"This man did," cried the farmer.

"Let me go," said John Slape, "and I'll find Bill. And Bill's friends. Bill's three friends. They told me what to do."

"They've left you, man," said the conductor. "They've elected you to represent them on this limb here. But we'll find them too."

"You won't find them without me," John Slape argued in the extremity of his position.

"Rather let them off," said the conductor, "than risk losing the hanging of the man who wrecked the train."

John Slape began to protest. "No, it's Bill that—" But the conductor pulled the noose taut, and John Slape's voice was choked off.

The farmer had disappeared a few moments before, and he returned leading his horse. Philo had to slip behind another tree to avoid being seen by the farmer. The animal was led into the lighted circle and John Slape hoisted onto its back.

John Slape's continuing protests were rendered incoherent by the rope around his neck.

"You are guilty, man, and you're to be hanged," said the conductor of the train, he being the senior of the employees there. He stepped into the center of the circle and slapped the hindquarters of the animal. It did not move, and John Slape, in his nervousness, produced a strangled laugh.

The farmer called out "Giyap!" and the horse took off. In its flight into the forest, it knocked over one of the lanterns and set fire to some dry brush on the ground. The farmer and one of the trainmen trod on the fire to put it out.

John Slape had fallen with hardly an audible sound. His heavy body brought the rope to a strong tension. He began spinning at the end of it.

He gurgled. There was a small tear in the flesh of his throat – no more than a black line in the lantern glare. The tear began to extend. Suddenly blood, forced out by arterial movement, spouted fountainlike two feet out from his body. The body still turning with the rope, the blood formed a gleaming circle on the ground beneath the tree limb.

The body twitched. Momentarily, the blood's flow lessened. It poured down beneath Slape's shirt, soaking it, and then his trousers too. Then it began to drip from his boots onto the ground directly beneath him. The blood became a circle with a large dot at its center. It continued to flow for about two minutes. The muscular spasms of the dead man were irregular and slight – but enough to splash his impromptu jury with his gore.

Five minutes later the rope was loosened, and the corpse of John Slape was lowered to the ground. He was buried on the spot marked by his own blood.

Philo still watched from behind the tree, and when the men had all gone away, she went forward to the place and thoughtfully rubbed her boot in the soil that still gleamed with John Slape's blood.

Hannah and Katie yet remained. She stood on the spot where John Slape was buried, and turned round and round, looking into the black forest for evidence of the Slape women.

Chapter 48

MR. BLAKEY HIRES PHILO

Philo, with the case of Nedda Maitland's jewels on her lap, rode in a wagon to Highland, where Henry had been laid senseless on the floor of the schoolroom that had been turned into a temporary hospital. She sat beside his pallet for the remainder of the night, holding his hand, too weary even to weep, but was not vouchsafed a single articulate word from his lips. The doctor would not give her firm hope that he would live.

In the morning, she telegraphed the Varleys that Nedda Maitland was dead and that Henry lay dangerously ill. Jacob and Caroline Varley arrived the following afternoon and pushed Philo out of the way.

"We blame you for this," said Caroline Varley with more savagery than logic. "Why were *you* not injured?"

Philo stood steadfastly before the lady. "Mrs. Maitland was killed in the falling of a timber. Henry was knocked in the head by a thief who was attempting to steal Mrs. Maitland's jewels."

"Where are my sister's jewels?" Caroline Varley demanded, with gleaming eyes.

"I have them," said Philo.

"Give them over," said Jacob Varley. "By rights they belong to me as her brother."

"I think they belong to Henry," said Philo, who knew that Nedda Maitland's will left the bulk of her property to her son and only legacies to her brother and his family.

"Henry will not live," said Jacob. "And if he does, I think he will be in no condition to worry with such. Philo, give the jewels to Mrs. Varley."

On the whole, Philo thought it best to go along with this. She was Henry's affianced wife, it was true, but the Varleys knew nothing of this and would disbelieve her – or affect to disbelieve her – if she told them so. In any event, she had no claim upon the jewels. She wondered whether she ought not hold back the diamonds, which were, after all, a free gift from Nedda, but then reflected that the gift was contingent upon the wedding. And having watched by Henry's side, she realized that Jacob Varley's cold prediction was very likely to come true, that Henry would die from the blow administered by John Slape. She must then, in all conscience, return the diamonds.

Philo took the case from beneath the chair where she had sat for two days watching over Henry. She opened it, and took from it the coral he had given her.

"Thief!" cried Caroline Varley in astonishment, drawing the attention of the entire improvised hospital.

Philo attached the chain to her neck and the rings to her ears. "Henry brought me these from Brazil," she said calmly. "They are mine."

"Give them back!" said Jacob Varley. "You are lying, Philo."

Philo looked down at her dress. It was ripped in several places, and she had had only partial success in scraping from it the mud that had dried there. All her other clothing had been lost in the destruction of the baggage car. The shining coral jewelry seemed ludicrously extravagant against the dun outfit that alone remained to her. Yet if there were to be no more to remind her of her proposal of marriage, then she had no intention of giving them over.

"You may ask Mrs. Maitland's maids, if you want corroboration of my claim to these jewels," said Philo. The three maids had had places in the rear coaches of the wrecked train and were shaken but uninjured. Philo had sent them back to their families in New York.

"The law will restore our property to us," said Caroline Varley pompously, and turned her back on Philo.

"You may return to New York," said Jacob Varley. "You are no longer wanted here."

"But Henry—"

"*Mr. Maitland* will be well provided for," said Caroline Varley with finality. "We will take him to New Egypt. Jewel and I will be his constant nurses. Good day, Miss Drax."

Philo's impulse was to fight the Varleys and demand to remain with Henry; but her only claim upon him was their engagement – and the only witness to that engagement, Nedda Maitland, lay on ice in the baggage room of the station, waiting for her brother to signify where her corpse should be sent. The Varleys *were* Henry's only relatives, and to them belonged the privilege and the pleasure of watching over his inert form. When and if he recovered there would be time enough to reassert her claim; but Philo, looking at him, pale and still, on a pad on the bare wooden floor, had little hope that she would ever see him again outside of a coffin. She turned, in the greatest despair she had ever known, and walked out of the schoolroom.

The air tasted of autumn. The maples had begun to show yellow on their crowns, and Philo felt that the Saratoga summer was already years behind her.

She returned to New York on the next train, wondering all the way where she should go when she arrived. Once more, through the agency of the Slapes, she had lost everything that was hopeful and everyone who was dear. But this time at least, she had had the satisfaction of seeing one of them die for it. She remained not a whit sorry for John Slape, and, though the memory of it was terrible, she was glad to have been witness to his hanging. She wondered at her new hardness of heart.

It was necessary that she return first to Twenty-sixth Street to gather what little clothing and belongings she had not taken with her to Saratoga. She half expected to find the house boarded up, but the same servant in his accustomed livery opened the door to her, and all three maids were at their posts. All their expressions were somber though, for they had loved Nedda Maitland. Upstairs Philo washed and changed her dress – for the first time in four days. The maid who was helping her then informed her that Mrs. Maitland's lawyer was in the parlor and wished to speak with her.

This lawyer's name was Mr. Blakey, and Philo had always liked him. After the usual exchange of condolences and inquiries into Henry's condition, Mr. Blakey said,

"Now, Miss Drax, if I might ask a delicate question. . . ."

"Yes?"

"What do you intend to do now?"

"I have no idea in the world, Mr. Blakey."

"Have you money?"

"None."

"Have you prospects?"

"None."

"I thought as much. Then we must see what *can* be done for you."

Philo breathed relief but wondered at the generosity of this relative stranger.

"I would ask you, Miss Drax, to remain here at the house for a time. As a kind of overseer to the servants and to assist me in gathering Mrs. Maitland's papers. Her estate was a large one, as I'm sure you're aware, and I would like, when Henry recovers – for I am certain that he will – for everything to be in order."

"I can't help but feel, Mr. Blakey, that this is being done as a favor to me."

"Not a particle. I need your assistance, Miss Drax, every bit as much as you need mine. Your salary—"

Philo waved her hand, as if recompense did not signify. " – will be augmented by one-half, to compensate for the increased responsibility of your position."

"Mr. Blakey, I should be honest with you—"

"Do."

"The Varleys will not be pleased to hear that I have remained in this house. The Varleys do not take kindly to me."

For the first time, Mr. Blakey smiled. "*I* am executor of this estate, Miss Drax, and I hire whom I please for the administration of it."

Philo nodded in acquiescence. She would struggle no more against an appointment that was entirely to her liking.

Thus after Nedda Maitland's funeral Philo remained on Twenty-sixth Street, and when the Varleys heard of it in New Egypt, they *were* angry. Jacob Varley fired off a letter to Mr. Blakey, and Mr. Blakey replied calmly and by return post that Miss Drax was in every way suited to the responsibilities with which she had been entrusted. Caroline Varley was certain that the house would be ransacked for valuables, and everything that was portable and worth more than fifty cents would be changed into gold to line that young woman's pockets. Jewel shrugged and said she didn't care what happened to that poky old house – but Jewel could afford to say this, because Henry Maitland lay in the chamber next hers. And when he recovered his senses and his health, Jewel intended that he should marry her, in the front parlor.

Henry's health improved more quickly than his senses, as the case proved. The scrapes and cuts he had received became no more than small white scars, the wound on his head no more than a livid red scar – but his consciousness returned scarcely at all. He lay in bed with his eyes wide open and staring but without emotion and without intelligence. His mouth opened for food, and his throat swallowed, but no more could be expected of him. And so he remained for seven weeks, from the tenth of September, when he had been brought to New Egypt on the cars, until the first of November, when he spoke again for the first time and asked for Philo.

Jewel placed her hand quickly over his mouth, and whispered, "Hush! Hush! Dear Cousin Henry. Philo has stolen all your mother's jewels and taken a packet for California!"

One morning in October, when Philo had been living on Twenty-sixth Street alone for nearly six weeks, wondering all the while what Henry's condition might be, she found that one of the letters in the morning post had been directed to her, forwarded from Mrs. Classon's.

The script on the envelope she recognized as Mr. Killip's, and she opened the letter eagerly. It read:

Oct. 21, 1871

Dear Miss Philo,

A hurried note. A man from Goshen visiting his married son in Boston swears to me that he ran across Hannah Slape on the street there. He went up to her and called her by her name, but she refused to acknowledge him. He is certain however to the identity. He has no idea where she lodges or how she occupies herself or whether her husband and stepdaughter are with her. I have not notified any authorities, for there are no charges outstanding against the Slapes in New Jersey. I have done what I could to remove you from the lists of criminals to be apprehended upon sight and have some hope that, in time, you will be cleared of all suspicion. I cannot advise you to go to Boston after the Slapes, for they are a dangerous family; but on the other hand I would not heavily dissuade you from such a course. I was pleased to hear of your altered fortune, and I trust it continues. Please let me hear from you, with news, if any, about the Slapes.

Sincerely yours,
Dan'l Killip

Philo sank into a chair. John was dead, and now she had found out Hannah's hiding place. Doubtlessly, Katie was with her.

Philo's first intent was to notify the police authorities, who wanted the Slapes for the murders of the young women found in the Christopher Street cellar, but Philo realized that she had no more information to provide than that a man she didn't even know thought he had seen Hannah on the street in Boston. She surmised too, from past experience, that the police would ignore her information or only desultorily pass it on to Boston. And how would the Boston force go about trying to locate a woman who was very likely going under a false name?

Philo remembered that Mr. Blakey's firm did considerable business in Boston. That very morning she visited his office and there found several recent newspapers from that city. Philo, not confiding in Mr. Blakey's clerk her motive, went carefully through the advertisements of clairvoyants and mediums. In the second paper she examined, Philo found the following:

MISS PARROCK – Clairvoyant, from Philadelphia; tells name of future husband and wife, number and sex of children; also medical or business clairvoyant. 102A Myrtle Street.

Philo thanked Mr. Blakey's clerk and scribbled a note for the lawyer saying that she would be away for a couple of days, looking up old acquaintances in Boston.

PART X
BOSTON

Chapter 49

THE ABANDONED FATHER

When John Slape had left New York on the morning that his daughter murdered Ella LaFavour, he reluctantly followed the advice of his wife and daughter and went to Philadelphia. It had been several years since John Slape had been on his own, and he did not relish returning to that obscure, knockabout time.

For John Slape life was seen at a distance, through a fog, in indistinct colors. He was able to understand hammers, and cellar graves, and pantomime clowns who appeared suddenly out of star traps in a puff of green smoke; but to ask the man to follow the laws of the State of New York regarding criminal culpability, or to understand the meaning of the words "accessory" and "conspirator" in a judicial proceeding, or to follow in its minor machinations the plot of *True to her Trust* was to expect too much.

Hannah had written out the name of the hotel where he was to stay on a scrap of paper, and by showing this to strangers he got directed there. He secured a room; he sat in the room and stared out at the traffic in the street below. He missed Christopher Street; he thought with fondness of No. 253, with its cellar graves. In his mind, he retraced the path from Katie's parlor up to the top of the house, through the hole in the wall, and down five flights of stairs again, through that dim, empty building. He remembered those inert burdens on his shoulders and the blood that sometimes trickled down his neck.

He attended the theater every night – but Hannah wasn't there to explain to him what was happening on the stage, so he didn't enjoy himself as much as he had in New York. He ate his meals in an eating saloon near his hotel, always sitting near the window so that he could watch the traffic from a different angle. Hannah and Katie weren't there to tell him not to drink, so he drank – mostly in the back room of the same saloon, behind the green-baize curtain where the billiard tables were. He didn't play himself, but he began to bet upon the outcomes of certain games, and within two weeks he had lost all his money.

It took several hours for the meaning of this to register on him with any force. He knew that Hannah had plenty of cash and would not hesitate to send him more, but then he realized that Hannah did not know that he lacked for funds. And he could not tell her, because he did not know where she was. He thought of sending a telegram to Hannah Slape – Boston, but remembered that she and Katie had declared their intention of assuming false names. He asked at the hotel desk if perhaps any money had arrived for him in the last few days and was disappointed to find that none had.

The hotel clerk eyed him suspiciously and alerted the owner that it was very likely that Mr. John Goshen – Hannah had suggested a familiar name for her husband to assume so that he would be less likely to forget it – would be unable to pay his bill.

That evening John was questioned by the owner of the hotel, admitted his inability to pay, and was thrown out onto the street. He hadn't even fifteen cents to get into a theater, and the very men who had won hundreds of dollars from him in the billiard back room refused to lend him more than fifty cents together.

John therefore had enough money to go to the theater, and did so, but without any other refuge he returned to the billiard room afterward. He was approached then by a man whom he had seen there before, but whose name he had either never learnt or subsequently forgot.

The man shook hands cordially with John Slape and bought him a glass of whiskey. He also brought the bottle to a table, where John followed him.

"Talked to you t'other forenoon," the man said, and introduced himself as Bill Reagan.

John nodded, though he remembered nothing.

"Talked of the War and railroads. Said you were a savage down in Virginia."

"I was," said John. John Slape had very little idea of subtlety in human relationships and did not see that Bill Reagan was driving at something.

"Hear you're flat."

John Slape jingled the nickels in his pocket. "That's all I got," he said.

"Where you put up?"

"Nowheres."

"Come to my place."

"All right," replied John with a grin. He had a place to stay for the night. This was a friendly man, and perhaps Bill Reagan would even tell him what to do about getting money from his wife in Boston.

John went with his new friend to a dirty little room in a house that leaned precariously out over the river, but before he could ask Bill Reagan what he should do in regard to Hannah, Bill Reagan said, "How'd you like to swell around town with your pockets full of gold?"

"I would."

"You know how to mend track?"

John nodded.

"You know how to fix track so it *wants* mending?"

John hesitated, then nodded again.

Bill Reagan sat back with a broad smile, certain that John Slape understood his intent. But John sat so stolidly across the red deal table from him, and stared so earnestly at him over the guttering candle flame, that Reagan realized, after a minute or so of silence, that he would have to spell out the entire matter in detail.

He did so, describing the trains that went from Saratoga to New York, the number of their passengers, their money and jewels, the ease of waylaying the train in some deserted spot along the river route the track followed.

"I'd do it," said John, when he had heard all, "but I don't have the fare to get up there."

Bill Reagan paid John Slape's fare to Milton, New York, where they put up at the little hotel that had been built within sight of the West Shore Railway. Pretending to be sportsmen, they walked out of the hotel early in the morning with guns on their shoulders and disappeared into the forest. Following the track of the railway north, they scouted out the most remote spot –

halfway between Milton and Highland exactly – for the train to be wrecked. Slape marked the rails and ties that would be best disengaged, and Reagan shot a few rabbits so that they would not return to the hotel empty-handed.

Three confederates were telegraphed and arrived singly over the next couple of days. On Monday morning, the fourth of September, John Slape went out of the hotel early and alone, walked up the railway line, and sat in the shade of the tree, watching the trains from Saratoga go by, one by one. It was at this time he was seen by the farmer's little daughter, gathering berries in a nearby copse. Just at dusk, John was joined by his confederates, who had left the hotel singly, all dressed in their best – thus better to mingle with the passengers of the wrecked train – and they assisted him in drawing the pins from the rails and removing the ties.

They all returned to John's comfortable place beneath the tree and waited for the four o'clock train from Saratoga to come by. When they heard its approach, they were careful to back away into the forest in order not to be injured by explosive metal and flying glass.

Of the five men involved in the scheme, only John Slape was caught. And by the time that he was seen by Philo, the other four had filled their pockets and emptied them again several times into sacks which they had brought with them. John Slape's confederates walked to New Paltz that night, and from there, next morning, took a train back to Philadelphia. At the station in New Paltz, they were sorry to hear of John Slape's capture, for his pockets had been filled with gold and jewels and negotiable bonds. They were less disturbed to know of his death – for a dead man did not tell the names of his confederates.

Chapter 50

MISS PONDER AND FIDELE

In order to remain as inconspicuous as possible, Hannah Slape, upon arriving in Boston with her stepdaughter, rented only a basement flat in a house on Myrtle Street a few hundred yards northeast of the State House but far from fashion. This cramped, damp space consisted of a parlor at the front, with two large windows right at the level of the street, a bedchamber behind this that was really no more than a wide passageway, and a kitchen at the back that was larger than either.

Katie hated the place, complained of its smallness, of the smells from the courtyard, of the noise from the street. Carriage wheels and horses' hooves sounded only a couple of feet from the windows, and at all hours of the day and night, the curious peered in. But more than the inconvenience of their quarters, Katie complained of inactivity. She wanted to tell fortunes. It was her calling, she maintained to Hannah, and what she did gladly.

Hannah reminded Katie that her description had been printed in papers all across the country and a list of her victims prepared for the delectation of a reading public long inured to sanguinary horrors. To put out her old placard in the Myrtle Street window would doubtless bring inquiries from the police.

Yet after two weeks spent in close quarters with Katie, it was finally Hannah herself who suggested again that she resume her old profession. Hannah composed an advertisement, calling Katie "Miss Parrock," and inserted it into the next day's *Herald*. A sign painter on Charles Street made up a placard with the same promises on it for a dollar and a half, and Katie was in business once more. Simply a new name in the lists brought in the custom of those ladies who had tried all the others already, and those impressed sent others. On Hannah's advice, Katie was more discreet than formerly, and was deliberately vaguer in her prognostications than she might have been.

Katie worked in the parlor at the front of the flat. Hannah sat in the bedroom or in the kitchen, silent and unmoving, hid behind a green linen portiere, listening to her daughter – and ready to interrupt should Katie begin to reveal something that was better kept secret.

After some of the sessions Katie would fling aside the portiere and stomp from one end of the flat to the other.

"She had money, Mar! She had three hundred dollars stuck down her front. I wish I had my hammer!"

It was necessary to soothe Katie at these times and calm her passion. Who knew how far voices carried in Boston? It was a quieter and closer place than New York.

"Wouldn't do us no good," Hannah would say. "Where would we bury her? In the courtyard, with all the neighbors watching? Who'd dig her grave? Katie, got plenty of money. Wait a while – soon be in New York again. Buy a new house, with a dirt floor in the cellar . . ."

And this, with a promise of another evening at the theater, mollified Katie for a time. She'd draw the curtains open and sit at the window, smiling at passersby who paused to read the sign and peer through the glass panes.

The summer passed, and autumn came on. Katie asked every day, "When do we go back to New York?"

"When it's cold," Hannah replied. She anticipated that the five hundred dollars that she had given her husband would last him at least until the first of December. By then, she considered, her family would have been forgotten by the public and the police. They would search out John in Philadelphia and be a family once more. Hannah thought it would be best ultimately to take up residence in some city other than New York – Baltimore or Washington perhaps. But of this she said nothing to Katie, knowing with what eagerness her stepdaughter anticipated a return to the island of Manhattan.

Katie accepted the plan, as she accepted all that Hannah suggested. But she asked, "What about the girl?"

"What girl?"

"The hired girl, Mar. The old man's granddaughter. My cousin. She saw me. She knows who we are."

Hannah shrugged.

"I want to find her out," said Katie. "I think she ought to be buried in the cellar."

"Don't have a cellar any more," said Hannah. She looked around. "*Live* in a cellar."

Katie closed her eyes. "I see her on a boat." When she opened them again, wickedness sparkled there. "I think we ought to tie her up in a sack and throw her in a river," she said.

"Got to find her first," said Hannah. "Can't get caught," she warned.

"Break her legs so she can't swim, and tie her in a sack and throw her in a river," cried Katie, and clapped her hands in gleeful expectation.

One morning toward the middle of October, Katie answered a knock at the door. A lady of an age more advanced than she would have liked one to think stood trembling on the walk and peering down the steps into the dark recessed doorway of No. 102a. She cradled a yapping terrier and whispered soothingly to it, though this did not quiet the animal in the least.

"Are you Miss Parrock?" she whispered, and looked up and down the street.

"Walk in please," said Katie.

With a nervous little laugh, the lady descended the steps and entered the parlor. Hannah had already retreated behind the portiere and had settled down to a copy of the *New York Clipper*, which she always read with a sigh for the theatrical splendors of New York.

The lady's dog, whom she addressed as Fidele, snarled at Katie in an absurdly high pitch. Katie couldn't repress a grimace – the dog was small, but Katie hated it – but the fortune-teller turned so that her customer would not see her disgust.

"He don't make friends easy," the lady said with a smile of apology. "I am Miss Ponder."

"Sit down, please," said Katie. "You're fifty-one next Christmas, and you're being courted by a man who's twenty-six years old."

The lady nearly fell into her chair. "Yes," she whispered, convinced suddenly and utterly of Katie's powers. "Does he love me?"

Katie paused, searching not for the true answer, but rather for the most advantageous reply.

"He has gambling debts," she said at last.

"Then he's marrying me for my money!" Miss Ponder shrieked, and clapped her hands over her ears. Fidele, her mistress's sure grip for a moment loosened, took the opportunity to jump down from her lap. The dog, yapping frightfully, ran round the table three times, snapping at both her mistress and at Katie.

Katie snarled back and kicked the dog.

Fidele, weighing no more than five pounds, sailed across the room and was knocked against the wall. The animal slid dazed to the floor.

"Fidele!" cried Miss Ponder in anguish.

"Sit down!" said Katie, wishing she had kicked the dog even harder. "He visits a lady on Goodwin Place every Saturday afternoon."

"It is his sister!"

"No!"

Fidele staggered behind the portiere.

Hannah looked up from the paper. She had retained an aversion to dogs since her poodle-stunting days. She took a pepper pot from the table and flung it at the dog. Fidele rushed forward as if crazed, leapt at Hannah, and through three layers of cloth, set her teeth into the flesh of Hannah's right leg.

Hannah growled and attempted to shake the dog off, but Fidele held on tightly. She reached down, took Fidele in both hands, and pulled her away. She drew in her breath tightly as she felt the skin of her leg torn.

"Damn you, dog!" she hissed, and lifted the dog high. Fidele snarled and yapped and twisted in Hannah's hands, but couldn't get loose.

In the front room Miss Ponder heard the scuffle and wasn't to be prevented from protecting precious Fidele. Forgetting her unfaithful, mercenary fiancé, she stood from the table, and before Katie could stop her, had pulled aside the portiere, calling "My darling, my darling . . . !"

At that moment, Hannah, who had decided that she could not put down the terrier without its biting or attempting to bite her again, had lifted the squealing, slathering animal high. Miss Ponder rushed in and stopped, appalled. Hannah looked at her – with alarm, knowing she was about to do that which she ought not – and brought the animal down hard onto a pointed edge of the stove.

The corner pierced the dog's belly, and blood spewed out over Hannah's apron.

Miss Ponder screamed and rushed forward.

Hannah dropped the dog on the floor. It hissed, and blew blood from its nostrils, and foamed blood at its mouth.

Miss Ponder bent over the dog, and Hannah backed away, saying nothing.

She stared at Katie, who stood in the doorway twisting the cloth of the portiere in her hands held behind her.

"You've murdered Fidele!" shrieked Miss Ponder over the dog still twitching in its death throes.

Hannah watched the dog's eyes glaze over.

"It's near dead," she said.

"I'll have the law," Miss Ponder hissed, with tears in her eyes.

Katie's smile faded. She rushed forward into the kitchen, took from the stove the kettle of water that was on the boil, and poured the contents over the woman's head. Miss Ponder shrieked, and Katie spilled the boiling water directly into her mouth. Miss Ponder fell onto the floor on top of Fidele. Her skin was already bright red and puckered.

Miss Ponder was frantic; blinded, unable to scream because her mouth and throat were seared, unable to stand because she was crippled with the pain. Kicking, she overturned a chair on top of her. She flailed with arms that were no more than extensions of pain and shook her boiled, blinded head from side to side.

Steam rose from her body.

Katie took a large skillet in which Hannah had prepared their breakfast and emptied out the cooling grease over the woman's writhing form. Then carefully stepping round her to get behind, Katie brought down the broad flat bottom of the skillet as hard as she could on Miss Ponder's face.

With the first blow she crushed her nose, cheekbones, and chin. With a second, delivered at an angle, she caved in Miss Ponder's temple.

The body convulsed twice – but Katie and Hannah knew from experience that Miss Ponder was already dead.

Chapter 51

FIDELE'S REVENGE

Hannah removed the placard from the window and drew the curtains. She turned angrily to Katie. "What do you think we're to do now?"

Katie shrugged.

"Told you, no hammers!"

"It wasn't no hammer!" Katie protested.

But there was still the corpse of Miss Ponder lying in a pool of steaming water on the kitchen floor. Her head was propped on Fidele's slit belly as on a pillow. Her skin was ripped and black from being seared by the boiling water. Her dress was stained with blood and congealed fat.

"Where are we to put her?" cried Hannah.

"Let's leave her," suggested Katie. "Let's go back to New York."

Hannah shook her head. "No," she said, "the police are still after us there, can't go back there yet."

Katie sat down at the table and amused herself by pouring cold tea from one cup into another and then back again.

There was a knock at the door. Hannah peered through the curtain. "It's another lady to see you."

"Let her walk in," said Katie.

Hannah pointed impatiently toward the kitchen.

"That's why we have a curtain," said Katie with imperturbable logic. "Go back and wait and let me tell her fortune."

Hannah did so and sat beside the corpse for twenty minutes, while Katie told a spinster that she would never find a man to marry and that all her nephews made fun of her nose.

When that second lady had departed in tears, Katie drew aside the portiere and went into the bedroom. She swung on the doorjamb and grinned at Hannah.

"Seventy-five cents!" she said. "Can we go to see Young America tonight?"

Young America was an acrobat who had won Katie Slape's heart. He was booked all that week at the Boston Museum Theatre, and Katie had gone to see him every evening.

"Help me with this," said Hannah. She held up a large canvas bag, the seams of which she had been reinforcing with thick cotton thread.

"Put her in, you mean?"

Hannah nodded.

There was some difficulty in this since Miss Ponder's limbs had stiffened in the last hour and both legs had to be broken in order to fit her in the sack. The dog, entirely rigid, was placed in her crossed arms.

Hannah sewed the bag at the top, and she and Katie then carried it through a little-used side door in the flat. At the back of a narrow storage room, behind a number of labeled crates, they hung it from a large hook that was embedded in the wall.

Hannah acquiesced in Katie's desire to see Young America in his last performance in Boston – on the condition that she clean the kitchen floor.

Though the weather had been decidedly cool, the bodies of Miss Ponder and Fidele began to stink within only a few days, even before the wound which the dog had inflicted on Hannah's leg had entirely healed. Their neighbors upstairs complained of the odor, and Hannah explained that she had recently set out poison for rats, and that some of the vermin had evidently expired in holes and corners. Katie and Hannah were themselves not immune to the disagreeable smell, and to cover it they cooked molasses and burned scented candles.

About ten days after this murder, which Katie had been warned was not under any circumstances to be repeated, Hannah came down with a severe cold. About the same time, the marks of Fidele's teeth, which had disappeared, reappeared as two jagged crescents. Then that injured leg began to swell and be painful to the touch. On Tuesday and Wednesday the pain increased, and the swelling ascended to her thigh. Hannah begged Katie for water, but at the sight of the pitcher that Katie brought, Hannah's throat began to convulse, and it would not stop until Katie had hidden it in the next room. Katie brought in a teaspoonful of the liquid, but when she put the spoon into her mother's mouth, Hannah's teeth clamped shut over the stem and broke it in two. Katie had to pry open her mother's jaws to extricate the bowl. On Thursday Katie went for the doctor whose sign was raised on a house within sight of Katie's basement windows. Dr. Fogg examined Hannah, then ordered a consultation. Within three hours, during which time Hannah called incessantly for water and then began to scream every time that Katie put her hand to the pump, Drs. Clark, Thaxter, Tuckerman and Walker arrived at Myrtle Street and could do no more than watch Hannah Slape – in her distraction, Katie had revealed their true name – grow repeatedly convulsed.

Hannah was pronounced a victim of hydrophobia.

The marks on her leg confirmed this opinion. The dog that had bitten her was rabid.

Katie was questioned but, in her confusion, could not remember what it was permitted her to say and what it was imperative she keep secret. So she remained silent and, when pressed, maintained she knew nothing at all.

Since nothing could be done, the doctors adjudged Katie a competent nurse for Hannah, and Katie remained alone with her stepmother. Hannah grew weaker by the hour. She found no comfort at all except by lying upon the floor in the parlor, this despite dampness and chill. She ate nothing but cold boiled potatoes.

She called incessantly for water, but Katie gave up any pretense of listening to this plea; for as soon as she saw the liquid or even heard it being poured in another room, Hannah went into dreadful spasms.

On Thursday night it rained, and Hannah screamed for three hours. At last she lost consciousness.

On Friday morning, as Katie sat turning over the cards of an old greasy pack she had brought with her from New York, Hannah had a spasm so powerful that it lifted her entirely off the floor, and Katie gaped in amazement. Hannah had jumped as high as anything that Young America himself was capable of.

"Oh, Mar!" cried Katie in admiration. "Do it again! Do it again!"

Dr. Fogg stopped in that afternoon and pronounced Hannah's symptoms even more unfavorable.

"Hydrophobia is the most painful death I can think of," he said in an undertone to Katie. "I had rather be clawed to death by a tiger than bitten by a mad dog. I only hope that the dog was destroyed."

Katie smiled and assured him that the dog would never bite anyone else.

Hannah moved scarcely at all for the next several hours. Then, in the night, Katie was wakened by her mother's hoarse whisper, begging for water.

"No, Mar!" cried Katie, exasperated with the illness. "I ain't getting you any. So don't hector me no more about it!"

Katie was weary of nursing, weary of her stepmother's demands. On Saturday morning, while Hannah lay in a coma on the floor of the parlor, Katie packed her clothing on top of Philo's fortune in the carpetbag and walked out of the flat, not bothering even to secure the door behind her. Within the hour she was on her way to Philadelphia, purchasing apples and oranges of a train-boy who didn't like the look in her eyes.

She missed meeting Philo on the platform by three-quarters of an hour. The New York train arrived in Boston at half past eleven, and Philo emerged with her wicker travelling case. She put up at the Parker House and, after inquiring about the way to Myrtle Street, discovered that Katie and Hannah were only four or five streets away. She had only to go up to the State House, then down the other side of Beacon Hill.

Philo put down her black veil and with some trepidation set out to find Hannah and Katie. However, she hadn't her former fear of them. Her knowledge that John Slape was dead and her memory of his death served in some way to protect her.

She found Myrtle Street without difficulty and approached the doorway of No. 102a with caution. She saw it first from the opposite side of the street and noted that the door was ajar. She waited for a few moments – not as long as she thought she should, but she was impatient – then crossed over and strolled past with as much insouciance as she could muster.

She could see nothing through the crack in the doorway. She slowed before the windows and peered in.

The sun, almost directly overhead, shone through the window from over her shoulder, and Philo could see black-stockinged feet protruding from underneath the table.

Philo assumed the Slapes had found one victim more. No longer thinking of her own safety, she flung the door of the flat open wide. She was astonished to find it was Hannah who lay underneath the table.

Her dress was stained with sickness, and the entire room stank. There was bloody foam on Hannah's mouth, and one of her hands convulsively gripped the leg of a chair. Her eyes were open but glazed. It was obvious, even to Philo, that Hannah Slape was near to death.

Philo was staggered. Now she wondered what she had expected to find here in Boston. Hannah and Katie, perhaps living high on the fortune they had stolen from her, not yet apprised of John Slape's death, confident of their safety – yet here was Hannah alone, and Hannah was dying.

Philo lifted the table out of the way and moved the chairs aside, leaving only the one anchored in Hannah's convulsive grip.

The dying woman's eyes unclouded for a moment, and she stared at Philo.

"Water," she whispered.

Philo went into the kitchen and pumped a glassful. She brought it back and, raising Hannah into a sitting position, held the glass to her lips.

But when Hannah opened her mouth, foul, discolored phlegm poured out over Philo's hand and the water was spilled onto her dress.

Hannah lost consciousness, and Philo lowered her to the floor.

At that moment a man appeared in the doorway.

"Is she dead yet?" he asked.

Philo, wondering, shook her head.

"I'm Dr. Fogg," he said. "Where is the daughter?"

"Was the daughter here?" cried Philo.

"This morning she was," replied the doctor.

Hannah began to choke. Her eyes flew open, her head twisted up off the floor, she spat up a great quantity of the brown phlegm and convulsively tried to take in more breath. The chair leg was still caught in her fist; she lifted it high above her head and brought it down as suddenly. The chair was smashed on the threadbare rug. Hannah Slape fell back dead, with bloody foam covering her mouth.

Hannah Jepson Slape was the name that went on the death certificate. Philo paid for the undertaker, the burial plot, and the brief service that was read over Hannah's ravaged body. Philo did not tell the police that the dead woman was wanted in New York for the murders of seven young women and a child.

Philo returned to New York the day after Hannah's body was laid in the earth. She had seen John and Hannah Slape die deaths more terrible than she could have wished on them had they stolen her fortune ten times over.

Yet Philo was not the least shaken in her resolve to find Katie Slape. Katie alone remained.

Hannah and Katie were quickly forgotten in Boston, even by the neighbors who lived directly above. Katie's advertisement no longer appeared in the papers, and those ladies who had been most impressed by the young woman's clairvoyant prowess could not discover her again. Neither mother nor daughter was at all remembered until the following spring when a woman, who had stored her children's lighter clothing for the winter season, went into the cellar storage room, moved aside some crates, and saw a canvas sack suspended from a hook, with long ropes of slime, shining in the dim morning light, dangling from the bottom.

PART XI

NEW YORK VS. NEW EGYPT

Chapter 52

KATIE ALONE

Katie Slape was stronger-willed than her father, more cunning and more alert. But when it came down to the basic business of getting from one side of a city to another, she wasn't much more to be relied upon than the unfortunate John Slape. Leaving her stepmother to die alone in the basement flat on Myrtle Street, Katie took up the carpetbag and walked to the railway station, stopping to ask directions three times upon her way.

She purchased a ticket to Philadelphia, waited an hour on a hard bench, and sat stiffly upright in the cars for the sixteen hours of the journey, fearful that someone would attempt to steal her case and placard. Katie was in no easy frame of mind. She wished it had been her father who had died instead of Hannah. Hannah told you what to do and where to go. Hannah said "Yes, now" and "No, later." Hannah kept the police away, and Hannah could read to you out of the papers. Katie wasn't sure why she was going to find her father, because he couldn't do any of those things any more than she herself could – but perhaps they two together *could* find someone to take Hannah's place.

She had fallen into a troubled sleep on the train, worried that someone would attempt to wrest the carpetbag out of her sweaty, unconscious grasp. The stove was at the end of the car and Katie in the middle. Moreover there was a draft at her window, and she was uncomfortably chilled. Her dreams were feverish, disconnected, silent. She dreamt of Hannah's teeth snapping off the bowl of the spoon that contained the water she had begged for, she dreamt of Miss Ponder biting her leg just as Fidele had bitten her stepmother's, she dreamt of the hired girl from Goshen, who came smiling to the window of the basement apartment, reached in, and snatched away Katie's treasured placard. Though Katie ran after her, she could never catch up. Then Katie dreamt of her father, lying beneath a vast tree with a rope around his neck. Katie came close to her father in that dream, bent down over him, and looked into his face. His eyes snapped open, and nothing was there but two bubbling wells of blood that overflowed and obscured his face. Katie stepped back, and the blood continued to flow out of his sockets, flooding the earth, until he began to float in it – to float and then to sink.

Katie woke suddenly with the knowledge that her father was dead. She had not interpreted her dream as prophetic, or as a vision of the circumstances of her father's death – but rather with that dream had come the absolute certainty that he *was* dead.

There was no need then to look for him in Philadelphia. She got off the train in New York.

She walked in a straight line until, because of water, she could walk no farther. This peregrination left her on Fulton Street within sight of the Brooklyn ferry, a location which, with its crowd and its smells and its noises reminded her of Christopher Street. Therefore on Fulton Street she asked for a hotel. At the first two she was rejected, since single ladies of irreproachable character did not travel alone, but at the third she was smart enough to tell the clerk that, her mother having died in Boston, she was waiting here for her father to return to her from California. Her chamber rent was fifty cents a day, but this did not include meals.

Katie sat very still on Fulton Street, trying to think out what was best for her to do. There was danger, she knew, in remaining in New York, for in New York were those who could recognize her as the daughter of the family that had inhabited No. 251 Christopher Street. Yet she felt more comfortable here, and was far more at her ease than she had been in Boston, even with Hannah to protect her.

Her money kept her and would have sustained her for the remainder of her life, but the idleness began to prey upon her. She asked the manager of the hotel if she could place her placard in some conspicuous place in the lobby, but this was refused her. Then she reflected that it was perhaps by this placard she would be found out, and she must search out a way to ply her trade that did not involve advertising. After thinking over this problem for a few days, she suddenly remembered that once when she and her parents had gone to Brooklyn for a performance of *Le Voyage en Suisse* by the Hanlon-Lees troupe of acrobats, she and Hannah, sitting in the ladies' cabin on the Brooklyn ferry, had been approached by a fortune-teller.

Five minutes after that memory was dredged up to the surface of Katie's consciousness, she put on her hat and went over to the Brooklyn ferry. She purchased a five-cent ticket and seated herself in the ladies' cabin. Not trusting the security of the hotel room where she was put up, she brought the carpetbag along with her.

The ferry ride from New York over to Brooklyn took no more than fifteen minutes, but ten more were consumed on either side, with mooring up and casting off, letting off carriages, dealing with recalcitrant animals, frightened ladies, and lost children. For inclement weather there were separate ladies' and gentlemen's cabins. The gentlemen's cabin contained only gentlemen, but the ladies' cabin was mixed, and entertained all ladies and those gentlemen who did not wish to smoke.

It was about two o'clock on a Tuesday afternoon that Katie paid her fare to get onto the Brooklyn ferry, and she was sorely disappointed to find, when she had seated herself on one of the red plush cushions, that there was already a fortune-teller in attendance there: a lady wearing a black crepe dress and a melancholy smile who moved round the compartment, spoke in a low musical voice to all the ladies present and to a number of the gentlemen, asking if they wished to have the future revealed. Katie watched her with barely suppressed anger and was not even comforted by the reflection that in such a crowd as this her hammer would have been of no use.

The lady in the black crepe dress came at last round to Katie. Katie smiled and placed a fifty-cent piece in the lady's hand.

"You wish to know the name of the man you will marry?" said the lady.

"I'll never marry," said Katie. She beckoned the lady closer, and when the fortune-teller leaned forward, Katie whispered in her ear, "The crepe is humbug. You ain't in mourning. Your husband run off with a whore. And you've got a cancer in your neck."

Katie grinned, and the lady in crepe – despite the cold and the cold spray – hurried out onto the deck.

Katie turned to the lady sitting next to her. "Tell your fortune, ma'am? Only a quarter."

Katie worked the Brooklyn ferry every afternoon, making sometimes as few as four, sometimes as many as eight trips back and forth. Her best target were the ladies of Brooklyn who had spent a few hours shopping along the Ladies' Mile and were returning home with their purchases. Katie wondered why these – whose lives contained no surprises whatever, other than that they or their husbands might die suddenly and soon or that their children would be imprisoned for ghastly crimes – were always the most eager to know the future. At the beginning or at the end of the workday, the ferry was crowded, and she could not operate in the privacy that was best for her. Sometimes, merely as a change, she would work in the evenings, and for fifty cents tell the fortunes of spooning couples, shopgirls, and counter clerks.

She made more than enough money to support herself. Therefore Philo's fortune in bank notes remained undisturbed at the bottom of the carpetbag. The bag itself became a kind of appendage to Katie: it was no longer heavy, it was no longer a nuisance, it was no longer even thought of by her. Once she went to see Young America at the Brooklyn Museum, but when she was told she would have to check her carpetbag before she went into the house, she tore up her ticket and went home again.

Chapter 53

HENRY'S MESSAGE

Jacob and Caroline Varley came to New York to see Mr. Blakey about the progress toward the settling of Nedda Maitland's estate. They stayed in Nedda's house, putting up with the abhorred presence of Philo Drax rather than with the charges of a hotel. Caroline complained, "I do not know why you could not have gone off somewhere for a few days while we were here."

"I saw no reason to," replied Philo calmly. "I am paid to live here and take care of the house until Mr. Maitland can decide what is to be done with it."

"Mr. Maitland is mending nicely under Jewel's constant ministrations," said Caroline, with a careful eye to gauge Philo's reaction to this remark. She gave none. "I suspect there may be a wedding somewhere about New Egypt in the spring. Or perhaps," she added less vaguely, and looking around the parlor, "we should have it in *here*. . . ."

Philo fingered the coral rings in her ears.

The Varleys returned to New Egypt, and Philo would do no more than send her best wishes for Henry Maitland's swift and complete recovery. Any tenderer message would never be relayed, she knew, and anything less would have been gleefully reported by the Varleys as downright coldness.

Philo was helpless. She could not send a letter, for that letter would be impounded by either Jewel or Caroline Varley. She could not go herself, for she would never be allowed into the room where Henry was bedded. She must only wait at a distance and trust that her silence was not misinterpreted.

Fortunately for Philo, it happened that a couple of weeks later, toward the middle of November, Mr. Blakey was required to travel to Trenton on business. He told her that on his return he would look in at New Egypt. "I would be happy to transmit any message or letter that you would care to entrust to me," he said.

To Mr. Blakey Philo had revealed the secret of her engagement to Henry. It was to the credit of both that Mr. Blakey believed implicitly Philo's story of the proposal, Nedda's approbation, and the outright gift of the valuable Brazilian diamonds.

Philo sat down immediately and wrote the following letter.

November 16, 1871

Dear Henry,

There is so much to be said that I cannot begin to write it. I have not seen you since you lay unconscious on the floor of the schoolhouse in Highland, calling out in your dreams for your poor mother. I am living in your mother's house, employed by kind Mr. Blakey to keep it against your return, which I pray and trust will be very soon. I would be in New Egypt to look after you myself, but Jewel, I fancy, would take my interference ill. Mrs. Varley tells me that there is to be a wedding as soon as you are well, and that the bride's new initials will be JM. If this is so, then I congratulate you heartily. Please be certain that I receive an invitation. If it should *not* be so, then please to give JM who is not to be my sincerest condolences. I remain,

Yours always,
Philomela Drax

She had decided to take a tone of banter with him. She could not write so much as was in her heart. And she distrusted and disliked effusion. A longer letter than this might well have aroused the suspicions of the Varleys, and she trusted Henry to be assured of her affection.

When Mr. Blakey returned four days later, he came directly to Twenty-sixth Street. Philo questioned him eagerly.

"How is Henry?"

"Mending."

"Does he speak now?"

"Yes, for short spaces. Jewel watches him closely."

"Did you give him my letter?"

"Yes," replied Mr. Blakey with a smile. "He said he was mightily surprised to see it."

"Why should he say that?"

"Because Jewel had told him that you had absconded to California with all Nedda's jewels sewn into your clothing, and that you were last seen in a dance hall in San Francisco. I assured him that you were neither a thief, a dance-hall girl, nor an inhabitant of California. He said that he was glad to hear it – that he had always thought well of you."

Philo smiled. "Jewel was present for this? What was her response?"

"She was a little disconcerted," said the lawyer, "but said that though you might not be a thief, you were certainly wanted for murder in New Jersey."

At this Philo's smile fled. "She is correct, Mr. Blakey. I could not have visited Henry in New Jersey for fear of arrest."

"Nedda told me the story," said the lawyer. "I might as well tell you now that I have initiated a correspondence with Mr. Killip and the authorities in New Jersey in the hope of clearing your name there. But for now, I would advise you to remain on this side of the North River, and if you decide to summer somewhere next year, make it Newport or Saratoga instead of Long Branch."

After thanking the lawyer for his interest in her, Philo asked, "Was Henry able to send a message to me?"

"No," said Mr. Blakey. "Miss Jewel was in the room all the while I visited Henry. And Miss Jewel, as they say, has bright ears. However," said Mr. Blakey with a small smile, "he had a commission for *me*. . . ."

Philo looked up.

"He gave me this—"

Mr. Blakey fished in his pocket and withdrew a ring, massy and gold, with a large canary diamond in the center of it.

"He asked me to have it reset for him."

Philo looked at the ring: it was the ring that Henry had worn on every occasion she had ever seen him. It had been given him by his mother on his majority.

"He said it should be made to match the diamonds that he had brought from Brazil."

"Caroline Varley has those diamonds," said Philo soberly.

"*I* have those diamonds," said Mr. Blakey. "I brought them back with me. They are part of Nedda's estate. Mrs. Varley was not pleased to give them up, I think, but she dared not argue with Henry in the house."

"Perhaps," said Philo with a smile, "Henry intends them *all* as a gift for Jewel."

"He does intend them for a wedding gift, I believe," said Mr. Blakey, "and as long as I'm here, I think I might as well take the measure of your finger, Miss Philo, just – you understand – for the sake of my records. . . ."

Chapter 54

ON THE BROOKLYN FERRY

Henry Maitland mended sufficiently to think of returning to New York. Jewel and Caroline and Jacob Varley all became lobbyists against this measure, but the doctor who came down once a week from New York to see Henry declared him fit to be moved again. He could leave New Egypt so long as he agreed to stay on Twenty-sixth Street, where he would receive sufficient care and attention.

Jewel remonstrated violently against this, and said that if nothing else had killed him in the past six months – what with voyages to Brazil, train wrecks, and murderous thieves – Philo Drax would. Caroline Varley gently reminded her nephew of the impropriety of remaining under the same roof with a young unmarried female.

To this Henry replied, "Jewel has reminded me often enough that Philo Drax is no more than a servant. I have lived all my life with female servants in the same house, and Philo Drax is only one more. Besides, I am, for the time being, an invalid and can do little more than sit in a chair in the sunlight."

"But your poor Mother!" cried Caroline Varley with sudden inspiration. "You cannot return to that house. It will be filled with painful memories!"

"Yes, no doubt it will," replied Henry, who had no intention of giving up his plans which called for Henry's doctor to fetch him back to New York from New Egypt.

The Varleys of course had wanted to come along on this journey, but the doctor wisely interfered and suggested that Henry be kept as quiet as possible on the journey back. On the day that the doctor left on his errand, it happened that the youngest child of the cook on Twenty-sixth Street died of a fever. The lady, who lived in Brooklyn, was in considerable distress, and with Mr. Blakey's permission, Philo thought to take the woman funds sufficient to cover the expenses of burial.

Therefore, with twenty-five dollars in her pocket – this was about double what would be wanted by the lady, but she was, in everyone's estimation, a *good* cook – and the happy thought in her heart that Henry Maitland would return to Twenty-sixth Street the following afternoon, Philo boarded the succession of stages that left her off at Fulton Street. She arrived just as the ferry was about to start its brief journey across the East River. The hands on deck held the ropes taut and allowed her to board, the last person onto the boat.

The day was chill and blustery. Philo went directly to the ladies' cabin, there to warm herself near the stove.

But she forgot the chill, and the newspaper she carried dropped from her hands. Directly upon entering the cabin, she saw Katie Slape, bending forward and putting some soft question to a lady seated with a baby in her lap.

Philo instinctively turned her face away, so that she would not be seen if Katie looked up. She picked up the newspaper and retreated into the farthest corner of the saloon. Holding up the paper before her, she peered round the edge of it and watched Katie. The fortune-teller was grasping the baby's two tiny hands in her own and was whispering earnestly in the mother's ear.

Philo sat very still, wondering at fate. She was in the same room with Katie Slape, who had murdered her grandfather, murdered her mother, stolen her fortune, and, in short, caused her vast misery. Yet this morning Philo was happy, thinking of Henry's return and his promise of marriage. And Katie Slape, who had worked so hard to overthrow her, was now an orphan. Philo had seen both her parents die – and it occurred to Philo suddenly that Katie might in truth be ignorant of the deaths of John and Hannah Slape. But where was Philo's money, if Katie was telling fortunes on the Brooklyn ferry, wearing a dress fashioned of material so decidedly cheap?

Yet if in some manner inexplicable to her and without her realizing it had happened, Philo's wheel of fortune had turned, and she stood at the top of the wheel, while Katie Slape was being crushed at the bottom, Philo still had no intention of forgetting her vow. She would not let Katie Slape remain in her peaceful anonymity. For many moments she wondered what she should do. She might approach Katie directly. Alone in a house on Christopher Street, Philo had feared for her life with the Slapes; but here she was protected by the presence of half a hundred persons. Yet, having decided to approach Katie, what could she say? Could she accuse Katie of murder and mayhem before those same protecting witnesses? They would think her insane, and their sympathy would fall on Katie.

With the consultation done, Katie rose, and Philo saw the carpetbag that had been hid behind the skirts of her dress. She was more astonished to see the satchel than she was to see Katie. She could not conceive it possible that any part of her fortune remained in the bag – surely Katie was not so foolish as to carry such a sum of money about with her!

Now it was imperative that Philo interfere – it was just possible that some part of her fortune remained intact. Best, she concluded, would be to find a policeman and tell him what she knew. The Slapes, though not much thought about now – other terrible murders had interceded of late in the papers – could not have been wholly forgotten. Philo suspected that there might be at least one policeman in the gentlemen's cabin, and she would have gone to fetch him but that Katie was seated very near the door, and Philo in going out would be certain to attract her notice.

There would be time, Philo decided, once the boat had reached the Brooklyn side. Even if Katie got off there – and Philo suspected that her enemy rode the ferry back and forth endlessly – there should be little difficulty in tracking her.

Having made this decision, Philo sat very still, though the effort cost her. She thought she had never been so nervous in all her life, and around the edge of the paper she stared at Katie Slape as if she had been a fabulous mythological creature, a sphinx or the Gorgon, dropped into the middle of nineteenth-century New York.

As the boat approached the landing in Brooklyn, the passengers drifted out of the cabin and took their places on the outer deck, each one eager to be the first ashore. Some, however, knowing of accidents that had occurred through just such haste, remained inside the cabin. The lady with the baby, whose fortune had been told, gave a coin to Katie, rose, and went out onto the deck.

Katie placed the coin in her porte-monnaie and looked around.

Philo cowered behind the paper.

Katie rose and came directly across the cabin toward her, the carpetbag swinging at her side.

Philo raised the paper higher.

Katie took from her bosom a little knife with a blade about four inches long; with it she sliced the paper down the middle. The halves of the paper fell from Philo's hands onto the floor.

The ladies who remained in the cabin cried out in alarm.

Katie grinned at Philo, leaned forward, and whispered, "Mar said I could use my hammer on you. But all I got's this knife. It's the knife I got *your* mar with."

Katie raised the knife high. Philo stood quickly and with both fists held tightly together struck Katie in the belly with all her mustered strength. Katie stiffened, and the knife fell from her hands. Philo jumped and picked it up. She held the handle tightly in her fist. Katie had almost recovered her breath. Philo said to her, "Katie, I saw your father die. I saw him hanged from a tree."

Katie straightened herself suddenly, drew in a sharp breath, and stared wildly at Philo. Philo did not flinch from her gaze. "Your mother died the death of a mad dog. I was there."

Katie swiped at Philo with the carpetbag. Philo jumped out of the way, and Katie rushed out of the cabin.

Philo looked round. Twenty women and a half a dozen men stood speechless and aghast. Holding the knife before her, Philo pursued Katie out onto the deck. The wind blew hard down the East River.

The boat was approaching the landing. Those on the forward edge – bootblacks, newsboys, and mechanics with their tin cans – prepared to jump the last few feet for the honor of being first ashore and quickest home. One ragged boy, urged on by a calculating friend, made the leap, and the crowd at the edge whistled at his prowess and daring.

Katie rushed through the crowd there. Taking fearless notice of the gap that yet remained between the ferry's deck and the wharf, she jumped.

She fell short of the other side. Catching on the edge of the wharf, however, and without even a cry for assistance, she began to hoist herself up.

The wheels of the ferry had been given one extra turn to aid the final speed, and the boat, with a last shudder, was rammed against the wharf.

Katie, who had almost lifted herself to safety, was caught between the lip of the ferry and the weathered boards of the wharf. She uttered one piercing shriek as she was cut in two. Her twitching legs dropped into the water beneath the wharf, and her lifeless trunk, exhaling air through her open mouth and pouring blood and quivering organs from the bottom, tumbled onto the deck of the ferry at Philo's feet. The carpetbag remained in her convulsive grasp.

Chapter 55

CONCLUSION

Henry Maitland married Philo Drax on Christmas Day, 1871. Jewel Varley *was* Philo's bridesmaid. The Varleys took the world as they found it, and when they received an invitation, engraved on vellum, to attend the wedding of Henry Adolphus Maitland and Philomela Drax, they sighed, sighed again, and then re-marked that at least Henry hadn't taken to himself an "uppity" bride. By "uppity" they meant one who would not recognize Henry's country cousins.

Philo also took the world as she found it. She knew that the Varleys, given their choices, would rather have seen her in a New Jersey jail than ensconced as the mistress of Twenty-sixth Street, but in the years to come, Philo never referred to the earlier animosity that had existed between her and the Varleys. Jewel married a lawyer to whom Henry had introduced her, and the lawyer eventually became a senator. Washington, everyone agreed, was a fit arena for Jewel's particular talents.

After a honeymoon in Rome and Milan, Philo and Henry settled into a quiet existence on Twenty-sixth Street. Early in

1873, Philo gave birth to her first child. It was a girl, and Philo called her Nedda.

Through the indefatigable assistance of Mr. Blakey, the carpet-bag and its contents were proved to be the rightful property of Philomela Drax Maitland, and when she needed it not at all, Philo came into the possession of her fortune. Even the bag had come back to her, though the pattern on one side was dimmed by large splotches of Katie Slape's dried blood. One evening, when she was alone on Twenty-sixty Street, Philo took out the bank notes and counted them. She had fallen heir to $26,720. She tied the notes in bundles, closed them into the bag once more, and then shoved it in the back of a wardrobe in her dressing room.

Philomela Maitland was not the Philo Drax of old. She had always moved through life as stiffly as if she had been pinioned to a stand in a photographer's studio. It had always seemed that she supported the world on her shoulders: responsible for her mother from as early as she could remember, for her poor murdered grandfather, for her own penniless self. And particularly, since coming across them on her grandfather's farm, she had been on her watch against the Slapes – and she had never slept with entire easiness, knowing they still wandered the earth.

She had seen all three of them die. She had seen John's body laid out beneath the vast tree in the Catskill forest; she had seen Hannah's convulsion-wracked corpse on the threadbare carpet in the basement flat in Boston; she had seen Katie's legless trunk jerking on the deck of the Brooklyn ferry. Despite that wicked family's crimes, their ending did not seem fit to her. She considered – though the thought was an evil one – that she would have liked to approach them in their sleep, with a kerchief and a bottle of chloroform: something quiet, dignified, and painless. She wished for them deaths which would have befitted not their crimes, but the dignity of Philo's own demand for vengeance. Yet the Slapes had died brutally, without dignity, in stupid, messy ways, and Philo could not help but feel that these terrible deaths reflected on her own insistence for revenge.

Every night she slept beneath their gallows.

Gradually, the feeling wore away. The Slapes, for all their

heinousness, became memories as innocuous as that of her mother. However, Philo didn't go to Brooklyn again until the bridge over the East River was opened twelve years later, and she never again looked on the house where Ella LaFavour had died. She saw the Varleys often, but never in New Egypt; and at Christmas she wrote to Mr. Killip, but she sold Parrock Farm without ever seeing it again. Charges of murder against her were dropped, but Philo never again travelled through New Jersey without uneasiness.

Her life seemed to have fallen into three distinct and very unequal divisions: her childhood in New Egypt – two decades of poverty and not much pleasure; the nine months in which the Slapes had had possession of her fortune (Could a time so important to her have occupied so little actual space on a calendar?); and the many many years she spent in quiet contentment as Henry Maitland's wife on Twenty-sixth Street.

She had four children, whose names were Nedda, Mary, Henry and Ella. Her husband Henry died of heart failure at Saratoga in 1891. Philo at that time, still on Twenty-sixth Street, moved into the room that had been Nedda's. She lived, quiet but quite happy, until 1919, when she perished in the influenza epidemic. When her daughters Nedda and Ella, then both married and both with children, went through their dead mother's things, they found at the back of an old wardrobe a carpetbag. And in the carpetbag they discovered, to their astonishment, somewhat more than twenty-six thousand dollars in old-fashioned currency. They could not imagine how such a sum would have come to be left and forgotten by their mother, who had been neither a forgetful nor an impractical woman. Ella's husband, a broker in Wall Street, examined the bank notes and made inquiries. The Bank of Cape May, which had issued the notes, had failed in the Panic of 1873. For more than forty years, Philo's carefully preserved fortune had been completely worthless.